CHARLEY AND TIM

AT

SCARUM SCHOOL.

LONDON: HOGARTH HOUSE, BOUVERIE STREET, FLEET STREET, E.C.

CHARLEY AND TIM

SCARUM SCHOOL.

CHARLEY AND TIM

AT

SCARUM SCHOOL.

BY THE AUTHOR OF "RALPH RATTLETON," "OCEAN OF ICE," &c., &c.

CHAPTER I.

A HERO IN DISGRACE.

' NATUR' is natur', sir."

The above sage expression was uttered by a wiry, grey-headed old man, attired in the style known as "half livery," apparently a gentleman's servant in a position of trust—one of the race now, unhappily. dying away, a member of the past age of servants, who spent their boyhood, prime, and old age in the same service, loyal and devoted throughout a long life, and faithful to the end.

He addressed himself to a gentleman of fine presence, seated at a library table, poring over an old book with the intensity of an earnest, studious reader.

The remark was unheeded, and the servant, with a prefatory "Ahem!" again ventured to observe :—

"Natur' is natur', sir."

Then the gentleman looked up.

"What did you say, Filer?"

Filer, with the indignant look which favourite servants at times indulge in, replied—

"Not bein' in the land of niggers, and in consequench not bein' a slave, I made so bold as to say that natur' is natur', Mr. Thorn—and I don't mind sayin' it agen—natur' is natur'."

His master looked puzzled, and passed his hand through his grey hair with a quick, impatient motion.

"If you will kindly be more explicit, Filer, I shall take it as a favour."

"There is no faviour," replied Filer; "I was a-speakin' of Master Charles—and I says agen, natur' is natur'."

"I understand you now, Filer, and I have no doubt there is a vast depth of philosophy in your declaration; but Master Charles has disgraced himself, and he must take the consequence."

"May I ax, sir," inquired Filer, looking as obstinate as you please, "*how* Master Charles have disgraced hisself?"

"You can read, Filer?" inquired Mr. Thorn.

"Thank the Lord," returned Filer, piously, "I'm a good 'un at print, and give me time I can get through writing if it's written fat."

"Then read that letter," said Mr. Thorn, pointing to one before him, and went on with his studies.

Filer, producing a case from a pocket somewhere in the tails of his coat, fixed on the bridge of his nose a good substantial pair of spectacles with horn rims, and taking up the letter, tried it in various ways until he got it right, and then began to read.

The communication was undoubtedly written "fat," in a good, plain, scholarly hand, and Filer had no difficulty in arriving at its meaning. It ran as follows :—

"Dr. Phosey presents his compliments to Mr. Thorn, and begs to inform him that arrangements have been made for the immediate return of his son to the parental roof. The establishment of Dr. Phosey is conducted on strict gentlemanly principles, and it is to be regretted that Master Thorn, during his short stay, has systematically and invariably ignored, derided, and held up to contumely and contempt, the rules laid down, not only for his welfare, but that of his fellow-pupils, and, therefore, the community at large. The system of Dr. Phosey forbids the use of the cane; but all that lectures, remonstrances, and punishments of a like nature could do, has been done, and the result has been eminently unsatisfactory. Master Thorn has been a disturbing element in the establishment; young gentlemen whose deportment had hitherto been all that could be desired, suddenly became corrupted and fell into backslidings of a painful nature. Four sheets of negro melodies, in company with some bones, were discovered in one of the pockets of a most promising pupil, and for two nights the strains of a vile melody concerning some individual of the name of Dan Tucker have been the means of disturbing the repose of all beneath the roof—masters, assistants, and the ordinary domestic servants. The shoeblack, a respectable lad from the neighbouring workhouse, is utterly ruined, his moral nature has been utterly corrupted by the unseemly levity of the pupils, and his constitution undermined by tarts, an unwholesome food hitherto a stranger beneath the roof of Dr. Phosey. This unhappy boy is at the present time in bed, lying in a state of rebellion and pimples, and in his box a paper has been discovered, showing that it was his ultimate intention to desert from his employment and become a *drummer in the army.* All this is undoubtedly the work of Master Thorn, and the painful step which has been taken was, therefore, imperative. Dr. Phosey encloses his account for present term, trusting that this unhappy affair will not, in any way, interrupt the pleasant terms existing between himself and Mr. Thorn.'

Although the writing was very legible, it took Filer some time to get through the lengthy epistle, but he achieved the feat, and stood before his master a fine specimen of indignant humanity.

"Of all the imperence——" he began.

Mr. Thorn looked up from his book, and, receiving the letter trembling in Filer's hand, asked him what he thought of it.

"The doctor's a hidiot," replied Filer, emphatically, "to write in this cheeky manner about Master Charles."

"The doctor is a very learned man," rejoined Mr. Thorn, gravely. "His establishment, although of limited extent, is considered one of the finest in the kingdom. A former pupil of his became Senior Wrangler last year."

"I'd wrangle him!" growled Filer, looking very wooden-headed, but intensely furious; "him and his bosh! Where can you find one like Master Charles?—a pictur' at any time and worth two—ten—a hundred doctors. Bring old Phosey here," added the old man, entirely losing his head; "shut him up in the pantry, and let me have a round with him!"

"Filer, you forget yourself," said Mr. Thorn, sternly.

"I can't help it, sir," returned Filer, recklessly, "I'm b'ilin' over. Bring Phosey here, and let us have a round!"

Here Filer squared in a terribly significant manner at the empty air and landed a heavy blow on an imaginary doctor's nose.

Mr. Thorn was very much annoyed, but Filer was an old and faithful servant, and he only said—

"You may go now, Filer. Master Charles will be here about five o'clock."

Filer bowed, and went out without another word.

Seeking his favourite place of retirement,

he put out the plate upon a table before him, and contemplated it with a shining countenance.

Whenever anything disturbed Filer, the sight of the plate under his charge always restored his equanimity—it was balm of Gilead to his wounded feelings.

"I've spoke my mind," he murmured, as he grew cooler. "The doctor's a hidiot, and Master Charles is a hangel. Lord! what I would give to have one round with the doctor here! I wonder what's his weight?"

This opened another field for contemplation, and the old servant of the Thorns fell into a musing mood, until the noise of carriage-wheels aroused him.

"Master Charles!" he cried, and, rushing out, intercepted a boy in buttons who was making eagerly for the door. "Get out of the way!" he cried, spinning Buttons into a corner of the hall; "like *your* imperence to think of such a thing."

"You ain't orfen so ready to answer the door," growled the boy; "you shove me again."

Filer was about to supplement his former proceeding with a severe castigation, when a loud knock at the door checked him, and, throwing it open, he stood face to face with his young master.

CHAPTER II.

CHARLEY THORN.

A HANDSOME boy, with a face clear as a May morning, with the sparkle of life and health in his eye, and strength in his supple limbs, cast a heap of rugs and overcoats upon the floor, and grasped the old servant by the hand.

"How are you, Filer?" he cried; "but, I needn't ask—hearty as ever. How do you do, Sam?"——this to young Buttons, who grinned amazingly. "Take my traps upstairs, will you? and, Filer, pay cabby; I'm cleared out—not a scrap left—give him something to drink, too."

Filer, lost in admiration of his young master, ignored the cabby for the time being, as he replied—

"Well! I never did see nothing grow like you afore; scarlet beans is a long way behind you."

"Yes," rejoined Charley, carelessly; "I'm pulling out a bit, but *do* settle with cabby, there's a good old chap, and then come and have a word with me, before I go in to father."

"I think you'd better," said Filer significantly; "that precious doctor have been a-warming up a decent hash for you."

"No doubt," returned Charley, laughing; "but come as soon as you can, you will find me in the pantry."

Our hero chose this place of retirement, as

it had been a favourite haunt of his whenever a consultation with Filer was necessary in the days he spent at home, and thither, in a few moments, came the old man.

"Now, first," said Charley, "tell me how my father took the news?"

"He took it," returned Filer, "like a lamb —same as he takes everything—he ain't the man to put his foot through a front winder over a trifle, 'specially when he's busy, as he is just now. He's tryin' to weigh the moon, and he'll do it, if any man can."

"Then he has said nothing."

"Well, he's said this much, Master Charles, that you'll go to a different school now, where they keep a 'tickler' for them as wants it."

"Any change will be welcome," replied Charley. "Well! I'll just run up, and when I come back, I'll tell you something about that precious crib. Ta-ta, Filer!"

"Adoo! Master Charles—horawoar," replied Filer, with the utmost gravity.

While Charley was absent, Filer laid out a very enticing lunch for his young master in the breakfast-room, wherein Charley shortly appeared, looking very little the worse for the ordeal he had undergone.

"I hope," said Filer, solemnly, "that the parental retrospective of your doings, Master Charles, were laid on light."

"My father was, as he is at all times, very kind; he is astounished and grieved at my sudden return from the bosom of Dr. Phosey —but he will get over that."

"And I suppose, you, Master Charles, will survive the blow?"

"Rather! What have you here, Filer?"

"That dish is potted beef, and the jar is marmalade. I've drawed, too, some of the best pale ale—this ain't a day for table-beer, Master Charles."

"It is not!" responded our hero, emphatically. "Pour some out, and put a good head on."

"And while you pecks, Master Charles, will you be so kind as to give me some idear of old Phosey's unairthly crib. His name is p'ison to me; but, no matter. Purceed, Master Charles, I'm all attention."

"As soon as I got down to that place, at midsummer," Charley began, having helped himself liberally to beef, "I saw it wouldn't do—wouldn't pay at any price. I never saw such a lot of duffers as the boys looked. I say 'looked,' Filer, because some of them were not bad when a fellow came to know 'em. But I never was so startled as when they first came under my blessed vision."

"Was they lookin' starved, Master Charles? Some of them schools do regerlate the wittles to a hair."

"It wasn't that, Filer. The grub, as far

as it went, was tidy, and, with what we brought ourselves, we were fairly filled out, but it was the stiffness of the lot—tall hats, high collars, tight boots, and gloves! Gloves, Filer, when they went into the playground, to walk their hours of leisure solemnly away. You see, Filer, it was a gentlemanly establishment."

"If I were a gent, I'd be merry and free," murmured Filer to himself.

"Laughing, talking above a whisper, whistling, and so on, was infra dig.," continued Charley, "and we were all Misters. Ha, ha! Filer, there was one Mister not quite seven years old; and when the wind was high, it was a sight to see him staggering about under the weight of his chimney-pot. Ha ha!"

"How long did he live?" asked Filer, anxiously.

"He's alive now," answered Charley, "but going down the high-road to idiotcy. Cut me a little more beef, Filer; it's prime. Well, from the first moment I met Phosey, I knew we should not agree. He was, I assure you, more like a hippopotamus than a man, and the most addle-headed, arrogant old humbug that ever filled his head with Greek roots and Latin quotations.

"I'm not going to trouble you with all that followed, Filer; it was pull master, pull pupil, from first to last. When I went, every hat was stiff and shiny; and I left behind me a collection of stove-pipe abominations that any old-clothes dealer would turn up his nose at. 'Incited by Mister Thorn,' as old Phosey said, 'a conspiracy was formed, and, at a given signal, every boy sat upon his particular tile'—Phosey didn't say 'tile'; but they are tiles, for all that—'and ruined them for ever.'"

"What a figger you would cut in a French Revolution!" exclaimed Filer, admiringly. "But, Master Charles, in Phosey's letter to your papa, he calls you Master Thorn."

"Under the circumstances, Filer, he would naturally do so. My father is Mr. Thorn; but I assure you that at school we were all Misters."

"Purceed, Master Charles, the hexplanation is satisfacterry."

"There was an awful row about the chimney-pots," rejoined Charley, "but at Dr. Phosey's the cane is a stranger; instead of having a stinger and getting over it, you are set five hundred lines of Virgil to translate, or something else that keeps you at it until bed-time. That night we were kept hard at it until it was time to turn in. Supper was tabooed, and we got between the sheets both hungry and cold, the most miserable lot of duffers that ever lived."

"Supper a'int considered a 'elthy meal," hinted Filer.

"Don't talk nonsense, Filer, *we* wanted supper preciously bad, and Phosey knew it was the worst punishment; but bless you! it did not do us much good, the first seeds were sown, and larking sprung up like anything."

"Which is nateral unto youth," rejoined Filer.

"Just so; having destroyed our *chapeaux*, or rather made them unpresentable to the public, we were deprived of our daily walk, which we didn't care a rap about, for it's no great treat to stalk through the town, two and two, chaffed by every butcher's boy, so we kept to the playground, which was the best fun after all. No solemn walkings about there. No! leap frog, toe in the ring, watchmen and thieves became the order of the day; in fact, Filer, Dr. Phosey's academy was turned head over heels."

"He said you corrupted the shoe-black."

"Poor little Jimmy!" said Charley; "a miserable little fellow from the workhouse, who had nothing but half a dozen empty blacking-bottles to pass away his leisure time. He hadn't much of that, poor fellow! I bought him a book or two, not washy stuff, but jolly things, and one he read was about a soldier's life, and he wanted to be a drummer."

"So said Phosey, in his wolluminous letter," remarked Filer.

"Poor little fellow!" said Charley, again, "I was sorry to leave him behind, he was so lonely and had but few friends; but there, it's no use thinking or talking, I've turned my back on Phosey's for ever. What do you think my father will do with me—you ought to know, Filer?"

"I think this, Master Charles, that he'll choose a place where there'll be less Wirgil and more tickler, *alias* cane; he don't want to be hard on you, but he was whopped hisself, and he's been a successful man, so he thinks it won't do you no harm."

"Anything but a second edition of Phosey," returned our hero, "*that* I could not stand. Perish the thought! Ha! ha! away with him to the deepest dungeon 'neath the castle moat! Don't you think I should make a good actor, Filer?"

"I ain't much up in that line," replied Filer, cautiously; "but I've no doubt whatsumever you tries to do, you'll do it. Hactors, as a rule, ain't up to much—there was one as lived opposite here, when the theayter were open, and he never paid no rent, but gave his unsuspecting wictim of a landlady a horder for a private box one night when he weren't hacting, and when she came back he was gone—likewise the bed linen—also two teaspoons, a salt-cellar, and a chimney ornament."

"He wasn't a real actor," said Charley, contemptuously.

"He weren't a ghost," insisted Filer, "that I'll swear; for I seed him fight a baker who called for his bill."

"He was a scamp, not an actor, Filer."

"He was both, Master Charles. Have any more beef?"

"No, thank you."

"Some marmalade?"

"Nothing more, Filer—clear away."

From that time, up to Christmas, Charley Thorn lived at home. conducting himself, on the whole, in a very quiet and creditable manner.

Mr. Thorn never once alluded to the delinquencies of his son. Charley had no mother to mourn over his backslidings, and Filer rather sympathised with whatever his young master did, so the time passed very pleasantly for our hero.

One day, early in January, Filer beckoned Charley into the pantry, a sure sign that he had something of importance to communicate.

"Master Charles," he said, cautiously closing the door, "the trick is done."

"What trick?"

"Your doom is sealed," answered Filer, breathless with excitement; "and I think you are in for something werry warm."

"Don't keep me in suspense, Filer," exclaimed Charley, "but tell me what it is."

"I've got a letter for the post," rejoined Filer, "and here it is."

Charley took the envelope and read, "Crawshay Crammer, Esq., Scarum School, Winkle-by-the-Sea."

"There's a name," exclaimed Filer; "and there's an address."

"But it may be only writing for terms Filer."

"No, Master Charles, the thing is settled, I have master's word for it."

"And suppose it is, what is there to fear at Scarum School?"

"Ah; you haven't seen all," returned Filer, gloomily; "read the advertisement of this Mr. Crammer, it's turned me all of a cold chill."

Filer drew a paper from his pocket, and with a shudder pointed out to Charley the following advertisement—

"UNRULY YOUTHS.—Mr. Crawshay Crammer, of Scarum School, Winkle-by-the-Sea, undertakes, without the exercise of more than needful coercion, to check the rebellious dispositions of unruly children. Mr. Crammer's principle has proved remarkably efficacious, and parents or guardians may confidently rely upon the beneficial results of a few months' stay of *any* pupil beneath the roof of Scarum School. References to friends of former pupils forwarded on application. Address as above."

"Now, what do you think of that?" asked Filer.

"Don't know," answered Charley, ruefully; "it is a strange advertisement."

"It's a staggerer," rejoined Filer. "Now here, the needful co—co—coercion—coercion, Master Charles! The meaning of that is, unlimited whopping, beginning as soon as you are out of bed, and ending somewhere shortly arter midnight. Mr. Thorn ought—"

"One moment, Filer," interposed Charley, "not a word against my father. I am sure he does it all for the best."

"He's a innercent lamb, and that's the truth," said Filer, wiping the perspiration from his forehead. "But I'll stand by you."

"I am sure you will, Filer."

"Fifty years ago, come the 14th of March," said Filer, speaking very fast, his face all aglow with excitement, "I was a ragged boy—so ragged that a'most as much of me was exposed to the public as was hid by my clothes. I was knocked here, kicked there, twisted about by this party, punched by that party, outil I was as nigh going mad as could be. Sitting down on a doorstep was a criminal offence, and offering to carry a carpet-bag was often looked upon as a piece of unexampled willany. I growed so wretched that I went one day to look at the water, and I was so small that I had to climb one of the stone seats of the bridge to look over."

"You had no parents then, Filer?"

"Never knowed 'em, Master Charles. Well, I was that miserable that I went with the awful intent of committing suicide, and putting a stop to all the badgering that I had endoored. While I was a-looking at the water, a gentleman taps me on the shoulder, and says, 'What's the matter, my lad?' 'I'm hungry, and chivvied to death,' I says. 'Poor little fellow,' he says; 'what crime have you committed?' I ups and tells him that I ain't committed no crime 'cept being poor and having no friends. 'Poor fellow,' he says again, 'come home with me and I'll stand by you.' Master Charles, that gentleman was your grandfather."

"I've heard the story before," said Charley, with tears of sympathy in his eyes.

"'I'll stand by you,' he says, rejoined Filer; "and he kept his word; and when he died, his son, your father, Master Charles, stood by me. Now I'm going to stand by you—if that Crammer lays it too heavy on you, don't write to anybody but me, and I'll wait upon him in a way that'll astonish him

a bit. I don't think that he'll want more than one round with me."

Poor Filer, too harmless to hurt a fly, and a complete stranger to the noble art of self-defence, looked amazingly fierce as he uttered this threat, and Charley, taking the will for the deed, shook hands, and said he was sure he might rely upon him.

"You may," rejoined Filer, "through wheels and woes, until death do us part. But I must say adoo!—there's some wine as came in yesterday to put away—but remember this, Master Charles, I stands by you for evermore."

———

CHAPTER III.

TIM TURNDOWN.

FOR three days Mr. Thorn said nothing to his son about Scarum School—at the expiration of that time a letter arrived with the post-mark of Winkle-by-the-Sea.

It seemed to give Mr. Thorn great satisfaction, and in the course of breakfast, he enlightened Charley upon the contents thereof.

"As I am going away for a few weeks," he said, "I wrote to know if you could be received in the school at once. Mr. Crammer says that the school does not begin for ten days, but his house is open to you, and although he will be absent in town collecting new pupils, his housekeeper will attend to your requirements."

Charley bowed in silence—he could not express any particular delight at the proposed change, and therefore held his peace.

"A few days by yourself," continued Mr. Thorn, "will make the place familiar to you: and meeting the pupils as they return one by one, will be better than being thrown at once into the midst of a body of strangers. Mr. Crammer has a large school—over a hundred boys."

"All untameable, sir?" said Charley, with a sly look.

"Many of them originally unruly," replied his father, gravely;" but Mr. Crammer assures me that now their conduct is all that the most fastidious parent or guardian could desire."

"I'm going amongst a precious lot," thought Charley. "I'm in for it; but I'll not funk it." Then he said aloud, "I am sure, sir, that you have made the best arrangement that could be made."

"And I hope, Charles, you will prove worthy of it."

"I hope so too, sir;" but Charley's face reflected his words but in a minute degree.

He felt that Scarum School would be no haven of rest for his troubled youth.

Winkle-by-the-Sea was forty miles away, and accessible only by coach.

Mr. Thorn being much engaged, it was arranged that the faithful Filer should see the new pupil to his destination; and one cold, sullen morning, the pair took their seats upon the High flyer, a coach of great fame in those parts.

It was, as Charley remarked, "preciously cold;" but he preferred the outside, as it gave him a view of the landscape; and Filer was too devoted a servant to hint at his old bones, and the desirability of taking a snug seat inside.

They sat by the guard—the coachman was a little too heavy for Charley, at present—and whiled away the time with anecdotes and scraps of cheery conversation.

The guard had many a story to tell—old friends of his, but new to our travellers, who accepted all his long-winded yarns as utterances from the mouth of a prophet; Filer especially placing implicit faith in all he heard of highwaymen, accidents during floods and deep snows, and other stock narratives of all the coach-guards of the kingdom.

Twenty miles of the road had been covered, when the snow began to fall; and in a few minutes the coach presented the appearance of a gigantic ornament for a twelfth-cake, liberally coated with sugar.

This, to Charley, was fun; but poor Filer suffered a martyrdom, and by the time they reached Winkle-by-the-Sea, he would have made a great sensation, could he have been exhibited as the only real living specimen of the blue mummy from the East.

"Whereabouts is Sca—Sca—rum School?" he asked of the guard, as well as his chattering teeth would allow him.

"Are you going to take this lad there?"

"I am going," interposed Charley; it's a good school, isn't it?"

"Very good," answered the guard, drily.

"It's well conducted, I suppose?" asked Filer, "and all the boys are lambs?"

"I can't say nothing about the conducting of the school," replied the guard, "because there is a law about libel; but I can say this about the boys, they ain't lambs?"

"What are they, then?"

"Trojans! himps! demons, if you like! anything but lambs! I pities a boy as goes among 'em at first."

"Oh!" exclaimed Filer, blankly; "and what sort o' man is Mr. Crammer?"

"I've said his boys is himps," replied the guard, "and he's the proper party to be at the head of 'em. I can't say no more."

"Come along, Filer," cried Charley, tossing his "tip" to the guard; "let us get to this precious place."

"You can't miss it," the guard shouted after them, "it stands alone on the cliff."

As it was yet early in the afternoon Charley's luggage was left at the booking-office to be called for, and he and Filer walked through the town towards the school.

Winkle-by-the-Sea was a large, rambling seaport town, with a jumble of streets full of ricketty houses, swarming with seafaring people of every degree. Outside, near the sea, were a few genteel houses built for visitors, but Winkle-by-the-Sea was not a favourite place of resort, and half the buildings were in a languishing state, several being but half finished.

There was an air of gloom and decay, not pleasant to a stranger, and the wintry scene around made this gloom doubly impressive.

"I suppose that is Scarum School," said Charley, pointing to a large red-brick house, surrounded by a tolerably high wall.

"It might be a prison or a mad-house," growled Filer, "if one goes by the looks of it."

"It's winter, you know," said Charley, trying to look cheerful; "this must be very jolly in the summer."

"Werry jolly," growled Filer; "here we are, Master Charles; that's the lodge, I suppose, close to the iron gate?"

"Yes; and there is a brass plate, 'Mr. Crammer, Scarum School.' Ring the bell, Filer."

Filer pulled the handle, and immediately the door of the lodge flew open.

A small hump-backed man looked up at them, and squeaked—

"Well?"

"Is this Scarum School?" inquired Filer, for the want of something better to say.

"It is; who are you, and what do you want?"

"This is Master Thorn."

"Oh! the new pupil—come in."

The voice of the little man was very harsh, and he appeared to be very irritable; but there was the appearance of long suffering and much endurance in his face, and Charley felt kindly towards him.

"Margery's got your bed ready; she expected you earlier," said the little man—"come this way."

He led them across a huge barren playground to the red house, and rang a bell by a side door.

In response, a tall, masculine-looking woman of forty appeared, and, without inquiring who they were, asked them to come in.

Charley and Filer entered the house, but the little hump-backed man returned to the lodge.

"Come into my rooms for a moment,"

said the woman. "I'm housekeeper here, and my name is Mrs. Margery—don't forget that, Mrs. Margery. Do you want any tea?"

"No, ma'am," replied Charley.

He was having his fill of other things.

"Can I offer you anything?" demanded Mrs. Margery, turning so suddenly upon Filer that she made that truly brave old servitor jump in his shoes.

"I think not, mum," replied Filer, slowly.

"In that case," said Mrs. Margery, "you need not wait. I'm worried to death to get the place ready for them precious boys. Master Thorn—you see I know your name—you can remain here or walk in the grounds, as you please."

"I think I will walk for a little while," said Charley.

"But where are your boxes?"

"Left at the booking-office, ma'am, to be sent for."

"Good gracious!" exclaimed Mrs. Margery, "why didn't you bring them? Ask Mops—that's the porter at the gate—to fetch them."

Charley and Filer then left the house and crossed the "grounds" in silence—the hearts of both rather too full to speak.

When they reached the lodge, Filer turned upon his young master, and looked him solemnly in the face.

"Master Charles," he said, "of all the downright dullerest places I ever——"

"Don't say a word, Filer," interposed Charley, "I'll brighten it up a bit. Good-bye, and write to me sometimes—I'll write to you."

"Them commoonications will be received with enthoosiasm," replied Filer. "Adoo, Master Charles—hoarywoar."

Charles felt very dull; but he put on a smile, and bidding Filer send Mops for his traps, walked slowly across the ground. We called it barren, and barren indeed it was, despite half a dozen trees clustered together in the corner farthest from the lodge. The bare branches, rocked by the breeze, sent forth mournful music in unison with the sound of the restless sea beating on the rocky shore.

Charley paused and looked up at the leaden sky where the clouds held out promise of a further supply of snow; from these he glanced at the trees, and became conscious of an object moving behind one of the nearest.

It was apparently something, or somebody in hiding, and Charley was but mortal, and therefore curious. With his hands in his pockets, he lounged towards the object, and presently had a full view of it.

A short, thick-set boy, whose remarkable stoutness was made more apparent by a skeleton suit of clothes.

For the benefit of our readers who are unacquainted with this barbarism of a bye-gone age, we will give a slight description of that peculiar attire.

A skeleton suit consisted of a jacket and trousers, both very tight-fitting, the jacket buttoning upon the trousers, and closed up in front by a row of brass buttons. When this apparel was popular, the youth of the period wore frill collars, and the youth whom Charley then beheld wore a frill collar also. His cap had the monstrous peak and huge round top which Germans affect to the present day.

Charley made plenty of noise as he approached, but the wearer of the skeleton suit never turned his eyes towards him, but calmly pursued the occupation of cutting two enormous initials, more than two feet long, on the bark of the tree.

Our hero went up to his side, still unheeded, and watched the work of the youthful engraver in silence; but this became unbearable, and at last he inquired—

"What's your name?"

"What's yours?" asked the other, with his eye steadfast upon his work.

"Mine's Charley Thorn," replied Charley, laughing.

"And mine's Tim Turndown," rejoined the other, as he gave the finishing touch to a mighty T.

CHAPTER IV.
SCARUM SCHOOL.

WHEN the important announcement with which we closed our last chapter was made, the owner turned upon Charley as if he expected to see him prostrated or injured in some way by the shock, but Charley was perfectly calm.

"It's a curious name," he said.

"It is," replied Tim, "and I'm a curious chap. Are you an old un here?"

"No, just come."

"New boy?"

"Yes."

"So am I," rejoined Tim, "let us shake hands."

Charley thought his companion a strange fellow, but he went through the ceremony heartily.

"Have you a father?" asked Tim.

"Yes, and a capital father he is."

"A mother?"

"No."

"There we are equal," said Tim; "but you lick me in fathers, you've one more than I have. I've none."

"That's jolly hard, old fellow,"

"So it is—but I have an uncle."

"What sort of fellow is he?"

"I don't want to say anything against him," said Tim; "but if he'd come here one day and pitch himself over this cliff, *I'd let him be.*"

"How long have you been here?" Charley asked, after a pause.

"Came yesterday."

"What sort of a crib is it? Who is in the house?"

"There's Margery, the housekeeper," replied Tim; "sweet creetur'—Oh, my!—don't she cut bread and butter? and ain't the butter nice, when you get a taste of it? There's two or three girl servants, and Mops at the lodge, and that's all—no, there's one of the ushers sleeps here, but he goes out early and comes in late, so I haven't seen him."

"You look rather cold," said Charley; "let us walk about."

"I *am* cold," returned Tim; "who wouldn't be in such precious togs as these? Look at em—skin-tight. I'm not a boy, I'm a polony. This is my uncle's idea—he says *he* wore 'em when he was a boy, and they were good enough for him, so they ought to be good enough for me—blow him!"

Tim was possessed of a very serious cast of countenance, one of those faces which rarely change under the influence of emotion. He anathematized his uncle, as he had requested the honour of shaking hands with Charley, without moving a muscle.

"It isn't only the fit," continued Tim, "but did you ever see a boy of this pattern? Shan't I stand alone here? Will there be another like me? If I could put my uncle in a suit like it, I'd have it *sewn up*—he should live in 'em. Look at the rig—cast your eye on the buttons—would you stand it? Oh! won't they have a precious lark with me," he groaned, "when they all come back, and I a new un, too!"

"I'll stand by you, Tim," cried Charley, clapping him on the back; "they shan't worry you while I've a leg to stand on."

"Well, upon my word, I'm grateful," rejoined Tim; "you will stand by me through thick and thin?"

"Like a brick."

"Give us your fist again, Charley. I'm yours for ever. See how I'll stand by you in other things! I don't mind school lickings, and when I can I'll take yours for you."

"All right, Tim, friends from this moment."

"How long are you here for, Charley?"

"Don't know."

"Are you going home in the holidays?"

"I should think so! catch me stopping at such a crib as this."

Tim whistled softly to himself a few bars of a negro melody; he then smote himself deliberately on the breast, and replied—

"I don't think there was ever such a precious miserable duffer as I am. I'm here for two years, *holidays and all*; but I shan't stand it. I'll—I'll kill my uncle, and run away to sea."

"We have months to talk that over in," said Charley, kindly—he was really touched by Tim's distress; "but ain't you getting peckish, old chap?"

"I am, rather."

"Good! here's my box, and inside of it is a plummy cake."

"Is that the box Mops is going to carry to the house?"

"Yes."

"Stop him," cried Tim, breathlessly; "if that old woman gets it, we're done. Stop! Mr. Mops, stop!"

The porter, hearing the cry, stopped, and perceiving the boys were running towards him, set down the box.

"What do you want?" he asked.

"Something out of my box, said Charley, "before it goes to the house."

"Ho! I see," rejoined the porter, with a grim smile, "but it can't be done."

"If you please, there's a good fellow," pleaded Charley.

"Well," exclaimed the porter, running his eyes over the windows of the house, "I'll risk it, but if *she* saw me, my place wouldn't be worth a shilling.

"Thank you, Mops; you're very kind."

"Come back to the lodge"—and when safe inside he thus addressed the boys:—

"You've said I am kind. Well, that's all right. Now look'ee here. When school begins, you be kind to me."

"Upon my word I will," said Charley.

"Don't make game o' my affliction, and don't drive me mad with larkin' when I've got the rheumatism on me."

"I could not think of such a thing," rejoined Charley, indignantly.

"I'd sooner have another uncle," added Tim.

"Ah! you all say so at first," said Mops with a sigh, "and when you get together 'tis forgotten; but there, out with your cake, and while I run up to the house with the box, eat what you want, and put the rest in the cupboard. There ain't no mice, and I've done with cakes many a long year."

"Sure you won't *have* a piece, Mops?" asked Charley, as he cut into his treasure.

"No, not a morsel."

"All right; now, Tim, peg away."

Tim pegged away with considerable effect until his skeleton suit became unbearable and the lower buttons had to be released.

and when Mops came back from the school-house he was still hard at it.

"You seem to have a good appetite," said Charley.

"I have," replied Tim, "about four sizes too big I should think; one more slice, Charley."

"You'll make yourself ill."

"A little one."

This request Charley granted, and put the remainder of his cake away. Mops, who had refused to partake, freely accepted a shilling Charley offered him. Mops had one weakness, and it was rum.

As it was now growing dusk, the porter hinted that Mrs. Margery might be expecting them, and her temper being what he called "a reg'lar buster," the boys thought it advisable to return to the school. There they found weak tea and bread and butter provided, of which neither, to her astonishment, could partake, but Tim surreptitiously stowed away a couple of slices "to munch in the bedroom."

"Supper," he whispered to Charley, "was a swindle there, and not enough to keep a child on his feet."

The evening they spent by themselves in the schoolroom, a veritable barn of a place, with a Lilliputian fire, and at nine o'clock they had the swindling supper and were sent to bed.

CHAPTER V.

ONLY A LARK.

THE dormitory to which Charley and Tim retired was a long narrow room containing twenty bedsteads. The couches of our friends were covered with a fair amount of linen, the rest were empty, and, ranged by the wall, looked like eighteen skeletons of defunct beds.

The candle allowed them was the fag end of a tallow dip, which only made darkness more visible, and altogether this place was as cheerless and comfortless as need be.

"A jolly dull hole this," said Charley.

"Not half so bad as last night," rejoined Tim, "when I was here alone. Criminey! it was a treat."

"I should think so," said Charley, wriggling between the sheets, with sundry gasps; "well, I'm tired, old chap. Good-night!"

"Good-night, Charley! I shall sleep easy, now."

And Tim, in two minutes, sent forth such sounds from his little snub nose, that the very room echoed again.

Charley was not slow in following him. Boys soon get over novelty, and before Tim had reached to his usual nasal pitch of perfection, he was in the land of dreams.

Throughout the night the snow fell fast, covering the shore and cliff with its purity, hiding the holes, and smoothing the roughness of the coarser earth; and when the boys awoke at daylight, they sprang delighted from their beds.

The snow, which pinches the old and punishes the poor, is "only fun" to youngsters.

"We'll have a lark to-day!" cried Tim; "nothing like a snow-ball—it's crummy."

"But there are only ourselves," said Charley.

"Let us pitch into Mops," suggested Tim.

"You remember what we promised yesterday?"

"Blow that; besides, the snow won't hurt him."

"I shan't touch Mops," said Charley, resolutely; "he's a cripple."

"Then we'll give it to some of 'em outside. We can get over the wall by the trees. We shan't be missed!"

"But how shall we get back?"

"Knock at the door of the lodge, and bolt in when Mops opens it. He won't split!"

"I don't think he will," answered Charley; "and if he does, it's only a thrashing! Anything is better than being poked in here all day."

Shortly after the breakfast hour, two youths might have been seen crossing the playground of Scarum School.

Arriving in the corner of the playground, the tallest rapidly climbed a tree, crept along a branch that overhung the highway, and dropped down.

He was followed, in a more laborious fashion, by a youth of exceeding rotundity, who narrowly escaped a broken neck several times during the journey, and when he dropped to the ground, fell, not on his feet, but on the broad of his back.

Fortunately the snow lay thickly, or under the combined effects of the fall, and the pressure of the skeleton suit, the career of Master Tim Turndown might there and then have come to an untimely termination.

"I never did see such luck as mine," he growled, as soon as he was able to speak; "such busters as I get always. Anything broke behind, Charley?"

"No," replied his chum, "not a rag rent."

"I heard something crack," muttered Tim, trying in vain to get a view of his back, "but it may be only stitches. Hallo! here's somebody coming."

"That's what the clown says," rejoined Charley. "Where?"

"Up the path leading from the beach."

"I see him now."

"Let's go behind the wall and make up a tight un or two," said Tim, and the two conspirators retired behind the wall to carry out the nefarious suggestion.

The unsuspecting "somebody coming" was a tall gaunt man in a threadbare suit, and a hat whose summers and winters were manifold. He bore under his arm a huge green gingham, and in his hand he carried a book, which he read with much gusto and delight.

He was walking slowly, halting every now and then to impre s some particular passage on his memory. thereby enabling Charley and Tim to get up a good stock of "tight uns" for his especial benefit.

As he advanced nearer, Charley, who was peeping round the corner, could see that the face of the reader was lighted up with enthusiasm; that he turned his eyes up like the suffering duck during an elementary disturbance, and waved his disengaged hand with the air of marked approval.

"Dear me," he exclaimed, as he got within ear-shot of the boys, "this is very striking."

So was the snowball launched by Charley straight as an arrow from a bow. It smote the enthusiastic reader on the nose, and brought a thousand varieties of cheap illuminations into his eyes.

"Hooroar!" shouted Tim, "here's another. Don't be afraid, sir, we're only larking."

"Larking, you villains!" roared the infuriated man; "I'll lark you, let me get near you."

He dodged to and fro, waving his gingham, and breathing threats most dire; but his enemies were too much for him — the "tight uns" were aimed too true, and beaten at all points, he finally retired to the wall, and placing his back against it, cried for quarter.

"Have another one," suggested Tim, dancing like a fat imp before him, "a little one."

"This is infamous," gasped the injured party, "preposterous. Where is the liberty of the subject;—the—the Magna Charta? Will you leave off?"

"I've only one more, sir," said Charley, politely, "and it's a pity to waste it."

And then the "last little lot" found a resting-place between the hapless victim's chin and comforter.

"I can endure no more," he shouted, and charged at them like a mad bull.

They fled. Charley escaped without difficulty; but Tim, who, like most unwieldy animals, required time to turn round, was not so fortunate.

The green gingham fell heavily on him just below the place where the two portions of the skeleton suit united.

"Take that, you villain," gasped the

stranger, unable to pursue. "It is well for you that I am somewhat exhausted."

"Yah!" sneered Tim; "hit a boy with a gingham!"

"I would break your neck, if I could," was the reply.

At a safe distance from the assaulted one, the boys stood and watched him replace his hat, pick up his book, and shake the snow from his attire.

This done, the stranger walked straight to the lodge of Scarum School, and knocked at the door.

"He knows us," gasped Tim, "and is gone to make a report."

"Nonsense," said Charley; "he's gone to make inquiry about the terms. See, Mops has asked him in."

"But he must know something."

"Nonsense. Let us go into the town, and have some fun."

The two truants went into the straggling town of Winkle-by-the-Sea, and whiled away the time after the manner of their hearts.

They pelted boys when they could, and men when there were no boys to pelt.

They did their share in the manufacture of a slide opposite a publican's door, the said publican charging out upon them every three minutes, and upsetting the youths who were "keeping the pot a-boiling."

They gave the finishing touches to a snow man outside the grammar-school, and put a snow ball into a letter-box; and then it was time to return home.

"Dinner at one," said Tim, "and it now wants twenty minutes. We shall do it beautifully."

They scampered home full of glee, rosy and healthy as a couple of cherubs, forgetful of their early morning adventure until Tim knocked at the door of the lodge; then Charley remembered it.

"It's just as well, Tim," he said, "to know who the fellow is. I'll ask Mops."

"Do," said Tim; "I'm sure he's been pitching into us strong."

When Mops opened the door, he stared "considerable some," as the Yankees say, to behold before him two lads he expected were in the safe keeping of Scarum School.

"You've been out," he said.

"We have," replied Charley, coolly, "or we shouldn't be here."

"I can't pass this over," remonstrat Mops. "How did you get out?"

"Over the wall."

"Ah!"

"Yes," said Tim; "it was one, two, and three and a jump."

"I must report you," said Mops, doubtfully shaking his head.

"Of course you must," rejoined Charley;

"we don't want to get you into a mess. You let a gentleman in this morning."

"How long ago?"

"About two and a half hours, perhaps three."

"A gentleman with a large gingham umbrella, a book and—a—perhaps a little snow about him. Who was it?"

"Mr. Matthew Pendulum, the usher."

"Lor!" gasped Tim, and leaned against the wall limp as a defunct starfish.

CHAPTER VI.

THE GENTLE LAMBS OF SCARUM SCHOOL.

"WHEW!" whistled Charley. "I think we've been and gone and made a considerable mess of it."

"Don't say we—it's me," groaned Tim. "I've done it."

"Bosh! we are both in it."

"So we are," said Tim; "but he may forget you—could he forget me in this beastly toggery? Oh! What sort of man is he, Mops?"

"If you've offended him, look out for squalls," answered Mops, sententiously.

"Offended him!" returned Tim; "we've smothered him with snow. I gave him two right uns in one ear, and Charley nearly stifled him. Just my luck. Is he in now, Mops?"

"No; he went in and brushed hisself, and went out, lookin' werry furus—I thought somebody had been brushin' his fur the wrong way."

"It can't be helped," said Charley. "Now, Tim, let us go in—dinner must be ready."

During the rest of the day they saw nothing of Mr. Pendulum, but after they had retired for the night, they heard him go past the dormitory door with a heavy footstep, which made Tim quake. The next day passed, and he did not appear; then they took heart, and went into the playground, where they amused themselves with the erection of a snow hut, but did not venture beyond the precincts of the school.

"If we keep out of his sight," said Charley, consolingly, "he may forget it."

"So he may," rejoined Tim, and then they tried to forget their little error.

A few days, monotonous in themselves, and of no interest to our readers, passed, and then the gentle lambs of Scarum School began to re-appear.

The first came in the evening, and presented himself *sans* ceremony to the new pupils in the school-room.

He was a quick-looking boy, with freckles, and he talked very rapidly, as if time, like his supper, was allowanced.

"Hallo! my birds," he cried, "how are you?"

"Flourishing," replied Charley, "how are you?"

"Blooming!" rejoined the other. "I always am as soon as I get away from home—it's so awfully dull there."

"This place is dull enough," returned Charley.

"Of course it is, my noble; but wait until they are all back—we shall be lively enough then. Oh! they are a prime lot of fellows—all incurables, of course;—but Crammer can't cure them."

"I have heard that Crammer is very severe," hinted Charley.

"So he is, after a fashion!" returned the other; "but pooh!" snapping his fingers—"we don't care a rap for him. Both of you new?—what's your names?"

Charley and Tim gave them readily.

"My name is Bob Martin; they call me Skitty," rejoined the last comer. "I say, Thorn, you look one of the right sort, but I don't think much of your chum—too crummy!"

"Don't you be cheeky" said Tim, looking at him very solemnly.

"Why not?"

"Because I don't like it."

"If that's the only reason, you had better shut up," said Bob Martin, frankly; "you will have lots of things you don't like here, I can tell you."

"But I won't have it," insisted Tim.

"You must, unless you fight; and one round would about wind you, I guess. But we needn't quarrel unless you like. If you do like, name your time and friend, and I'm your man."

There was a genial liberality in this offer that quite touched Charley's heart.

He looked upon Bob Martin as a good fellow, and told him so.

"Thank you," replied Bob; "I return the compliment. There is one thing you will have to do as soon as they are back—*you* must fight somebody."

"Why?"

"There is no particular reason," replied Bob, after a moment's consideration, "except that it is the rule. You will have several volunteer to oblige you, and you can pick your man. I think I hear some more of them on the stairs."

The door opened and four or five boys bounded into the room; they did not appear to be the victims of oppression and tyranny, but were overflowing with animal life and spirits.

"Here we are," cried Bob, dexterously turning a wheel. "How are you, Grimmer? How's the bull-dog, Samson? Sister quite well, Leicester?"

The last addressed was a handsome lad

with delicately-formed features, and curly flaxen hair, the sort of boy one would expect to have handsome sisters. He answered Bob Martin's query in a satisfactory manner, and that youth continued—

"Here's two new Incurables, my boys; stand up, my chicks; Charley Thorn and Tim Turndown, at your service, gentlemen. Don't bend too much when you bow, or you will make creases in your fat."

"Don't chaff him too much," interposed Charley, laughing; "Tim is a good fellow."

"What's the price of his frills by the dozen?" asked Grimmer—a sharp youth with a sarcastic style of face.

"Who bought his buttons?" asked Samson.

"I knew it," groaned Tim; "but there," he added, with a sudden fury, "come on, the whole lot; stand out of the way, Charley, I'll fight 'em."

"No, no," said Bob Martin, "we never fight the first night. You are not a duffer, I can see, so we won't chaff you any more—until to-morrow. Who's got anything to eat?"

"I've a heap of flat puffs," replied Grimmer, "but I can't touch them until we go upstairs. They are in my box."

"How did you get them in? Wasn't old Margery about?"

"Was she ever away?" asked Grimmer.

"No, boys! I had a false bottom made to my box, and they are snug enough."

A general murmur of admiration arose from his listeners. Grimmer smiled upon them with the proud consciousness of being a great inventor.

"I made it myself," he continued, "out of the top of an old kitchen table. There was a row at home when they found I had cut it up, but they never knew where it went to."

"I have a dozen new pairs of socks full of blackjack and bull's-eyes," said Samson; "but I dare not risk the pastry. The last time, when I brought it in my shirts, the jam came through the fronts. I couldn't go to church, I was in such a mess, and Crammer laid it on stiff."

"What have you, Leicester?" inquired Bob Martin.

"Four pounds sewn in the belt of my trousers," returned the boy. "Margery couldn't find it, though she did turn my pockets out. Uncle Jack gave it me on the quiet."

"I've an uncle," groaned Tim.

"What does he give you?" asked Bob.

"Whack on the head when I'm near him; long letters of abuse when I'm away," replied Tim.

The boys laughed; it might be death to Tim, but it was fun to them.

"I expected to see something very different to you fellows," said Charley, when the laughter had subsided. "I went by the advertisement, and expected nothing but a life of misery here."

"It's a good game to advertise that way," explained Bob Martin; "most fathers think their youngsters troublesome, and so they send them down here as an experiment; when they find the boys don't complain they keep them here."

CHAPTER VII.
NUMBER SIX DORMITORY

"WHAT sort of fellow is Mr. Pendulum?" inquired Tim.

"Very nice, if you *don't put him out,*" replied Bob Martin.

"And if he is put out?"

"Then he's very warm indeed—he's venom!"

"Oh!" exclaimed Tim, and fell into a musing state, as to the probable result of his snowball performance.

The boys now arrived thick and fast, until the crowded school-room rivalled Babel in the confusion of tongues; but there was no skylarking, nothing more than an exchange of reminiscences from home.

There was a great variety without a doubt at Scarum School—good, bad, and indifferent, were there—good tempered lads, sullen lads, and every other phase of humanity, as there is in the grown-up world.

"Has Mr. Crammer returned?" asked a weak-eyed lanky boy, addressing Bob Martin.

"He has *not* returned, Mr. Lobby Panks!" replied Bob; "you are in a precious hurry to see him. Have you picked up some news already?"

"Lobby Panks," as he was called, was the sneak of the school, the general reporter to the head master, when information was required. The shot from Bob went home, and he slunk away.

"I hate that fellow," growled Bob; "there goes the gong for supper—who's on for tommy and curdled milk?"

Hungry or not, the boys all descended to the dining-room, a long bare apartment, with no furniture beyond the long deal table, the forms for the boys, and a chair at each end for those who presided.

At one end sat Mrs. Margery, the housekeeper; at the other, Mr. Matthew Pendulum, the tutor.

Poor Tim, he knew him at once, and sought a seat remote from him, but ill-luck and the persistence of the old pupils, who objected to sit nearer the tutor than was absolutely necessary, forced Tim to a vacant seat upon the left hand of the outraged man.

For a time Mr. Pendulum was fully engaged in serving out maximums of bread, and minimums of cheese, but when the plates were all supplied, he sat calmly down and surveyed the pupils with an air of paternity.

Tim was in a dreadful state of mind; without looking at the great man, he was conscious of his eye approaching him by slow degrees, and soon the orbs of Mr. Pendulum fell upon him.

The tutor started and stared. Tim swallowed a huge piece of bread without mastication, and choked himself.

"A new boy, I perceive," said the tutor, when Tim had in a measure recovered himself. "What is your name?"

"Timothy Turndown, sir."

"Haven't I seen—you—somewhere—before?"

The question was asked in slow, measured accents. Tim felt that all concealment was futile.

"I think you have, sir," he said.

"*Outside* the school?"

"Yes, sir," said Tim.

"Very good," rejoined Mr. Pendulum; "proceed with your supper, Turndown."

Tim, wretched beyond expression, looked down the rank of boys facing him, where Charley was seated between Harry Leicester and Bob Martin.

Having succeeded in catching his friend's eye, Tim winked very slowly, and *accidentally* pointed his knife towards the tutor.

Charley had long ago marked his man, and only smiled in reply.

"That's all very well," thought Tim; "but I am in for it, as usual."

After supper Mr. Pendulum addressed a few words to the boys, having reference to the opening of the school, and the desirability of their conducting themselves in a becoming manner, and making themselves a credit to Scarum School; then dismissed them for the night.

Charley found that Grimmer, Samson, Harry Leicester, and Bob Martin were all occupants of the same dormitory, a discovery which gave him exceeding delight.

Tim was too much depressed to take pleasure in any discovery, and said so.

"Fancy my being shoved next to him to-night," he said, "and he knew me at once. 'Didn't I see you outside?' he says. 'Of course I did.' And won't he see me inside? Lor!"

"Ten minutes for undressing," shouted Bob Martin. "Now then, first night. Who'll be the hare?"

"What's up?" asked Charley.

"Hare and hounds over the beds for five minutes," replied Bob. "We give the hare three beds start. Now then, who leads?"

"I'm on," shouted Charley; "catch me who can!"

A rough-and-tumble race ensued—Charley vaulting over the beds with the agility of a deer; Bob Martin and Harry Leicester leading the pursuit.

Suddenly the door was thrown open, and Mr. Pendulum rushed in.

Tim, unhappily in the rear of the hounds, was directly in his way, and forthwith the tutor fell foul of him.

"This is a pretty beginning, Turndown," he said, holding him at arm's length; "but I must make an example of you."

A carefully-balanced cane gave the skeleton suit a severe dusting.

Tim took it without a cry. The rest stood looking on, as quiet as mice.

"Now, perhaps, you will all go quietly to bed," said the tutor, and left the room.

"You're a good plucked un," said Bob Martin; "give us your hand."

They all shook hands with him, and Tim was, in a measure, consoled; but he had his wounds to attend to.

"Candle-fat is a good thing," he said; and the superfluous tallow of the cotton candle was forthwith applied to the afflicted part.

"Now, into bed, boys," said Bob Martin; "I hear Mops coming round for the candles."

In the twinkling of an eye every youth was between the sheets, and, when Mops opened the door, they were apparently in sound repose.

"Good night, gentlemen," he said.

A chorus of snoring replies; and the old man went out, muttering something about their being beauties and no mistake."

Charley knew enough of school life to know that the evening's entertainment was not yet over; but being a stranger, he left it to others to take the lead.

He had not long to wait ere the voice of Bob Martin was heard:

"Harry, tip us the first verse—the usual song, you know. We always sing first nights."

"Is it allowed?" asked Charley.

"You will soon see," replied Bob, with a chuckle. "Now, Harry, lead off."

Harry Leicester then, in a clear, musical voice, sang the following song:—

> The boys that are now mustered here,
>   Are unruly as a rule—
> To cure them of their sinfulness,
>   They're sent to Scarum School.
> But all that Scarum School can do—
>   Whacks, penalties, and pains—
> Will never wipe their sins away,
>   Or bind them up in chains.

"So, heigho! for liberty and chorus, boys."

But all that Scarum School can do—
Whacks, penalties, and pains—
Will never wipe their sins away,
Or bind them up in chains.

The graceful melody was quickly taken up by the other dormitories, and soon the house was alive with music.

But not for long; for the banging of doors showed that the hawks were about, and the door of Number Six again opened to reveal the usher, with a bull's-eye lantern and a wrathful face.

"Who's singing here?"

No reply, save the sounds of gentle slumber from the peaceful.

The light travelled round from bed to bed, until it fell upon Tim; one eye was open, and he was detected.

"You were singing?" said the usher.

"I can't sing," returned Tim.

"You can sing!"

"I can't!" replied Tim, growing desperate under oppression.

"I will see about that," said the usher, turning down the sheets, and forthwith drew sweet sounds from the guilty one. "Who was singing with you?"

"Nobody. None of us can sing."

"Who was it, then?"

"Don't know; perhaps it was Mops, or the cats."

This reply was too much, especially as sundry gasping chuckles were heard in various parts of the room.

"I shall make this night's conduct a subject of especial enquiry," he said. "Mr. Crammer returns in two days; I shall lay it before him."

There was no response to this; and Mr. Pendulum retired for the last time that night.

In reckless defiance, they sang the song again, but were undisturbed; and finding this, the inhabitants of Number Six proceeded to further outrages.

"Let's cob Lobby Panks," suggested Bob Martin.

"What's he done?" asked Charley, with a yawn.

"Nothing yet; but he's sure to be up to something in a day or two. Sneaking is his line."

"How will you work it?"

"Seize him in bed, gag him, and bring him here. Who'll help me?"

There was no lack of volunteers.

Even Charley and Tim offered to become members of the foraging party; but as they were strangers in the house, and might lose their way, their services were not accepted.

"All in good time," said Bob; "we shall want you another day."

He then led out a small party of marauders in their night-dresses. They were back almost immediately, bearing a white bundle in their arms; this was Lobby Panks, bound and gagged with a sheet and a pillow-case.

"Put him on the floor, there," said Bob Martin; "we will try him first. Charley, you be judge. Tim, you can be the jury."

Both offices suiting the boys immensely, they readily acquiesced.

Charley sat up in the bed with a white cotton handkerchief over his head, to represent a wig; Tim settled himself to listen to the evidence against the prisoner.

It was a moonlight night, and a broad ray came through the window, the blinds being drawn by Harry Leicester. Altogether, the proceedings had a wild, weird aspect, and were therefore intensely enjoyable.

CHAPTER VIII.

THE TRIAL AND SENTENCE.—THE FINALE.

"FIRST witness!" said Bob Martin, speaking like a whispering usher of a court of law.

Lobby Panks here gave a wriggle and a groan, and Grimmer, who did constable duty over him, gave him an admonitory shake.

"If you interrupt the court," he said, "you are sure to get it warmer—so be quiet!"

The first witness was a youth whose name was strange to the judge and jury—otherwise Charley and Tim—he gave it as Richard Harty.

"The duffer at the bar," he said, "peached upon me last half, when I fastened Mr. Crammer's bedroom door up, and called 'Fire!' through the key-hole. I had a licking for it—a regular bender—was sore for a week, and savage for a month!"

"Have you any questions to ask the witness?" asked Charley, sweetly.

Lobby Panks rolled his eyes about and kicked.

"He says No," interpreted Grimmer.

"Good! the next witness."

The next was Harry Leicester, who deposed to Lobby having betrayed the secret of a large store of fireworks, and thereby caused the confiscation thereof.

"I gave sixpence for one lovely cracker," said Harry, mournfully; "and it was let off in the private back-yard, for the benefit of Toddy Crammer!"

"Who is Toddy Crammer?" asked the learned judge.

"The eldest son of our beloved head master," rejoined Harry Leicester, "and precious imp he is. He'll return with his respected parient."

The prisoner was asked, as before, if he had anything to say to the witness, but this time he remained sulky and still.

"This conduct won't do you any good," said Grimmer, shaking him; "contempt of court is a bad thing at Scarum School!"

Lobby Panks evidently thought so by the expression of his eyes, but he made no apology; perhaps, under the circumstances, he would have had a difficulty in doing so.

"My lord," said Bob Martin, who had relations in the law, and knew the ordinary mode of procedure, "if I desired to do so, I could multiply the number of my witnesses tenfold, and prove the vagabond shivering at the bar to be the greatest sneak and duffer that ever had the prospect of getting a cobbing. My lord, and gentleman of the jury, the case is clear, the time is short, and it's getting colder every minute; so while you settle the matter, I will, with your leave, get into bed."

Without waiting for leave, Bob rolled himself up like a hedgehog, while Grimmer, in sonorous tones, asked the gentleman of the jury for his verdict. Tim had, however, fallen asleep, and answered with a nasal sound of unimportant meaning.

"Now, then, wake up!" cried Grimmer, "is the prisoner guilty or not guilty?"

Tim, opening his eyes, rubbed them, and answered—

"Awfully guilty—give it to him warm!"

Charley then leaned back on his pillow, and passed sentence.

"Lobby Panks, you have, after a long and patient trial, been found guilty of sneaking and peaching, and as nothing could be more duffing or deserving of punishment, the sentence of the court is, that you be cobbed forthwith, and acting upon the recommendation of an enlightened jury—who is snoring again—wake him up, Grimmer—acting upon the recommendation of the jury, I trust you will get it hot."

A few willing executioners volunteered their services, and the wretched Panks was cobbed without delay. He took his punishment with many sighs, tears, and groans, and when it was over, they thrust him outside the dormitory with the recommendation to cut it at once.

"It's a case of great necessity," said Bob Martin, "for he's a regular beggar to upset everything; he has the eyes and ears of half a dozen, and he makes good use of 'em."

"What's the row now?"

A cry of terror and a scream rang through the house; it was followed by the voice of Mrs. Margery shouting for help.

"Thieves! fire! burglars! help!"

Then came a protest in the weak voice of the cobbed victim.

"It's only me, ma'am!"

"Who are you?"

"Master Panks, ma'am. I couldn't see you in the dark, and you fell over me ma'am!"

"What are you doing here?"

"I've been dragged from my bed, ma'am, and beaten upon my—my—cobbed, ma'am."

"Don't talk such low slang to me, sir," rejoined the dame, indignantly; "I shall report your conduct to Mr. Crammer. If Mr. Pendulum did his duty, he would prevent this, instead of hiding away in his room, as if he were ashamed of you. *Mr. Pendulum!*"

No answer was vouchsafed to her scream. Lobby Panks sniffed deprecatingly.

"Why don't you go to bed?" cried the enraged woman; "let me get hold of you. It's a good thing for you that my candle is out."

They heard her groping about until she fell again over some boxes in the passage, but Panks apparently succeeded in making his escape, and after a few mutterings directed at the school in general, the housekeeper retired.

"They'll carpet Panks to-morrow, I suppose," said Charley.

"Sure to," replied Leicester.

"He will peach about his trial."

"Let him, nobody will believe him, and if they do it won't matter to us. Mr. Crammer seldom punishes us unless he bowls us out himself, and then it's dance, boatman, dance, with some of us, I can tell you."

"Stop that row," growled Grimmer; "I'm getting sleepy."

"Good night, old boy."

"Good night."

And in a few minutes Number Six Dormitory was in sweet repose.

CHAPTER IX.

TIM DISTINGUISHES HIMSELF.

MOST of our readers have doubtless experienced many first mornings at school after the holidays. The boys have not yet settled to their work, and the holidays still hang about master and ushers, lessons are scamped or totally ignored, and no serious business is expected until the second day.

It had invariably been so at Scarum School, but, to the astonishment of the elder boys, Mr. Pendulum, on taking his seat, made the following announcement:

"Boys, the holidays have been of more than usual duration, owing to the lamented indisposition of the respected head of this establishment. As I trust and believe that you have devoted the additional time to your studies, I expect to find you perfect. First class, English grammar."

First class stood up and blundered about in the mazes of Lindley Murray; many delinquents were there, but dismissed with a mild reproof. The same with the others, who were sent back in like form. Many of the boys were still absent, but sixty stood up in the various classes—a goodly number to pass an examination with a dose of "tickler" in those days.

Neither Charley nor Tim stood up, being new boys and not appointed to a class.

At Mr. Pendulum's request, they now stood forward.

A brief examination of Charley resulted in his being appointed to the first class.

Then came the ordeal for Tim, with a result not quite so satisfactory.

"Turndown," said Mr. Pendulum, "attend to me."

Tim fixed his eyes upon him, as a hapless sparrow would stare at a rattlesnake.

"How far are you in geography?"

Tim took so long to reflect, that the usher extended his left hand towards "tickler;" then he answered hastily—

"Nowhere, sir."

"Nowhere! What do you mean by that?"

"Never learned it, sir."

"H'm! a lamentable state of ignorance. How about English grammar?"

"Never learnt it, sir."

"Arithmetic?"

"I'm in addition, sir."

"Indeed. How much does nine and seven make?"

Tim was proceeding to work this terrible sum out upon his fingers, when the sudden elevation of the cane checked him.

"How much does eight and seven make?"

"You said nine and seven before, sir."

"I did *not*," answered the usher, bringing the cane down upon the desk violently. "How dare you contradict me, sir? How much is nine and six?"

Poor Tim was now utterly confused, and, driven to desperation, he replied—

"Twenty-three."

Mr. Pendulum smiled grimly.

"Where have you been to school?" he asked.

"Nowhere, sir—at least, nowhere particular, sir."

"What do you mean by that?"

"When I came from the infant-school, my uncle took me to teach, sir."

"And what has he taught you?"

"I don't know, sir," replied Tim, turning cold as Mr. Pendulum groped in his desk.

The usher produced a large sheet of foolscap, which he dexterously twisted into a sugar-loaf form, and, pasting the sides together, formed a very striking head-dress.

"It's plain to me, Turndown," he said, "that you are a complete dunce. We allow no dunces here; and I mean to shame you out of your ignorance."

Tim rubbed his hands thoughtfully together, and winked his little round eyes, but otherwise betrayed no emotion.

"There," said the usher, fixing the cap upon his head, "that will do; stand upon that box for the rest of the morning."

Tim marched slowly across the school, under a fire of broad grins, and slowly mounted upon a tall box, the observed of all observers.

Standing there, he was so droll a spectacle that even Charley smiled.

Tim's face seemed to be moulded in iron.

"Is this a usual game?" whispered Charley.

"No; quite new. Got up especially for Tim. Look at him; he's going to sleep; he'll fall off. Where's my shooter? Bob, cover me, will you, while I wake him up?"

Tim was indeed going into a somnolescent state when a friendly pea smote him on the nose and aroused him. The pea rebounded to the usher's desk, and trickled slowly down. Mr. Pendulum fixed an eye upon his victim. Tim returned his gaze with a stony stare.

"You be careful, sir," said the usher; "put your hands behind you."

"What have I done?" demanded the injured Tim.

Mr. Pendulum made no reply, but placed the pea among his penholders, to bear future record against Tim's villanies.

In the course of half an hour, the writing books were served out, and the usher went round from boy to boy to watch his progress during the copying labours. In this he was interrupted by Mops, who came into the room, hat in hand.

"A gentleman to see you, sir," he said.

"To see me, Mops?"

"Yes, sir; he wanted Mr. Crammer, but as he's not at home, Mrs. Margery thought he had better see you."

"Thank you, Mops; I will come directly. Boys," he said, addressing his promising charges, "I trust you will not disgrace this establishment during my absence. Should this gentleman have brought a new pupil, any noise or riot may prove detrimental to Mr. Crammer. As that gentleman is absent and the second usher not yet engaged, I must rely upon your love of order."

"As for you," he added, addressing Tim, "move but an inch and I will punish you severely."

He left the room, and in a moment every boy had left his desk. Tim, heedless of the warning, rolled from his pedestal, and cut a caper.

"Who's for a lark?" he cried; "give us a back, Charley."

Charley promised, obliged him, and Tim vaulted over with unexpected agility.

"Ain't this a lark?" he said; "I say, did you ever see an Indian war-dance?"

"Never!" chorussed half a score of voices.

"Then I'll show you one," said Tim. "Here, give me some of old Pendulum's quill pens; stick them round this hat, ten in the crown—now then, look out."

Charley sat facing him on the form, the others gathered around, tolerably quiet.

"Steady it is," cried Tim; "one, two, three, and off. Whoop-la!"

It was a sight to behold the little fat fellow in the skeleton suit performing wondrous feats with his arms and legs, learned goodness alone knows where; he twisted, turned, stamped, and whirled in fine style, uttering at intervals imaginary war whoops.

"Bravo!" cried the spectators, as he halted for a breath; "good again, Tim."

"I've not half done yet,' rejoined Tim, "that's the peaceful part of the dance. I'm going in for the bloodthirsty next. Here we are. Whoop!"

"Look out for Mr. Pendulum," said Harry Leicester.

"Blow old Pendulum," replied Tim, recklessly.

"Here we go—hi--there—whoop!—The—Indian war-dance---gentlemen. Blow old Pendulum! Who's he?"

A staggering blow on the side of the head sent Tim reeling to the further end of the school; there he fell upon the floor, and recovering a little, beheld the enraged tutor standing before him, and the spectators of the war-dance quietly sneaking to their seats.

"This conduct is infamous!" said the tutor; "stand up, sir!"

Tim stood up, and Mr. Pendulum raised his arm to strike, but he let it fall.

"No," he said; "Mr. Crammer shall settle this. He will know how to deal with you. A pretty scene this," he said, "to introduce a stranger to. Smith," he addressed, turning towards the door, "come in!"

A tall boy, apparently about fifteen years of age, emerged from the shadow of the doorway, and stood beside the usher.

"Young gentlemen," he said, "a new comrade—Julius Cæsar Smith!"

CHAPTER X.

CHARLEY CALLED UPON.—HE REPLIES.

THE new pupil was not a pleasant-looking boy; he had good features and a well-built figure, but his expression was bad, and as he looked around the room he scowled upon the pupils in what may be called a baronial style.

"This is Lord Soapdish!" whispered Bob Martin.

"Or his grandmother!" rejoined Harry Leicester.

"Or an emissary from the court of His Serene Highness Prince Tittlebat!" added Charley. "Look out, Bob! he's going to sit by you!"

"You will find room here," said Mr. Pendulum, and the haughty one was forthwith installed next to the lively Bob—introduced as it were into the midst of a nest of hornets—for Grimmer was on the other side, and Samson, Charley, and Harry Leicester opposite.

Julius Cæsar Smith deigned to cast no look upon his companions, but busied himself with arranging his books in his desk—that done to his satisfaction, he put down the lid, opened his English History, and began to read.

"Is your lordship's family quite well?" asked Bob, with an air of anxiety.

Julius Cæsar looked up, and frowned.

"My family is quite well," he said.

"No measles, or fits, or whooping-cough, among 'em, lately?" continued Bob.

"Or tumbled into a starch basin?" added Harry Leicester.

"Or caught cold in the back?" said Grimmer.

The face of the new pupil flushed, but he made no reply, and the charge was renewed, Charley opening the ball this time.

"Your uncle," he said, "I hope, has recovered?"

"From what?"

"The indignity of bearing the name of Smith; your lordship in person must feel it keenly."

"If you will have the kindness to address me in a becoming manner," rejoined the stranger, "I will answer you—Oh!"

"If you make that row," said Bob Martin, "'tickler' and you will come together."

"You pricked me, sir."

"I did, with a pin. Behold the little article which has ruffled his lordship."

"You will repent this," muttered Julius Cæsar Smith, grinding his teeth. "My pa, though reduced, hoped he had placed me among gentlemen."

"Do you insinuate that we are not?" quickly inquired Charley.

"I mean to say that you are a low, paltry beggar," returned the other.

"And you are an upstart cad, Mr. Julius Cæsar Smith, and I will take some of the stiffness out of your back as soon as school is over."

" I am at your service," replied the other, bowing magnificently.

"A fight!—scrumptious!" said Bob Martin, with a sympathetic wriggle.

With electrical rapidity the news passed round the school, and reached even Tim upon his perch.

"A fight!—jolly!—scrumptious!" and so on, commented the lads.

And from that moment every thought of lessons departed from them.

Mr. Pendulum had a hard time of it.

Class after class came up and went down in disgrace, and a long list of names with black marks against them was prepared for the edification of Mr. Crammer upon his return.

This troubled the boys very little.

Absorbed in the coming fight, they ignored the prospect of future punishment, and discussed in whispers the merits of the two antagonists.

Both were strangers; but Charley had been four-and-twenty hours at Scarum School, and had already gained many friends.

Julius Cæsar Smith had but just arrived, and had not made a very favourable impression, but he was not without supporters.

Connoisseurs, the heroes of a score of fights, declared that he had more muscle and was stouter built than Charley, and had a further advantage of being the eldest; so the coming contest was looked forward to with a vast amount of interest.

At twelve o'clock the school was dismissed, books and slates disappeared like magic, and, although a slight snow was falling, and the wind blowing keenly, every boy made at once for the grounds.

There was but one spot where such a contest could come off, and that was between the south side of the school and the wall, where they would be secure from all observation, save that of Mops.

But Mops was all right. The boys knew he never peached when other similar affairs had come off, and the combatants were assured that interruption was impossible.

Charley, surrounded by Tim, Harry Leicester, Bob Martin, and others, was the first to strip. Julius Cæsar Smith seemed in no hurry about it, but leisurely surveyed the faces of those around him.

"It seems to me," he said, "that my opponent has plenty of friends—will no one support me?"

Of course they would! A dozen stepped to his side in a moment, and choosing one—Pangford by name—Cæsar began to "peel."

As he stripped off his jacket and waistcoat, and rolled up his shirt sleeves, well-developed muscles met the admiring gaze of the boys, and many of them cast pitying glances at Charley, who was much slighter built, but clean skinned and as wiry as a hare.

Tim, ardently supporting his friend, had brought a bottle of water and a sponge, and with ulterior views in respect of a black eye, opened his pocket-knife and laid it on the snow to cool.

"It may be wanted, Charley," he said, with a significant wink, "for he's a tough un."

Charley smiled confidently.

"I shall want something more than that to bring me round," he said, "when I give in."

"As for giving in," rejoined Bob Martin, "you can't do it. It's against your nature; but if you will take my advice, fight low and guard your ribs. If he winds you it's all over. Keep your right for defence the first few rounds and let him have your left. Now then, he's ready!—go in and win! Boys, keep the ring."

Bob pushed back a few ardent spectators, and then the two antagonists stood face to face.

It was a moment of breathless interest.

They eyed each other cautiously as they approached within distance; suddenly their hands and arms were up, and Charley led off smartly with his left.

It fell short, but just touched the chin of Julius Cæsar; his dark brows closed over his eyes with a sullen expression, and he rushed in to close.

But Charley was not to be had that way, he knew that he was scarcely a match for his foe in a wrestle, so he dodged dexterously under his arm, turned smartly round, and, planting a blow on the side of his head, laid him in the snow.

"That's the way, Charley!" cried Tim, in ecstacies, as our hero retired to his corner; "about half a dozen like that will settle him."

"No fear of that," answered Charley; "I've my work cut out and so has he. Roll my sleeves tighter."

When time was called, Charley forced the fighting at once, and Julius Cæsar remained solely on his guard. The blow on the side of his head was a stinger, and he was taking time to recover himself. He was no mean boxer, and Charley, after many feints, only succeeded in giving one "rib-bender."

This woke up Julius Cæsar, and he rushed in, apparently to close as before, but he suddenly pulled up short when he expected Charley would dodge, hoping to get him into chancery. Again was he disappointed.

Charley saw the move, and instead of ducking his head, leaped forward and gave Julius a terrific facer, straight between the eyes, and he went down like an ox.

"The fight's over," cried Tim, his voice rising above the triumphant shouts of the boys, "he's done for."

"Stop that capering," rejoined Charley, "and give me a little water. He's not done for yet."

It was so. Terrific as the blow had been, and it was one many men would have winced under, Julius answered readily to the call of "Time!" and stepped out with his dark brows almost hidden by the swelling above his eyes.

He was cool still, and uttered no word, but Charley saw that his teeth were tightly set, and resolved to fight on the defensive.

"If he gets me in his clutches," he thought, "I'm done."

Slowly round and round they stepped, each watching for some relaxation in the vigilance of his opponent, but without any success for at least a couple of minutes, then Charley thought he saw an opening, and rushed in.

This time he was mistaken. Julius Cæsar was doing a bit of good generalship, and only dropped his guard for a moment to induce Charley to make a rush.

This was done; he was on the alert in a moment, and caught our hero in his arms.

For many years afterwards boys in Scarum School talked of that struggle. As the actual witnesses of it departed, they handed it down to their successors until it became legendary in the school-house on the cliff.

With every muscle strained to the utmost, and limbs locked, they strove for the mastery; their bodies slowly rocking to and fro, never budged an inch, while the boys stood in breathless silence for the issue.

Presently the ground was shifted, and Julius Cæsar stepped back a pace.

This was apparently an advantage to Charley, but he gained little by it; strive as he might, he could not throw his foe from his firm, statue-like footing.

"This can't last," whispered Tim.

"No," rejoined Bob Martin; "one must go directly. If Charley falls, have him up in a moment and sponge his face."

The tactics of the youngsters now changed; they shifted legs, and violently exerted themselves to bring about a fall.

Round and round they spun, trampling the snow beneath their feet, and breathing hurriedly between their set teeth.

This could not last; signs of fatigue began to set in; it became painfully apparent to Charley's friends he was getting blown, and Tim was about to say as much to Bob when Julius, with a cry of triumph, lifted Charley fairly off his feet and dashed him to the ground.

It was a cruel fall, and no cheer followed the victor as he walked to his corner with a look of one who has satisfied a deadly hatred.

Tim and Bob rushed forward and raised Charley in their arms.

He was insensible.

"Here's a pretty go," moaned Tim, "Charley's licked."

"Don't snivel," muttered Bob; "but sponge him well, while I rub his hands. That's it—eyes open already. How are you, Charley?"

"A little giddy, old fellow," replied our hero; "but I'm ready."

"Keep still; you have a few moments. Give him a drink, Tim."

When the warning cry came from the opposite corner, Charley staggered into the arena, and all around looked upon his defeat as certain.

Tim showed violent demonstrations towards blubbering, and began loosening the buttons of his skeleton suit.

"What are you up to?" growled Bob Martin.

"He's not going to be murdered before my eyes," muttered Tim. "I shall slip into that fellow, Smith, myself."

"You do nothing of the sort," said Bob, pushing him back. "Charley's not beat yet—look at him—he's getting his second wind."

Charley certainly backed up amazingly in a few moments, and Julius Cæsar, who had relied upon an easy and immediate victory, was assured of his error by two blows, one on the lips and the other on the cheek, following each other rapidly.

The confident smile he had assumed fled, and his old look of ferocity returned, and he launched out several wild blows, any one of which, if it had reached our hero, would have ended the combat. But Charley kept warily out of reach, contenting himself with giving a left-hander whenever an opportunity arrived.

This round ended without their closing, both combatants, being winded by their sparring exertions. Julius Cæsar went into his corner and sat in gloomy silence. Charley hinted to Bob and Tim that "he was coming round and felt stronger than ever."

"Second wind is always best," said Bob Martin, "and I think if you go now upon another tack you'll win. His eyes are swelling, and you only want to wind him now—half-a-dozen rib plasters will do it."

"I'd kick him," said Tim, viciously.

"Like a young ass," said Bob. "There's your man rising; don't let him be the first in the field."

Charley went in as advised and severely peppered the ribs of Master J. C. Smith, who, finding one of his eyes closing fast, and his breath going, made a frantic effort to grapple his foe. He failed and got his head into chancery.

A yell of delight rent the air, and in the judgment of those learned in such matters Julius Cæsar was beaten.

"Bravo, Thorn! Well done, Charley! Now he's settled!" were the cheering cries, when a louder voice than all broke in, and Mr. Matthew Pendulum stood before them.

Charley was erect; but Julius lay panting on the ground, blood streaming from his nose, and one eye blinking with undiminished ferocity.

"What is the meaning of this?" demanded Mr. Pendulum, angrily; "is this the proper way to begin a studious course? What will Mr. Crammer think of it when he returns?"

No answer—and not a boy even shifted his seat. Most of them knew what was coming.

"Thorn, Turndown, Martin, Smith, and Pangford, you will retire to the cell—you know it, Martin," added the tutor, significantly; "lead the way"

Bob only waited until Charley and Julius had put on their jackets, and then marched off with an imperturbable countenance, and the rest of the boys broke up into twos and threes and strolled about the ground until dinner time.

The cell, as Mr. Pendulum called it, was a long room at the back of the house, kept entirely bare except upon such occasions as will presently appear. It had three windows almost level with the cliff, with strong iron bars as safeguards and preventives to youths of an exploring turn of mind, and the glass was painted outside to hide all view of the beautiful sea.

It was, in fact, the punishment place, the "black hole" of Scarum School, where youthful prisoners were sent to await judgments on their high crimes and misdemeanours, and afterwards, to use the professional words, "served their time."

It was only for the highest breaches of discipline that culprits were sent there; and although, as the tutor significantly pointed out, Master Bob Martin knew the way there, he had only twice before made an acquaintance with this desirable place of retirement.

It was, indeed, a cheerless room. The fire-place in the corner was bricked up, and the bare walls and ceiling were entirely unrelieved by any ornament or fittings whatever.

They found the door ajar, and when the troupe of culprits entered, Bob pushed it to, and it closed with a spring which could be only opened on the outside, thus adding to its resemblance to a prison.

"Here, gentlemen," said Bob, "is our place of rest; make yourselves at home"

"I say, old fellow," said Charley, addressing his late opponent, "now that the fight's over, let's be friends. Give us your fist."

Julius Smith scowled like the baron in the play, and retired to a corner, where he sat down in dignified silence

Tim immediately improved the opportunity.

"Now, Smith, he said, walking up and standing before him with his legs wide apart, "you had better doctor that eye of yours. Have you got a knife?"

No answer.

"Lie down and cool it on the floor," suggested Tim; "or there's the hearthstone. You *will* have a precious peeper to-morrow."

Julius Cæsar looked at him loweringly; but uttered not a word.

CHAPTER XI.

THE CELL.—MR. CRAMMER RETURNS.

"ONCE I had an eye like that," said Tim, with a communicative air—"got it from a young butcher, because I called him 'Suet.' I put it against the pump for an hour, and brought it right beautiful."

"Go to your friends," muttered Smith.

"A chap of your rank ought not to have a black eye," pursued Tim, ignoring the advice; "what would your aristocratic father and your anxious mother say? Your lordship must feel that if—"

"Will nobody take this fat fool away?" roared Julius Cæsar.

"Eh! what's that?" rejoined Tim, "fat fool! Charley, hold my jacket, and lend me your braces to keep my bags up, and I'll have a go in with him."

"Nonsense," laughed Charley, pushing Tim back, "he would murder you."

"Would he?" replied Tim, "let him try it. Who's he? Baron Putty, I suppose, or Lord Scraps, or His Royal Highness the Dook of Cork. Yah! who got a licking and a black eye?"

"Keep him quiet, will you?" growled Julius Cæsar Smith, savagely. "I don't want any cheek from a fellow like him."

"Who'll stand by me?" demanded Tim, fiercely. "Will you lend me your braces, Charley? Here, hold this beastly jacket, and I'll fight without 'em. Talk to me in that style? Come here and let me close that other eye."

"You can't fight here," said Bob Martin; "drop it for to-day; you began it, Tim, you know."

"So I did," rejoined Tim, cooling down; "but I'm not fat, only reasonably stout, am I?"

"Certainly not, old boy; now drop it."

"It's preciously cold," said Tim, after a

gloomy silence : " let's have a game of some sort."

"Go it, 'Touch' is the thing," cried Charley ; " here, Tim, you've got it."

All but the gloomy, venomous owner of the black eye, immediately began scampering about the room, setting their blood aglow, while Julius Cæsar, shrouded in his dignity, sat and shivered in the corner.

The game was interrupted by Mops, who brought in five portions of bread and cheese, and a jug of water. The old man put them on the floor, and was about to depart when Bob checked him.

"What's this, Mops ? "

"Dinner for five."

" Where's the pudding ? "

" There ain't none to-day."

" Why not ? "

" You arn't to have none."

" And no beer ? "

"Nothing 'o that sort," said Mops, shaking his head. "Mr. Pendulum said he should be exceeding of his dooty if he gave you any luxuries."

"But how can a fellow dine off this ? " demanded Bob, in disgust.

"You needn't if you don't like it," hinted Mops.

Charley went up to the porter and whispered in his ear.

"Couldn't do it," replied the old man, shaking his head. " I should have the sack straight."

"Who would peach here ? " asked Charley, "who'd be mean enough ? "

"I have been peached on," replied Mops, sadly, "and by them as I've trusted most. I've got notice if I does anything ag'in rules ag'in I'm to go, and then there's the work'us and nothin' else for me."

"You're right enough this time," urged Charley ; "trust us, old fellow, if you never trust another."

"Well, I will. I'll shove it through the door," said Mops, " and you mustn't leave a crumb."

"No fear."

"What's the game ? " inquired Bob, when the porter was gone.

"You will see in a minute," replied Charley ; "put that rough tommy in the corner."

In a few minutes the door was quietly opened, and something wrapped in a piece of newspaper was thrust in.

Charley opened it, and revealed a good remnant of his cake, at the sight of which Tim, Bob, and Pangford cut triumphant capers.

"Now," said Charley, " we will divide it into five parts."

"You need not cut any for me," said Julius Cæsar, sulkily.

"Why not, old boy ? "

" I don't want any."

"Don't be an ass."

" I won't have any."

"Then we cut it into four," said Charley, calmly ; "and now, boys, peg away."

"I think his lordship is a-pining for a cut of salmon," whispered Tim, with his mouth full, "or a weal pie."

"Hold your tongue, Tim," said Charley, laughing ; "mind you, he will have his revenge for all this chaff."

"I'm not afraid of him," rejoined Tim, adding to himself, "if you stand by me."

The welcome meal disposed of, every crumb was carefully swept away, to keep faith with Mops, and sundry exercises were indulged in, to scare away the cold.

Julius Cæsar Smith, after sitting until he was almost cramped, rose up and walked slowly to and fro. Tim, in the most accidental manner in the world, ran against him, and shot him into a corner.

"Keep out of the way," said Tim, indignantly.

A magnificent scowl spread over the other's face as he leaned against the wall watching the game with contempt.

"You can have your fling," he said ; " I will settle with you by-and-by."

Nothing more was said, and Tim, in the excitement of the game, forgot the threat. It must have been about three o'clock when Mops re-appeared and announced that Mr. Crawshay Crammer had returned, and earnestly desired the honour of their company for a few minutes.

"Now," said Bob, tightening a belt he wore, "we are in for it. "How is he, Mops ? "

"Mr. Crammer," replied the porter, "have been disapp'inted of a pupil, and he's oncommon savage."

"Stop a moment," rejoined Bob, " I'll take it up another hole. Do you wear a belt, Charley ? "

"Yes."

"Pull it in then, and all you that have one do the same."

"I've nothing but brass buttons," groaned Tim. "I'm a ready-made article for a whacking, I am."

"Come along, gentlemen," urged Mops, "Mr. Crammer don't like to be kept a-waitin'."

The master of Scarum School awaited their coming in the breakfast parlour, and when the boys entered, he rapidly scanned their faces, especially those of the three strangers.

Charley expected to find a lowering, brutal

man; but Mr. Crammer was nothing of the kind. He had a handsome face, a soft smile, and a musical voice. His attire was neat and gentlemanly, and his linen spotless. As sleek as a cat, and at times as cruel.

"Well, young gentlemen," he said, in a clear, pleasant tone of voice, "I hear a very bad report of you. Who are the principal offenders?"

Julius Cæsar Smith, *alias* Lord Scraps, alone offered a reply.

"I was annoyed," he said, "as soon as I took my seat, and challenged to fight."

"Who challenged you?"

"Master Thorn."

"Is that true, Thorn?" asked Mr. Crammer with his most pleasant smile.

"Quite true, sir; the quarrel arose out of a few words.

"Very good. Then you, Smith, are in a measure exempt," said Mr. Crammer. "You will learn Cato's Soliloquy on Death before you retire to-night. Return to your studies."

Julius Cæsar left the room, and Mr. Crammer proceeded—

"The rest of this affair I know of. The report comes from a source I cannot, and have no right to doubt. Ring the bell, Martin."

Bob complied, and one of the housemaids appeared.

"Put two beds in the cell, Mary," said Mr. Crammer, sweetly, "at once, if you please. You, Thorn and Turndown, will pass three days there. I see I must be stern with you. Martin and Pangford, come here."

Bob and the other came forward, and being desired to bend, received from Mr. Crammer as neat a thrashing as any youth could desire. He did it smiling all the while, and only desisted when fairly tired out.

"Return to your studies," he said, "and be brought before me again within a month if you dare!"

Bob's face rivalled the full moon as he retired, but he managed to squeeze out a private wink for the benefit of Charley, and an encouraging nod for Tim. Pangford, blinded by his tears, could see nothing, and made a futile effort to get out of the room through the cheffonier. Mr. Crammer led him to the door, and dismissed him with a box on the ear, which aroused a noise in the head like a jangling peal of bells.

The master returned to the room, and without bestowing a glance upon his pupils, sat down to write. Charley and Tim eyed each other in a gloomy, meditative manner.

Mr. Crammer filled a sheet of foolscap with a fair round hand, which he read over with much apparent gusto, and then proceeded to enlighten the boys.

"I do everything on a system," he said, "and here I have written out rules for you during your incarceration. Attend! Turndown, why are you rolling your eyes?"

"Was I rolling my eyes, sir?" asked Tim, starting.

"Answer me, and don't ask questions," replied Mr. Crammer, "or ——" he pointed towards a slender cane with much significance. "Now attend!"

"Masters Thorn and Turndown will, during their three days' incarceration in the cell, rise with the first gong in the morning, make their beds, and put the room generally in order—then, until the breakfast hour, they will prepare their lessons. After breakfast I will hear them in person. As they will have much time on their hands, all lessons will be *trebled* and heard in three portions, viz., morn, noon, and night. Any further relaxation from the course of duty will be visited by other punishments according to the rules of Scarum School."

"This," said Mr. Crammer, "I will have pasted in the cell. You will then have no excuse for backsliding. Ring the bell, Thorn."

The bell was within a few inches of his hand; but Mr. Crammer was apparently a man who loved to take things easy, and Charley, crossing the room, rang the bell. Mary again responded.

"The cell ready, Mary?"

"Yes, sir."

"Show these young gentlemen into it, and send Mops to me."

"Yes, sir."

Mary was a buxom country lass, evidently possessed of a sympathetic heart, for she looked at the boys with much commiseration as they crossed the hall.

"What ha' you been a doing of?" she asked.

"Had a fight," said Charley. "Will you wait upon us, Mary?"

Mary shook her head.

"You'll ha' plenty of 'em waitin' on you beside me," she said; "but I pities you, for it's awfully cold there when the wind blows from the sea."

"I shall keep in bed," said Tim.

"You can't," returned the girl; "they be in and out a dozen times a day, and there be a *peep-hole in the door*; but don't say as I said so," she added, "or Mrs. Margery will be down on me."

Charley thanked Mary for her sympathy, and told that she need not fear he would betray her. Tim vowed he would die first.

"If you gets any little things, such as a bit o' pie or meat, wrapped up with your dinner," whispered Mary, "eat 'em up clean. Mrs. Margery be a sharp un; but there be sharper than her."

THE WHEEL OF TORTURE.

"You are a brick, Mary," said Charley; "give us your hand."

They both shook hands with Mary and entered their prison-house.

The door closed behind them.

"Here's a go," whistled Tim; "here's a precious crib to be shut up in for three days."

"I'm not going to keep here three days," rejoined Charley.

"You must."

"I won't!'

"Then Mr. Crammer must change his mind."

"Not he; but I'm not going to be stuck here, I tell you."

"What's your game?" asked Tim, after a moment's reflection.

"Look at that window, Tim."

"I see it."

"What is beyond?"

"The cliff and the sea, I suppose."

"Then we will go out and enjoy the cliff and the sea."

"Oh! come, drop it," cried Tim. "Just look at the shadow of those iron bars."

"Yes, I see them."

"And the window is nailed down."

"No, dear boy, it is *screwed*, and pocket-knives will loosen screws, Tim. Iron bars are never nailed—so there we are, patience

3

and a couple of hours will do all we want."

"But our lessons, Charley—trebled you know."

"Learn them overnight, or leave them. Bless you, Tim, I mean to enjoy a walk to-morrow morning."

"Do you, really? It's risky, old boy," said Tim aghast.

"So are other things we do, Tim. I think there is enough land to steal round the house; if there is not, I mean to go down the cliff."

"It's as upright as a wall."

"It looks so; but it is a sand cliff, and I never yet saw one without a foothold. Chalk cliffs are the boys to beat you. Now, to work! You listen at the door, Tim, and I'll go to work upon the screws."

Tim lay down by the door, and Charley out with his knife. He tested the screws and found them all firmly imbedded and covered with rust; but he did not despair, and, by judicious scraping, had one in the course of half an hour in condition for working.

During this time Tim kept faithful watch; but, the duty being arduous, he asked Charley for a moment's rest, and they walked together up and down the room.

"What do you think of this crib, Charley?" asked Tim.

"The school?"

"Yes!"

"Oh! not so bad as I thought, and I think we shall find plenty of fun about. This is a deuced sight better than old Phosey's, with his tall hats, chokers, and other swindles—wait until we know the fellows a little more."

"But this dodge of shutting a fellow up," urged Tim.

"Is not pleasant," replied Charley; "but we are not duffers enough to cave in. I mean to have a jolly run to-morrow morning. There's somebody by the door!"

The handle was quietly turned, and a hand, holding a small piece of paper, appeared. Charley recognised it as Mary's hand, and, holding it fast for a moment, whispered—

"Who is it from, Mary?"

"From Mops!" replied the girl; "don't stop me, please, you don't know the risk I run!"

Charley let her go, and went to the window to read the communication, for it was growing dusk.

He opened it, and saw a few lines in the cramped handwriting of an illiterate man. A blank expression came over his face, and, with tears in his eyes, he read the following—

"I don't reeprooche you Young Genelmen but i am an hold man and beein' turned away i must go to the work'us—you ought not to hev sold a old man and a cripple."

"Now, what may this mean?" demanded Charley.

"He's got the sack," replied Tim.

"But why?"

"Don't know—unless it's the cake!"

"That's it, Tim; but who has done it?"

"It ain't Martin, in course?"

"Certainly not!"

"Nor Pangford?"

"I should think not!"

"Then I know who it is," said Tim, "it's Lord Scraps!"

CHAPTER XII.
A MORNING'S STROLL.

"WHOEVER did it," said Charley, "was a confounded sneak. Poor old Mops!"

"Poor old Mops!" repeated Tim.

"If it is Smith," said Charley, deliberately, "we shall have another difference to settle."

But as they could not positively lay it to the charge of that individual, they returned to their labours in doubt.

In a short space of time Charley had the screws of the window loosened, and, cautiously raising the sash, proceeded to operate upon the iron bars.

Tim, in a recumbent position, kept careful watch, but darkness had grown upon them and they were still undisturbed; then Charley had done all that was needed, the lower screws could be removed at any moment, and the bars swung aside at will.

"I'm glad it's over," said Charley; "it was precious hard work."

"And mine was precious cold work," rejoined Tim; "but we won't grumble, our path of liberty is open."

"We are free!" cried Charley, striking a powerful dramatic attitude.

As it was quite dark they closed the window, and sat down upon one of the beds arranged for their convenience, talking over certain subjects of interest to them until Mr. Pendulum put in an appearance with a further supply of bread and cheese, and water; books, and a tallow candle.

He looked with an evil eye upon the captives, they in their turn bestowed anything but loving glances upon him.

"This," he said, "is bread and cheese."

He paused as if for a reply, but got none.

"You will get no meat here," continued the usher, "it is against our rules; you hear me, Thorn?"

"Yes, sir."

"And you, Turndown?"

"I ain't deaf, sir."

"None of your insolence," said the usher sternly.

Tim sniffed indignantly.

"You began badly here," continued Mr.

Pendulum, "and it seems probable that you will go from bad to worse."

"I ain't got much better," said Tim, shortly; "no chap could on bread and cheese."

"Here are your lessons," returned the usher, ignoring the last remark, "you will study them, and when you have all by heart you may go to bed—not before."

He left them alone in their glory after this admonition, and closed the door with a bang.

"Don't move yet," said Charley, "he is squinting at us through the peep-hole!"

"Oh! that I'd a squirt!" said Tim; "but never mind, let him peep."

Tim felt inclined for open rebellion, but Charley advocated the better course of studying their lessons.

"We have nothing else to do," he said, "and a short stay here is all I want—so pitch into them, Tim."

"It's all very well for you, Charley, but I'm such a thickhead."

"Go it, Tim, and I will help you."

Tim put his shoulder to the wheel, and in the course of the evening, with the help of Charley, arrived at a dim knowledge of his lessons. They then jumped into their respective beds and slept soundly.

The faint light of the early dawn sufficed to arouse Charley, and having given his chum a friendly dig in the ribs, they sprang up and were dressed in a twinkling.

Up went the sash, and the loose bars being pushed aside, gave free egress to their bodies, and out they sprang.

It was not the usual style of morning selected for a walk; the sky was cloudy, cold, and cheerless; the sea rough and noisy, and the wind boisterous; but this mattered little to the lads, they wanted freedom and there it was.

We have said that Scarum School was built upon a cliff; but, as our readers will readily understand, not upon the extreme verge of it; nearly twenty feet intervened between the house and the precipice, so that the escape of the young captives was easy when once the house was left behind.

They skirted the wall, keeping close under its shadow, and made straight for the open country, to the left of the town of Winkle-by-the-Sea.

With respect to their proceedings they had formed no definite plan; in fact, they could not, as they were utter strangers to the locality.

A quick run brought them to the gate of a field; the land thereabouts was very rich, and cultivated almost down to the sea; and ignoring a notice that all trespassers would be prosecuted with the utmost rigour of the law, they entered and followed a path mapped out for them by the iron-shod feet of some labouring men.

"This is the sort of morning to give us an appetite," said Charley.

"It is," said Tim; "not that I want an appetite given to me, I always have one."

"I say, Tim?"

"Well, old boy."

"What shall we have for breakfast?"

"What we had last night for supper; bread, curdled milk, and water."

"Suppose we have a change."

"Of what?"

"What do you say to a new laid egg or two?"

"Oh, criminey! but where shall we get them?"

"There's a farm yonder."

"And a barn."

"And some stables; there must be chickens."

"And where there are chickens there are eggs, Charley."

"Just so. Come on."

"But suppose they catch us, Charley?"

"Then we pay the penalty, as the outlaws of old did, and take a whopping."

There is a law against picking and stealing, and a strong one, too; but the boys did not wait to consider whether it was a crime or not, they wanted eggs, and the mere taking of them was excellent fun.

"Come out of the track," said Charley, "and let us work our way by the hedges; there are sure to be some yokels about."

The farmhouse stood in the second field, surrounded by a group of barns and granaries, with small places for the residence of certain poultry and fowls strutting about the yard. One old hen was cackling and flapping her wings in a tremendous manner.

"Just laid," whispered Tim, as he peeped through the hedge; "they always make an awful fuss about it."

"We must have that egg," rejoined Charley.

"I'll go," said Tim. "I saw her come out of that little hole in the barn door. You keep watch."

"All right, Tim; but keep your eyes open."

"I'm down," said Tim, and crawling through the gap, ran across the open ground to the barn door. This stood ajar, and Charley beheld his friend, after a cautious peep, force it slowly open until it admitted of the passage of his body, and then he disappeared.

"All smooth and serene," thought Charley, with a chuckle, and waiting for his comrade to re-appear.

One minute, and no Tim.

Two minutes, and no Tim.

Three, four, five, six, ten minutes, and the fat form of the owner of the skeleton suit did not return.

"What is he up to?" thought Charley; "the place must be dark, and he cannot find the eggs."

Another pause, and Charley's anxiety became almost unbearable.

"I must go up and see what has become of him," he said. "I can't see anybody about; so here goes."

He had another look round before he ventured, and then he followed in the footsteps of his friend. Arriving at the door, he peered through the opening. All still and rather dark, and no signs of Tim.

"Strange!" he thought, "where can he be gone to? Tim!"

He spoke in a whisper, but the word plainly echoed in the roof. There was no answer except a faint rustling among some straw to the right.

"Tim!"

This time something like a stifled groan responded. Charley began to feel alarmed.

"He's got into some mess, with his usual luck," he thought; "put his legs in a chaff-cutting or steam thrashing machine. I must go in."

Burdened with doubts and apprehensions respecting the safety of his chum, Charley hastily entered.

The next moment a pair of strong arms were thrown around him, a rope was cast over his shoulders, and a hoarse voice exclaimed, in chuckling accents—

"Dang it, I've got thee both. Mike, give t' rope another turn, for these warmints be as slippery as eels."

Mike was a heavily-built farm labourer, who stood grinning in front of the astounded prisoner. He obeyed the instructions given him, and another turn was passed round our hero.

He then pushed open the barn door, and a flood of light rushing in, revealed Tim lying on a heap of straw, bound and gagged, and on the verge of a fit of apoplexy.

Charley was laid beside him, and then he saw that the other man was a labourer also, a huge, round-shouldered specimen of manhood, with goggle eyes, protruded from his head in the excess of his enjoyment.

"Run, Mike," he said, "and wake up measter. Tell 'un that we're got the poachers at last—the young warmints. I'll keep an eye upon 'em, and if one moves, let 'em look to the fork."

He held a pitchfork before their eyes for a warning, while Mike, gasping and grinning, lumbered across the yard to wake his master and give him the welcome news.

In two minutes the farmer came, whip in hand—a sturdy, thick-set, dogged-looking fellow, without one solitary gleam of mercy in his eyes.

CHAPTER XIII.
THE WHEEL OF TORTURE.

"UNGAG that chap," said the farmer, pointing to Tim, "and let us hear what they've to say for theirselves."

It was fortunate he gave these instructions, for Tim was black in the face and almost gone; Charley had not been gagged, and, therefore, was comparatively free from suffering.

"Now, what's your name?" demanded the farmer, examining the lash of his whip in a casual manner.

Tim looked at Charley, whose eyes plainly said, "Don't answer," and in consequence, he remained silent.

"Ye'd better say," said the farmer, threateningly. "Now then, your name?"

He might as well have talked to stone—Tim was immovable, so the farmer turned to Charley—

"What is your name?"

"Herne the hunter."

"What?"

"Herne the hunter; born at Windsor Castle, seventeen hundred and four, afterwards mayor of Putney Green!"

"That's cheek," said the farmer, addressing the labourer called Mike.

"It be," rejoined Mike, "darned cheek!"

"I'll have it out of yer," growled the farmer. "You can't come stealin' here with compunity."

"In course you can't!" assented Mike; "nobody can't—and shan't!"

"We have stolen nothing," said Charley.

"But you were goin' to steal summat."

"Prove it," said Charley.

"Prove it," said Tim.

"Well," returned the farmer, tilting his hat up and scratching his head, "I wasn't here, but Mike can prove it—can't yer, Mike?"

"I'll swear to anything you axes me, measter," said Mike, with a grin. "I can't do more."

"But weren't they stealing?"

"I copped 'em afore they touched nothin', measter," returned Mike; "I seed 'em a comin' across the fallow field, and I ses to myself, ses I, 'They be the chaps as hev been a walkin' orf all the heggs lately,' so I calls to Jim—didn't I, Jim?"

"You did, Mike," assented Jim.

"And I says to Jim, 'Here be them poaching thieves a-comin' ag'in,' and Jim says—didn't you, Jim?"

"I did!" replied Jim, with wondrous readiness.

"Jim says, 'Let's lay down here and nab 'em when they comes in.' We did it—didn't Jim?"

"We did," consented Jim; "ha, ha!"

"The fat un comed fust," continued Mike;

"I has my hand over his mouth sharp, Jim ties his legs, for he did kick to be —I'll bet I've got a sight o' skin scraped my left leg, dang him! Then t'other rly-headed chap comes, and we nabs him—didn't we, Jim?"

"We did," again assented that able assistant.

"And we chucks him down," grinned Mike, "and then I comed for you, measter—didn't I, Jim?"

"You did?" replied the corroborative Jim.

"And that's all, measter?" said Mike.

"Now then, will ye give your names?" asked the farmer.

"No!" replied the prisoners, together.

"Then I'll have it out of you," he replied, savagely; "take 'em out, and tie 'em to the cart wheel yon. We'll see whether you will speak or not."

The two bore out their helpless captives, and bound them to the wheel. Charley began to feel that trouble was in store.

"Go 'ee to the farm, Mike," said the farmer, "and bring t'other whip. I'll use both on 'em on these young warmints. Stand 'ee out of the way, Jim—now will 'ee give your names, for the last time?"

"You have no right to do this," said Charley, struggling with his bonds. "At the worst, we were only trespassers. You have no right to do it."

"Your names?"

"I will not give them."

The whip fell for the first time upon Tim —of course, he was sure to have it—but ere it was raised again, another voice was heard.

"What are ye doin', Farmer Baker?"

"Who be 'ee?" cried the farmer, turning in the direction of the speaker. "Why, it's Mops o' the school—be these any of your cubs?"

"I've left the school, sir," said the exporter, quietly; "but I know these lads, and you must not ill-treat 'em."

"Dang it, they come a-poachin' here,"

"I don't care for that," said Mops, firmly; "you mus'n't take the law into your own hands. You touch 'em again, I'll go down to the justices, and have 'ee afore 'em in the twinklin' of an eye."

Farmer Baker looked puzzled. Morally, he was perhaps right, but legally, he knew he was wrong—but he was a prudent man, and feared the law.

"Cut 'em free, Jim," he said "but it's danged hard a man can't be left at pease. Look 'ee here," he added, addressing the boys, who were now free; "I'll call down and see 'ee at the school."

"We shall be happy to see you," said Charley, bowing low.

"Bring's a few eggs with you," suggested Tim, "or a fowl, or a cream cheese."

"I give you five minutes to get clear o' the land," said Farmer Baker, sternly; "arter that, I loose my dogs. Ye've no business here."

He was evidently in earnest, and they prudently retreated. Mops would have hastened away, but Charley called him back.

"Don't go away, Mops," he said; "I've something to say to you."

"I don't want no thanks," muttered the old man; "good morning, Master Thorn."

"But it is something else I want to speak to you about. You sent me a letter, Mops."

"I don't want to hear nothing about it—it is a sore point with me, young gen'elmen."

"Do you believe I betrayed you, Mops?"

"I can't say, Master Thorn—somebody did."

"Can you for a moment suspect Tim? Look at him, does he look like a fellow to peach?"

"I tell 'ee, Master Thorn, I don't know. Somebody told Mr. Crammer, and he dismissed I without warnin'. I'm old, and it don't matter much where I spend the few days I've got left, but——"

The old man broke down, and hot tears rolled from his eyes.

Charley could not help feeling for him keenly. Tim's eyes had tears to match, ready on the shortest notice.

"Pull up for a moment," said Charley, halting; "we are clear of that old beggar's grounds. Now listen to me, Mops; upon my word we had nothing to do with it. I would not have betrayed you to have saved my life. Would you, Tim?"

"Never!" rejoined Tim, fervently.

"I believe 'ee, gentlemen," said Mops, fervently; "we will say no more about it."

"But I have not done with it, Mops," said Charley; "tell me where I can write to you. You won't go to the workhouse straight?"

"No, sir. I've got a pound or so by me, but I'm old, and that will soon go. Besides, there ain't much work as a cripple can get."

"Keep up your pecker, Mops," said Charley, encouragingly; "where shall I write to you?"

"I've a brother, ostler at the Nag's Head, send the letter there."

"I won't forget, Mops; thank you for coming up this morning, and good-bye for the present."

They took a kind leave of the old man, and scampered across the open ground towards Scarum School.

"There goes eight o'clock," said Tim, as a distant church bell pealed the hour, "capital time. Crammer is not out of bed yet."

"I don't see any sign of anybody stirring."

"Come closer to the wall, Charley; somebody is sure to be about."

They crept close to the wall round by the edge of the cliff, and Charley pushed the bars aside and raised the sash.

"Done it neat," said Tim, with a chuckle, "I shouldn't mind a walk like this every morning."

Barely had the words escaped his lips, when the head and shoulders of a man appeared by the open window, and the light revealed the calm, placid, genial countenance of—

Mr. Crammer!

CHAPTER XIV.

A MYSTERY.

"Good morning, gentlemen," said the schoolmaster, sweetly.

Neither of the boys was able to reply; his sudden and unexpected appearance completely overpowered them.

"Don't stand there," continued Mr. Crammer, "the morning air is chill, and you may catch cold."

"It—it—is cold—sir," rejoined Tim; but Charley, although he had recovered, refused to speak a word.

"May I inquire whither you have directed your perambulations?" inquired Mr. Crammer.

Still Charley did not answer, but Tim ventured on a reply.

"We've been, sir, out—of—into—across the way—over there."

"Indeed!" exclaimed the schoolmaster, evidently gratified with this lucid explanation.

"Yes, sir," replied Tim, wiping his face with a red cotton pocket-handkerchief, "that's where we've been."

"But come in," said Mr. Crammer, withdrawing from the window; and, as there was nothing else to be done, in they went.

"You don't appear to care much for this style of punishment," said Mr. Crammer, looking round the room.

"I do not, sir," answered Charley, frankly.

"You like something shorter and—and sweeter?"

No answer.

They knew that something shorter and sweeter meant "Tickler;" and Mr. Crammer's right hand was behind him.

"Turndown," said the schoolmaster, turning suddenly upon Tim, "bend."

Tim bent; and a swishing sound, intermingled with gasps of agony, ensued.

Tim resumed the perpendicular, with a face like a rising sun.

"Thorn," said Mr. Crammer, after a few moments' breathing time, "will you follow suit?"

Charley saw that there was no help for and when the performance was over, stood calm and unruffled, to receive any further verbal or physical punishment.

Mr. Crammer pointed to the door.

"You can join the breakfast table," he said; and, glad of an end to their lone confinement, they hurried away.

"That's a tickler, isn't it?" whispered Tim, with one hand upon the afflicted part.

"Pooh!" exclaimed Charley. "If Scarum School has nothing worse than that, I shan't care."

"You are a tough un!" exclaimed Tim, admiringly.

"Tol-lol," rejoined Charley.

When they entered the breakfast-room, there was no cheer of welcome; but the eyes of the gentle lambs of Scarum School glistened with delight, especially those in the head of Bob Martin.

Two faces expressed no joy, those of Julius Cæsar Smith, and Lobby Panks: the former, because he had already learned to hate our hero; the latter, because he seldom expressed joy at anything.

Bob Martin made room for Charley, and our hero took his seat.

"What's shortened your days in limbo?" asked Bob, in a whisper.

"Such a lark," rejoined Charley; "tell you all about it by-and-by."

"Silence there," shouted Mr. Pendulum; and Mrs. Margery indignantly rattled the sugar-tongs in the basin.

"This place is a perfect bear-garden!" said the usher, angrily. "Will you be silent, Turndown?"

Poor Tim was only choking; but this was construed into a breach of the peace, and set down against him accordingly.

"Don't muddle yourself," muttered Bob, addressing himself to the usher; "it might prove fatal, and we should be so sorry to lose you."

"Who is speaking now?" demanded the usher, looking at the delinquent.

"Can I have any more bread and butter, sir?" replied Bob.

"Pass the plate, Leicester," said Mr. Pendulum, "and silence, once again."

Tim recovered from his choking fit; and the meal proceeded with a silence only broken by the rattling of cups and saucers.

Mr. Pendulum kept his eyes roaming from side to side; but the sharpest scrutiny did not enable him to detect a disturber of the public peace.

A quarter of an hour was allowed between the meal and the duties of the school, spent by Charley in relating to an admiring circle in the playground their adventure of the morning, Tim standing by and bearing witness as to his veracity, as Jim had done that morning at the farm.

"If the farmer doesn't call," said Bob, when the story had concluded, amid a vast amount of satisfaction, "all's over—I know Mr. Crammer well, but if he shows up, you must have another dose."

"I can stand it," said Charley; but Tim thought of his rotundity, and sighed.

"If I could only get something inside these beastly clothes, I wouldn't care," he said; "but I can't; there isn't room for a sheet of writing paper."

"There is not," rejoined Grimmer, measuring Tim with his eye; "your skin doesn't fit better."

The bell interrupted the conversation, and the boys trooped in and took their seats at the various desks. Mr. Crammer was seated at the upper desk, Mr. Pendulum at the lower one; by the side of the head master stood a small, undersized boy, about thirteen years of age.

"That's Toddy Crammer," whispered Bob.

Charley looked at the boy curiously. There was much of his father in him, he was decidedly good-looking, with one exceptional feature, his eyes, which were small and restless as those of a ferret. Master Toddy Crammer was evidently a young gentleman to be avoided.

"Don't like the look of him," said Charley.

"You'll like him less when you know him more," was Bob's rejoinder.

The voice of the head master summoned the first class, Mr. Pendulum called the second; all of the latter came except Lobby Panks, he never left his seat, but appeared to be making strenuous exertions to do so.

"Panks, come here."

"I can't, sir."

"Why not?"

"I—I—don't know, sir. I—I—seem to be sticking here."

Both the masters descended, and by their united exertions, Lobby was removed from the form.

"Cobbler's wax," said Mr. Crammer, lightly touching the seat with his hand.

"It is cobbler's wax," rejoined Mr. Pendulum, as if a great discovery had been made.

"How came this here, Panks?"

"Please, sir, I don't know."

"Then you ought to."

And in the absence of the real culprit, whose discovery the master knew was very problematical, Master Panks received two smartish cuts from "Tickler," and with waxy inexpressibles, took his place in the class.

"If I find out the author of these tricks," said Mr. Crammer, "he and I will probably disagree."

Nothing more was said at the time, and the lesson proceeded. Just as the two classes were being dismissed, a small bell hanging above Mr. Crammer's head rang. This was the usual signal for him to learn when visitors came, or his presence was required below.

Mr. Crammer rose from the desk and went out. During his absence, the usher kept the lads in order, and there was of course nothing approaching the scene of disorder which had transpired the day before.

In a few minutes Mr. Crammer came back without the semblance of a smile upon his face, and those who knew him well felt that something very serious had occurred.

"Attention there," he said, smiting his desk with the cane, "I have something very serious to say to you, boys; a theft has been committed in this house."

A dead silence followed this announcement, a theft was a serious thing.

"Mrs. Margery informs me," continued Mr. Crammer, "that since last evening, most probably in the middle of the night, the store cupboard was deliberately broken open, and three pots of jam removed therefrom."

There was a surreptitious licking of lips as the listeners thought of the spoil, but no single face betrayed the slightest sign of guilt.

"A theft is a theft, whether it is jewels or jam," pursued Mr. Crammer, and Charley's face flushed as he thought of the morning's expedition, "and if I find out the culprit I will punish him severely. I shall now question you one by one. Martin, are you guilty?"

"No, sir."

"You, Leicester?"

"No, sir."

And in this way he went through the entire school, and every boy answered frankly and at once.

Mr. Crammer was puzzled—the act was of such an outrageous nature that no boy could have withstood a cross-examination. The simple act of taking jam was nothing—boys all do that when they get a fair chance, but the lock had been deliberately and scientifically forced, and the sacred stores of Mrs. Margery coolly rifled.

Judging by their faces, the lads were not the culprits. As for the domestic servants, they slept in a far-off wing of the building, and had no access to the room where pickles and jams were kept. No! it could not be any of them. Who then was the thief?

Ay, there was the rub. Charley and Tim would have been suspected, but for their being confined in the cell, which precluded the possibility of their being the culprits. It was true they had absented themselves that morning in a most unwarrantable manner, broken *out* in fact, but this was a case of breaking *in,* and they could not be associated with it in any possible way.

Then a most absurd idea dawned upon the head master. Mr. Crammer was naturally a suspicious man, and for a moment he suspected Mr. Pendulum.

Ushers were but mortal, and many grown-up mortals were fond of jam.

It is probable that Mr. Crammer would have given vent to his suspicion in words, but for the tinkling of the private bell above his head. Deferring any further remark he might have to make on the subject of the missing jam, he again retired.

Tim scrawled something on a scrap of paper, and passed it to Charley.

Charley opened it and read :

"It's old Baker ; look out for warmings,"

Charley was puzzled, and looked towards Tim.

That rubicund youth drew an egg upon his slate, and held it up.

Charley understood him then, and meekly and patiently awaited for Mr. Crammer's return.

He came, with an angelic smile upon his face, and called them out.

The two culprits needed no accusation, and he made none, but simply desiring them to adopt a favourable position for the performance, laid on "Tickler" in a most artistic manner.

When it was over he simply said—

"With Mr. Baker's compliments !"

And Charley and Tim, with strong doubts respecting their being able to sit with comfort. returned to their seats.

CHAPTER XV.

A LETTER FROM FILER—MORE MYSTERIES— WHO IS THE CULPRIT?

CHARLEY did not forget Mops, but wrote off to Filer at once, and, delicately reminding him of his early days, besought him to do something for the ex-porter, who was in sore distress.

Filer lost no time in replying, for a letter directed in round-hand to Charley came by the next post.

It was an extraordinary epistle, and we cannot do better than lay it before our readers in full.

"MASTER CHARLES,—your leter come lass Night and i thinc That hit r onely Like you toe thinc hof a pore ole cripel—james is gon he wos a rud boy and a kic on the shines i doant stan From noobodi which it was a buster he guv me just aboove the soc an i went doon has if i ad been shot—he is Now carryin cools and wedgertables aboot for a low dealer and Mops may cum as soon as he like to be a odd man an boy about the hous—

"Yours trooly—

"FILER.

"p.s.—mr. Thorn hev hallmos wayed the mone, but he's a stopping ontil he finds out whot sort of stuff the man in It is made hov.

"p.p.s.—this is a joak."

Charley sent a few lines to the Nag's Head, and within a few hours had the satisfaction of hearing that Mops, on the receipt of his note, immediately departed.

In the meantime, matters at Scarum School did not improve. The absence of a porter enabled the boys to do much as they liked in the playground, and growing bold, secret excursions to go into the town were planned.

The first was undertaken by Charley and Bob Martin, who, armed with some of Harry Leicester's money, obtained the condiments for a bedroom feast, which went off with great success—and would have remained unknown but for Tim, who, startled by a false alarm, got into bed in company with a raspberry tart, and left there a record which brought upon him a dose of "Tickler" on the following day.

Tim only murmured "Just my luck," and consoled himself with a few bull's eyes—the remnants of the feast.

On the following morning the clashing gong awoke Tim, and as it was his turn to fetch the water, he groped about in the darkness of a wintry morning, in search of his stockings.

Not on the right hand—not on the left !

"Some game this," thought Tim, savagely ; "but I'm not going to get out of bed until I find 'em !"

He groped again, leaning out of bed to the utmost extent of his little round body— but no stockings—no shoes—and not a sign of any article of attire.

"I say !" roared Tim, "who's prigged my things ?"

"What's the row ?" asked Bob Martin.

"None of your larks," said Tim, "it's my turn to fetch water."

"Then fetch it !" growled Bob, "and don't make that row about it."

"How can I fetch it ?" muttered Tim, "when somebody's having a lark with my toggery ?"

"Why don't you get out of bed ?"

"It's so freezing cold!"

"Bosh!" cried Bob, springing out of bed, "here, wait until I've got my—— Hallo! —where are my things?"

"Yours gone, too?"

"Every scrap! I put 'em on the foot of the bed last night. This is some of Charley's gammon."

"It's nothing of the sort," rejoined that young gentleman, "I've been sound asleep ever since I got into bed. Confound it— where are *my* things?"

The cry was taken up by other voices in the dormitory, and then it became apparent that the whole of the eighteen occupants had lost their attire.

"Here's a pretty go! Bob, what's to be done now?"

"Put on other things, I suppose!"

"Can't, Mrs. Margery keeps them all. I say, let us lie in bed until they come after us."

"Very good," said Bob, "it's no fault of ours—capital idea, that."

They lay there, speculating upon the probable culprits, until the second gong sounded; then they heard the pattering feet of the boys hurrying from the other dormitories.

"We are in it alone," said Charley; "don't I wish I knew who did it?"

"It must be Lord Soapdish," said Tim, "showing his venom."

"His lordship is not of a larkish nature," rejoined Charley. "Hush! I hear footsteps."

The door swung open, and Mr. Pendulum, visible in the faint morning light, stood there, the personification of wrath.

"What is the meaning of this?" he demanded. "What new phase of your rebellious natures? Get up at once."

"We can't, sir."

"Why not?"

"Our clothes are stolen."

"What!" exclaimed Mr. Pendulum, aghast, "your clothes stolen?"

"Everything, sir!" rejoined Charley. "Socks, boots, jackets, caps—everything."

"Pooh, pooh!" exclaimed Mr. Pendulum, after a moment's pause of wonderment. "I must have you get up at once."

"In our night-shirts?" inquired Bob Martin, with great simplicity.

"Well, no; I suppose not," returned the usher, looking puzzled. "Let me see. Mrs. Margery keeps your Sunday apparel, does she not?"

"Yes, sir."

"Then I will speak to her at once."

When he was gone, Tim lay down in his bed and groaned.

"What's the matter with you?" demanded Harry Leicester.

"Don't ask me," moaned Tim.

"Are you whining about your skeleton suit?"

"Well, yes, I am," growled Tim, indignant at the charge of whining; "and good reason, too. *I haven't another scrap of toggery here!*"

"Well, that's nothing. We can lend you some."

"You will?" cried Tim, delighted.

"With pleasure."

In a few minutes Mr. Pendulum returned, in company with one of the servants, who remained outside, with her arms full of clothing, which the usher distributed in portions, as the coats, jackets, &c., were recognized.

When all were supplied but Tim, he turned upon that unfortunate youth.

"You have no second suit, I hear," he said.

"No, sir."

"Why not?"

"My uncle says *he* never had more than one suit in his life, and that ought to be enough for me."

"Your uncle is—a—a——Are you not ashamed of yourself to show up at a respectable establishment in this state?"

Tim reflected for a few minutes, as if the question required consideration, and then replied—

"I don't know that I am. *I* can't help it, sir."

"It's my belief," said Mr. Pendulum, lowering upon him, "that you are a shameless, depraved boy, and, but for decency of attire being enforced by the laws of the land, you would willingly run about in a savage state."

Tim offered no reply to this estimate of his character, but he sniffed protestingly.

"I have made arrangements for your being properly apparelled," pursued the usher. "Master Crammer has kindly consented to lend you some of his attire until the missing clothes are recovered."

"But, sir——" began Tim.

"I will convey your thanks to the young gentleman who has been so kind," rejoined the usher. "Ha! here is Mary with the suit. Dress as quickly as you can, boys, for after breakfast this disgraceful affair will be fully inquired into."

"Now, look here," said Tim, indignantly, appealing to the room, when the usher was gone, "would you wear these clothes?"

"You must," said Charley; "you can't refuse."

"But they're old, and darned, and patched," urged Tim.

"It is only for a few hours."

"And then, he isn't half my size. I shall have a fit, if I get into these."

"Sharp's the word" cried Bob Martin.

"Get some water, Tim; we haven't a drop in our jug."

"Who'll get it for me?" implored Tim. "Oh, here's a pair of bags! Short and tight. Look at my legs."

"I'll get the water," said Harry Leicester, laughing at the figure cut by the wretched Tim. "Leave the top button alone; you will never be able to reach that."

Tim growled out a youthful anathema upon all buttons in connection with the attire of Master Crammer, and went on with his dressing.

The clothes of the rest, being their own, were of course as comfortable as usual, and rather enjoying the joke than otherwise they went down to breakfast as the third gong was sounding.

Tim limped behind, his youthful eyes filled with tears of pain and indignation.

Mr. Crammer was in the breakfast-room, in the place of Mrs. Margery, who was occupied in searching the house for the missing clothes.

Mr. Crammer looked gloomy, and "Tickler" lay beside him.

The meal passed off in silence, and without any allusion to the morning's discovery, and Mr. Pendulum was about to say the concluding grace when the housekeeper entered the room and beckoned Mr. Crammer out.

In a few moments the master returned with a very white face, and mildly desired Mr. Pendulum to favour him with his company for a few moments.

The excitement, which had worked upon the school for the last hour or so, now arose to fever heat; and when the voice of the master, usher, and housekeeper, were heard in angry discussion, the majority of the boys were driven to a pitch of frenzy.

"What can it be?" "They've found the clothes!" "Something else gone!" cried a dozen voices.

And several of the boys went quietly towards the door.

"Stand out of the way!" cried Bob Martin, unable to contain himself. "One is enough to find out what is the matter, and I'll do it!"

He softly turned the handle of the door and went out.

During his absence the boys remained dumb as mice, their excitement was so intense.

Master Bob came back very promptly, and instead of proclaiming his news fell upon the floor and rolled and shrieked with delight.

This was unendurable, and a dozen hands dragged him to his feet.

"What is it, Bob?" "Do tell us!" "We can't stand this!" they cried.

"Oh! lor'!" gasped Bob; "give me time—such a go!—they've found the toggery."

"Where?"

"Under—oh! lor'! ha! ha!—under—ha! ha!—such a game!"

"I'll strangle you," cried Charley, "if you don't out with it."

"They've found it all—under—*Mr. Pendulum's bed!*"

CHAPTER XVI.
GRIDDLE, THE PORTER.

A WILD shriek of laughter followed Bob's announcement, in the midst of which Mr. Crammer returned to the room.

That gentleman had evidently lost his usual placidity, for, without any preliminary address, he rushed down upon "Tickler," and, having fairly grasped that weapon, laid about him manfully.

Lobby Panks, who had advanced with the deliberate intention of informing about Bob having left the room, received the first brunt of the attack in the form of a couple of vicious cuts on the calves of his legs, which brought from his lips a most unmelodious howl.

Warned by this signal of distress, the other boys scampered to various parts of the room, all but Tim, who, being hampered by the attire of Crammer junior, received his full share and something over, before he could beat a retreat.

After this a few more sacrifices to "Tickler" were offered up, and the indignant master of Scarum School dismissed them to the play-ground.

"All but those," he said, "who have occasion to change their attire. The boys of No. 6 dormitory will find their clothes above."

The boys of No. 6 hurried back to their bedroom, where the clothes lay in a heap, Tim's skeleton suit crowning the pile.

"I never knew the value of these things before," said Tim, as he buttoned up his particular jacket, "never dreamt that I should miss 'em so."

"Better than Toddy Crammer's," said Charley.

"I should think so," rejoined Tim, surveying those garments in disgust.

By the time they were dressed the school bell rang, and their usual morning's time for recreation was lost, but the fun before and after breakfast amply compensated them for any loss they might have sustained.

The lessons passed over very quietly, the boys were well up to their work, the master and usher gloomily silent, each evidently occupied with his own thoughts.

In the afternoon it was announced by Bob

Martin, a very active scout upon all occasions, that a new porter had arrived ; "a regular cure," he said, and shortly after lessons the school became acquainted with the new arrival.

They gathered round his little lodge, and after several futile efforts to get a peep at him through the windows Charley knocked at the door.

It opened, and there stood before them a gaunt, wiry man between forty and fifty, with a head like a bad unfinished carving, the grain coarse, and knots and pimples all over it.

"How are you ?" inquired Charley, pleasantly.

The man looked at him without any change in his expression, and slowly allowed his eyes to wander over the rest of the boys, taking in their looks one by one.

"My name's Griddle," he said, at length ; "you let me alone, and I lets you alone. Give me cheek and I can give cheek too. If it comes to blows, I'm there a little. All boys is warmints, and I puts my foot on 'em, so cut."

Bang ! went the door in their faces, and Griddle returned to his seat by the fire.

"Cheerful," said Bob Martin, after a pause ; "I think there will be some games with Griddle."

"Ought to be," said Charley.

"Look here !" said Tim, "you may stand what you like ; I'm not going to be griddled ; let's have a lark with him—I'll begin !"

Tim stooped down, and putting his mouth to the keyhole, shouted,—

"Yah ! old Griddle. I am a-looking at you. How's your mother ?"

The reply was given immediately.

The door flew open, and Tim received a staggering blow on the side of the head, and went down like a stone.

"You ain't no right to do that," he shouted.

"Right or no right," said Griddle, firmly, "I does it ; you let me alone, and I lets you alone."

The door closed again, and a body of select friends picked up the discomfited Tim.

"You call yourselves men," he said, indignantly, "to stand by and see me get a oner like that !"

"It came so sharp," rejoined Charley, laughing, "that we had no time to stop it."

"Besides, we were waiting for your lark," grinned Bob.

"You won't wait long," said Tim ; "old Griddle will live to repent that smite. Dash it ! my head is singing like winking—never had such a oner—it was worse than Pendulum's. Is my ear red ?"

"On fire, Tim !"

"Old Griddle will suffer for it, I tell you ; it's war to the knife !"

"Tell him so through the keyhole," suggested Julius Cæsar Smith, who was standing quietly by.

"Did you speak to me ?" demanded Tim.

"I did."

"Why ?"

"Because I chose to."

"Isn't one licking enough for you ?" inquired Tim ; "or do you want me to give you another ?"

"I have yet to receive the first thrashing," said Julius, with the same exasperating composure ; "and I should not lower myself to fight a fat boy from a show !"

"Let me get at him !" roared Tim, as Bob held him back ; "fat boy from a show—I can't stand that !"

"You will kindly withdraw that observation," said Charley, bowing to his old antagonist.

Julius Cæsar folded his arms, and smiled contemptuously.

"I belong to a race," he said, "which never recalls !"

"Bunkum !" said Charley ; "confound your race. Will you apologize ?"

"Not I."

"You shall !"

"I won't."

"It is growing dark—too late for a fight to day," hinted Bob.

"There is light enough for me to speak," said Charley ; "we can, if we wish it, fight to-morrow. Look here, my lads, I want a word with you. You all remember Mops ?"

To be sure they did.

"The poor old man was a cripple," said Charley, "the sort of man who would have a difficulty in getting a living in most places. He was sent away a few days ago. Do you know why ?"

The general body did not, and answered "No !"

"I will tell you," said Charley ; "he did a kind act against the rules and was peached upon."

A yell of execration followed this announcement, and Julius Cæsar Smith's brow darkened.

"He was peached upon," pursued Charley —"basely betrayed ; and there is the beggar who peached. Do you deny it ?"

He turned upon Julius, and suddenly confronted him with the accusation, and the culprit did not flinch, but his face, to his very lips, turned white.

"Do you deny it ?" demanded Charley.

"I do not care to take the trouble," replied Julius Cæsar ; "there is no need to do so."

"What do you mean by that ?"

"This," replied Julius, fiercely, "that you are a liar, and everybody knows it."

Without any further preliminary, the boys closed, and, in full view of the house, a fierce fight ensued.

It was getting dark, or they must inevitably have been seen.

As it was, the battle raged for ten minutes without interruption.

Bob loved fair play, and, exerting himself, managed to form a semblance of a ring, and appoint supporters to the combatants.

"Pangford," he said, "you look after your man. Harry, keep an eye upon Charley; now he's down. None of that, Smith; if you kick him on the ground, we'll gang you! Up again Charley."

"I slipped," returned our hero. "I'm as fresh as a lark. Call time, for he is getting winded."

"A fat boy from a show!" murmured Tim. "Go it, Charley. Kill the beast."

Again they rushed in.

It was too dark for scientific work, and give and take was the order of the fight.

Blow after blow rained upon the head and face of Julius Cæsar, and Charley received a succession of smartish taps, which brought the blood from his nose, and starlights in his eyes, but neither thought of giving in.

Julius, panting fiercely, lunged out in every direction, half his blows missing fire : but Charley was more cautious, and seldom let out without landing somewhere.

Darker grew the shadows of night, and the struggling boys became invisible to the outside portion of the ring.

They could only gather from the exclamations of those in front how the fight was going on.

Suddenly there was a lull, and passionate sobs broke from the lips of one of the antagonists.

They pressed forward, and beheld Julius Cæsar Smith lying on his face.

Either he would not or was unable to respond to the call of time.

Julius Cæsar Smith was beaten.

"Bravo, Charley!" cried Bob, as he helped his friend on with his coat. "The last one did it—straight from the shoulder, and caught him well under the chin."

"He is a good plucked un," rejoined Charley, "and I am sorry for his defeat."

But Tim was not, and said so.

He had been stigmatized not only as a fat boy, but as one who exhibited his rotundity before the public, and Tim was venomous.

"If you had killed him," he said, "I would have danced like winking."

We have said that Julius Cæsar Smith was beaten—and so he was.

The young gentleman of noble blood was soundly thrashed, and, to quote the words of Grimmer, "doubled up, dished, floored, fibbed all over, and punched out of time."

Pangford had much ado to get him on to his feet ; and, when he was at length prevailed on to rise, he was sobbing under the pain and sense of defeat.

"Here's a go," said Grimmer; "he's snivelling !"

"So he is," rejoined Pangford, in disgust. "Pah! and to think that I've seconded him."

"Now, Molly," said Grimmer, addressing the defeated youth, "put on your coat, or you will catch cold, and then what will your mammy say ? "

"Drop it !" said Charley, in a low tone, as he joined the group; "no fellow could have fought better."

"Perhaps you are right, Thorn," rejoined Grimmer ; "he certainly stood up well."

"And let us respect him for it. Smith, will you shake hands with me now ?"

Julius Cæsar shook his head, turned on his heel, and walked away.

"Tears of pride, more than anything else," said Charley , "I've whopped him, and his aristocratic nature doesn't like it."

"Hallo there's been a fight here."

It was Griddle who spoke, who had noiselessly emerged from his lodge.

He held a stout stick in his hand, and peered among the group, as if in search of the culprits.

"You've got a nose, you have," said Bob, scornfully.

"But there's been a fight," persisted Griddle.

"Just so."

"Is it all over ?"

"An hour ago, and all the pugilists are in bed."

"It's a good job for 'em it's over," growled Griddle, holding up his stick. "I've got orders to stop all fights, and I'll do it."

"How ?" asked Charley.

"Fight again, and you'll see," said Griddle. "I've got orders not to report in sich small matters, and I don't mean to do it. If I sees fights I stops 'em—werry quick."

"You don't hit me," said Charley.

"Or me ! or me !" chorussed a score others.

"I don't say whether I shall hit you or whether I sha'n't," returned Griddle ; "but you fight, and see how I'll stop it. Why, there's hacts of parlyment ag'in breaches of the peace, and them hacts says as any man have a right to step in and restore order. See if I don't do it—and werry quick, too. Dooty is dooty, and I stands by it, but in other things, you let me alone and I lets you alone."

So saying, Mr. Griddle waved his weapon in the air, and retired to the sanctity of his lodge.

A LITTLE DIFFERENCE WITH A SWEEP.

CHAPTER XVII.

A CONSULTATION.—MR. CRAMMER PUZZLED.

THAT night a small but efficient circle of conspirators were called together after lessons.

The following were of the party, and their place of meeting was the schoolroom :—Bob Martin, Grimmer, Samson, Harry Leicester, Pangford, Charley, and Tim, and the object of their meeting was to consult over the arrival and conduct of Griddle.

"It's plain to me," said Bob, opening the proceedings, "that he's a regular Tartar, and we sha'n't have a bit of peace when he is near as ? "

"But is it possible," interposed Charley, "that Mr. Crammer gives the fellow powers to pitch into us when he likes ? "

"Poor Mops had the same," said Grimmer, "but he never acted upon them—too weak, I suppose."

"Too good-hearted, Grimmer."

"Well, it may be so; anyhow, he let us do as we liked when we were outside, but this fellow won't."

"There's hacts of parlyment ag'in it," said Bob Martin, mimicking the porter.

And a general laugh followed.

"Such being the case," said Charley, "what is to be done ? "

"Roast him out of the place," suggested Samson.

"But how."

"A hundred ways."

"Then all put their heads to work," said Bob Martin, "and to-morrow night we will meet again and each lay his plan before the rest, and select the first to act upon by vote."

This was agreed upon, and a number of the other lads coming in the usual general fun of the evening leisure hours went on.

We trust our readers have now a pretty fair idea of Scarum School and its pupils.

We have presented to them Mr. Crawshay Crammer—polite, jovial, but cruel; Mr. Pendulum, the usher, well up to his work, but irritable; Dame Margery, and Mary, the servant, we know; many of the boys are growing familiar, and the rest call for no particular description at present.

As they rise and fall in the scale of fun and adventure, so will they appear and disappear; the sneak, the coward, the brave and bold, shall each have their turn, and their merits or demerits shall be put before our supporters, and left to their judgment.

Our heroes are not in any way extravagant fellows. Charley has his failings, but he has his good qualities; he is a clean-limbed, sound-hearted, plucky youngster, and nothing more.

As for Tim, we know what he is—badly-reared and trained, slighted and snubbed at the only place he could call a home. turned into a guy by the prejudices of a wooden-headed relation; in fact, as Charley said, he is a "poor, unfortunate, uncle-ridden youngster."

But Tim is not a duffer—he is dull, but not a downright fool, he is stout and unwieldy, but he is prepared to march to battle with the most lissome, and when the pinch comes, Tim will not be settled by a single blow.

At present we have only seen him uttering defiant challenges, as it were, throwing down the glove to the strongest; but wait awhile, and Tim shall come out in fisticuffs in a way which will astonish you, my young readers; the "fat boy" is bound to make a lasting name in the annals of Scarum School.

Back to our story.

The next morning Mr. Crammer was again at the breakfast-table with "Tickler" beside him, and the expression of his face showed that something more outrageous than the deed of the morning before had taken place.

"What can it be ? " was the whisper which passed around, and every boy kept his eyes upon the Great Mogul, as he gloomily scanned the table-cloth, apparently solving some mental problem.

" Before leaving the table," he said, after grace, "I want to say a few words to you, boys. I regret to have to make further announcement of a third outrage, and to give you fair warning that, if I discover the culprit or culprits, I will soundly thrash and dismiss him or them from the school ! "

"Last night," he continued, taking "Tickler" in his hand, and gently stroking it, " *my* bedroom was invaded, and *my* clothes removed ; also those of my son Todman, who has a small bed in the corner, as most of you boys are undoubtedly aware. That such an outrage could have been committed here," cried the master, angrily, smiting the table, and creating an electrical jump among the pupils, " is incredible ; the audacity—and—and infamy of the act is unparalleled, but I am determined it shall not go unpunished. If the perpetrator confesses, it may be the better for him ; if any accomplice will reveal the name of his co-partners in crime, he shall be forgiven ; but if this reticence is continued, let the guilty one beware ! "

A dead silence followed this address.

Lobby Panks shifted uneasily in his seat, but the rest remained motionless and silent.

"Will nobody speak ? " again demanded the master.

Not a sound.

"I am determined to fathom this affair," continued Mr. Crammer ; " or you shall all suffer for it, all out-door exercises and holidays are stopped for the present. Mr. Pendulum, we will resume our studies at once."

This was a heavy blow, for what is life to a boy without fresh air and sunshine?

The hearts of all the listeners sank within them as this fiat went forth from the lips of the master of Scarum School.

No out-door exercises or holidays!—it was monstrous.

"Who the deuce can it be?" muttered Bob Martin, as he took his seat in the schoolroom.

"Not me," said Charley; "I have nothing to do with it."

"Nor I," said Harry Leicester.

And so said all who sat near him.

"It is the strangest move I ever heard of," said Bob; "although we have had some strange moves here at one time or the other. Do you remember Langley running away, Harry?"

"Rather!" replied Leicester.

"He was a strange moody sort of chap," continued Bob, addressing Charley in a low tone—"never played any game or chummed with any one. Nobody knew anything of his family, whether he had father, mother, sister or brother, or where he lived or where he came from, and you could as soon have got a tooth out of his head as anything about his life before he came amongst us."

"A sulky sort of fellow?" said Charley.

"He was more than sulky; he was awfully moody; we used to call him the Brigand, and he was as obstinate as a mule, not only with us, but with Crammer, Pendulum, and Tubs, who was our second usher then. If he didn't know his lessons he didn't care; and when he made up his mind not to answer, ten "Ticklers" couldn't get a word out of him —could they, Harry?"

"Not a letter. But speak lower, old boy; Pendulum is casting a vicious ogle this way."

"They tried the cell with him," continued Bob, speaking as desired, "and short commons, and all sorts of games. One morning, after three days in the cell, he was missing, and wasn't heard of for three blessed weeks. Crammer was in an awful state," continued Bob, "for he got a good screw with the fellow, whose friends, it turned out afterwards, were abroad. Up and down the country he sent notices of his disappearance; the police went into the case, and at last they found him—driving a donkey with a travelling tinker, and *singing a song!*"

"Singing a song?" repeated Charley.

"Fact, old boy, I assure you—Langley was singing; but when they collared him he turned sulky again. When they brought him in here again, he began to blubber; and that was the only time I or anybody else, to the best of my belief, ever saw him shed a tear."

"What has become of him?"

"He went away last half," replied Bob, "to spend the holidays with some distant relations in town, people of whom we had never heard a word."

"Is he coming back?"

"Don't know," said Bob; "you see he was such a close chap that nobody never knew anything about him. There's plenty of time yet; fellows who go to town for their holidays always stop a week or so over, but if he don't it won't trouble me much."

"I should like to see him," said Charley, whose curiosity was aroused.

"There ain't much in him when you get used to him," said Bob, indifferently. "I like lively fellows much better."

"Silence there," roared Mr. Pendulum.

"Take care of your bellows, sir," muttered Bob.

Then, putting his pen to his forehead, he fixed his eye upon the ceiling, as if deeply engrossed in mighty mental calculations.

But the usher was not to be deceived.

"You were talking, as usual, Martin," he said, with an angry look.

"Was I, sir?" asked the innocent Bob.

"You know you were," retorted Mr. Pendulum, angrily. "Let me catch you at it again!"

CHAPTER XVIII.

MAT LANGLEY.

Bob muttered something about the desirability of Mr. Pendulum going forthwith to Jericho, and winking at Charley, dived into his "History of the Earth and Animated Nature."

"Talk of the old gentleman and he is sure to appear," whispered Harry Leicester, after five minutes' attention to his books.

"What's up?" inquired Bob.

"Look towards the door."

Bob, after a glance at the usher, to see how he was occupied, turned slowly round, and beheld a boy slowly sauntering through the doorway.

Charley looked too, and recognised the lad at once, although he had never seen him before.

It was impossible to mistake the owner of that moody, heavy face and slouching gait.

There was the hero of Bob Martin's story; but, if confirmation were needed, Harry Leicester gave it, for he touched Charley lightly on the arm, and whispered—

"That's Langley."

Charley felt keenly interested in the last arrival, notwithstanding the rather forbidding expression of his face, and mentally resolved to make an effort to form his acquaintance.

Langley, or Mat Langley, as he was generally called, walked straight to a vacant seat in a far corner of the room, with which he seemed to be familiar, and sat down without a nod or a look for any of the boys. Spreading out his books, he, with his head resting on his hands, apparently applied himself to study their contents.

"That's his way," whispered Bob, who had been watching him also; "to look at him you would think that he meant to be well up with his work, but no, he will remain for an hour at a time over a book in that style, and when he goes up doesn't know a word about it."

"Day-dreaming," suggested Charley.

"I suppose it is," rejoined Bob, "or stupidity, or a little of both, perhaps. You wait until he goes up, and then see what a mess he will make of it."

This proved to be true. In the course of half an hour Mat was summoned by Mr. Pendulum for a "solitary dose of lessons," as Harry Leicester called it, and hopelessly broke down.

The queries he scarcely troubled himself to answer, and when he did so, spoke in a listless way, as if it were no particular business of his, from which he could reap neither profit nor reward.

He made the usher very angry; but neither angry looks nor words affected him, and having received a preliminary thrashing, a sort of opening entertainment of the season, he went quietly back to his desk, and became absorbed as before.

This was nothing new to most of the boys, but it was a great novelty to Charley.

This strange, gloomy lad began to have a fascination for him, and he longed for the close of the morning's duties, when he would be able to have a word or two with this strange lad.

It so happened that it was a half-holiday, a grand feature at Scarum School, for the boys were allowed upon such occasions to wander at will, within certain bounds; but it was viewed in a different way by the farmers and other inhabitants, who kept records of such days as the inhabitants of the east did of the periodical ravenous descent of locusts.

Complaints were continually being sent in, and Mr. Crammer thrashed the offenders when he could find them, promising amendment, and a more strict surveillance for the future, but Mr. Crammer was an easy-going, lazy man, and when the next holiday arrived, the horde of depredators turned out as before.

Upon this occasion Bob Martin had arranged a raid upon a small village school,

especially the sanctum of certain louts, who were educated at the expense of the lord of the manor, and Charley was invited to become a member of the invading fraternity.

To the profound astonishment of Bob, this offer was refused, Charley saying that he wanted to stay behind for awhile, and would follow up anon.

The conduct of our hero towards Julius Cæsar Smith forbade any one suspecting him of being a coward, otherwise his refusal would have caused no light expressions of disgust; as it was, Bob organised his little party, including Tim, by his express desire, and scampered off as soon as dinner was over.

All the lads but Charley and Mat Langley apparently had appointments or missions to fulfil, and were soon far away over the fields, or down in the town of Winkle-by-the-Sea.

Mat Langley simply sat in the schoolroom until they were all gone, and then sauntered out with his hands in his pockets.

In a minute Charley was by his side.

"Capital day for a run," said Charley, cheerfully.

Mat turned a very queer look upon him, gave a grunt and walked on.

"Look here, Langley," pursued Charley, "I want a word with you. It's wretched to see a young fellow like you moping about in this fashion."

"It can't hurt you," growled Mat.

"But it does."

"Don't lie!" returned Mat. "You leave me alone."

"What is the matter now?" said Charley, laying a hand upon his shoulder. "Come, do be more chummy, let us have a stroll into the town."

"I'd rather be alone," said Mat shortly.

"That's nonsense, a fellow is always miserable alone."

"I'm not."

"You don't look very happy. *Do* cheer up a bit."

"I hate everything and everybody," returned Mat, with a suddenly-aroused ferocity, "books, masters, ushers, boys, and all."

"That's bad," rejoined Charley.

"Why am I stowed up here?" returned Mat, "the school is worse than a prison to me. I want to be free, to go where I like, and when I like. Why didn't they leave me with the tinker? *I* wouldn't have come back."

"Most tinkers are vagabonds," said Charley.

"I like vagabonds," returned Mat.

"Why?"

"Because they do as they like. They don't care for the law or anything. They're bold, and free, and roving like. They've got no trouble or care, and everybody is afraid of of them."

"*I* am not afraid of any tinker," said Charley.

"Well, no, perhaps you are not," returned Mat, who had grown more communicative, and, therefore, more genial; "but you see I don't mean tinkers in particular, but those fellows who go about and do nothing, and live happier than princes and kings."

"Who are they?"

"Well, that I can't exactly say," said Mat, with a puzzled look; but I have read about them, you know, in lots of books."

"Why, Langley, old boy," said Charley, with a merry laugh, "you are romantic."

"Am I?" asked Mat, with a doubtful shake of the head.

"To be sure you are. I can tell you the state of your mind to a shade. You walk about picturing all sorts of scenes of adventure in which you are the hero."

"I do, and that's a fact," returned Mat, slowly.

"Whenever you are awake," continued Charley, "day and night, in school and out of school, you are always thinking of these things, and nothing else."

"That's true."

"Now just listen to me," said Charley; "this dreaming is very bad, it will never do you any good, and will be sure to do you harm. You must come out of your shell, and act and think with the rest of us, and you'll be a fellow of another pattern. I'm certain you have got it in you."

"Do you think so?" said Mat Langley.

"I am certain of it. So just make up your mind to spend an hour with me, and see if an hour of real fun is not worth all the day-dreaming in the world. Bob Martin has gone to the village to pitch into the louts —if we are smart, we shall be able to join the row."

Mat pondered for a moment, his old habits clinging to him, and he felt he would rather be alone; but Charley was not to be beaten off, he struck again while the iron was hot, and obtained a victory.

"If you don't go," he said, "I shall stay here with you."

And then Mat gave in.

"I'll go," he replied, "and really thank you for taking so much interest in me."

"Come on," cried Charley; "now pull yourself together, and make up your mind for a smart trot."

Charley felt proud of his success, especially when he perceived the hitherto moody face of Mat Langley lit up by smiles of anticipated pleasure. He then saw how different a fellow Mat was to what a casual observer would expect, and already numbered him among his select chums.

The boys went straight across the open to the outskirts of the town, when they turned down a lane leading to a small cluster of houses called "the village."

There the victims of Bob's marauding expedition were to be found, and as they entered the narrow way, both Charley and Mat heard the shouts of combatants far down the lane.

Charley was in ecstacies, and Mat's face all aglow, and both increased their pace, hoping to share in the fray.

But they were late, the battle was over, and the defeated and disordered louts came coursing frantically up the path, followed by the victorious Bob and his compeers, Tim bringing up the rear.

The spirit was willing, but the flesh was heavy and weak, and Tim was unavoidably behind.

"Stand firm," cried Charley, "and stop them."

Mat planted his legs well apart, and stood his ground.

On came the louts, about eight in number, goaded to madness by the shouts in the rear, and prevented from a side retreat by the high stiff hedges on either side.

To halt was utter destruction, and there was a chance of their breaking the small opposing force in front, so they came madly rushing on.

The check was of course but momentary, for the two boys could not stand the weight of numbers, but it gave Bob and Harry Leicester time to come up and administer a few stingers ere their foes went howling on their way, leaving two recumbent in the ditch, exhibiting the mathematically arranged hobnails of their boots.

"Get up," said Bob, addressing one of the forlorn.

"Will yer hit me, then?" asked the lout.

"Not if you promise to touch your hat whenever you meet me."

The louts both promised this, and were allowed to depart; but broke faith as soon as they got a safe distance away. Turning towards their conquerors, each applied a thumb to his proboscis, and spread his fingers out, a masonic sign supposed to be expressive of unmitigated contempt.

"Never mind," shouted Bob; wait until we come down again—then I will put something else against your nose.

The louts uttered a hoarse laugh, and then, perceiving signs of further pursuit, turned again and fled as fast as their legs could carry them.

CHAPTER XIX.
TIM'S LITTLE ENCOUNTER.

THERE were now mustered together, Bob Martin, Harry Leicester, Charley, Tim, Mat, and five others, a goodly company for any expedition which might be proposed by any of their respective wits.

The advent of Mat Langley caused profound astonishment; but he met with a hearty welcome, and that over, the question was what should be the next move.

"Perhaps I may be allowed to propose something?" said Tim.

"Certainly."

"You remember Mike, don't you, Charley?"

"Farmer Baker's man?"

"That's him! Well, he lives in that cottage, with the white gate in front."

"Suppose he does—you can't hurt him. Besides, he is sure to be away."

"'Tain't him I want," said Tim; "but his son—such a kiddy—a sweep."

"Sweeps are generally good fighters," said Bob.

"Never mind," returned Tim. "I'm going in for him—you will stand by me?"

"Certainly, and see all fair; but how do you know that it is Mike's cottage?"

"Saw him go out with some bread and cheese and an onion an hour ago—just after that the boy came home."

"Come on then—we'll have him out," said Bob.

The cottage with the white gate was, indeed, in the occupation of Mike, his wife, and one sweet chick, a boy about fourteen, devoted to the profession of a sweep.

Mike, junior, was anything but a lamb; on the contrary, he was somewhat renowned for his ferocity, and was so much given to fistic encounters, that he was known among his friends and acquaintances as the "Slogger." Very few of those around him but what trembled, and feared him.

From infancy this son of Mike had fought his way up, losing no opportunity to batter, beat, bruise, and maim, in fair fight or otherwise, all the hapless youths who came within his clutches. A fight was his pride and glory—a victory his one great ideal of the summit of earthly bliss.

This youth having, on this particular day, returned from his morning's labour, and partaken of a rude, substantial meal, was standing by the door of the parental cottage, meditating on the advisability of going into the town, and calling upon a young tailor with whom he had a slight difference to settle, when the form of Tim Turndown appeared by the little white gate, and halted there.

Tim was fat and fair to see. His tightly-clothed form appeared prepared for punching. There was something terribly tempting about his look, and Mike junior licked his lips, anticipatory of a coming fistic feast.

"Be off!" he shouted, making the order as insulting as possible.

"Come out," said Tim.

"What for?"

"I want to fight you."

"How many pals have you got?"

Tim would not fib, although they were out of sight, so he answered—

"Four or five."

"Then I doesn't come," replied Mike junior. "I ain't to be done that way."

"You're afraid," sneered Tim.

"I bean't," returned the sweep; "if you gives me time to get a mate or two, to see as I isn't imposed on."

"Get 'em," said Tim, and come on to the green yonder in half an hour."

"Done!" said sooty, and Tim returned to his friends waiting under the shadow of an old oak tree.

"Well?" said Bob.

"On the green in half an hour," replied Tim.

"What sort of chap is he?"

"Taller than I am," returned Tim; "but he's thinner—the same sort o' fellow pulled out, you know."

"Oh!" exclaimed Bob, and winked at Charley in a forlorn manner. He was already gloomily prophetic as to the result.

Before the half-hour was up Tim and his supporters were at the trysting-place, and shortly after the son of Mike swaggered up with a small congregation of admiring louts.

The sweep was a cool, impudent varlet, and, nodding familiarly to the Scarum boys, asked how they were, and whether their mother was acquainted with the fact of their being from home.

"Don't jaw," said Bob Martin, sternly, "but get your things off."

"Peel for him!" rejoined the son of Mike, looking contemptuously at Tim, who was struggling with the buttons of the skeleton suit; "not I—when he's ready I am."

"Poor Tim!" whispered Bob to Charley, "this chap will eat him."

"I'm afraid so," returned Charley in the same tone.

"Couldn't one of us quarrel with him?" hinted Bob.

"Tim is the challenger," returned Charley, "and it wouldn't be honourable."

"That's true, but look at the fellow, active as a cat."

The sweep justified this encomium by turning sundry somersaults, probably with the intention of getting his blood into full circulation, and when he advanced to meet Tim, he looked a model of juvenile brute force.

Poor Tim was determined, but the battle was all one way; the first round he received a stinger between the eyes, and another upon the chin, and went heavily to grass. Bob and Charley picked him up, and carried him to his corner, the son of Mike strutting back amidst the admiring leers of his chums.

"Better throw up the sponge," said Bob, gloomily.

"Tim's no match for him," added Charley.

"What's that?" interposed Tim, "give up at the first round!—Not I. Wait until I've got my second wind, and see what I will do to him."

"He would knock three winds out of you," muttered Bob, as time was called, and Tim, with a heavy bump on the top of his nose, rushed out gallantly to meet his foe.

The sweep launched out fiercely, and Tim stopped the blows, as the nigger of old did, with his ribs, eyes, and nose; objects around him assumed strange positions, a cottage hard by was in the air, his friends apparently were standing on their heads, and the trees near him seemed to be engaged in a wild waltz. Giddy and sick, he fell, but he was not defeated.

"I wish my second wind would come," he gasped, "as it did to you, Charley."

"Better give in, Tim," said Charley.

"Not yet," replied Tim, staggering to his feet; "I'll have one more round."

He had another, and it was the last. The sooty son of Mike had only to walk round the unwieldy Tim, and plant his blows wherever he chose. He planted them unmercifully and unsparingly, choosing vital parts with a scrupulous nicety that drove Bob Martin, Charley, and the others to frenzy, but it was an honourable combat, and they could not interfere.

Tim struck out with futile madness at the empty air, and when his cup of punishment was full, reeled, and with a short, gasping sob, fell insensible.

"Does he want any more?" grinned the son of Mike.

"No," returned Bob, savagely, "I throw up the sponge for him."

"I never fights more than one at a time," rejoined the sweep, "but at a future time, if any of you gents want a licking, you can have one."

"You have only to name the time," said Charley.

"Any time will soot me."

"Will this day fortnight do?"

"Yes, any time arter twelve."

"That'll do, then," said Charley; "you be here this day fortnight at two o'clock, and we will find a man for you."

The son of Mike nodded an acceptance of this challenge, and taking the arm of one of his supporters, in imitation of genteel life, strutted with burlesque magnificence away.

A little exertion sufficed to restore Tim to a partial comprehension of things around

him, but he had been punished heavily, and his mind was in a dreadful state of turmoil and confusion.

"I haven't learned my lesson, sir," he said, with a vacant stare; "but I think I'll take a little more pudding. What's the odds? Here's at him again."

"Come, come, Tim," said Bob; "pull yourself round—steady—that's it; how do you feel now?"

"Oh, ah! I remember," groaned Tim; "the sweep. Is he licked?"

None around him answered for a moment, and then Charley mercifully rejoined—

"Not quite, but the fight is over."

"The coward!" growled Tim, "to run away."

"He did not exactly run, Tim; the fact is, he was too heavy for you. The fight was all on one side."

"Ah! I see how it is," moaned Tim, "*I'm* licked by a sweep, and him the son of Mike."

"What does it matter?" said Charley, "be here this day fortnight, and see me take it out of him."

"If you wouldn't mind, Thorn," interposed Mat Langley, hesitating, "I should like to fight him."

"You?" said Bob, with a stare, "you have never had a row since you have been at school."

"I think I could lick him," said Mat quietly.

"You shall try," cried Charley, slapping him between the shoulders; "but," he added, whispering in his ear, "don't dream of victories, but go into training with Bob and me, and you will settle the fellow in no time."

Mat looked up into his face with a smile, and promised that he would in future act, and dream no more.

CHAPTER XX.

LOBBY PANKS GOES INTO BUSINESS, AND FINDS A RIVAL.

ABOUT this time Lobby Panks created a sensation in Scarum School, and he did it in this way.

One morning he produced a small circular, written in his own hand, and its substance and contents were after the manner following:—

FOREIGN STAMPS.   FOREIGN STAMPS.

Master Panks, having been appointed agent to the Jericho and Newfoundland Stamp Company, calls the attention of his friends to the following list of prices.

SIXPENNY PACKETS.—No. 1. Contains fifty well-assorted continentals, including consignments from North and South Germany,

Prussia, and the King of the Cannibal Islands.

No. 2. Contains fifty general varieties, consisting of old Bad uns, rare Danish, Portuguese, and South Australia. N.B. With this packet is presented a *very* rare stamp gratis.

No. 3. Contains forty used Colonial stamped envelopes, and a wrapper from Peking, directed to the Emperor of China, by Chingering Chumbo, the First Lord of the Chinese Waterworks. P.S.—No gammon about this packet.

A complete collection for young beginners, One Shilling and Sixpence ; including some real stunners from Malta, Gibraltar, the East and West Indies.

All Stamps Warranted Genuine.
NO FORGERIES !
Terms :—MONEY DOWN.

It was plain that Master Panks meant business, and the appearance of a small tray with very weak wooden legs, a bit of his own workmanship, in the playground during the hours for relaxation, confirmed this impression.

The stamps were wrapped up in neat little packets, or pasted on sheets ; but there was a great heap of loose ones, supposed to be very rare, and marked 3d. each.

Lobby Panks had hit upon a happy time. The mania for collecting had just begun, and he did a roaring trade. Boys sold old treasures to raise money, and invested the results in the contents of the tray of Lobby Panks. Lobby was going on in a fair way to become rich.

This was not unmarked by his fellow pupils, who were but mortal, and, therefore, freely hated one more successful in the art of collecting the filthy lucre ; but none hated Lobby Panks so much as Tim Turndown.

Tim immediately obtained the address of another great firm, and cunningly obtained the appointment to an agency. He was hard at work for two days with his circulars, and two more upon the construction of a tray, with legs, if possible, weaker than that of Lobby Panks, and then he burst upon the school in the full glory of a rival dealer. His circular created an immense sensation. Here it is—

REAL FOREIGN STAMPS ! !
ALL SPIFFERS ! No FORGERIES ! !

SIXPENNY PACKETS OF ONE HUNDRED, with all the best issues of Europe, and the islands of the Pacific Ocean. P.S.—Any purchaser finding a duffer in this packet will be entitled to receive ONE SHILLING.

SIXPENNY PACKETS.—No. 2. Consisting of eighty UNKNOWN varieties—all different. None of your common stuff among this lot ; but all real downright staggerers, to be had only of Timothy Turndown, Esquire, Agent to the Clerkenwell Green and Botany Bay Association for supplying purchasers with the real thing. P.S.—One of these packets was presented by the Prince of Wales to his Royal brother on his last birthday. See the circular of the Association on view in the bedroom of Tim Turndown, Esquire.

FOUR THOUSAND VARIETIES ON VIEW, All at a penny each, and those who have any money had better show up sharp, as Timothy Turndown, Esquire, intends to retire on his property in a month's time.

NO CONNECTION WITH ANY OTHER DUFFER.
A WEEK'S TRUST GIVEN.

Tops, marbles, cricket bats, putty, and squirts taken in exchange.

This was a settler for Lobby Panks. The terms were far more liberal than he was able or willing to offer, and this, combined with the proclaimed Royal patronage, brought every collector around the triumphant Tim, and left the hapless Lobby alone in his glory.

The ill-blood hitherto existing between them now increased, and dark thoughts of mortal combat became engendered in the defeated dealer's mind.

"Now's your time, boys !" shouted Tim ; "this is the only shop where you can get a good sixpenn'orth. All stamps warranted genuine, and no connection with any other duffer !"

"Have you got a Shanghai ?" asked one of the boys.

"A Shanghai ?" replied Tim, looking over his stock ; "of course I have ; I've got everything. What sort o' chap is a Shanghai ?"

"Much he knows about stamp-dealing," sneered Lobby Panks, from behind his weak-legged stall.

Tim, ignoring the observation, repeated the question.

"If you don't know what a Shanghai is, you had better shut up," said the would-be purchaser, taking the part of the crusty Lobby.

"If you don't want nothing more than a Shanghai," rejoined Tim, growing suddenly independent, "you had better cut."

"What's the price of Hayti Islands ?" asked another.

"Hayti Islands," said Tim, with a merchant-like cock of his eye, "are very rare, and I'm out of them, but I expect another consignment by next post."

"I've got two Hayti Islands," shouted Lobby.

"Forgeries !" shouted Tim. "Here— look here—as I've not got a Hayti, take an Egyptian—werry rare and obsolete."

"Cheap as dirt, Egyptians are," replied the purchaser, "no good to anybody."

"Then if you ain't a-going to buy anything," said Tim, becoming suddenly indignant, "go to that idiot there ; *he's* hard up for a customer."

"What do you want ?" continued Tim, addressing a boy who was hovering about his stall like a bee over a flower.

"I want a sixpenny packet."

"Here you are," said Tim ; "hand over the coin."

"I haven't any money, and I want you to take this squirt in exchange."

"*This* squirt !" rejoined Tim, surveying the proposed exchange contemptuously, "it's broken."

"No, it isn't."

"I think it is. Chuck in a dozen buttons, and here's the packet."

After a little haggling the deal was effected, and Tim, lifting up his voice, shouted—

"Sold again, and got the squirt ; now's your time—who's for another packet ? "

Lobby Panks, in the meantime, driven to a state of frenzy by his rival's success, had been revolving in his mind half a dozen schemes for Tim's defeat.

Desperation overcame his natural meanness, and he reduced the price of his stock.

"Hi ! look here," he cried ; " sixpenny stamps reduced to fourpence, and a very rare stamp from the colonies thrown in. Every packet contains fifty, and all warranted genuine."

"Never mind him," shouted Tim, not to be beaten. "Sixpenny packets half price— here's a bargain for you, and no gammon."

"Who got licked by a sweep ?" asked Lobby Panks, half maddened.

"What's that you said ? "

"Who got licked by a sweep ? "

All thoughts of business immediately deserted Tim, and the next moment the weak-legged stand of Lobby Panks was high in the air, and the stamps scattered far and wide.

Lobby, now in a reckless state, promptly returned the compliment, and Tim's weak piece of carpenter's work followed the other. Then the two dealers closed.

Most of the boys gathered around, delighted with the fray ; but certain cunning collectors busied themselves with picking up the scattered stock, loose and in packets.

The combat was brief, for Panks was not made of fighting stuff ; but before it was over every stamp had disappeared, and the weak legs of the weak stands partly cut into tip-cats.

Tim took his loss philosophically, for he had been triumphant in the fray ; but Panks, with a bleeding nose and watering eyes, went prying about the grounds in search of some portion of his lost treasure.

But he looked in vain.

CHAPTER XXI.

TODDY'S MISHAP.

THE entire consignment was lost to him and his heirs for ever.

"It's a jolly shame to prig a fellow's stamps," said Tim ; "but I don't care much about 'em."

"I shall tell Mr. Crammer," snivelled Panks. "I'm not going to be robbed in this way."

"Who's robbed you ?" demanded a sweet youth, whose trousers pockets were positively bulky with plunder.

"I don't know," said Panks, wiping his eyes ; "but you're all in it. They—co—o —ost me nearly—four—shillings,—and I—I —haven't paid—for 'em yet."

"Be economical, then," said the young depredator. "Save up your money, and pay your way."

"It's my belief," whined Panks, "that you all got up a fight on purpose to rob me."

"What's that ? What did you say ? " demanded a score of voices.

"Steady there," said Bob Martin ; "here comes Mr. Pendulum."

The usher, passing through the midst of the boys on his way to the lodge, caught sight of the tearful face of Lobby Panks, and demanded the cause of his grief.

Lobby told him, raising the value of his stock to ten shillings.

"Infamous," said the usher, looking round at Bob and certain other culprits. "This affair must be investigated at once."

Mr. Pendulum lost no time in laying the report before his chief.

Mr. Crammer, however, did not betray that alacrity in punishing the culprit which might have been expected, the more especially as it was difficult to point out who the culprits really were.

Two dealers had quarrelled, true—stamps had been feloniously appropriated, true— but beyond this nothing could be ascertained.

It was difficult to fall foul of the whole school, and stand each separate boy upon his separate head, to compel him to disgorge his ill-gotten gains ; a process of searching would likewise have been difficult or impossible, with a proper regard for the dignity of the school, to carry out, so Mr. Crammer fell back upon the two originators of the disturbance, and asked them by what right they introduced stamp-dealing into the school.

The reply of each was characteristic ; Lobby Panks said he was very sorry, and Tim declared it was "just his luck ;" both answers, of course, gave offence, Tim's especially, so that youth being in for a run of luck, Mr. Crammer brought forth "Tickler" and laid about him unmercifully, until dealers regretted the hour when first they accepted agencies for this strange mania of the British empire.

Having been duly warned, the rivals retired to the sanctity of the schoolroom, where Tim took advantage of the absence of master and usher to favour Lobby Panks with a finishing touch upon his nose, which brought forth a few tears and a very respectable ruby flow.

Lobby threatened to report this unwarrantable proceeding; but Tim laughed him to scorn, expressing it as his decided opinion that with or without a report, he would have his dose of "Tickler."

Many strong comments were made upon the rough-and-ready justice of the master of Scarum School; but strange to say, the plunderers passed without any censure, which may be accounted for by the fact that the majority of the "gentle lambs" had all had a finger in the pie.

During these foregoing events the late mysterious robberies of clothes and jam had not been forgotten; Mr. Crammer being particularly mindful of those events. He had deputed Griddle to keep an eye upon the movements of the boys, and having named the matter to his son, Master Toddy Crammer, with spirit, entered upon a voyage of discovery.

He laid wait upon every possible occasion, listened at doors, peeped through keyholes, and performed innumerable other feats of a spying nature.

When two or three boys were gathered together, there was Toddy casually listening and endeavouring to pick up scraps of information, and was particularly attentive to the movements of Charley, Bob Martin, Grimmer, and other members of the *élite*.

Whenever they stopped to exchange a few words, there was Toddy, sidling and crawling around them until it became unbearable.

"Look here," said Charley, " I'm going to put a stop to this."

"I should think so," growled Grimmer.

"Wonder what he is doing?" asked Bob.

"Sneaking round to gather something for a report," said Charley; "and I am ready to give him something to talk about."

"What shall it be?"

"Wait until we get a chance. Hullo! I've idea," exclaimed Charley. "Come into passage; he will be sure to follow us."
What then?"

Gag him and shut him up in the pantry, key is always outside."

Right you are."

Half a dozen conspirators forthwith left the room, and ranged themselves in the dark on either side.

Meanwhile, Griddle was on the alert, for

Mr. Crammer had said that he "relied upon him"—a moral way of patting the porter on the back which was exceedingly gratifying to him.

So he prowled about the house, peering into holes and corners, like a liveried Puritan in search of hiding Royalists.

Mr. Crammer, sitting in his study poring over a book, was aroused by a tap at the door.

The person knocking being desired to come in, Mary entered.

"If you please, sir, Griddle wishes to speak to you."

"Then why doesn't Griddle come in?" demanded Mr. Crammer, with a frown; "he is not too bashful, I presume?"

"If you please, sir, he's keeping watch."

"Keeping watch!—where?"

"By the pantry door; he's found something, sir."

"I'll come directly, Mary."

He only remained a moment to try "Tickler," and then he followed the girl to the pantry, where he found Griddle waiting outside the door.

"What is it, Griddle?"

"I think we've got 'em, sir."

"Who?"

"The jam priggers—stealers, sir. I heard 'em only a minute ago, and I thought it best to send for you, sir, as I couldn't do nothing alone."

"Very good, Griddle, I commend your zeal. Remain here; I will enter alone."

Mr. Crammer entered, holding "Tickler" carefully poised, bent upon an immediate onslaught on the culprits, and then beheld ——his interesting offspring, knees and nose together, stuck fast in an empty meal-tub!

"Todman, what is the meaning of this?"

Toddy, with a dolorous whine, said it was " the boys."

"Be explicit, Todman; who has dared to commit this outrage?"

Then Toddy began his explanation.

He was coming along the passage in the dark, when a dozen hands where laid upon him, and a handkerchief bound about his eyes.

He was then hurried away amidst suppressed laughter, into the pantry, and forced into the tub. The handkerchief was whisked from his eyes, and his assailants disappeared like a flash of lightning.

"Then you saw none of them, Todman?" asked Mr. Crammer, gloomily.

"None, papa, but I think——"

"I cannot act upon your thinking, Todman—but stay, are you sure you have told me the whole truth?"

"Yes, papa."

"If you have been tempted hither by a longing for sweets and fallen into your present position while in the act of purloining, say so, my son, for the truth is always the best."

"Indeed, papa," replied Toddy, with tears in his eyes, "I have told nothing but the truth."

"Then come forth, my son," rejoined the schoolmaster, and giving Toddy a dexterous jerk, he brought him out of his uncomfortable position.

The promising son of the master of Scarum School was handed over to Griddle to be brushed, and the master himself retired to his sanctum, the serenity of his disposition greatly ruffled by this gross outrage upon his heir-apparent.

CHAPTER XXII.

A SERIOUS AFFAIR.

Two days passed without any event transpiring which we need record here. Matters, both with master and pupils, remaining *in statu quo*.

On the third morning a very serious event happened. Mr. Crammer woke up at dawn, and being desirous to ascertain the time, sought his watch, and found both it and the chain were stolen.

It was a valuable trinket, a family relic, which made the crime more exasperating, and Mr. Crammer was half beside himself with rage.

Mr. Pendulum, Mrs. Margery, all the domestics, and every pupil were summoned to hear the crime denounced, and when they heard the nature of it, there was not one who did not heartily deny any participation in the affair.

"The bounds of foolish jesting and boyish pranks are passed," said Mr. Crammer, with flashing eyes ; "I shall call in the officers of justice, and every portion of the house, and every box in it, shall be searched. If the culprit be discovered, no matter who it may be, if it is my own son, the law shall take its course."

A shudder ran through the boys, not one of whom could have any possible sympathy with the thief ; but beyond a general expression of sorrow for his loss, Mr. Crammer elicited nothing.

When the boys were dismissed, they broke up into little groups to discuss the event.

"It's odd to me," said Bob Martin, "somebody must be precious sly. I wonder who it is ?"

"Goodness knows !" rejoined Charley, diving into his pockets ; "but I think we ought to overhaul our lockers and things, some malicious fellow may have committed the robbery to plant it on another—such things can be done, you know."

He looked significantly at Julius Cæsar

Smith, who was walking moodily alone, in deep meditation.

"Confound it !—no," cried Bob. "A fellow can't be bad enough for *that*. The biggest thief in the world would shoulder his crime, I should think, if he were found out."

"Not always," said Tim. "I remember once being out for a walk, and getting into an orchard quite promiscuous—what are you laughing at ?"

"All right, Tim, go on."

"I got into this orchard in the most accidental way," continued Tim, "and before I could sniff the apples, and get out of the way of temptation, I heard a roar, and a dozen boys came rushing by, followed by a fat man with a whip—oh !" added Tim, with a wriggle, "wasn't it a whip ! Now, I assure you, my noble friends, that I didn't know one of the fellows from Adam, but they shouted—'Come on, Tim,' and naturally, I ran with them."

"Of course you did, Tim," said Bob with a wink.

"At the end of the orchard," continued Tim, "was a wall—a wall with spikes—the other fellows didn't seem to mind the spikes, but went over like a shot ; I blundered to the top, got caught behind, and there I hung. Just my luck," added Tim, looking solemnly around. "I got such a dose of the whip, that I thought I was flayed alive. An innocent boy ! I hung there until the fat man tired, and the real villains a-laughing like winking down below."

"Innocent Tim !" grinned Grimmer.

"Don't you believe me ?"

"As regards the thrashing ; but with the other I want a little salt."

"Just like the world," exclaimed Tim, profoundly disgusted.

"But who stole the watch?" interposed Bob.

It was a grave question, and for a wonder, gravely discussed, for every one felt keenly interested in the discovery of one who could be guilty of such a misdeed, but all the discussing had no further effect than to confound and muddle the few ideas already formed upon the subject.

Mr. Crammer kept his word respecting the employment of the police, and late in the afternoon, a functionary, philosophically chewing a piece of straw, was ushered into the schoolroom by the deferential Griddle.

"Before resorting to the more painful examinations of a personal nature," said Mr. Crammer, "I will have the house searched. Perhaps, during that time, the culprit may have time to reflect, and think proper to confess his guilt."

The officer and the master of Scarum School left the room, leaving Mr. Pendulum in charge.

studies were out of the question, neither the boys nor usher were capable of pursuing them, and gradually the voices of the boys arose from a wondering murmur to the open tone of general conversation.

"Silence!" cried Mr. Pendulum, suddenly awaking to this breach of discipline.

The talking immediately subsided; but only to return like a wave of the sea with re-doubled force, and Mr. Crammer returning, found the usher in the course of a mad charge upon the refractory speakers, dealing out im-partial doses of his particular "Tickler."

Behind the schoolmaster stood the officer, with a pile of clothes on his arm, and a watch in his hand. In the dead silence which ensued, the ticking of Mr. Crammer's valuable watch could be plainly heard.

"Boys," said Mr Crammer, "you perceive that the missing things have been found. I ask you, one and all, for the last time, can you tell me where?"

No reply.

"Officer," continued the schoolmaster, "you may go. Mr. Pendulum, we will re-sume our studies, if you please."

His voice trembled with suppressed anger; but he said no more; but the usual routine was pursued until the clock announced the hour for breaking off, then, without a word, he dismissed the pupils and retired.

CHAPTER XXIII.

MAT LANGLEY GOES INTO TRAINING.

In a few hours it became known where the lost things had been found.

It seemed that, after searching every other probable place, the detective had entered the cell, which our readers will remember as the place of punishment for refractory pupils, and there, behind the board covering the fire-place, he not only found the clothing of Mr. Crammer and his son, also the watch and chain, but a variety of other articles of a domestic nature which had not demanded any notice of disappearance, being in fact, unworthy of a thought.

Worn-out stove-brushes, empty blacking-bottles, pieces of hearthstone, scraps of soap, and articles of that nature were found, to-gether with a heap of old newspapers and other waste material from Mr. Crammer's study.

This was the greatest marvel of all. What object could any one have in collecting such material? What possible end could be gained? and Mr. Crammer, puzzled more than ever, wisely resolved to watch and wait.

He could do no more.

The cell was accessible from the outside, closing with a spring lock, and any one in the household could have entered, had they been so disposed, although culprits confined for sundry misdemeanours found it no easy matter to get out.

For the present we must dismiss this subject, although the time is drawing nigh for the solution of the mystery, and turn to Mat Langley, who is in earnest training in preparation for his forthcoming encounter with the sooty son of Mike.

Those familiar with Mat marvelled at the change Charley had wrought in him.

He no longer moped about, or sat with his head between his hands, but he joined his comrades during the play-hours with a light heart, and in school not only astonished the boys but dumbfounded Mr. Pendulum by going more than once entirely through his lessons without a blunder.

The interest he took in every sport in-creased day by day, and the sallow hue of his face disappearing under the healthy influence of his new-made friends, he became a very bright and rather handsome specimen of the young Briton.

"I think I shall lick the fellow," he said to Charley, with a bright smile, as he was doing a "constitutional" walk round the playground.

"Lick him!" repeated Charley, lightly; "of course you will; but don't forget one thing—he's a wide-awake fellow, and you must get to work with him sharp, don't dream about it."

"Not I," returned Mat; "I've done with dreaming; you've made another fellow of me, Charley—just feel this muscle."

"Hard as nails."

"So the tinker said. He was confident I should make a tough fellow."

"And so you will, Mat, but the toughest of fellows want training. Now come into shadow of the house, and let us have a spar a bit."

Charley took him aside, and put him up to certain fistic moves, for which Mat felt truly grateful, and Bob Martin coming up, gave a little instruction and advice.

"Keep your elbows well in," he said. "Smutty punished poor Tim about the ribs; keep your left more forward, and stand firm upon your right leg. Now, straight from the shoulder! Bravo! that was a nose-tapper. Ah! Charley."

"Confound your instructions!" returned our hero, with watery eyes; "and you, Mat, just remember that I am not a sweep, and we are only in play."

"Beg pardon," said Mat, with a grin; "but I really thought for the moment that I was pitching into the son of Mike."

"Don't think it any more, then, and play light."

In this way was Mat trained, and when

"YAH! YOU IMPS," SHOUTED GRIDDLE, "MY SHOULDER'S BROKEN—OH!"

the half-holiday arrived, he went forth with about a dozen supporters to meet the sooty foe.

The offspring of Mike was there, true to his appointment, with a very strong muster of yokel supporters, all in jubilant spirits, and confident of the overthrow of another foe; but their smiles grew narrower, and their vaunting less, when Mat stripped for the encounter.

Mat was a muscular little fellow, and thanks to the care of his friend, was in splendid condition, and he stood up before his foe with a smile of confidence which daunted the over-confident sweep.

Sooty, contrary to his usual rule, decided to remove some of his outer garments, and these being of a limited number, the removal of his jacket revealed his skin.

Tim hovered around Mat in a state of feverish expectancy, with a keen remembrance of certain stingers he had received.

"Don't spare him," he whispered, "the beggar didn't spare me."

"No fear," returned Mat; "I'll darken some part of him, black as he is. Now, Smutty, are you ready?"

Smutty slowly declared that he was quite ready, and Mat stepped into the arena, with his elbows well in, and his hands well advanced.

Sooty took up a place before him.

Mat, under instructions, forced the fighting, and leading off, gave the son of Mike a couple of blows which so confused him that he slipped to grass.

Cries of "Yah, duffer!" "Take him home!" &c., &c.

"Bravo!" cried Bob Martin. "Now, Charley, give Mat a little water—that's it. Time, there! put that nigger up again, you louts."

The sweep was not yet defeated, far from it; and exasperated by the title of nigger, he showed a really lively front for a moment or two.

But the well trained Mat speedily knocked him out of time, and sent him once more to Mother Earth.

Screams of approval from the Scarumites—gloomy looks of the louts—Sooty gasping and despondent.

"Time!" cried Bob.

"Stop a moment," replied a lout.

"Either put up your man, or toss up the sponge," returned Bob.

"Then here's my man," cried the lout.

And the sweep, in a decided funk, was again thrust forward.

The rest was soon performed.

Mat, fresh, cool, and confident, literally "walked round" his opponent, and did as he liked with him.

The son of Mike accepted his punishment manfully for a time; but at last, convinced that he was fighting against odds, he sat plump upon the ground and cried for quarter.

"Hooroar!" cried Tim, throwing his cap into the air.

"Never shout over a fallen foe," said Charley, gently; "it's not chivalric."

"Blow chivalry!" returned Tim. "He pummelled me, and made me sore for a week; and he hit vicious, too. So I says, Hooroar! and those who don't like it may do the other thing. Hooroar!"

"Ah! you may holler," said the sweep, from his corner; "but you keep clear o' me, for whensomever I cotches you on the quiet, I'll take this out of you."

"Bah!" returned Tim; "whenever I meet you, I'll give you a licking."

"You?"

"Yes, I; as easy as that," said Tim, snapping his fingers.

It was a boastful vaunt; but nevertheless, when they met again, Tim kept his word.

CHAPTER XXIV.

TIM TURNS APOTHECARY.

"GRIDDLE," said Mr. Crammer, "you came here with an excellent character, and I think I may rely upon you."

"You may, sir," said Griddle.

"For some time past, Griddle, Scarum School has been the scene of certain outrages, the author of which has escaped detection."

"So it seems, sir."

"Even the officer, a keen agent of the law, failed to detect the culprit. He discovered the property, and nothing more."

"Which any of us might have done, sir."

"True, Griddle; but listen to me and don't interrupt. Last night, in spite of all which occurred, these outrages were renewed. The face of my son, Todman, was blackened as he lay asleep."

"What a sacrilidge!" exclaimed Griddle, ignoring his master's instructions.

"Who it is that thus dares to defy all authority I am determined to find out. We must watch night and day. I will take the day, Griddle, and you the night."

"And my ordinary duties, sir?" hinted Griddle.

"You will perform as usual, with intervals of rest. Matters of this sort require a little zeal, and I rely upon you."

Griddle coughed behind his hand, this was not the sort of thing he expected.

"There is a p'int in this, sir," he said, "as rekrires some consideration. I speaks, sir, of the constitution of man, which won't do more than a sartain amount, let the man be ever so willing. Night work and day work together would be more than a common mortial like myself could bear."

"You will be paid extra, of course," said Mr. Crammer.

"In that case, sir," returned Griddle, brightening up, "I'm ready to begin at once."

"To-night, then, I shall expect you here, Griddle, in my study. I shall provide for you two bottles of lemonade and a few biscuits. Intoxicating liquors upon such an occasion are entirely out of the question."

"In course, in course, sir," replied Griddle, "I could not think o' touching them at any price."

Despite this fervent assurance, Griddle did not appear to relish the lemonade idea. It was certainly not his notion of the liquor required for a night watchman.

As Griddle crossed the ground towards his lodge, he halted a few moments to watch the boys at play.

"Now I wonders," he thought, "who is the himp as is at work; there's Martin bad enough for anything, and Thorn, and Turndown—for the matter o' that—all ready and ripe for anything. But if they lets me alone, I lets them alone. I should like to catch some of 'em at it."

"Good morning, Griddle," said Charley, as he was passing.

"Mornin', Master Thorn."

"You don't look well, Griddle."

"I am as well as man could hope to be among himps."

"Don't be personal, Griddle. Hallo! Bob."

"What is it?"

"Griddle says you are an imp."

"Make him apologize or pinch his calves," replied Bob, assiduously pursuing a game of knuckle-down.

"There ain't a boy in the school as durst do it," cried Griddle. "Oh! now you let me alone, and I lets you alone."

It was Charley who had taken momentary advantage of Griddle's back being turned and pinched his lean leg as he uttered his defiance.

"You can't bounce us," said Charley. "Go to your lodge."

"I'll bounce some of yer," whined Griddle, retreating. "You wait a few days, and see if I don't. Mr. Crammer have given me a dooty to perform, and see if I don't do it."

"Sneaking duty?"

"No it ain't, Master Thorn; but it's a duty I'm proud on."

Charley turned away, with a contemptuous shrug of his shoulders; and Griddle sought the retirement of his lodge.

Charley stood watching the skilful manœuvres of his friend Bob for some minutes, until a roar of delight from the farther corner of the ground attracted his attention.

A crowd of boys gathered around some object caught his eye, and he sauntered over.

He found that the cause of the excitement was Tim, with a wooden box, filled with small packets, slung around his neck.

"What now, Tim? More stamps?"

"No; I've changed the line. Stand back you fellows, and let me have a little air."

Having cleared a space, Tim settled his box comfortably, and thus proceeded—

"I have, my noble Britons, a patent pill for sale, cures everything. One taken before breakfast brightens your head, and brings out the lesson clear; two drives away pain; and 'Tickler' can't touch you if you take 'em regular. I'll back that if any boy takes two every morning for a week, that he can take the stiffest licking without a wink."

Tim was here interrupted by a laugh.

"I hate sniggering," continued the pill-vendor. "You can't say what they're like unless you try 'em. They are made from a recipe which has been in my family for a hundred years. What did you say, Grimmer?"

"I said 'Gammon!'" replied Grimmer.

"Did you?" said Tim. "Then it's like your ignorance and cheek. People without faith ought not to buy the pills; because they're no use without faith, and it might spoil the sale. I don't care whether you or any other chap says 'gammon'; the pills are right. Take one, two, or three now and then, and you could stand a pin run into the calf of your leg right up to the head. Only a penny a packet, and every packet contains forty."

"Let's look at them," said one of the spectators.

"They must not be exposed to the air," answered Tim, "until taken, or they lose their virtue. Have a packet, Panks?"

Panks, who had been looking on and listening with curiosity, drew back a little.

"Never mind the stamp shindy," urged Tim. "You have a packet; and if you find them right, I'll tell you how to make 'em. Only a penny a packet, and every packet contains forty."

"You're sure they stop all pain?"

"I'll stake my life on it, Panks. You don't know your Murray, I'm certain; and you're sure to have 'Tickler' about you this afternoon. Have a penn'orth?"

"Will you trust me?" asked Panks.

"I would," replied Tim, gravely, "if it didn't affect the pills; but when there's no money down, they won't act."

"Oh! that won't do," shouted several.

"I know it will," answered Tim; "it's a fact."

"Here, give us one," said Panks, pulling out his penny.

"Anybody else have a packet? Now, Muffet, have a penn'orth?"

"I've only a ha'penny," said the boy addressed.

"You can owe a part, but not the whole," said Tim. "Hand over; here's the packet. Thank you. Any more? No. But don't go away; I've something more for you."

"The pills I've just sold," he went on, "are my number ones. Very good, but not up to number two. Here's the sort of thing for everybody. They give strength, and any fellow who takes two every morning, will be able to lick the whole school and lift a hundred weight."

"Suppose we all took them?" asked a sceptical youth.

"I'm not running down the other pills," continued Tim, ignoring the question, "for they are very good; but these are rum uns, fifty in a packet, and only a penny."

"'Tain't fair," grumbled Panks, "you ought to have sold them first."

"You're not in the trade," said Tim, stoutly, "so shut up."

"Will you change mine?"

"We don't change anything at this establishment," said Tim. "Now, then, who'll have a penn'orth of the rum uns?"

After a deal of persuading, and Charley

buying a packet "to start the trade," two fresh victims fell into Tim's net, and then the school bell rang.

As Tim had insinuated, Lobby Panks was behind with his lessons, insomuch that he was sent back, and when the class was dismissed, he was recalled for "a solo."

"There he goes," whispered Charley, "and by jingo! he has taken three of Tim's pills."

"Much good may they do him," said Bob Martin, with a grunt.

"What are they made of?" asked Grimmer.

"Goodness knows," replied Charley; "but I strongly suspect the ingredients. Tim has been saving bits of bread these two days, and this morning he cut off a bit of soap and put it in his pocket."

A general "Ugh!" followed this explanation, but the general interest became absorbed in Lobby Panks.

That hapless and too confiding youth having, as declared above, taken three of the patent pills, stood before Mr. Crammer with his hands behind his back, and his right eye fixed upon "Tickler."

The lesson began.

From first to last, it was a series of blunders; half the questions Lobby answered incorrectly, upon the rest he was dumb.

"Tickler" was raised.

In less than a minute Lobby returned to his desk weeping and rubbing the afflicted parts.

"He got it hot," grinned Bob.

"So much for Tim's pills," said Harry Leicester.

"Don't run down the patent medicine yet," said Charley, "let us hear what the old boy has got to say about them when the school is over."

"It's a jolly swindle," growled Grimmer, who had placed a limited faith in the patent article. "I never saw Panks wriggle so much before, and he can wriggle a bit."

"It serves Panks rightly," grinned Harry Leicester, "he should have had number two, and taken a packet."

"If Tim don't shut up shop," said Bob, "somebody will be breaking his windows."

"Wait until the old man has made his defence," rejoined Charley.

When school was over Tim showed up in the playground with his box and packets as bold as brass—a howling mob of unbelievers crowded round him.

"Yah! you swindler," said one.

"You ought to be punched," said another.

"What's the row?" demanded Tim.

"What good are your pills?" asked one.

"Have you tried 'em?" demanded Tim.

"No, I ain't."

"Then buy a packet, or shut up."

"What good are they?"

"They ease suffering and harden the muscles."

"Bah!"

"I don't want any of your cheek."

"Who swindled the boy with pills?"

"Swindle, did I?" said Tim. "I say, Lobby, come here."

Panks, with the signs of recent suffering upon his intelligent countenance, advanced, glaring at Tim like a tortured youthful tiger.

"You bought some pills of me, Lobby?"

"You know I did."

"How many did you take?"

"Three."

"Hum! four is a better number. You found 'em all right?"

"No, I didn't."

"What was the matter with them?"

"They tasted like soap, and made me feel sick."

"Physic never tastes nice," said Tim; "but they did you good!"

"No, they didn't," returned Panks. "'Tickler' stung me more than ever; I'm sore all over."

"Did it?"

"Yes, it did."

"Then you've got no faith," said Tim, "and the next time you want a pill don't come to me. Now, who's for another penn'orth?"

A roar of laughter followed Tim's reply, and Lobby Panks, with a sniff, retired snivelling and secretly vowing vengeance on the youthful apothecary.

CHAPTER XXV.
GRIDDLE'S WATCH.

"GRIDDLE."

"Yes, sir."

"Here are the lemonade and biscuits, and a stool for you to sit upon. You will keep a strict watch."

"I will, sir."

"By keeping the door open, you will command a view of the lobby leading from the dormitories to the part of the house I occupy. You will, of course, have no light, the moon is at the full and the gallery will be sufficiently illuminated."

"In light or dark, sir, I am willin' to sarve you."

"I believe it, Griddle, and I am glad to hear it. Should you succeed in detecting any of the culprits, arouse me immediately."

"I will, sir."

As soon as Mr. Crammer was gone, Griddle kicked over the stool, and taking up a position in Mr. Crammer's easy chair, surveyed the festive lemonade preparations with contempt.

"Lemingade and biscuits," he muttered bitterly. "What does the ass think I'm made on?"

Then from his pocket Griddle drew a bottle of rum.

"Here's a licker," he said, "as you ought to found, Mr. Crammer, but for that meanness of your 'art, which I holds in serene contempt. Lemingade, indeed! wot next will the hidiot be dreaming of? An' a hard stool—does he think I'm made of ingy-rubber?"

A footstep in the passage aroused him from his reverie, and Griddle had barely stowed his bottle away, and demurely seated himself upon the despised stool, when Mr. Crammer re-appeared.

"Griddle."

"Yes, sir."

"I forgot to tell you that my suspicions point towards Master Thorn."

"I thort as much, sir. I'm inclined that way myself."

"Keep an eye upon the dormitory where he sleeps."

"I will, sir."

"Good night, Griddle."

"Good night, sir."

"Well, I hopes as you is gone at last," muttered Griddle, as the door closed. "It's bad enough to keep one up all night without keep coming back as if you was a sentry. I do hate the sneakin' ways of some men; but you did not see the bottle, artful as you was."

He went to the door and carefully listened.

At length, assured that Mr. Crammer was in his room and safe for the night, Griddle returned to his easy chair, and uncorked the bottle of his own providing.

"When rum is good, it's prime," he murmured, after a prefatory sip, "and I don't know a place where they sell it better than at the 'Coach and 'Osses.' Griddle, here's your good 'elth, for you are a man out of a thousand, that's what you are. Once you was a beadle, Griddle, and you've been things which we don't want to mention, but you are a stunner for all that, and here's your 'elth again. When I think of what you were, and what you are," he said, after a third application to the bottle, "I'm 'lectrified—that's what I am; but it won't do to get too much elevated with pride, for it always hath a fall. What a lovely moon! I likes a lovely moon, and I'll drink it's 'elth. Your 'elth, my lovely moon, combined with the Mrs. Griddle which was to be. Was to be, did I say?" he added, in a maudlin manner, after a few additional sips; "lor', how I did love that woman! but she guv her 'art to a brick-layer, and chucked me overboard. It broke

my 'art, but I forgives her. Maria, I forgives you, lovely as thou art."

And thus Griddle began his watch.

How he passed the night let the events of the following morning tell.

The bright grey light of an early spring morning was peeping through the windows as the bell rung by Mrs. Margery aroused Mary, the housemaid, and two of her fellow-servants from sleep.

The call of duty being imperative, they arose, and walking downstairs yawning, began their daily tasks.

Mary's duty led her to Mr. Crammer's private room, and, opening the door, she entered.

There a sight met her wondering gaze which at first impelled a scream to her lips, but it changed to a merry laugh when she fully realized the scene before her.

Mr. Crammer's easy chair was over, and on the ground lay Griddle, clasping a globe fondly in his arms.

He was not asleep, for, as she entered, he turned upon her a lack-lustre eye, and smiled a sickly smile.

"Oh! Mr. Griddle," she exclaimed.

"Mary," he murmured.

"Yes; it's Mary; but how came you here?"

"It's all 'fection," he murmured—"it's all dewotion. Mary, I loves you dearly."

"La! Mr. Griddle," simpered Mary, "you are old enough to be my father."

"What's age?" demanded the porter, struggling into a sitting position; "time can't 'radicate love like mine. Mary—Mary—I loves yer."

"You mustn't talk nonsense, Mr. Griddle. If Mr. Crammer knew you were here, he would be very angry."

"Mary," replied the porter, leaning back against the overturned chair; "un'erceive yerself. Misser Crammer knows I'm here. He knows I love yer. I tol' him so lars' night; and Misser Crammer behave like a brick. What does he say, Mary? 'You're a good feller, Griddle,' he ses, 'and I want to see yer happy. Come in early and 'pose to the gal of yer 'art.' That's what Crammer ses, an', Mary, I'm here. I loves yer, Mary."

"How strange of him, Mr. Griddle!" said Mary, playing with the corner of her apron.

"'Tain't strans when yer know all," returned Griddle; "he take a interest in us boof; he want to see yer happy. 'Griddle,' he ses, 'you'll make her a lovely husband, marry soon as yer can. Will you have me, Mary?"

"I thank you very much, Mr. Griddle," said Mary, with another simper, "but I couldn't."

"Couldn't?" repeated Griddle, struggling to his feet, "why not?"

"I'm—I'm engaged to Mr. Roper, the ostler."

"Blow Roper! break it off," cried Griddle, ferociously.

"I couldn't, Mr. Griddle, I really couldn't. I'm very sorry for you, but——"

"Will yer break it off?"

"Indeed I could not."

"Then I'll end my miserable 'sistence," said Griddle, wandering wildly about the room, and knocking down the other globe and a chair or two; "woman, stand out of my way."

"Oh! what would you do?" asked Mary, holding up the broom to bar his way.

"That can't signerfy to you. Out of my way, woman," returned the porter, "am I allers to be diserp'inted? What's life to me? Stan' out of my way, Mary."

She was too much alarmed to check him, and he staggered into the passage, and made his way towards the back door.

Mary followed in a trembling, tearful state, wondering what would be the issue of her refusal.

Griddle, accustomed to the place, readily drew back the bolts and darted out. Then he turned and once more addressed the frightened girl.

"Mary, will yer have me?"

"Oh! indeed, Mr. Griddle, I couldn't."

"Then farewell, thou lovely critter," cried Griddle, rushing madly towards the water-butt.

Mary waited to behold no more, but rushed into the house screaming, her cries penetrating the chamber of the master of Scarum School, who was completing his toilet.

Out he dashed to meet Mr. Pendulum, and the two rushed below.

"What's the matter?" demanded Mr. Crammer of Mary, who was still screaming.

"Oh! Mr. Griddle, sir."

"What of him?"

"He's dead—drownded."

"Where?"

"Oh, sir! I'm very sorry."

"Where is he? What do you mean, you aggravating girl? Where is Griddle?"

"In the back yard, sir. This way, sir."

And tottering, with tears in her eyes, into the back yard, she introduced her master to the latter half of Griddle, hanging from the water butt, and kicking convulsively.

"Give me a hand, Mr. Pendulum," cried the master, hastily—"overturn the butt as it is, now then, together."

Over went the butt, discharging a large quantity of water, and the form of the half-suffocated Griddle, his face bloated and ghastly from the night's potations and the morning's experiment.

"Griddle, you fool," cried Mr. Crammer, furiously, "what is the meaning of this?"

Griddle gasped and rolled his eyes, and smiled a sickly smile.

"Misser Crammer and Misser Penerlum," he said, "my duty to you, gents both."

"He's been drinking," exclaimed the tutor, in disgust.

"All that lemerade," returned Griddle, "If you hadn't lef that out this wouldn't have 'appened, Misser Crammer, an' I feels I can't forgive yer. If you ain't careful, Misser Crammer, you'll lose a old an' faithful servant."

"How annoying!" muttered Mr. Crammer, "Griddle, go to the lodge and lie down, I will see you by-and-by. Mr. Pendulum, I think we will keep this matter as quiet as we can. The absurdity of the man! Mary."

"Yes, sir."

"You will please talk as little about this affair as possible. This wretched man has apparently been drinking. Have you dusted my room yet?"

"No, sir."

"I will just look in for a moment, then you can put it to rights at once."

When Mr. Crammer entered his private study, he found the little confirmation needed to show the cause of Griddle's disaster. There were the overturned globes, and furniture, and upon the table an empty rum bottle, but the lemonade and biscuits remained untouched.

CHAPTER XXVI.

STRANGE NOISES—THE MYSTERY INDEED.

CAREFUL as Mr. Crammer designed to be, the story of Griddle's watch and the results spread about the school, and when Griddle came forth after sleeping off his debauch, he found a strong muster of young friends awaiting him.

"What'll you take for the water-butt?" inquired one.

"Oh! Mary, I love you!" exclaimed another.

"It's all the lemonade," added Charley, and a voice in the rear finished the porter off by calling him, "Boosy Griddle."

The porter stood in the sunlight, blinking like an owl, endeavouring to measure the strength of his opponents, but his head still reeled from the effects of his potations and strange bath, and sinking against the wall, he could only feebly mutter—

"You let me alone, and I lets you alone."

"Why didn't you marry Mary right off?" demanded Bob Martin; "I'm ashamed of you deceiving the poor girl so."

THERE WAS THE BODY OF THE DESPAIRING GRIDDLE HANGING FROM THE WATER BUTT.

"I shall be round a bit by-and-by," muttered Griddle, "and then I'll pay you off."

"Oh! you're a model porter, ain't you?"

"Have a packet of Tim's pills," chimed in a voice in the rear.

And a scream of laughter followed.

"As soon as this precious head of mine gets a bit square," growled Griddle, "I'll have you all up afore Mr. Crammer. Why don't you let me alone, if I let's you alone?"

"You swipy old villain!"

"Who said that?"

"Lobby Panks."

"It wasn't," roared Lobby. "It was Charley Thorn."

"I'll put you both down," said Griddle, solemnly, "as soon as I can write."

Having baited the worthy porter for about an hour, they left him in peace; and whether Griddle ever reported them or not they never knew.

But certain it is that Mr. Crammer never named it; and equally certain was it, that for some reasons of his own, he overlooked the disgraceful conduct of his night-watcher; for Griddle, contrary to the general opinion, stayed on.

Shortly after this, a fearful mystery uprose in Scarum School.

The beginning was this:—

Tim, who slept near the door of the bed-room, was awakened by a sound in the lobby outside.

It sounded like the pattering of rain.

Tim sat up, and listened.

Pit-a-pat! pit-a-pat! pit-a-pat!

"It's somebody walking about with naked feet," thought Tim, sitting up. "Charley!"

"What's the row?" asked Charley, waking up.

"Somebody in the lobby."

"Crammer, or Pendulum."

"No, it is not. Listen."

"Pit-a-pat! pit-a-pat! pit-a-pat!

Now slow; then with a quick, trotting action, as in a hurry; but never going far away.

Backwards and forwards before the dormitory door.

"It certainly is a strange noise," said Charley. "Some of the fellows up to some game."

"No, it isn't," rejoined Tim, with the very hair of his head lifted up. "I—I—think it's a ghost."

"Bosh!"

"You wouldn't say so if you was near the door."

"You can come to my bed if you like, Bob."

"I'm not in the humour for larking," growled that worthy; "I'm tired."

"Wake up, sleepy. Do you hear that noise outside?"

Bob, thus adjured, yawned, and sat up in his bed.

Pit-a-pat! pit-a-pat! pit-a-pat!

Now slower; then quicker; but ever before that dormitory door.

"You may say what you like," said Tim, diving under the sheets; "it's a ghost."

"It isn't," said Charley.

"It is."

"Don't be foolish, Tim."

"No live fellow could make such a horrible noise."

By this time the whole of the eighteen occupants of the room were awake, in various stages of surprise and horror.

Who or what could it be?

Pit-a-pat! pit-a-pat! again, again, backwards and forwards before the door.

It sounded very strange in the stillness of the night, though none could doubt but that it arose from some person with naked feet.

"I wonder what's—the—the—time?" asked one of the boys, his teeth chattering in his head most musically.

"Near daylight," returned Charley. "I can see the grey light in the sky."

"Hadn't somebody better peep out, and see what it is?" suggested Bob.

The sole reply he received was the ever-lasting pit-a-pat! pit-a-pat! of the mysterious visitor outside.

"I wish it was daylight," groaned somebody in the corner.

"Look here," said Charley, springing out of bed, "I'm not going to stand this. I'll see what it is."

Bracing up his nerves, Charley boldly opened the door, but immediately fell back.

"What is it?" asked Tim, in a thrilling whisper. "Something long and white," replied Charley, shuddering. "It looks awful."

Pit-a-pat! pit-a-pat!

All the plainer for the door being open.

Tim rolled himself up like a hedgehog, and was seen no more.

"I'm not afraid," said Charley, retreating a few steps; "but I don't like a thing of this sort. I can't hear it now, can you, Bob?"

Bob growled something from under the bed-clothes; and Charley, finding that he was alone, quietly closed the door, and retreated to bed.

"I can't stand alone," he thought, looking round the dormitory, where nothing in the form of humanity was visible except outlines under the sheets, so I will get into bed."

Which he accordingly did, and rolled himself up like his fellow pupils.

They heard nothing more that night.

A strange whisper of the mystery floated around the room on the following day.

Boys walked about in silent companionship, and looked pale.

But none ventured to speak to the authorities on the subject; and then another night came.

Sleep, for an hour or so, was out of the question; but by degrees the boys fell off, and heard nothing until they were awakened again by Tim.

"There it is again," gasped our friend. "Listen, all of you."

CHAPTER XXVII.

A LITTLE MORE ABOUT THE GHOST.

THERE it was again, with the thrilling pit-pat! pit-a-pat! and ever before their door.

Charley lay still for awhile listening.

Then he spoke to his most reliable chum.

"Bob!"

"Well, old chap."

"Will you make a rush with me, and see what it is?"

"Can we do any good?"

"We can't do any harm."

"Suppose it is a real ghost?"

"I never heard of one, Bob; and if there are such things, they would know better than to keep up that idiotic trot before our door. Get up; and let us rush out together."

Done," said Bob, desperately.

And the pair, anxious to avoid losing a moment, lest their courage should grow cool, jumped out of bed, and dashed into the lobby.

A wild cry, or rather shriek, followed; and they both staggered back into the room, and fell to the ground.

A loud cry followed the sudden return of Bob and Charley to the dormitory—a cry which rang in the ears of Tim, and the other lumps of humanity cowering beneath the clothes, like a death-knell.

At first it seemed to them that the two boys had rashly intruded upon the perambulations of a ghost, and had been stricken dead for their temerity; but Charley's voice quickly dispelled this supposition.

"That's a ghost!" he cried—"deuce a bit, Bob; ghosts don't strike out straight from the shoulder."

"He's given me one on the nose, whoever it is," rejoined Bob, ruefully. "Did you see what it was like?"

"Something tall and white."

"Just what it appeared to me."

"May I inquire the reason of your being out of bed?"

It was Mr. Crammer's voice; and Mr. Crammer stood before them in dressing-gown and slippers, as polite, or even more so than usual.

"I—I—yes, sir—I don't know," stammered Bob, his teeth chattering in his head.

"Very lucid," sneered Mr. Crammer.

Then turning to Charley, he continued—

"Perhaps you, Thorn, can tell me?"

"We heard a noise outside, sir."

"Undoubtedly."

"And got up to see what it was, sir."

"Indeed."

"And we found upon the landing a——"

"What?"

"We found a—a——"

"Pray don't hesitate," said Mr Crammer, calmly. "Whatever you saw need be no secret here."

"We saw a ghost, sir."

Mr. Crammer smiled a sardonic smile.

"A ghost, did you?"

"I don't say it was a real ghost, sir—in fact, I think it wasn't," rejoined Charley; "for it struck both of us sharply in the face, and knocked us down. But it was something tall and white, and, at first sight, looked like a ghost."

Mr. Crammer looked down upon him thoughtfully, scraping his chin with his right hand.

"Go on," he said seeing Charley hesitated.

"There—there is nothing more to say," rejoined Charley.

Again did Mr. Crammer smile, casting a vicious glance at the boys staring at him from the beds.

"These tricks," he said, "I intend to put down. You may play the fool to a limited extent in the daytime, if you please, but at night I am determined not to endure it. Get into bed at once."

The boys lost no time in complying, and Mr. Crammer went out, softly closing the door behind him.

"Now, what may that mean?" asked Bob.

"Whoppings all round," answered Tim, from his corner.

"It's plain he doesn't believe us," rejoined Charley; "but what will be the end of it I cannot say—'Tickler,' of course, and something more, but what the something more will be I cannot guess."

"The smoother he is," said Harry Leicester, "the more he means mischief. Like a cat, his purring is dangerous."

"What could it have been outside?" asked Grimmer.

"It looked awful," rejoined Bob.

"White, wasn't it?"

"Very white."

"Any eyes?"

"Two, I thought; but I hadn't time to look before I got the stinger on my nose."

"Horns?"

"Didn't see any."

"Then it wasn't a ghost," said Tim, decidedly; "for ghosts without horns don't smite people. I remember once seeing a ghost—some years ago, when I was quite a young un——"

"You are an old one now," grinned Charley.

"When I was quite a young un," persisted Tim, "I saw a ghost—such a whopper! he was standing at the corner of four cross roads, and I was going home with my uncle, when——"

The story Tim would have told died away upon his lips, for the door of the bedroom opened, and Mr. Crammer entered.

Without a word, without any intimation whatever of his being annoyed, he turned down the counterpane and gave Tim a very solid dose of his favourite weapon, and then as quietly retired, leaving the object of his visit, as Tim afterwards expressed it, "so sore that he hadn't a single side to lay on."

"Not much of the ghost about that," chuckled Harry Leicester.

"Hush!" returned Charley; "look at poor old Tim wriggling."

"Who wouldn't wriggle," gasped the afflicted one, "if he had such a dose as this? I swear I'll kill old Crammer and run away."

"Not you. To-morrow you will forgive him, and forget all about it."

"Shall I ?" growled Tim. "That's all you know. Oh, lor! I never felt anything like this. I believe he has broke the skin."

Warned by this condign punishment, the dormitory soon settled quietly again, and one by one the boys dropped to sleep again—Tim last, his aching bones keeping him from balmy slumbers.

On the morrow, it was plain that serious steps would soon be taken by the master, unless the various outrages received a full solution.

Charley, Bob, and the other occupants of the bedroom, including Tim, were again examined, and stuck so sturdily to their tale, that Mr. Crammer could not help believing in them.

"I shall come to the bottom of this," he said, in conclusion; "and woe be to the culprits. As for you, sir," he added, turning to Tim, "you dare to tell another story in your bedroom, and I will dismiss you from the school."

Tim meekly accepted this warning, and retired with his brethren.

Once outside, he made a pantomimic demonstration towards the study with his fingers and thumb, assisted by his nose—the whole supposed to express the keenest contempt for the master of Scarum School.

Unfortunately for him, Mr. Crammer opened the door to give a parting injunction to his pupils, and caught him in the very act.

He called Tim into the study, from which, almost immediately, arose the wailings of the afflicted.

"I never did see such a fellow as Tim," said Bob, pityingly. "If there is a hole about, he is sure to get into it. We were going peaceably away, but he must take a sight. Just like him."

It was then about seven o'clock in the evening, too early in the year to permit of their being in the playground; so they adjourned to the schoolroom, where Tim, with gritty furrows about his eyes, presently joined them.

"Did you ever see anything like that?" were his first words.

"Serve you right!" growled Charley. "Just as if you wanted to perform so near the lion's den."

"I was overcome by my feelings," returned Tim. "I hate the brute."

"Has Mr. Crammer been beating you again?" asked Lobby Panks, with an air of interest.

"He has," returned Tim, "been laying it on thick. But what is that to you?"

"Did he hurt you?" asked Lobby, kindly.

"Just," replied Tim.

"Why not have taken a few pills first?" asked Lobby.

Tim's answer was not given verbally.

He simply walked up to the questioner, and dealt him a stiffish blow about the ribs.

"You are always knocking me about," whined Lobby.

"I'll trample you to death," growled Tim, "if you don't keep civil. Do you want any more?"

"Hold hard!" broke in Bob, in a thrilling whisper. "There is somebody listening at the door. Come closer, Charley. Can you hear anything?"

"Yes; like hard breathing."

"If they are listening, they must be leaning. I'll open the door suddenly, and let them in."

No sooner said than done.

The latch was quickly turned, and the head of Griddle fell through the opening.

The next instant Charley, perceiving who it was, rushed forward, and, with the assistance of a few friends, held him fast.

"Now then," gasped Griddle, "wot's the wicious game? You let me—oh!—alone, and—oh!—I lets you alone. Yah! you wicious brutes! to squeadge a old man like me."

"You sneaking spy!" returned Charley, "Now then, boys, all together; give him another."

"Oh! oh! ah!" gasped Griddle. "I—never—yah!—you imps! Oh!—my shoulder's broken."

They gave him another squeeze, and let him go.

Then Griddle disappeared, [vowing vengeance upon his assaulters.

The story was laid before Mr. Crammer but that gentleman declined to take any steps in the matter—in fact, he could not, for Griddle had committed a crime in playing the part of a spy, and a greater one by allowing himself to be detected.

CHAPTER XXVIII.
THE SECOND USHER.

A FEW days later a little sensation was created by the arrival of a gentleman to fill the place of second usher.

His appearance was heralded by Griddle staggering across the hall and upstairs with a box of huge dimensions, almost large enough to contain the court-dresses of a dozen ladies. As Griddle worked his way upwards he puffed, growled, and cursed in an undertone, alternately, and when he reached the first landing he halted for a rest.

To him then appeared Tim, who was on his way to the schoolroom for an hour's evening study.

"You look hot," said Tim.

"Ain't that box big enough to make a man look hot?" grunted Griddle.

"Whose box is it?"

"Read it yourself—the letters is big enough."

Tim stooped down, and on the front of the box read—

"MR. JONAS TIDD."

"What sort of man is he?" inquired the inquisitive Tim.

"He ain't come in yet," returned Griddle, "he's settling with the cabby. Now are you satisfied?"

Tim said he was satisfied, and departed to spread the tidings among the pupils.

"Another usher arrived!" he shouted, as he entered the schoolroom.

"What's he like?" "Who is he?" "Old or young?" and a volley of other queries poured upon him.

"Haven't seen him," replied Tim, as soon as he could get in a word; "but he'll turn up soon. Old Griddle is carrying up his box—such a whopper! I should say he was a swell."

"A big box may have very little in it," sagely twitted Bob.

"But it's heavy," urged Tim. "If you was to see the state Griddle is in you wouldn't think it empty."

"Well, the sooner he shows up and lets us see what he is like, the better," said Bob.

This desire was speedily satisfied, for in a few minutes Mr. Crammer entered, followed by a tall, sallow-faced man of five-and-forty, or thereabouts. His hair, which was very dark, he wore long, almost to his shoulders, and his great height—for he was very tall— was somewhat reduced by a slight stoop.

"Young gentlemen," said Mr. Crammer, "your new usher, Mr. Jonas Tidd."

Bob Martin, as the oldest pupil, stepped forward to greet him.

Mr. Tidd acknowleged his few words of welcome with a magnificent bow, such as princes give at court.

"Stuck up," thought Bob.

"Stupid!" was the mental comment of most of the boys.

"Mr. Tidd," said the master of Scarum School, "it will be a portion of your duty to spend the evening here. The pupils have had too much freedom of late. A want of help has compelled me to be somewhat lax of late."

Again Mr. Jonas Tidd bowed, "or the prince acknowledged the salute of another noble." Then Mr. Crammer retired, and Mr. Jonas Tidd took his seat by the fire.

A dead silence ensued.

The boys clustered in knots, cast glances upon the intruder which had little welcome in them, while he, with knitted brows, gazed thoughtfully at the glowing coals.

Sitting there, he did not appear in a very enviable light. His tall, bony frame, his long black hair, and fixed eyes reflecting the fire, gave him a wild, weird look, such as the astrologers and hermits of old were supposed to have, which had but little keeping with the school and the fresh young faces around him.

Soon the ice was broken, and the boys began to whisper. Rebellious glances were darted towards the strange man, who sat apparently unconscious of all around him.

Were they to have this giant at their evening revels—this mountain of flesh ever attendant upon them? Dark and dire were the looks engendered by their thoughts.

Presently the whispering became a murmur, then the murmur deepened and finally swelled into a roar.

Then he looked up.

"Boys," he said, in a deep tone, "be quiet."

A few of the most timid held their tongues—the rest dropped their voices, and the usher, apparently satisfied, resumed his contemplation of the fire.

Once again the murmurs arose, deepened, and swelled into a roar.

Then once more the usher looked up.

"Boys," he said again, "be quiet."

This time but few obeyed him—rebellion had taken root, and was springing up fast. They resented this intrusion of the gaunt man with the matted hair. Hitherto, the schoolroom, during certain hours of the evening, had been their own, their only sanctum during their waking hours, and now here was a tall, forbidding-looking man instructed to sit in their midst—to report, perhaps, their every word and deed. It was too bad.

Now Mr. Tidd looked up as the talking increased, and looked slowly round the room, taking each boy in his turn in his basilisk eye.

A few met his gaze, among them Bob Martin, Charley, Tim, and Harry Leicester. He singled out the latter for an address.

"What is your name?"

"Leicester, sir."

"Then come here, Leicester," said the usher, "and let me say to you what I hope will suffice for all. You know why I am here?"

No reply.

"To keep order," continued the usher, "and without I have your help the matter will be impossible. If we quarrel, the result may end disastrously for me, and perhaps painfully for you. You may be dismissed the school, and I—I—lose a chance of getting my daily bread."

The boys were quiet enough now, impressed by the deep, sonorous tones of the stranger.

"I don't want to freeze up your young

lives," he went on; "within the bounds of reason, enjoy your leisure hours—Heaven forbid that I should stint the young of a moment's enjoyment!—but remember this rioting is not fun, and rebellion is rather a serious form of amusement."

"Not a bad sort of fellow," whispered Charley.

"I don't think he is," returned Bob.

"Go and say something to him. Harry seems to be quite shut up.

Bob made a comical grimace deprecative of his powers of oratory, but he went.

"Mr. Tidd," he said, "if we hurt your feelings a little while ago we are very sorry; but—but we like to have a little time to ourselves, and it seems so—so hard——"

"Say no more," returned Mr. Tidd, kindly; "I perfectly understand you. When I am here think only of me with consideration, and keep exuberant spirits within bounds. I have no desire to check enjoyment—in fact I will assist you; are you fond of acting?"

"Charades, sir?"

"Anything; but, above all, the plays of glorious old Shakspeare?" said the tutor, a light dancing in his eyes. "Do you like the character of mad Lear?"

"Never read much about him," returned Bob with a gentle cough, and an irresistible wink at Charley.

"Then I will sometimes read to you," returned the usher, warming up into another man. "You shall taste of the sweets of the immortal bard. You shall weep with Juliet, mourn with Mark Antony, philosophize with Hamlet, rejoice with Bassanio, and be merry with Falstaff."

"I shall be most happy to do whatever is agreeable," returned Bob, who scarcely knew what to make of this unexpected outburst.

"But I am tired to-night," continued Mr. Tidd, "and will forbear. Break off, boys, and disport yourselves."

"I think we have got a treat here," said Bob, as soon as he got quietly into a corner with his friends.

"Good-natured chap," said Harry Leicester.

"I can't think where I've seen him before," said Mat Langley, thoughtfully, "but I have seen him."

"Look at him now," broke in Grimmer, "staring at the fire in that wild manner. He may do something here; perhaps kill Crammer."

"Or smother Pendulum with a bolster."

"When I first saw him," said Tim, "I felt inclined to bolt."

"To do what?"

"Bolt—run away—skedaddle."

"Yah! you fool," growled Mat Langley.

"Before you make up your mind to bolt, just think of what is before you."

"You bolted."

"Yes, and came back."

"Brought back."

"Well, it's the same. But running away is no joke, I can tell you."

"I say, Mat," said Bob, "you never told us the story of your adventures. Spin the yarn now."

"Nothing worth telling," rejoined Mat, modestly.

"That's all bosh. You must have seen something when you were away."

"I certainly did."

"Then, why not out with it?"

"Because I don't want it to spread over the school."

"It won't be spread over the school. All chums here, you know?"

"Come in a little closer, then."

They gathered around Mat, who leaned against the wall, and, in a calm, matter-of-fact tone, told the following story:—

"Old Crammer had been taking it out of me most unmercifully. I was black and blue from neck to heel, and when I was in bed too sore even to sleep. I lay thinking how I should prevent such another awful licking.

"Suddenly the thought came upon me, 'Why not run away?—many a lad has done it before, and made great fortunes.'

"Nearly all night I lay pondering on this, but it was daylight before I resolved to turn my back on Scarum School.

"I got out of bed and dressed quietly, keeping an eye all the time upon the fellows sleeping in the same room, but as they were all fast asleep and snoring prodigiously, I had little need of fear on their account.

"I slept then on the first-floor dormitory, and to drop into the garden was no difficult matter. So after packing up a few things I thought absolutely necessary, I opened the window gently, and the next instant was among Crammer's favourite rose bushes.

"I have heard a great deal about the beauty of early morn, the sun rising from the sea, and all that sort of thing, but you may guess, boys, that I had no eye for anything of that sort, although it was one of the most glorious mornings I had ever seen, but I turned my back on the sea and rising sun, and set off for the woods, and, as I implicitly believed, to make my fortune.

"The bruises and wheals that Crammer had made with his confounded 'Tickler' ached, and aggravated me to such an extent that at first I felt inclined to go back; but then I thought it would be but to receive a second edition; and after an hour's walk the pain decreased, and I determined to go on.

"MAY I AX THE MEANING O' THEM WORDS?" ASKED GRIDDLE.

"I had brought no food of any description with me, and after I had left Scarum School about two hours I began to feel as if I wanted my breakfast, and I can tell you it was not at all comforting to know that you fellows were pegging away, while I was a hungry runaway.

"There was a hill before me, and this I climbed, but not a house was in sight, and I sat down in despair, calling myself a fool and a jackass for attempting to tramp the country without knowing anything about it.

"As I sat thinking what I should do, I suddenly saw smoke arising from behind a clump of bushes.

"'Where there's smoke there's generally fire,' I said to myself, getting up, 'and maybe somebody has lighted it—a gipsy perhaps, or some poor hungry wretch like myself.'

"Proceeding to the spot from whence the smoke rose, I saw an old man in shabby garments and a battered hat; he sat warming his hands over a small brazier, and around him were strewn a quantity of dilapidated kettles and saucepans.

"A glance told me that the old man was a travelling tinker, and as I had always heard that tinkers, as a class, are generous-hearted, I essayed to speak to him."

"'Good morning,' said I; 'cold, is it not?'

"'Hullo,' he returned, raising his head, 'I weren't aware that anybody was about. What cheer?'

"'Very little,' I returned. 'I'm as cold as a fish in a block of ice.'

"'Then come to the fire,' said the tinker, 'it's very small, but if you begin at the toes, and warm upwards, you'll be as warm as a toast.'

"It is scarcely necessary for me to say that I accepted the old man's invitation, and sat down on the opposite side of the brazier.

"'Well, now we're comfortable,' said the tinker, 'perhaps you won't think me rude if I axes where you come from.'

"I did not know what to say, for although not liking to tell the old chap a fib, I dared not tell the truth; but the tinker came to my rescue.

"'I ain't got no right to ax no questions,' he said, 'and I won't do it. Maybe you're hungry, and can pick a bit?'

"'You have hit the right nail on the head,' I returned; 'I don't remember being so hungry before.'

"Mine host rose and took from one of the bushes a kind of wallet, from which he produced a piece of ham, three or four eggs, and a loaf of bread.

"Then he had a search among the ruined tinware distributed around, and, at last, finding one waterproof, or nearly so, set off to a spring hard by for a supply of water, which was afterwards boiled over the brazier.

"When everything was ready, and we sat down to breakfast, the sun had risen, and was throwing its warmth around, the birds sang in the trees and bushes, and there was a warm southerly breeze from the sea.

"I never felt so jolly in my life, and wondered why I had not turned tinker long ago, and, with my mouth full of ham and egg, pitied you poor wretches shut up with old Crammer and 'Tickler.'

"During the meal I spoke more coldly, told mine host that I was determined to see the world—in fact, as the term goes, to rough it—and asked him if I might be allowed to travel with him, expressing my willingness, as the advertisements say, 'to make myself generally useful.'

"'You ain't done nothin' wrong?' said the tinker, after pondering on my proposition for a few seconds—'you ain't done nothin' as is likely to get you into jail?'

"I felt rather riled at this; but as beggars must not be choosers, I swallowed what I considered an insult, and assured him that his fears were groundless."

"'Then I'm willin',' he said; 'and we'll share and share alike. I shall push on to a willage about four miles ahead, and where we'll shake down for the night—that is, if we have a good day. Some willages,' mused the old man, 'they makes a rush upon a chap when he's flush, and not inclined to work; and another time, a man may walk through a dozen places without gettin' so much as a biler to solder—but sich is life!'

"'What shall I do?' I asked, interrupting the soliloquy, feeling rather dubious as to how I should perform my part of the business.

"'You'll carry the kittle and the b'ilers,' replied the tinker; 'and I'll take the brazier, tools, and the grub; that's fair, ain't it? But fust, afore we move, I must know your name.'

"'Call me Mike,' I said; 'that's near enough.'

"'Werry good, Mike,' returned the tinker; 'my name is Sam Crooks, but call me Sam—plain Sam.'

"I collected the tinware, and, stringing them on a piece of rope, was about to march off, when Sam alarmed me by bawling for me to stop.

"'Hold hard!' he roared, and I dropped my burden, thinking Mr. Crammer, or some of his myrmidons, had appeared in sight; 'this won't do—my face black and yours white.'

"I understood his meaning, and soon gratified Sam by blacking myself as black as a Christy minstrel, and together we set out for the distant village.

"Jacktown was the name of the place for which we were bound, a curious tumble-down little place, with a solitary street winding about like a corkscrew, and a few formal red-brick houses scattered about on the outskirts, looking like Noah's arks without the boat parts.

"It was market day, and Sam was busy, and I did all I could to help him, but that wasn't much.

"However, we got through the day jolly enough, having lived like two princes, and I was as happy as the hours were long.

"About six in the evening, Sam announced his intention of 'knocking off,' and as soon as the fire was extinguished and the brazier cool we set off to spend the evening at the Dog and Whistle, the principal inn of the place.

"'Werry sorry, Sam,' said the landlord, who appeared to know my friend perfectly. 'Werry sorry, but I'm full, from attic to cellar. It's market day, you know, and then again, some as would ha' gone home have put up, for they say a storm is risin'.'

"For the first time, I now noticed that a fleecy haze overspread the sky; but I had seen the same thing many times before, and laughed at the idea of the storm; but Sam's face wore an anxious expression after he had scanned the clouds, and swinging the brazier over his shoulder, said—

"'We must get in somewhere, lad—there's summat comin'. It mayn't be only a shower, and it may be a deluge.'

"But every inn was as full as the Dog and Whistle, and as no one else would take us in at any price—for who would care about housing pair of tinkers?—we were compelled to turn our backs upon the village.

"'We'll try a farmhouse or two,' said Sam, with something like a sigh; 'but I don't hope for much, as they are a werry suspicious lot down 'ere. Hallo! thunder, by jingo! If we ain't quick we shall have the storm upon us.'

"Before us stood a farmhouse, with a number of comfortable-looking barns and outhouses surrounding, and Sam and I, weary and footsore, dragged our limbs up to the door, and craved a lodging for the night, if even in one of the barns.

"'Not I, indeed,' said the farmer whom we addressed. 'I've lost quite enough fowls already, thank ye. Tramps is dangerous, and I never encourage them. You may be honest, but that ain't nothing to me, whether you are or not.'

"'There's another peal of thunder,' said Sam, as we turned away, sick at heart, from the door, 'and we're in for it as sure as water will run out of a b'iler with a hole in it; but it ain't a bit o' use givin' way, we must make the best of matters.'

"The sky was now overcast, and lightning began to quiver amongst the hills, and every minute the thunder became louder and louder; then the clouds turned inky black, and the wind suddenly rose and whistled through the trees, and as suddenly dropped, and all was still.

"The rain then began to fall; first a few heavy drops pattering loudly on the dusty roadway and parched foliage, and then it came down with tremendous force, and in less time than it takes me to tell it, the road was transformed into a river.

"Both Sam and I were wet to the skin, and half stupefied by the flashes of lightning, and roaring of the thunder, but we struggled on and again entered the village.

"A dog-cart, containing two persons wrapped up in overcoats, passed us on the way, and drew up at the door of the Dog and Whistle.

"We, in our turn, entered the bar, and then proceeded to the parlour to endeavour to comfort ourselves, but imagine my horror when Crammer himself confronted me.

"He knew me at once, and taking me by the hand, wished me good evening.

"'I trust you have made the day enjoyable. You shall have a *hot* tea when you arrive home.'

"The other party I saw in the dog-cart then drew nigh, and to my horror it was a police-officer.

"'Well, gov'nor,' he said, turning to Crammer, 'so you've caught un. Shall I put the darbies on the young warmint?'

"'Dear me, no!'" said Mr. Crammer.

'My pupil will return with me, even as a lamb with its shepherd. And who,' continued the old hypocrite, patting me on the back, 'is your friend?'

"I explained.

"'Wot's all this?' said Sam Crooks at last. 'Mike——'

"'Master Matthew Langley,' uttered Crammer, bowing and smiling, 'of Scarum School.'

"'Oh!' returned Sam, sitting down, and gazing from me to Crammer. 'That's how the wind is, is it?—the young warmint.'

"Crammer took me back that night as soon as the storm was over, and after I had partaken of my *hot* tea I went to bed ten times worse than on the night before; and the next morning when I rose I registered a vow never to run away or turn tinker again.'"

CHAPTER XXIX.

THE ART OF LETTER WRITING.

ONE of the most interesting arrivals, the most welcome of visitors at the School of Scarum, was the letter-bag.

Mr. Crammer certainly did more than many masters of the strict school.

He allowed his pupils to receive their letters unopened; and youths writing home for remittances always received them, if they were forwarded.

We—that is, all you who have been to a boarding school—know full well how frequently and earnestly those plaints were made, and what excuses were made for irregular dips into the pockets of parents and guardians.

As the half lengthened, so these appeals increased in number and power, especially on the part of those who were invariably successful.

These letters were seldom, if ever, written in secret; but when funds ran short, a solemn council was generally held, and a course of action decided on, resulting in a neat little batch of letters for transit through Her Majesty's post.

Bob Martin was considered the most pathetic letter writer, Harry Leicester the most lively; and Lobby Panks' effusions generally took the form of an appeal made by a prisoner under sentence of death imploring for a remission of his punishment.

It was Lobby's natural whine, and whine he did upon each and every occasion.

From a variety of causes, among them the utter failure of the stamp and pill trades, money ran very short at Scarum School; and a few niggard youths who always had money —there are some such in every school—made enormous bargains in the way of bats, peg-tops, and other youthful treasures, sold under pressure of the times.

Tim was so far reduced that he parted with every available button, leaving only a sufficient number to keep his clothing in a decent position on his portly frame.

Charley hadn't a rap.

Grimmer, Martin, Leicester, and all the others were in the same condition.

And then one of the general council meetings was held, with Bob Martin in the chair.

He opened the meeting in a fashion peculiar to himself.

Rapping the desk with Mr. Pendulum's private and personal ruler, he thus addressed the school:—

"Now, all you fellows who've got any writing paper and envelopes, shell out."

A few rather soiled and crumpled specimens of stationery were produced; and, by careful sorting, sufficient for a letter from each of the boys was doled out, Julius Cæsar Smith alone holding out, and Tim declining under the plea that it "was as much as his life was worth to ask his precious uncle for a brown."

"The next thing," said Bob, "is stamps —who's got any?"

This was a more difficult matter, for stamps were almost equivalent to currency, and not more than a dozen could be found.

"The next thing," continued the president, "is to choose the fellows who are most likely to draw some coin. Charley, how will you get on?"

"I think I can get some," answered our hero.

"One stamp for you, then. Harry, how about you?"

"I never failed yet."

"Then there's one for you. Grimmer?"

"I'm generally lucky," replied Grimmer; "but Crammer has sent home a letter about my evil ways, and I'd rather not try it on."

"Very good. Will you have one, Mat?"

"Yes. I've a friend or two in London."

"Right you are."

In this way the stamps, all but one, were dealt out, and this, Tim, to the profound astonishment of his friends, suddenly claimed.

"I'll have a shy at it," he said; "it isn't possible to make my uncle more crabby than he naturally is, and if he should be ill, and think he is going to die, he may repent, and send me something."

"A little in that," said Bob, and the last stamp was dealt out to our fat friend.

"Now," continued Bob, "the next move is the letter—you who can't get up a respectable affair, or think it too much trouble, can copy one which I will draw up, and I shall charge twopence to every fellow who brings in the coin. Who wants a letter?'

All but Harry Leicester, Tim, and Charley decided to avail themselves of this offer, and Bob sat down to write.

In a quarter of an hour he had the epistle ready, and stood up to read it, subject, of course, to general approval.

"Silence, there," he said. "Now boys, listen—'My dear——' the blank," he explained, "you can fill up as you please—depends upon whether it is father, mother, uncle, friends, or guardians, you are pitching into—keep quiet, Panks, or get out of the room."

Panks, who was having a little difference with Grimmer, who unceremoniously elbowed him into the rear, immediately subsided, and Bob continued—

"'My dear ——

"'I am glad to say that I am getting on very nicely with my lessons, and this morning Mr. Crammer said I should soon be at the top of the school. This is a very nice place, but Mr. Crammer is very strict, especially about my dress, and he told me after I came from church last Sunday, that my gloves were very shabby. I took all the boys in the class down yesterday, and now stand at the head, where I intend to keep if I possibly can, although it will be hard work, as we are all very industrious, and work like steam after school hours.'"

"Isn't 'steam' rather slangy?" put in Grimmer.

"Ain't you rather stupid?" returned Bob, "how should steam be slang? You might as well ask me if rump-steaks are tripe. Be quiet and listen."

"'I think it is just possible I may gain a prize this half, and I could make certain of it if I had a new ruler and some red ink to make my lessons look neat. Mr. Crammer likes to see things neat, and Mr. Pendulum is quite an artist in this way; but I cannot have either ruler or ink, as they are not allowed, and I have no money left. We have a new usher, Mr. Jonas Tidd, who seems to be a very kind and learned gentleman—he promises to help me on, so all is very nice with me, and all I want is a few shillings *by return of post without fail.* So no more from your affectionate'—and so on.

"There!" exclaimed Bob, with the conscious pride of a man of talent; "what do you think of that?"

There was only one dissentient—Loony Panks—and he did not think it was "kind enough." Being asked for an explanation of the term, and failing to give one, he was recommended to go to Bath and spend his twopence in stale buns—a piece of advice he took in high dudgeon, and retired to a corner in a fit of sulks.

The rest set to work upon this precious

effusion, copying it in various specimens of handwriting.

In the meantime, Harry Leicester had written a lively epistle to an elder brother; Charley had scribbled one to Filer, and Tim, with much labour, had composed what he considered to be a respectful appeal to his uncle.

We give the two last specimens—Charley's first—

"Dear old Filer,—

"I'm quite stumped—cleared out as neat as wax, and all the fellows are in the same state; we have not a brown, and toffy is as scarce as gold-dust on the sea-shore. You must get me some, and send at once, for I want no end of things. If you just give my dear father a hint, it will be all that is required. This school is not a bad sort of crib after all—the untamed youths are not bad, take them for all in all, although we have some jolly sneaks amongst us, and a proud, stuck-up fellow who gave me a bit of cheek, and I gave him a licking, which you will be glad to hear—not easily though, for he stood out well, and gave me a few stingers such as I don't want over again. I have a jolly chum—Bob Martin, and a comical one—Tim Turndown, besides a number of others of the right sort; and if you can manage to run over some day, I will introduce you, and they will give you such a reception as will make you young again. Write as soon as you can—at once, I mean.

"Truly yours, dear Filer,
"CHARLES THORN."

Tim's letter was of a heavier order of structure, and altogether more elaborately conceived. Writing to his uncle was like treading upon unknown ground, and required a deal of caution.

The effusion ran as follows—

"My dear Uncle,—

"If I might ask for a little money, will you send me some at once, as all my buttons are off my clothes, and I want more to eat than I can get here. My duty to you, sir, and my best respects, and I think it will be better to send money or stamps, as we are not allowed to go out and change cheques and post-office orders. Mr. Crammer and Mr. Pendulum send their best respects, and hope that your gout is better; the same with me, and long may you live to enjoy it. So I conclude,

"Your affectionate nephew,
"TIMOTHY TURNDOWN."

"I think that'll touch him," murmured Tim; "it's kind and affectionate, and to the point—the allusion to the gout is nice and delicate—yes! he'll shell out, I'm sure."

Lobby Panks also despatched a letter, and the post-office of Winkle-by-the-Sea was that night richer by twelve epistles from the promising youths of Scarum School.

CHAPTER XXX.
GRIDDLE ASSERTS HIMSELF.

WHILE the replies to the letters were pending, two events took place at Scarum School which we relate, to enable our readers to perceive that changes are at hand.

The first relates to the potent Griddle.

For several days after the water-butt adventure, he maintained a dogged reserve, seldom dining at the house unless specially required, and keeping to his lodge when the playful youths appeared in the grounds.

The consequence was that much of his work was neglected, and Mr. Crammer grew dissatisfied, insomuch that he despatched his only son to command Griddle to appear and answer for his delinquencies.

Master Todman—or Toddy, as he was better known—crossed the playground without farther mishap than a small piece of putty, thrown by an undetected hand, which caught him deftly on the ear.

Opening the door of Griddle's lodge, without ceremony, he entered.

The position he naturally expected to find Griddle in, if he expected at all, was on his feet, or sitting in his chair—but nothing of the sort, the porter was lying on his back upon the hearth-rug, with his feet in the fender, snoring prodigiously.

Master Toddy was alarmed, thoughts of Griddle's being murdered flashed across his brain; he looked for the flowing blood, but it was not there.

Was Griddle in a fit?

Toddy crept closer, and looked down upon the prostrate form.

If he was in a fit, it was a peaceful one; for Griddle's face was calm, and although he breathed heavily, his respirations were regular.

"He must be sleeping," thought Toddy, gently shaking him.

This mild attempt failing, Mr. Crammer's son and heir administered four or five sound punches in the ribs; and then Griddle opened his eyes.

He stared at the ceiling for a moment, then brought his optics slowly to bear on lower objects, until they rested on Toddy.

"That you, Masser Crammer?" murmured Griddle, with a sickly smile. "Very kind of you to come and see poor ole man."

"Papa wants you immediately," said Toddy.

"Your papa can't have me 'mediately," returned Griddle. "He must wait till this confounded room gets straight."

"You are lying on your back, Griddle," hinted Toddy.

"So I am, Masser Crammer," rejoined Griddle, slowly getting into a sitting position. "Skewrious thing for man to lay on his back. Wonder how I got there!"

Master Toddy said nothing, but he looked very hard at a bottle and glass upon the table.

Griddle followed the direction of his looks, and smiled mournfully.

"Cramps," he said. "Awful cramps I gets, jes' under the fourth rib. Nothin' like pep'mint, Masser Crammer."

Toddy said not a word, but he looked wondrous wise; and Griddle went on—

"I gets little simplethy from anybody. 'What's cramps?' they ses. 'Nothin' more than a little pain here and there.' All I ses is, that I 'ope they'll have 'em."

"You are keeping papa waiting," said Toddy, anything but favourably impressed by this explanation.

"I'll be with'm in a moment," rejoined Griddle; "as soon as I get rid of the after-pains o' them cramps."

Master Toddy said no more; and hastening to the presence of his father, imparted what he had seen, adding, by way of a rider, that he believed Griddle "was very much intoxicated."

Mr. Crammer dismissed his son, and, with a lowering brow, awaited the coming of the recreant porter.

In about ten minutes Griddle arrived, none the better for having acted up to the Spanish proverb, and "taken a hair of the dog that bit him."

"Misser Crammer," he said, making strenuous efforts to keep a respectable balance, "you sent for me, sir."

"I did," returned the schoolmaster. "Your household duties have been much neglected during the past few days. Give me a reason."

"I'm a miser'ble man," said Griddle, with tears in his eyes; "a neglected, miser'ble wretch, without a friend in the world."

"That is no answer. The knives and forks, you have not touched for days. That work has, therefore, devolved upon the housemaid."

"It's the lease she could do, Misser Crammer, after breaking my 'art."

"Breaking your fiddlestick. I am disappointed with you, Griddle. You grieve; you are not sober; you are not well-conducted."

"Misser Crammer," said Griddle, drawing himself up, "you forget yourself; you forget the man you air addressin'."

"I am speaking to my servant," rejoined Mr. Crammer, sternly.

"You are addressin' more than that," said Griddle. "You are talkin' to a man reduced from a beadle to a school-porter; a

man suddenly carse down from a lellivated spear, and chucked clean on his back afore a tyrant master and a 'ole family of bottle-imps. Misser Crammer, you are too 'ard upon a old and faithful servant—you are indeed, sir, and you'll live to repent it."

"Go, and sleep yourself sober; then come again to me."

"May I ax the meaning o' them words?"

"I mean, Griddle, that you are in a beastly state of intoxication, and unfit to speak to any respectable person, upon any subject whatever."

The effect of these words upon Griddle was at once apparent.

Squaring himself up, he assumed an attitude of self-defence, and requested Mr. Crammer to "Come on."

"When I thinks of what I were, and what I am," he said, "my blood biles. A man as has had the lockin' up of tramps and wagrants in general to be cheeked by a school-master is too much. Mortial flesh and blood can't stand it. If you're a man, come out o' that cheer and come on."

Mr. Crammer was alarmed—he arose and stepped towards the bell pull. Griddle, perceiving his object, stepped between, squaring and sparring with an amount of science one might have expected from an Ojibbeway Indian.

"It's fair play atween man and man," he said. "Come on, you old willain—'tossicated am I? Come on."

But the master of Scarum School declined this offer, and kept the table between him and his furious domestic, until an opportunity was afforded to reach the door. Then he retreated hastily, and locked Griddle in.

His next step was to secure the aid of the ushers, with whom he quickly returned, and valorously posting himself in the rear, bade them enter and seize the culprit.

This was all very well for him, but rather disagreeable for the ushers, Mr. Pendulum especially, who had as much dread of a fight as a child has of fire.

Mr. Jonas Tidd was not so timid, but he was far from being an advocate of the fistic art.

"Don't you think, sir," said Mr. Pendulum, in fearing tones, "that we had better have the police in? The fellow is raging about like an infuriated bull."

"Have you no regard for the credit of the establishment? Winkle-by-the-Sea is a small place, and scandal spreads fast. I command you to enter—remove the fellow from the premises at once."

"Suppose we were to rush upon him," said Mr. Jonas Tidd, "we might maim him mortally."

"Something must be done," returned Mr.

Crammer, angrily; " the fellow is destroying everything in the room."

Indeed, Griddle appeared to be performing some extraordinary feats, chairs were tumbling about, and twice had there been a smash of crockery and glass.

" Come on. Follow me," said Mr. Jonas Tidd, with a sudden resolution. " I'll have the fellow out in a jiffy."

Mr. Crammer unlocked the door, and the usher rushed in.

Ere Mr. Pendulum could ascertain the whereabouts of the foe, he received a stinging blow under the left eye, and went over to grass—that is, to the doormat. Mr. Tidd, however, succeeded in grappling with the furious Griddle, and the two, locked in each other's arms, reeled about the room, adding to the damage already created.

Griddle was not a weak man, and drink had made him furious, but Mr. Tidd was also of the muscular description of man, and the first alarm over, he succeeded in securing the refractory domestic, and pinned him upon the sofa.

When this was done, Mr. Pendulum arose, and he and Mr. Crammer valorously came forward and lent their manly aid.

" How many on you?" cried Griddle, who was literally foaming. " I'll bring a haction for this—there goes my weskut strings. Yah! you cowards."

" Ring the bell, Mr. Pendulum," said the schoolmaster, " and get the boys into the schoolroom, then we will thrust this fellow forth."

The usher hastened to obey, and having formed the boys, returned to his post. Then the final struggle began.

Griddle would not walk, but obliged his assailants with the full benefit of his dead weight, screaming and vowing vengeance upon them.

Numbers prevailed, they got him into the hall, then into the grounds, and across to the lodge, his heels leaving a track almost as deep as a cart rut, and finally he was thrown into the roadway, a wrecked and ruined porter.

" I will send your things down to the inn," said Mr. Crammer, at parting; " but you show your face here again and I will give you in charge."

They closed and locked the door, but Griddle immediately ran at it with the force of a battering ram, and the lodge quivered again, and a couple of stones came through the window like shots from a gun.

" A violent fellow!" said Mr. Crammer, pale and breathless; " I have narrowly escaped with my life."

They waited a few moments for a second charge, but Griddle made none, he had pro-

bably ran against the door with his head foremost, and found the balance of advantage on the side of the door, and thereupon desisted from any further attempt. Mr. Jonas Tidd, peering cautiously through the broken window, beheld him ruefully holding his head in one hand, and shaking the other, clenched, at Scarum School.

" I think we may leave him now," said Mr. Tidd; " he will probably go quietly away."

So they returned to the school, and having smoothed their ruffled plumes, resumed the duties of the day.

Scarcely had the second class begun when the housekeeper's bell above Mr. Crammer's desk was violently rung. Master and ushers exchanged glances, and hurried out in a body, leaving the pupils, who had witnessed Griddle's struggles in the ground from the window, in a state of frenzied excitement.

In the passage the three gentlemen encountered Mrs. Margery in a disordered headdress, her afternoon toilet had apparently been interrupted, and her face quivering with agitation.

" Oh! if you please, Mr. Crammer——"

" What is it?—woman, speak."

" That Griddle, sir; he's climbed through the scullery window, and is now in the kitchen. I saw you take him out, sir, all the servants saw it, and they've run out of the kitchen to save their lives."

" A desperate man, a murderous villain!" said Mr. Crammer, trembling like a leaf; " what is to be done, gentlemen?"

" Arm ourselves and drive him forth," rejoined Mr. Jonas Tidd, striking a powerful attitude; " we are three to one, why should we fear?"

" I have some stout sticks in my bedroom," said Mr. Crammer, " we will arm at once."

The stout sticks were of about the same consistency as an Irish shillelagh, in fact, Mr. Crammer had brought them from the Sister Isle a year or so before. Armed with these, the three gentlemen descended to the kitchen, and listened cautiously at the door.

Not a sound—not a word.

" He has retreated again," said Mr. Crammer, and threw open the door.

But, no! there was Griddle, leaning against the dresser, no longer furious, but mild, abject, and weeping copiously.

Then his three opponents became valorous indeed.

Mr. Crammer boldly advanced to the middle of the kitchen, and demanded an explanation of the porter's extraordinary conduct.

" Misser Crammer," returned Griddle, wiping his eyes with the back of his hand, " it was all cramps and the rum I took to cure 'em. I axes yer parding, and if you'll overlook it this time, I'll jine the band of 'ope, and endoor the cramps for hever."

"How did you return, sir?"

"I climbed the wall, Misser Crammer," was the reply; "and here I come to ax your parding, and 'ope as how you'll overlook it this time; I'm a teetot'lar from this hour. I'm never wicious 'cept in drink, and when people lets me alone, I lets them alone. I hope you'll forgive me, sir."

Mr. Crawshay Crammer paused a moment. School porters were scarce, and Griddle, on the whole, had been a good servant; besides, he had promised to amend, and abjure strong drinks for ever.

"I suspend my judgment for awhile," he said, at length, "to see how you behave. Let but a shadow of this scene occur again, I will not only discharge you, but hand you over to be dealt with according to law."

In this way, a peace was patched up, and Griddle resumed his daily duties at Scarum School.

CHAPTER XXXI.

REPLIES FOR AND AGAINST.

THE second incident alluded to at the beginning of the previous chapter requires but a very few words of explanation.

Our readers will remember that Mr. Jonas Tidd was appointed as warder or keeper to the pupils during their evenings of leisure in the schoolroom, and that his presence was looked upon in the light of an intrusion.

But this feeling was quickly expelled by Mr. Jonas Tidd himself.

One evening, when the boys were sitting rather quietly in groups, he asked them why they did not do something to amuse themselves.

They answered, through Bob Martin, that they did not know what to do.

"Are you fond of acting?" asked Mr. Jonas Tidd.

Of course they were; charades and so on were always capital fun at Christmas parties.

"Charades are all very well," returned Mr. Tidd, with a contemptuous curl of his lip; "but I will teach you something better than that. I know something about acting; in fact, I—I—never mind, I will teach you how to act. We will choose a play from Shakespeare, and certain members of you shall play the parts—what say you?"

What could they do but hail the proposition with delight?

"Glorious old Will!" cried Mr. Jonas Tidd—"the greatest of all poets, Nature's masterpiece. We will play *Richard the Third*; but, first of all, let me hear you each recite an impromptu piece, so that I may judge of your ability and power."

Thus passed the first evening, and as the result of these novel studies will appear in the sequel, we will leave the subject for the present.

The morning for the replies to the letters came, and by the side of Charley's plate was an epistle directed in the tortuous handwriting of Filer. Martin, Harry Leicester, and Tim also had one each, but the rest for the present were doomed to disappointment.

Filer enclosed a sovereign from Mr. Thorn, and after a variety of domestic incidents of no particular importance, concluded as follows:—

"Mops is a huseful servant, and, althow he his a cripel, he stode up agenst two burglair chaps who got into the howse and tried to steel the plait. Mops hav too black eyes, but both the chaps is Took, and hav been afore the Magerstraits, a couple of big willins as ever I see."

"He means the burglars, I suppose, and not the magistrates," said Charley, who was comparing notes with his friends after breakfast; "but it was very plucky of Mops."

"I think the burglars might have dropped in here," said Bob Martin, significantly, "and Mops would not have grieved much."

"Perhaps so—what's your luck, Bob?"

"Five shillings and four sides of advice, with a small pamphlet from my sister about the good little boy who saved his pennies and died worth a million of money."

"I don't believe in those fellows," rejoined Harry Leicester, "it's a swindle altogether; what's the good of raking and scraping every copper together; spend it, say I, like a brick."

"Hear, hear!" cried Tim.

"How much have you got?" asked Charley.

"Listen," replied Tim, folding back a letter written with a quill pen upon blue official paper; "if you can make anything out of it, it's more than I can."

"'Nephew Timothy—

"'Your letter requires a little investigation, and I shall take the first opportunity to make it.

"'RALPH TURNDOWN.'

"That's neat and nice, isn't it?" exclaimed Tim; "who's got noddle enough to make anything out of it?"

"I sniff a letter to Mr. Crammer in it," said Harry Leicester.

"Do you think so?" rejoined Tim, breaking out in a cold sweat; "what a fool I was to write! I might have known the old curmudgeon wouldn't shell out a brown. Hallo! there goes Panks. Any letter, Lobby?"

Panks answered with a rueful shake of the head.

"Not a word," he said.

"Sure to come next post," said Tim, "perhaps they are doing you up a big hamper."

"I am more likely to have a hamper than money," rejoined Lobby.

"When it comes," returned Tim, kindly, "let me know, and I'll help you with it."

Panks muttered something, whether in the affirmative or negative, Tim could not say, but he let him go. A project had crept into his youthful mind. Drawing Charley aside, he begged the favour of a loan of sixpence.

"You can have a shilling," said Charley, "as soon as I can get change. Mary is going down to the village directly."

"Ask her to bring me some note-paper and envelopes."

"Going to write to nunkey again?"

"No, Charley, I fancy not. I am not going to write for money—something very different."

Charley put his hands upon Tim's shoulders, and looked steadily into his eyes.

"Come, old boy," he said, "none of that."

"What do you mean?" demanded Tim.

"None of your spooning, Tim—you ought to know better."

"Now do I look like a fellow to spoon?" asked Tim, with an injured air. "Do you think I would go dangling about after a lot of girls?"

"I should hope not, Tim."

"Upon my word, Charley, you vex me; I feel savage. Me spooning!—what next will you think of? I'm ashamed of you."

"Well, all right, Tim—don't get roughed; but it certainly did look like it, you know."

In the course of the day Tim received his paper and envelopes, with a few stamps; and on the following morning Lobby Panks received the following production:—

"High Street, Winkle-by-the-Sea,
"March 31st, 18——.

"Dear Sir,—I am instructed by Mrs. Panks to let you have four tarts weekly for a month; which will be better than your having them all together, as they will be fresher. Please call for the first lot to-morrow.

"Yours truly,
"A. DOUGHTY."

The unsuspecting Lobby hugged this letter to his breast, and said nought to his schoolmates. The morrow was a half-holiday, which would give him the opportunity of quietly sneaking down and enjoying them alone.

Now this Mr. Doughty was a man who had made a considerable fortune among the best families, by supplying breakfast, supper, and wedding parties; and being a narrow-minded and chuckle-headed country tradesman, was, in his own estimation, a very important personage indeed.

His shop was too aristocratic for the boys; none ever ventured within its precincts; in fact, it was doubtful if Mr. Doughty, who attended to the shop in person, would have waited upon them, the place being a fashionable lounge for the small-fry aristocracy of Winkle-by-the-Sea.

Panks did not think of this, he only remembered that when his mother came to see him, as she did several times during the half, living but a few miles away, she often lunched at the place, the only shop in the town of the class; and it was, therefore, with no misgiving, that Lobby entered at high noon and elbowed his way through a group of ladies to the counter.

Mr. Doughty, who was bowing, smiling, and expatiating upon the weather to some of his favourite customers, caught sight of him, and being assured by his demeanour that Lobby belonged to no party there, asked Lobby sharply what he wanted.

"My four tarts," replied Lobby, promptly.

"When were they ordered?" asked Mr. Doughty, thinking it was a family order.

"Yesterday, I think," replied Lobby. "I will take two raspberry, one gooseberry, and a currant jam. Mother says that I am to have them every week for a month."

A light dawned upon him, and the great confectioner frowned.

The only doubt he had was whether Lobby was the joker, or only the victim.

He glared at his desk, and the daily calendar caught his eye.

Then Mr. Doughty smiled, not graciously, but sardonically.

"Wait a minute, my lad," he said, "and I will attend to you."

Lobby waited patiently while the ladies consumed sundry tarts and a couple of bottles of lemonade, that charming cooling drink despised by Griddle.

This done, they left, bowed to the door by Mr. Doughty.

The confectioner turned.

He and Lobby were alone.

"My lad," he said, "what did you ask for?"

"Four tarts. Two rasp——"

"I remember now," said Mr. Doughty, taking hold of Panks by the collar; "two raspberry. There they are!" Here he administered two openhanders on a portion of Panks which shall be nameless. "Here's the gooseberry!" Another smack. "That's the currant jam! with a little un in, to help you to keep your eye on the 1st of April in future, you fool!"

With a feeling of having been stung all over, Panks staggered into the street, plump into the midst of a bevy of his schoolmates, headed by that arch-joker Tim Turndown.

CHAPTER XXXII.

A VISITOR.

"DEAR me," exclaimed Tim, "if this isn't Panks!"

"Yes, it's Panks," returned that youth, with a vicious look.

"What are you doing here?"

"What's that to you?"

"Don't be rude, Lobby. The fact is you've had a tuck out of tarts."

"He has had a tuck out of something," rejoined Bob Martin, who was a member of the party, with Charley and a few other particular friends.

"Of course you don't know what is the matter," said Lobby Panks, "but mind you don't get into trouble about that letter."

"What letter?" asked Tim, innocently.

"The letter you put Mr. Doughty's name to—that's committing forgery.

"If you accuse me of forgery," returned Tim, "I'll—I'll make you prove it."

"So I can," said Lobby, drawing a letter from his jacket pocket, "look here. I must have been a fool not to have known the writing—it is yours, and you have signed Mr. Doughty's name—mind you don't get into trouble."

"I signed old Doughty's name!" cried Tim," what next I wonder?"

"Here it is."

"Let me see it?"

The unsuspecting Panks put it within reach of Tim, who grasped it, and coolly tore it into a hundred pieces.

"There," he said, scattering them about, "prove it, will you?"

"That's mean, to do a dirty trick and be ashamed of it."

"Lobby Panks," said Tim, standing with his legs very wide apart, "withdraw those words."

"I sha'n't."

"Then here's at you," cried Tim, and closed with his old foe.

"Drop it," said Bob Martin, pushing his way between them, "you can't fight in the High Street; if you must knock each other about, do it like gentlemen, out in the country."

"I'm not going to fight," said Panks.

"You must," returned Tim, "or apologize."

"I sha'n't do either," said Panks, and sauntered away.

"Let him go," interposed Charley, as Tim made an effort to follow him, "remember the quarrel arose from your own joke."

"So it did," said Tim, smiling immediately. "Didn't he come out of the shop in a hurry? Ha! ha! and didn't old Doughty look savage?"

"Rather! Now that little performance is over, what is the next step? We've the best part of the day before us."

"Suppose we go down to the beach and play pirates," suggested Tim.

"Not a bad idea," assented Charley; "there's a cave among the rocks. I'll be the pirate chief, and will defend it with my men —you, Tim, can be the coastguard."

"And get licked," grumbled Tim.

"Of course," rejoined Charley; "the coastguard always get licked in story books, but remember this, Tim, the coastguard is alive and kicking still."

"Well it don't matter," said Tim; "it's a lark anyhow. Who'll be a coastguardsman?"

"Settle it when we get down to the beach."

Away they scampered through the streets of the town, round by the boats to the sands, strewn here and there with huge stones fallen from the frowning cliff above.

The spot Charley alluded to lay some distance from the town, and not far from Scarum School. It was a place they could see from the windows of the house, and had the reputation of being haunted by the ghosts of departed smugglers.

In the summer time, when visitors mustered at Winkle-by-the-Sea, it was a favourite place of resort for lovers and students, who made collections of young lobsters, crabs, starfish, and seaweed, the huge masses of rock offering shelter for quiet spooning, and forming banks for innumerable little pools where the young fish disported themselves when the tide was out.

Now it was too early in the year for visitors, and the boys hoped to have this desirable spot to themselves; but lo! and behold, as they neared the smuggler's cave an elderly gentleman rose before their vision, seated on a piece of rock, quietly reading a book.

"It's like them old uns," said Tim, pulling up, "they are sure to get in the way. There he is, right in the track of the cave. We can't attack it without running over him, and if we only go within a mile of the brute, he'll shout out, 'Be quiet there, can't you,' and perhaps drop upon some of us with that stick of his."

"It's very aggravating," rejoined Bob Martin, "we can't ask him to move, and he is in the way."

"Let's have a lark with him," suggested Tim.

"What can we do?"

"I'll creep up and hang a lot of seaweed on the back buttons of his coat. Then we'll say something at him and run away."

"You daren't do it, Tim."

"That's all you know; look here, and keep quiet."

He crept over the soft sand, and stole behind the unconscious gentleman.

The boys saw Tim with wonderful care, tying two large tails of weed upon the buttons of his coat, and stoop for a second supply; when the gentleman suddenly arose to his feet and turned round.

"He's in for it," cried Bob Martin.

"Why doesn't he run?" rejoined Charley; "look at the fool. Come away, Tim."

But no; Tim stood like one petrified, while the old gentleman slowly and deliberately advanced and laid a hand upon his collar. Tim appeared to surrender himself without an effort.

"He's dragging him away," shouted Charley; "now boys, a rescue."

"A rescue!—a rescue!" they cried, and arming themselves with huge bundles of the damp weed, they bore down upon captor and captive.

Tim heard them coming, and turned upon them with a look which they remembered for many a day.

His lips moved as if he were speaking, but he uttered no sound.

"Leave hold of him, sir," cried Charley, aiming a bunch of weed rolled up like a snowball at the old gentleman's hat.

The aim was true, and the hat bounded merrily before a brisk breeze.

"Confound you!" roared the old gentleman, "I'll make you repent of this, you young scoundrels."

"Let him go then," cried Bob Martin, administering a second dose full in the shirt front of Tim's captor.

Again Tim appeared to be making a frantic effort to speak, but, as before, no sound came.

"There's another dose for you," cried Harry Leicester, throwing a star-fish about a foot in diameter.

This fine specimen of marine produce caught the old gentleman full in the face, and he roared like a mad bull.

"Every bone in your bodies shall ache for this," he cried. "Pooh—puff—faugh! You imps! you monsters! you devils!"

"Shy away, boys, until he lets go," cried Charley; "smother him. Why don't you kick out, Tim?"

Then Tim, for the first time, found his tongue, and bellowed out—

"Why don't you keep quiet? It's my uncle!"

This startling announcement made the boys positively reel, with the exception of Bob Martin; and he, with about seven pounds of seaweed elevated in the air, pulled up and remained motionless, as if turned to stone.

The first surprise over, Harry Leicester, followed by the main body of assailants, walked away, whistling, leaving only Charley and Bob upon the ground.

Bob's arm slowly sank to his side, his grasp relaxed, and the seaweed fell upon the sand.

Mr. Ralph Turndown wiped his face with a huge red cotton handkerchief, puffing and blowing like a grampus.

For the better performance of this needful act, he released Tim; but his nephew had no more thought of flying, than he had of turning a Catherine-wheel.

As for Bob and Charley, they remained, as they afterwards declared, simply because "they could not help it."

"So," said Mr. Turndown, surveying them with knitted brows, "this is your general style of conduct, is it?"

"We are very sorry, sir," replied Bob Martin. "We had no idea you were a relation of Tim's."

"Indeed," grimly responded Mr. Turndown; "and do you think that betters your case? You are pupils of Scarum School?"

"Yes, sir."

"Your names?"

"Charles Thorn, and Robert Martin."

"Very good," rejoined Tim's uncle, making a memorandum of their names. "I will remember you when I have settled with my nephew. I came down to see Mr. Crammer, and, finding he was absent for an hour, I strolled here; I am glad of it. My eyes are opened. Nephew Timothy, follow me."

The enraged Mr. Ralph Turndown swung round on his heel, and strode towards the pathway leading up the cliff.

The weed upon the back buttons of his coat still remained; but Tim, meekly and patiently crawling in the rear, had neither the courage to remove it quietly, nor confess his guilt to his outraged relation.

And in this order they ascended the rough footway, and disappeared.

"Bob!"

"Charley!"

"Here's a game."

"Pickles!"

"I never saw a man look so tigerish."

"A precious wolf!"

"Poor old Tim!"

"Yes! and for the matter of that, poor Bob Martin!"

"And poor Charley Thorn! 'Tickler' all round, or I'm King of the Cannibal Islands!"

CHAPTER XXXIII.

A SENTENCE—"COME, PREPARE!"

LIKE unto a prisoner led to execution went the gallant Tim.

The cool, curt letter he received from his

uncle had given rise to certain misgivings, but all wide and foreign, as most matters are of our daily lives, to the actual event.

A letter from Mr. Ralph and from Mr. Crammer would have been bad enough ; but here was something terrible—Tim's uncle in person come to denounce him.

"It isn't that I'm so much afraid of 'Tickler,'" he thought ; "but he will want something worse—perhaps he will take me away from school altogether—I could hardly bear that yet."

Tears rose to his eyes as he thought of parting with the lads to whom he had, in a few short weeks, become attached.

Charley, Bob, Harry Leicester, Grimmer, all had their several claims upon him, and his heart ached at the thought of a possible separation.

So he went trembling on behind, the coat of his uncle garnished with two tails of sea-weed.

At the door of the lodge Mr. Ralph Turndown knocked with the air of a man upon an important mission, and Griddle opened to him.

"Mr. Crammer in ?"

"Yes, sir, just returned ; and he'll be 'appy to see you. This way, sir. 'Scuse me, sir, something on your coat."

And Griddle removed and held up before Tim's uncle the ornaments he had worn.

Mr. Ralph Turndown glared—glared as only a man suffering from a huge fury pent up in a small body can, and there and then he forgot the difference of their respective ages, and shook his fist in the face of his nephew Tim.

"It was a dark hour for me," he said, "when you were left in my charge, and this shall prove a dark hour for you."

"The games they is up to at all times," said Griddle, with a propitiatory smile, "you wouldn't believe, sir. The life I leads is worse than a bear at a bull-fight ; but lor', sir—"

"Get out of my way," cried Tim's uncle, giving Griddle an unceremonious push. "If you cannot lead the way to Mr. Crammer, point it out."

"Beg parding, sir," said Griddle, aloud ; then, under his breath—"Of all the cranky gents I ever met, you are the most crankiest, bar none."

Mr. Crammer was in, and received Mr. Turndown with smiling face. Tim he honoured with a request to shut the door, and then offered his visitor a chair.

"Judging by your looks, sir, you have a complaint to make."

"I have, sir."

"Is it of me, sir ?"

"That I will leave you to guess—first hear me. You, sir, I believe, advertise yourself as a strict disciplinarian—one who rules with a rod of iron and keeps rebellion down."

"My advertisement," said Mr. Crammer, smoothly, "is, in my establishment, carried out to the letter."

"I will not deny it," said Tim's uncle, "until I have heard your defence ; but first, look at that boy."

Mr. Crammer looked at Tim, who presented the appearance of a puffed lobster. The master of Scarum School frowned—he saw that something was wrong, but could scarcely tell what, and he thought it the best to look displeased.

"What were my instructions," pursued Mr. Turndown, "when I sent him here ?"

"They were of a very strict nature."

"Did I not tell you to keep him down ?"

"You did, sir."

"Were not my instructions very strict that he should have all the nonsense taken out of him—that he should be cured of every boyish propensity, and sent back to me a model youth, fit for the world and the ways of men, so that I might be able to get back a little of the money he has cost me ?"

"I believe you stated as much, sir ; but we must have time, sir—we must have time."

"I grant that," said Tim's uncle ; "I did not—do not expect him to be made the correct thing at once ; but he does not improve. At home he was never jocular—he dared not have been ; but here he plays the tricks of a clown and a fool, and worse than all, does not hesitate to play them on me."

Mr. Crammer looked astonished, as indeed he was ; but being still somewhat in the dark, quietly waited for more.

"But half an hour ago," pursued Mr. Ralph Turndown, "he learns that I am here —comes down to me upon the beach—and how does he greet me? With love and duty? —no ! With respect ?—no ! He walks straight up to me, covers me with sea-weed, throws a stale fish of some sort full in my face, and yells at me like a wild Indian. Mr. Crammer," added the old gentleman, violently smiting the table with his hand, "may I ask if this is the result of your strict course of discipline ? Are your pupils instructed to insult their relations, to cast stones at those who give them bread ?"

"Really—ahem !" replied Mr. Crammer, "you astonish—overwhelm me. That Master Turndown should have so far forgotten the precepts and practice of this school is excessively painful to me, but it is an isolated case of disobedience, sir, I assure you. My other pupils are models, sir—models in every way."

"Indeed !" sneered Mr. Ralph Turndown!

THE GROUND BENEATH THEM SUDDENLY GAVE WAY.

"Permit me to have a word to say upon that point. My graceless, worthless nephew, there, had two assistants in his diabolical work, who not only audaciously assaulted me, but gave their names with the cool impudence of mountebanks, sir. I have them here, and I will read them to you."

Mr. Ralph Turndown then brought forth his pocket book and read aloud—

"Charles Thorn and Robert Martin."

"These are the gentlemen," he said—"two of your perfect pupils."

"Sir," rejoined Mr. Crammer, after a slight pause, "I am astounded at these revelations, coming from a source I cannot doubt. The whole matter is a surprise to me, and the misconduct of these young gentlemen shall be severely punished. Have you any complaint against the rest?"

"Many more lads, whether of this school

or not I cannot say, combined to insult me; they fled without giving their names. I must leave you to make the needful inquiries."

"I will attend to it, Mr. Turndown; and now with regard to your nephew?"

"One word more," interposed Tim's uncle, "and that with regard to the food you provide, sir; I pay you to feed my nephew here."

Mr. Crammer turned a dark and lowering frown upon Tim, who remembered his letter and shuddered with fear.

"I provide a good table for all in this house," said the schoolmaster.

"And yet, sir, I am bothered about an insufficiency of food. Sir, here is my nephew's letter—read it."

After a brief perusal of that precious piece of composition, Mr. Crammer looked again at Tim—with a face stamped with "Tickler" unlimited.

"The charge is utterly false," he said. "Turndown, look at me."

"Ye—-yes, sir," gasped Tim.

"Have you sufficient food here, sir ?"

"All—all I want, sir."

"Then what is the meaning of this letter?"

Tim occupied one moment to think, and then blustered out the truth.

"I wanted some pocket-money, sir," he said, "and my uncle never allows me any."

"Enough!" said Mr. Ralph Turndown, "I will hear no more of it. I am outraged in my tenderest feelings. Pocket-money! Bah! why should I lead the child of my brother, whom I promised to love, cherish, and protect, into dissolute ways? Already he has learned to lie; but the Old Man must be driven out of him, lest he fall into the pit of Tophet. Punish him at once, sir; punish him severely."

"I am willing to be guided by you as to the course I ought to pursue," said Mr. Crammer.

"Give him a week's solitary confinement," said Mr. Ralph Turndown, "and thrash him well every morning—the first instalment I will witness. Nephew Timothy, prepare."

Tim, with a dolorous countenance, made the little preparation needful—all the lighter on account of his paucity of buttons, and Mr. Crammer took "Tickler" in his hand, and elevated it in the air.

Scant mercy was meted out to the rubicund youth, but he held his own until the last blow was administered, and then he gave vent to his feelings in a mortal shriek of pain.

"You will remember this," said his uncle, grimly; "the respect due to me will, perhaps, be shown the next time we meet. Mr. Crammer, good day, and do not forget, sir, a week's solitary confinement, and a repetition of to-day's punishment every morning."

"Good day, sir."

CHAPTER XXXIV.

TIM IN CONFINEMENT.—THE LAST OF JULIUS CÆSAR.

THE unhappy victim of his own practical joke, Tim Turndown was promptly led away to the solitude of the cell, and left there to reflect upon his position, and ease his aching bones as best he could.

In sober truth, his thoughts were none of the best. What little spark of love or reverence for his uncle he had cherished in his breast was that day extinguished, and while he rubbed his aching limbs he vowed solemnly that he would seize the first opportunity to run away and injure his uncle and Scarum School for ever.

"I couldn't—be—be—worse off if—i—I was a nigger," he sobbed; "I wish I was a nigger, and then I might get killed right off. The beast !—the brute ! As for old Crammer, I'll buy the pistol down at the pawnshop, and shoot him. He's taken the skin off, I know. Yah ! you coward !"

He shook his fist at the door, and after another volley of reproach poured upon his late assailant he became calmer. The fact was, the pain of his castigation was departing, and when the physical sense of it was over, Tim, being a good-natured little fellow, always either forgave or forgot.

Then he sat down to think out a plan of escape, but the thought of his chums unsettled him, they were his only friends in all the wide world, and he felt he could not leave them. The resolution to run away died out as other similar resolutions have done, and he resolved to take his punishment with as much forbearance as possible.

"It's only a week," he thought, "and then I'll be among them again."

In the course of the afternoon, Griddle came in with a mattress and other things needful, and made his bed. It was a task congenial to the porter, who betrayed an unwonted hilarity during its performance, and whenever he looked at Tim chuckled outright.

Tim bore it philosophically, and pretended not to heed this unnecessary demonstration, but Griddle was not a man to be denied a little amusement when the object from which it was to be abstracted was helpless and weak.

"Nice man that uncle of yourn !" he said, as he spread the counterpane.

A lofty look and an indignant sniff was all Tim cared to give in return.

"Jest the sort o' man," pursued Griddle, "who, when he comes to see anybody, would be sure to *leave 'em something to remember him by.*"

"Mind your own business," grunted Tim.

"I should be proud of such a uncle," continued Griddle, in a meditative manner. "There's many a poor boy without a uncle, as would be glad of such a one. I'm a orphan myself; but I——"

"You've made the bed," interrupted Tim, "and now get out."

"I shall get out or come in," said Griddle, deliberately seating himself on the side of the bed, "just when I please. When I seed that man come in, a-holdin' you by the collar, almost like a—a mother, I ses to myself, 'There's a man to be loved by a nevvy, if that nevvy's got a feelin' 'art. There's a look about the man,' I ses, 'as shows him to be brimful o' good-natur'; the sort o' man to chuck his gold and coppers about, and smother you, as I may say, in the flowery roses of kindness.' Perhaps he's been a-smotherin' you."

"No, he hain't," answered Tim, shortly.

"Then, I'm wrong," said Griddle. "But when I fust looked at you, I thout you'd been sheddin' tears—the tears of joy. But I'm wrong ; perhaps it's a cold."

"What if it is ?" demanded Tim.

"Nothin'; only this," replied Griddle, "that if you had caught a cold, it was rum that your uncle, who comed here and *gave you somethin' hot.* hadn't cured it."

And, with a hoarse chuckle at his own poor wit, Griddle arose, made a profound bow to Tim, and beat a retreat.

He only appeared once again that evening, when he brought the prisoner's supper ; and being apparently in a great hurry, he spared Tim from any further witticisms.

That night our friend went to bed with the pleasant consciousness that in the morning he would receive, by way of morning orisons, a second dose of the famous weapon which had so effectually scored his frame that day ; but he was not the style of lad to be troubled long with gloomy thoughts, and he soon fell asleep.

With the morning, however, came back the anticipation of "Tickler."

He awoke long before it was light, and lay thinking—thinking over a score of schemes to assuage the pain he knew was in store for him.

"I'm sore all over now," he thought, "and I can't stand it to-day."

But he knew that it must come ; and the hours which he wished to be so long sped by on the swiftest wings.

As the clock struck eight, a footstep in the passage awoke the stillness ; and Tim, knowing that his time was come, turned cold all over.

The latch was drawn back, and Mr. Jonas Tidd entered.

He bore in his hand a cane, and his looks were very severe.

"Turndown," he said, "I am deputed by Mr. Crammer to give you a severe flogging every morning during the week. This is not unexpected, is it ?"

"No, sir," replied Tim ; "but it is very cruel."

"I have nothing to do with that," said Mr. Tidd, calmly. "I must punish, as a matter of duty ; and, see, I leave the door open, so that Mr. Crammer may hear your cries, and know that I have fulfilled my allotted task."

"I won't cry out if he kills me," thought Tim ; "who could have thought that Mr. Tidd was such a brute ?"

"Are you ready, Turndown ? "

"Yes, sir."

"Then carry out your name upon your attire."

"Don't give it me on the naked skin, sir." pleaded Tim, "I was nearly flayed alive yesterday."

"I shall give it where I please," said the usher ; "my duty is to flog, and yours is to cry out as loud as you can."

And then, to Tim's profound astonishment, Mr. Jonas Tidd deliberately winked. A light began to dawn upon our young friend.

"Are you ready, Turndown ? "

"Quite, sir."

"Then bawl away."

The cane rose and fell, and Tim shrieked with might and main ; but when the work was over he had not a tear in his eye, and his face was one broad smile.

He understood Mr. Tidd now, he had not given a blow sufficiently heavy to crush a fly.

"It's—it's very kind of you," began Tim.

"Hush, my boy, not a word—no thanks, no anything, but when Griddle comes in with the breakfast, let him find you in tears ; call me a cruel brute, anything, or it may get me into trouble—you understand."

Tim, with a grateful look, nodded assent, and Mr. Tidd, resuming his frown, retired.

"What a brick he is !" thought Tim ; "upon my word, he's a noble fellow."

But there was a different idea current in the school that day ; the boys had heard Tim's cries, and learned the fact that Mr. Jonas Tidd was appointed deputy executioner, and their spirit rose against him.

"Don't let him humbug us again," said Charley. "I'll have none of his grins, and mouthing Shakespeare."

"A brick at his head would do him good," muttered Bob Martin ; "if I were a couple of inches taller I would offer to fight him."

In this way nearly every boy, especially the particular friends of Tim, commented on the conduct of the usher.

He soon marked a change in their conduct ; they did not come so promptly to his call for the classes, they bungled and stumbled purposely when all was clear before them, and gave him all the trouble they possibly could, and when the evening came, and they returned from the playground to the school, everybody drew away from the side of the room where the usher was sitting, as if he had been a leper, or smitten with the plague.

He saw it, and knew the meaning of it all ; but a quiet smile upon his face was all the sign he gave.

"Come, boys," he said, "let us to our usual reading to-night. Martin, I must hear you with your part—*Richmond*, I believe."

"I can't read to-night," answered Bob, abruptly, "I've got a headache."

"You, Thorn, then."

"No, sir, I'm tired of Shakespeare."

"Very good." said Mr. Tidd, quietly taking up a book, " as you will, my boys."

For a moment Charley felt something like remorse, for he had taken a liking to the usher ; but the remembrance of Tim's cries steeled his heart, and he kept as far away as he could from Mr. Tidd throughout the evening.

On the following day two events occurred, one of which caused considerable sensation, but little sorrow in the school.

The first was the public punishment and lecturing of Charley and Bob for their share in the attack upon Mr. Ralph Turndown, but whether Mr. Crammer was in an unusually kind mood, or whether he considered the martyrdom of Tim sufficient to atone for that outrage, we cannot say, but certain it is that our two friends were let off very easy—with half a dozen touches of " Tickler" and a hundred lines of Virgil, which was, compared to many other punishments administered at Scarum School, a complete farce.

The other event was the retirement of Julius Cæsar Smith.

From the time of his arrival he failed to make friends ; his pride made him obnoxious to pupils, master, and ushers ; the slightest thing offended his dignity, which he never failed to display upon each and every occasion.

On the second day of Tim's confinement, Julius Cæsar, for the first time, was brought within the range of " Tickler." As a rule, he was a ready and apt scholar, and being of a sullen and retiring disposition, never committed himself in any of those boyish pranks which kept his *confrères* in continual hot water ; but on this particular day his lessons were unlearnt, and being questioned thereon by Mr. Crammer, answered that " he was not in the humour."

The cool, audacious reply stung the schoolmaster to the quick, and diving into his desk, he brought out the universal corrector.

"Now, sir," he said, "have the kindness to repeat that observation ? "

"What will be the consequences, sir ? " asked Julius Cæsar, calmly.

"You need scarcely ask that," said Mr. Crammer ; " you know full well."

"I must warn you, sir," rejoined Julius Cæsar, " that I will not be beaten."

"You will be if you are insolent here, sir, and bandy words with me. Once more, why have you not learned your lessons ? "

"I was not in the humour," answered Julius Cæsar, and " Tickler" swished down upon him.

He bore the first cut with apparent calmness ; but ere the second could be given, he snatched a penknife from the desk and threw it at Mr. Crammer's face. Fortunately, it missed its mark ; but the blade being fixed in the handle, it stuck quivering in the panel of a cupboard behind the master of Scarum School.

This was an outrage of no common description, and Mr. Crammer showed him no mercy ; he beat him until he cried—beat him until he lay down breathless on the floor, and beat him until the ushers, alarmed, interfered and dragged the boy out of the way.

"Take him from my sight ! " said Mr. Crammer. "He has Spanish blood in him. Leave that knife there, Mr. Pendulum, to be a warning to all of such dastard blood."

So the knife was left fixed there for many a day, and the legend of it was the theme of many a hour's evening chat.

Julius Cæsar was locked in his bedroom ; but he contrived, with the assistance of a few sheets and blankets, to make his escape.

Two days later, there came a letter from his father threatening Mr. Crammer with all the pains and penalties of the law, for the outrage upon his son. Mr. Crammer sent in answer back, the boxes of the sweet-tempered youth, and a brief account of the penknife episode, and a few words of warning respecting the probable termination of the career of Julius Cæsar, unless he amended his ways.

"The use of the knife," the letter said, " is abhorrent to every true Englishman, and especially in one so young. I could never forgive him, and the task of educating him would at all times be revolting to my nature. I trust I shall never see him or the like of him again."

After this Mr. Smith wrote no more, probably seeing the justice of the master's plaint, and Julius Cæsar was struck out of the books of Scarum School for ever.

CHAPTER XXXV.

"RICHARD THE THIRD."

TIME lagged heavily enough with Tim, but thanks to Mr. Jonas Tidd, things were better and brighter than they might otherwise have been.

He lent the boy a few entertaining books of the old school, such as " Sandford and Merton," " Peter Parley's Annual," and " Don Quixote " (revised for family use), to while the time away, and every morning the howling and flogging farce was repeated.

But to the last Tim had a sorrowful time of it ; escape was impossible, for since the day when he and Charley levanted from that same room, a cunning carpenter had been there, who had removed the screws and put in long and strong nails to the iron bars of the window.

The shouts of the boys at play oft reached his ears, and then he would picture the glories of the playground—marbles, peg-tops, the game of touch, until he felt like a hungry wild beast sniffing, but debarred from, the flesh of oxen.

Then Tim would walk up and down his prison-house fretting and fuming, and calling down all sorts of horrors upon the head of his cantankerous uncle.

"He might be kinder to me," thought Tim, "for my mother loved him, I know; she used to say he was her favourite brother —her kind-hearted brother. I wonder what could have changed him so?"

We will tell you, Tim, what has wrought such a change in him; contact with the hard world, the fight for wealth, and a cultivated greed of gain; men are not born curmudgeons, the worst of us have or had good traits once upon a time; the best have their spots; all men have the seeds of good and evil in them, and that which is cultivated most will assuredly flourish.

There was one small spot of relief in the room—upon the window, where the colouring on the outside had been worn or washed away.

By flattening his nose upon the glass, Tim could peep through and watch the ships sailing out at sea, and here Tim passed many of his waking hours.

So persistent was he at his post, that had his confinement been of much longer duration, Tim would have permanently flattened his nose, and had the development of the lineaments, without the colour of a Hottentot. But the seven days ended at last, and at high noon Mr. Jonas Tidd opened the door of his prison-house, and told him he was at liberty to seek the play-ground.

Scarcely staying to thank his friend, so eager was he to get once more among his playmates, he rushed into the ground and was immediately surrounded by a throng of eager questioners.

"Keep off a minute!" he cried, struggling with the mass; "shake hands, Charley—now you, Bob; all right, Harry? Now just tell me the news, some of you; anything happened since I was chained up?—anything broke?"

"Julius Cæsar's gone."

"Good riddance. Anybody else?"

"No."

"Anybody come?"

"Nobody."

"That's all right; now it's no use you fellows crowding round me; I've nothing to tell you except this—I've been shut up a week, had my prog regular, learned my lessons, and taken my dose of 'Tickler' every morning."

"Yes, we heard you," said Charley, meaningly, "and Mr. Tidd hasn't gained much by it."

"What about Mr. Tidd?" asked Tim, quickly.

"Why we have sent him to Coventry, shown what we thought of his meanness and cruelty in a hundred ways, bothering him at class, lost our books, and all sorts of games."

"Just come this way," said Tim, drawing Charley to the seclusion of a corner. "So you have done all this?"

"Every bit."

"Then more fools you!"

"Hallo, Tim! what's this? Would you have us afraid of him?"

"No; but I'd have you know that he is the best and kindest fellow in the world. He only pretended to lay on 'Tickler,' and I howled so that he might not get into trouble."

"Phew!" whistled Charley, with a perplexed look; "here's a turn out. I *am* sorry."

"So you ought to be. What will you do?"

"Apologize as soon as we get together this evening. Upon my word, I never was so vexed."

The secret was also confided to Bob Martin and a few other particular chums; but as it might be dangerous to Mr. Jonas Tidd to let the whole school know it, Tim contented himself with informing them that he was not hurt a bit, and that he lifted up his voice more as a precautionary measure than from any pain he felt.

"If you take it silently," he said, "you always get it worse; I've found that out, and I've made up my mind to bellow like a bull in future."

In the evening Charley was the first boy in the schoolroom, where he found Mr. Jonas Tidd mending pens, to whom he offered a warm and sincere apology for his conduct of the past week.

"I could not understand your being cruel to Turndown, sir," he said, "especially after your general kindness to us."

"You were only led away," rejoined Mr. Tidd, "by what misguides half the world and makes fools of the rest—appearances. Friends, lovers, whole families, are sometimes broken up by a single misinterpretation of a word or deed, and never become united in this world again. Let it be a warning to you, Thorn, and remember this—a slow judgment of your neighbour is sure to be best in the long run."

Charley had broken the ice, and the boys and the usher were friends again.

It was plain that Mr. Tidd felt the change,

for his spirits rose high, and he volunteered, if the boys were quieter, to give them a treat that night.

"I have had some acquaintance with theatrical life," he said, "that is—ahem!—I have *friends* who have had some acquaintance with it; and, through them, I have acquired a little taste for the noble and enlightening art. What say you, shall I give you the death of Richard, the hunch-backed king?"

Anxious to do anything to please him, the boys declared they would be delighted.

"It was in happier times," said Mr. Tidd, with a soft smile, "when I last portrayed the character; but the times are out of joint; the sock and the buskin are exchanged for—ahem! Move those forms closer to the wall, and give me a clear space."

When all was ready, the boys clambered upon the desks; and Mr. Jonas Tidd, standing in the centre of the room, began his entertainment thus:—

Dishevelling his hair over his eyes, and bowing his back, he took a letter from his pocket; he then read the words which caused so much terror in the bosom of the arch-king:—

"Jocky of Norfolk, be not so bold,
    For Dickon, thy master, is bought and sold."

Then he rushed into the address to the nobles, warming as he went onward, speaking in a voice naturally sonorous, the smooth and easy lines of the immortal poet, ending with—

"Fight, gentlemen of England! fight bold yeomen!
    Draw, archers, draw your arrows to the head!
    Spur your proud horses hard, and ride in blood;
    Amaze the welkin with your broken staves!"

This brought down the house. The boys applauded roundly, and the strange usher seemed to draw fire from their youthful appreciation.

He forgot all—the schoolroom, the vicinity of Mr. Crammer, the charge he held—and was once again upon the boards.

Then came the last words of the frantic king:—

"A horse! a horse! my kingdom for a horse!
    Slave! I have set my life upon a cast,
    And I will stand the hazard of the die;
    I think there be six Richmonds in the field;
    Five have I slain to-day, instead of him:
    A horse! a horse! my kingdom for a horse!"

And then Mr. Jonas Tidd, with a cane in his hand, entered upon the sixth and last fight of the hump-backed king. He thrust and parried with the empty air, tramped to and fro, puffing and blowing for his life, until he received an imaginary stab, and then he fell upon the floor and grovelled in the agonies of a fictitious death.

The hands of the boys were raised for a round of applause, their mouths were open, ready for a cheer, when Mr. Pendulum's voice broke in:—

"Help—help! Here is Mr. Tidd in a fit. Help—help!"

CHAPTER XXXVI.

MR. CRAMMER NONPLUSSED.—THE GHOST AGAIN.

Now the cries of Mr. Pendulum aroused the whole house, and the domestics, headed by Griddle, rushed towards the schoolroom. Mr. Crammer, being absent at the time, did not appear.

Master Todman Crammer, however, was a member of the party, and followed quickly on the heels of the alarmed usher as he returned to the schoolroom.

"Mr. Tidd, I think you said?" he remarked.

"Yes, Mr. Tidd," replied Mr. Pendulum; "he was lying on his back rolling his eyes in a dreadful manner. Quick! quick! for I am certain he is dying for want of help."

They entered the schoolroom—usher, cook, porter, and all, and there was Mr. Tidd, not rolling in agony, but standing in the middle of the room calmly reciting, "My name is Norval!"

"That is the way it should be done, boys," he was saying; "never be in a hurry with your declamation. Dear me, Mr. Pendulum, what is the matter?"

"Are you not ill?" inquired the usher looking surprised, as he really was.

"Ill! no; what put that into your head?"

"A minute ago I saw you lying on the ground, as I thought, in a fit."

"I slipped and fell," rejoined Mr. Tidd, coolly, "during the early part of my evening's lecture on elocution, which I have started here to while away the hours, and to benefit the pupils—but nothing more!"

"It was a strange sort of slip," said Mr. Pendulum, thoughtfully, scraping his chin; "and you seemed to suffer from it."

"At any rate, I am well now," returned Mr. Tidd. "Boys! we will resume; mark well this passage:—

"'For I had heard of battles, and longed to follow to the field
Some warlike lord, and Heaven soon granted what my soul desired.'

"Speak the first line with enthusiasm, and the second with gratitude in the tone of your voice. Young Norval had——"

"I can't understand it," muttered Mr. Pendulum, who stood watching the usher, in doubt; "he was certainly suffering from something. If it were possible to get sober in thirty moments, I should say that Mr. Tidd was drunk—but he is sober enough now."

Failing with the usher, he turned upon the servants, and demanded with some asperity, "what they wanted there?"

"You hollered for us," rejoined Griddle, mildly.

"And cannot you see, now, that your services are not required?"

"It is aperient that they are not," returned Griddle.

"Then back to your work," said the head usher, "and lose no valuable time."

The servants bustled out, but Mr. Pendulum and Todman Crammer remained, both seeking some clue to the mystery. Mr. Tidd gave none, and the boys maintained on the whole an impassibility of faces which did them credit.

For the rest of the evening Mr. Tidd confined himself to very placid breathings of great poets, but Mr. Pendulum was far from satisfied, and when Mr. Crammer returned, he laid a report of the event before him.

"Tidd is a strange fellow," said Mr. Crammer, when he had heard all; "but he does his work well."

"May I ask, sir, without being impertinent, what sort of reference you had with him?"

"Pretty good," rejoined Mr. Crammer, indifferently; "he comes from a village school, where he has been master for some time. The establishment of a national school deprived him of his means of living, and he came here through the medium of the curate, Mr. Ringley."

"Indeed, sir!" said Mr. Pendulum; "I'm glad of that, for I've noticed something very strange about Mr. Tidd—eccentric, to say the least. Look at his big box!"

"True; I have been puzzled by that box myself," returned the schoolmaster; "it is large enough to hold sufficient clothes for half the house, and yet Mr. Tidd never has a change. Neither is the box empty, for it cost Griddle a severe effort to get it upstairs."

"I am afraid, sir, he won't turn out as you could wish."

"That is a problem, Pendulum, to be solved by time."

Although Mr. Crammer did not show it, he was more than doubtful about the antecedents of Mr. Jonas Tidd, having engaged him upon his personal recommendation, and a vague letter from the curate, for the simple reason that he was cheap—the salary of Mr. Tidd being about enough to find him with a decent amount of washing, leaving clothes entirely out of the question.

The schoolmaster remembered some of the unexplained practical jokes, and the ghost, and wondered if his new usher had anything to do with them.

Then he thought that some of the tricks had taken place before the usher's arrival, and, logically, the culprit could not therefore be him.

"They have been quieter lately," Mr. Crammer thought. "They are only waiting until the noise blows over, and then they will begin again, but they won't find me asleep, I'll warrant them."

That very night he was aroused from his first sleep by the screams of his firstborn, Master Toddy, who was sitting up in his crib, and yelling like a young pig in difficulties with a butcher.

"Good Heavens! Todman, what is the matter?"

"The—the ghost, father!"

"Nonsense!" answered Mr. Crammer, trembling in spite of himself. "Where?"

"It was sta—anding—at the—the foot of my bed, po—ointing straight at—at—my nose."

"This is becoming unbearable," muttered Mr. Crammer, as he struck a light. "What was it like, Todman?"

"Something—very—very tall—and white. I could just see it in the faint light—oh! oh! ah! there it is again on the landing," roared Todman, pointing through the bedroom door, which stood partly open.

Toddy dived somewhere under the bedclothes, and his father sprang from his couch.

He was not a nervous man, but there was a little hesitation in his steps as he peeped out.

All quiet and still.

"Todman must have been mistaken," he murmured, as he closed and locked the door.

"Rouse up, my boy; it is all your fancy."

"Oh, no—no—it isn't," answered Toddy, as he emerged from the bed-clothes.

"I assure you it is."

Bang!

It was a most terrific knock at the door, and caused Mr. Crammer to leap into the air, and jerk the candle out of the socket.

It fell to the ground, and went out, leaving him in darkness.

"This is—a—scurvy trick," he said, making a castanet-like music with his teeth, "I will punish all concerned in it, severely. Be—be quiet, Todman, and help me to find the candle."

Master Crammer needed the adjuration, for he was groaning aloud in agony of spirit.

He dared not have left the security of his bed for a bag of gold; and his father, muttering invectives upon the head of every pupil in the world, groped in vain for the lost candle.

Bang ! bang !

The noise so startled the groping school-master that he fell forward on his nose; but, quickly recovering, he rushed towards the door, turned the key, and opened it.

The passage was very dark, but he could faintly perceive a tall white figure, with arms extended, about half way down.

For a moment his brain reeled.

When he recovered, it was gone.

He could rely on himself no longer, but had sufficient wits left to avoid alarming the whole house.

With trembling limbs he returned to his room, recovered the candle, ignited it, and then aroused the ushers.

Both Mr. Pendulum and Mr. Tidd were undoubtedly in a sound sleep, for they could only stare at Mr. Crammer as he stood between the beds adjuring them to get up, for thieves or rogues were within the house.

"Have they stolen anything ? " asked Mr. Pendulum, recovering a bit.

"No—no. I don't know. I cannot say; but get up at once."

As they slipped on a few garments, Mr. Crammer explained to them what had taken place. Both the ushers looked very grave.

"Some foolish joke of the boys," said Mr. Tidd.

"It was no boy I saw in the passage," rejoined Mr. Crammer, decidedly; "the figure was at least six feet high."

"But the figure can be made up," hinted Mr. Pendulum.

"Not to appear and disappear in that extraordinary way. I really cannot comprehend it."

They went quietly about the passages, and passed through the dormitories, but there were no signs of any intruders, and every boy was undoubtedly fast asleep.

Toddy, who durst not remain alone in the bed-room, accompanied the party, clinging closely to the skirts of his father's dressing-gown. The fact of no solution to the mystery being discovered, convinced the youth that the visitor he had seen came from the spirit world, and his terror visibly increased, so much so that he trembled all over as if he had the ague.

"Todman, be still," said his father, sternly, when they returned to the ushers' room.

"I ca—an't, father."

"You must—you must," rejoined Mr. Crammer, himself pale as a muffin; "we shall catch them at it one of these nights."

"It certainly is very strange," said Mr. Tidd, thoughtfully; "boys are not so fond of being out of bed at this time. Can it be any of the domestic servants ? "

"They sleep in another part of the house," returned Mr. Crammer, "accessible only by a door of which Mrs. Margery keeps the key."

"Then I give it up," said Jonas Tidd; "and as it's rather cold, I will, with your leave, get again into bed."

"Mr. Pendulum," said the schoolmaster, "what is your opinion of this affair ? "

"Mine, sir, is like yours," said the usher, "and that is, that we are being humbugged by somebody, but by whom, or how, it is impossible at present to say."

"Well, then, we will leave it for the present," said Mr. Crammer. "Good night, gentlemen—or rather, good morning. Todman, if you shake in that way, you will tumble into pieces."

"I ca—can't help it," replied Toddy, "I —I—am so—so cold, and afraid of—of the ghost ! "

"Ghost be bothered ! " returned his father, dragging him away. "I'll ghost him, when I get a chance ! "

There was no further disturbance that night, although Mr. Crammer kept a watchful vigil until the morning dawned, when he fell into a fitful sleep, and dreamt that he had lost his way in a churchyard, where every tombstone became suddenly imbued with life, and danced a Scotch reel around him.

CHAPTER XXXVII.
A RAPID JOURNEY.

THE second ghost story got wind in the school, and formed the subject of a deal of conversation, many dismal forebodings arising therefrom, especially in the breasts of those who were rather more than ordinarily nervous, among whom Master Lobby Panks figured conspicuously.

There were not wanting youths willing to add to the terror of the times—youths who had a stock of authentic ghost stories always on hand, comprising a series of supernatural events which had either befallen themselves or some of their most intimate relations.

Charley laughed at the whole affair, and hinted that Mr. Crammer must have had an extra glass that night, but Bob Martin, who had a ghost in his family, would not hear of the idea.

"It's a ghost right enough," he said "and I'll bet I know what sort of a fellow it is."

"No doubt," grinned Harry Leicester, "perhaps you have a hand in it."

"Not I," answered Bob, seriously, "nor anybody in this house, I dare swear. It's the ghost of a smuggler, that's what it is— some chap killed years ago, and buried in the cliff, perhaps just on the very spot where this house is built."

"That's about it," rejoined Tim; "the smugglers' cave is under here, you know."

"So it is," put in Charley; "and as we have a holiday, what do you say to visiting it? The last time Tim met an old friend there, and spoiled the day's sport," he added, with a sly glance at the rubicund youth.

"You needn't mention it," rejoined Tim, drily. "I haven't forgotten it."

"Then hurrah for the smugglers' cave," cried Bob; "and I tell you what we'll do. We will spin ghost yarns inside our cave in the dark, and the first who bolts is to stand sixpennyworth of lollipops."

"We must have a victim then," said Harry Leicester. "Lobby Panks had a letter this morning, and there was money in it."

"I'll bring him," said Tim; "we have made up our little quarrels, and are like twins again."

As soon as the dinner was over, the boys were dismissed with instructions not to go into the town, and not to ramble either into the country or on the beach beyond certain bounds, on pain of coming in contact with the all-powerful "Tickler."

Promising to obey, they scampered off—some in the direction of the country, but the main body towards the sea—our friends showing up very prominently among them.

Tim had Lobby Panks in tow, who was only too glad to be associated with Bob Martin and others, who were considered to be the *élite* of the school.

"It's a beastly way round to the steps," said Tim; "let us go down the cliff."

"Rather steep, isn't it?" rejoined Harry Leicester.

"'Tis rather; but there's lots of knobs we can jump on. I got down all right the other morning."

"Let's try it, then."

The cliff was inspected, and really looked practicable. It was a stiffish slope towards the sea; but broken here and there, so as to give a tolerable foothold.

"There's nothing in it," said Tim, standing on the very verge. "You start from here—jump on to that bit, then slide down to the other knob—then—oh!—help!—help!"

The ground beneath him had suddenly given way—cliffs will crumble, we all know—and away went Tim, Lobby Panks, Charley, Bob Martin, and a few others, heels over head, down the face of the cliff.

Bumping, sliding, rolling, gasping, and shrieking, Tim led the way, flying from knob to knob like a cricket ball, until he reached the sands, where he rolled over and

until his brethren rolled upon him and checked his career.

Charley was first to his feet, crying—
"Anybody hurt?"

They were all hurt more or less, but none dangerously.

Tim had every particle of breath knocked out of his body by Lobby Panks, who finished his journey by pitching head first into the stomach of our friend.

A bleeding nose and scratched hands were the most serious casualties among them.

"I'll—I'll—give—you something for this," gasped Tim; "so you look out, Lobby."

"How could I help it?" whined Panks. "Could I tell that the ground would give way?"

"Couldn't you fall on somebody else?" demanded Tim.

"Let there be peace," interposed Harry Leicester, speaking through his nose. "Why should there be dissension in the camp?"

"Dissension be bothered!" muttered Tim, rising to his feet. "If his head had pitched into you, you would have found out how hard and thick it is. Dash it! there's the last button behind gone. Have you a bit of string, Charley?"

Charley had not, but Bob had; and Tim's apparel was thereby saved from dissolution, Bob fixing it with a neatness and dexterity which left nothing to be desired.

"Run for the cave," said Tim, "if you've quite done wiping your nose, Lobby. Tie up his little finger with the odd bit of string, Bob; that'll stop it."

"It's all right," said Lobby. "I'm quite ready."

The cave was quite deserted, and they took possession of it.

If ever smugglers had chosen this for a home, they must have been in great security, and satisfied with a limited hiding-place, the cave in question being not more than fifty or sixty feet deep.

It was very narrow at the mouth, but widened as it descended, which made it very gloomy, and gave it an air of romance to the fanciful minds of the boys.

It was rather cold, but dry.

It was arranged that they should sit down at the bottom, and spin their yarns.

Each of them had brought, in their pockets, and concealed about their persons, a little material for a fire, which was now collected, and ignited by Bob Martin.

"I saw some old bits of timber the last time I was here," said Bob, "apparently thrown in during a storm."

They found them lying in a corner—rotten and dry—capital fuel for a fire.

...ous blaze was rising, and the

Scarum boys reclining around it, felt as if they were indeed smugglers and outlaws of their country.

"I'll tell the first story," said Tim ; "and there's such a ghost in it as you never heard of."

"I don't like ghost stories," said Panks, glancing timidly at the dark corners of the cave—he had not been let into the secret of the object of the meeting.

"You must like them," rejoined Tim, coolly, "or put down sixpence for the good of the company."

"I'll not pay sixpence," said Panks, holding something very tightly in his pocket.

"Then sit still and listen," returned Tim ; all attention, you fellows ?"

Receiving a reply in the affirmative, Tim cleared his throat, and began :—

"There are certain people," said Tim, looking at Lobby, "who do not believe in ghosts. I *do*, for I know the story which I am going to tell to be perfectly true.

"Some years ago, when my father was alive, we lived in a very old house in the country. When we first went there every room in the house was smothered with dust, the windows and corners clogged with spider webs, and a musty smell pervaded the whole place.

"I can remember my father leading me by the hand, and his heavy footsteps resounding from room to room like thunder, and my pattering following as if the echo to the echo."

Here the merciless Tim stopped and glanced at Lobby, who, as pale as a sheet, and eyes of unnatural dimensions, glared upon his tormentor.

"Well," continued Tim, "the house was cleaned, and we soon took up our abode there ; but a gloom hung over the place ; when the sun shone, it cast a sickly light through the stained-glass windows, the wind screamed louder round the house than anywhere else, and at night to hear it moaning up the passages, sighing and sobbing like a fretful child, it was something awful to hear, and what is strange, it never ceased in the house.

"*When everything was calm outside*, within ere was something that went *sighing and oaning through the house*."

"I— I don't believe it, " gasped Lobby Panks, shifting uneasily.

"No," continued Tim, "that's the way with the ignorant ; but let me get on with my story. Fancy lying in bed and hearing the sound approach the door of the chamber, bursting into a roar and then subsiding into a whisper. My father kept a page. His name was Jem Watts, and as plucky a fellow as ever breathed. The other servants thought

the place was haunted, but Jem laughed at their fears, and said he should only like to see a ghost. If he had only known how soon his wish was to be gratified, I don't think he would have made that remark.

"One day in the depth of winter, both the other servants obtained permission to visit the country fair, and in the afternoon we set out also, leaving Jem to take care of the house.

"While we were out, a heavy snow-storm came on, which compelled us to put up at an inn.

"Hour after hour passed, and still the snow came down, until it lay a foot thick upon the ground.

"It was near midnight before the storm ceased ; but to think of going home was out of the question, and we had to sleep at the inn."

"What became of Jem ?" asked Lobby, faintly. "Did he see a——"

"I'm coming to that directly," said Tim. "Listen, and don't interrupt.

"Jem, as I have said before, was a plucky fellow ; but when he heard the rising storm, and saw the darkness closing in, and he alone in a house miles away from any other building, it is not to be wondered at that he felt a little queer.

"He sat in the kitchen trying to read, but the wind—screaming inside the house, and roaring like thunder without—distracted his thoughts.

"He pictured travellers waylaid and murdered, the churchyard, and other disagreeable things ; and a feeling seemed to cling to him that something awful was going to happen, when the clock struck ; and Jem, naturally thinking that we should not return, went to bed.

"He had been in bed about an hour, vainly endeavouring to go to sleep, when a loud knocking at the door startled him, and made him spring up in the bed.

"'I don't know that knock,' thought Jem. 'It doesn't belong to any one here.'

"Another tremendous clatter followed, shaking the house to its foundation.

"'I suppose I must see who it is,' groaned Jem, getting out of bed, and quickly dressing. 'It may be somebody from master. But I don't know why they want to hammer at the door like that.'

"Jem went downstairs, and, partly opening the door, inquired who was there.

"The next instant the door flew wide open, and Jem saw enter the hall *the black shadow of a man*."

Lobby, now green with fright, managed to stammer—

"How could a s——shadow be seen in the d—d—dark ?"

" Jem did not drop the candle," said Tim, coolly.

" It was the black shadow of a man, not thrown upon the wall, but walking upright, leaving blood-red footmarks, *which dried up immediately afterwards.*"

" Oh ! " gasped the victim. " Don't. I don't care about hearing any more."

" Jem," continued Lobby's tormentor, not heeding the supplication, " stood helpless against the wall, shaking with fright, glancing from the awful apparition to the horrible footmarks.

" Suddenly the phantom stopped, and, stooping down, appeared to be examining the stone flags in the hall ; and Jem screamed with terror when he saw one of them rise, and disclose the terrible sight of a headless skeleton.

" Nature could bear no more ; and Jem, throwing up his arms, fell in a swoon.

" The next morning, when we returned, we found the door fastened, but could make no one hear.

" A ladder was procured, and two men entered a window, and soon re-appeared, bearing the senseless form of Jem Watts.

" In a few hours he recovered, and told his story, pointing out the stone under which lay the skeleton.

" Some labourers were sent for, and the stone taken up, and——"

Here Lobby uttered a yell of terror, and fled from the cave.

" Oh, Tim," said Charley, " what a lot of whoppers ! Poor Lobby won't get over it in a month. Well, let us hear the last of it. What was under the stone ? "

" Nothing ! " grinned Tim. " And in the cellar they found an empty barrel, and two inches of beer on the floor."

CHAPTER XXXVIII.

AN OLD FRIEND.

" It is not a bad story of yours, Tim," said Bob Martin, " but I don't exactly understand the two inches of beer upon the floor."

" No more did my friends," returned Tim, " until they found that an opening had been made into the ordinary beer-cellar—where somebody had been to the tub and left the beer running."

" That wasn't a ghost," said Harry Leicester, decisively.

" It must have been," returned Tim, " unless it was Jem. He stuck to the ghost story, though, and as it was rather a respectable thing to have in the family, the affair was passed over."

" And yet strange things have been done," said Bob, musing ; " strange enough to raise a thousand ghosts. Mat knows a little about them."

Mat Langley, who had as usual proved a very quiet member of the party, nodded assent.

" Give us a yarn, Mat," urged Charley.

" I can tell you of a little thing," replied Mat, " which happened while I was in London. My friends are in the building line."

" So I've heard."

" And do a deal of work in the City and the West-end, but principally among the old inns, where alterations have to be made, which is a ticklish job, sometimes, I can tell you. I had not forgotten it, but I never told it, thinking that you might imagine I was gammoning you—so here goes :—

" I shall never forget it. I had cause enough to remember. One of the oddest things happened that ever I heard of, or read of either, and I dare say that you have never heard of anything like it.

" I went with my uncle to No. 90, Cobbett's Inn.

" It had been many years since the old place had been done up, that is to say, thoroughly ; though it had been painted once within the last twenty years—but they always paint chambers of a doubtful white, and this was over several other coats of paint, the accumulation of many years.

" On one side of the fireplace was a recess, while on the other there was none, and thinking it possible that one could be made on that side, my uncle ordered the men to ascertain if there was any impediment to it, or if it would injure the security of the house by breaking into the wall.

" This was accordingly done, when the men, in scraping the paint off, found that a chink ran round in the form of a door. Much surprised at this, they called my uncle, and consulted him.

" ' Eh ? ' said he, ' a door—did you say a door ? I never heard of one being there before. Are you sure ? '

" ' Not quite, sir ; but it is very strange if they have run this crevice round for the sake of ornament, and then stopped it up with putty ; besides, here is a keyhole, that has been very carefully stopped up.'

" ' Indeed ! '

" ' Look, sir.'

" ' Well, I am surprised.'

" ' That may be,' replied the painter, ' because I did not see it till I scraped the paint off, and very likely should not have done so then, but I chipped a piece of the putty out. But you'll have it opened, I suppose, sir ? ' said the man.

" ' Yes, yes, by all means ; it will make all the difference, and save much trouble if a cupboard or closet really exists.'

"'It will so.'

"I stood by, and recollect the job being done well enough.

"They had some trouble, for the door was thick, and made of very strong wood—oak, I think, and it had been well secured by some means which the men could not explain.

"They, however, after some trouble, opened the door, and then my uncle opened his eyes and looked in. I peeped over his shoulders, in case anything should happen that made a retreat necessary.

"It was a closet, dirty enough, and plenty of cobwebs, enough to make curtains to a four-post bedstead, and quite heavy enough.

"After a little examination, my uncle declared he could hardly believe his senses.

"'Will you walk in and see?' said one of the workmen.

"He went in, and it being dark, he very nearly tumbled down a hole.

"'Hilloa! there—help, help! I shall fall and be killed. Help!'

"The man ran into the closet, and seized my uncle by the back of the neck, and dragged him along the floor.

"'What is the matter, sir, what is the matter?' inquired the workmen.

"'The matter!' said my uncle, rubbing his shins, and brushing his coat; 'why, there's a great hole, it may be a well; at all events, I have had a narrow escape.'

"'A well?'

"'Yes, a well; go in and look at it, will you?—there, don't be afraid.'

"The workmen were not afraid, though they had no taste for dropping into a well, and they obtained a light, which I gave them —one of the office candles—and they examined the hole, saying,—

"'Here's an old pair of stairs or steps.'

"'Some steps?'

"'Yes,' said one of the men, 'and it looks rather a dingy place.'

"'Shall we go down and see?' inquired one of the workmen.

"'Yes,' added my uncle; 'go down and I will follow you.'

"They descended, but my uncle waited and looked at me, and I at him.

"'Ain't you going down?' he said.

"'Going down!' said I.

"'Yes.'

"'Why,' said I, 'it might be unwholesome, you know—the air might be damp.'

"'I'll come after you. Go down.'

"Well, there was no saying I wouldn't, so I peeped down, and hearing them talk, I soon followed, and found myself in a queer kind of place, a sort of cellar, or passage, or passages—it might be something else; but it was very cold and very damp.

"I can't give you much of an idea of it, but there was a kind of closet fitted up in it, or something that served the purpose.

"It was well done, the men said, and worth something. The place was completely festooned with cobwebs, that appeared like curtains. Indeed, they resembled crape, and the first thought that entered my mind was that the place had been hung with black some years.

"However, there were other places that went off in different directions, that led I don't know where, and I never had any curiosity to see, for the very look of the cobwebs was enough to deter one. They clung so strongly to my cap that they pulled it off my head, and caused me to duck, for fear my head might go with it.

"I never was good in adventures, but especially those which are uncertain in their termination, and I didn't know how soon one might drop into a hole, or a lot of bricks and mortar, or other heavy rubbish might fall upon me, and then there would be an end of my days.

"'Hilloa!' said one of the men, 'what have we here?'

"We instantly turned to the spot where the man was, when we saw a beer barrel, upon trestles, covered over with a kind of odd-looking things, that grow in dark, damp places.

"'Oh!' said another, 'beer, I dare say, or more likely it is wine.'

"'Oh! that is a lucky find,' said my uncle, 'we can be merry.'

"'Yes,' said one of the men; 'it will be a rare house-warming.'

"'This wants warming, I am sure,' replied one of his companions.

"So I thought, but they said nothing more then; but when we had all quitted the cellar, one went to my uncle, and said—

"'What's to be done about the beer, sir?'

"'What beer?' he exclaimed, tartly.

"'The men will want beer, sir, to drink you require them to make haste.'

"'Beer, indeed!'

"'Yes; are we to buy any?'

"'No—no, and yet——I don't see why we should. It is an imposition.'

"'But there's the beer downstairs.'

"'Do you think it's beer?'

"'I do.'

"'And very good?'

"'I can't say; but it's been kept long enough. It may be thin; but it is very old, and, I should think, strong.'

"'Very well. You may buy a tap when you go out, somewhere or other.'

"He went out and bought an old tap—it was a very good one—and returned, armed with a mallet and brown paper, and my

"PLAY."

uncle followed with the candle, a jug, and glass.

"The barrel was duly tapped—the tap went in very easily, but nobody noticed it—the beer was of darker colour than we had anticipated ; but, on tasting it, we found it of an extraordinary quality, and somewhat peculiar flavour—so peculiar, indeed, that the men would not drink it, and it was drawn off and thrown away.

"That done, I thought I might as well have the cask to sell, for my uncle used to put many little things like it in my way to give me a little pocket-money—and putting it in that light, I asked him for it.

"'Very well,' he replied, 'take it.'

"I immediately made a bargain with a man, who offered me six shillings for it, which, as it was very old, I took.

"He brought it upstairs. My uncle was there, and the men, and so were the clerks. It was very rotten, and burst to pieces, leaving a large bundle of something that looked like a bundle of rags, tied up, carefully concealed.

"'Hilloa !' said the man, 'what's this ? Why, if it ain't a body !'

"And sure enough it was. It had been a human being, corded up carefully to about a third of its size, bringing the knees to its chest, and the heels to its hips—the canvas was decomposed, and fell to bits—the bones and flesh parted, and the skull rolled on the floor, and as it did so, the flesh rolled off, leaving the bones bare.

"I never shall forget the faces I saw," concluded Mat; "it seemed as if they were all wondering how they would have felt had they drank the beer. There was a deal of bother about it—police and others came and examined the place all over, but they made nothing of it, as men who ought to have known declared that the place had been shut at least a hundred years—and so my story ends."

"And the fire being almost out," rejoined Bob, "it is getting precious cold ; let us make a move to the beach."

Thither they at once adjourned, where they found Lobby Panks with several other interesting youths, constructing a fort of sand.

Tim fell upon him at once.

"Lobby," he said, "shell out."

"What for ?"

"A tanner for funking," replied Tim ; "that's the price of running away from a ghost story."

"I hain't got any money," whined Panks.

"Then you refuse to pay ?"

"You haven't any right to my money if I have any."

"Perversity is the offspring of bloodshed and little minds," said Tim, with a hazy notion of some old proverb. "Make a ring, boys."

Panks began to cry, but his audience had hearts of stone—his tears fell upon a rocky place.

"You know I don't fight," he said.

"I'll have that tanner—out with it," returned Tim, and after a little further demurring, Panks produced it from the depths of his trousers pocket.

"Thanks," said Tim, spinning it in the air, "I value this more than a bob in the usual way."

"I'm to have some of the bull's-eyes," stipulated Panks.

"You shall—if bull's-eyes I buy ; but I have an idea of using it for something else. Ta-ta, boys—I'm going into the town."

"Out of bounds," sung out Charley after him.

"Out of Bath," returned Tim, waving his hand as he disappeared.

Charley, Bob, and Mat, sat upon the sand watching the construction of the fort, and talking to each other in an undertone, until one of the boys called out—

"Here comes Mr. Tidd ; now we shall have some fun."

Mr. Tidd came up and gave the pupils a

kindly greeting, but his object did not appear to be fun. Drawing Charley aside he whispered in his ear—

"Thorn, you are wanted at the house."

"Anything the matter ?"

"No, I think not—somebody from your home—a hard-visaged old man, with a face like a nut-cracker."

"It must be Filer," returned Charley ; "I hope nothing has happened to my—my father."

"I think you may make your mind easy about that—the old man said he only looked you up in what he called a 'cashyvill manner.'"

CHAPTER XXXIX.

NEWS FROM HOME.

IT was indeed old Filer awaiting the coming of Charley in the reception room for friends of the pupils.

He gave his young master the warmest of greetings, and in response to Charley's eager inquiries, declared that all was well at home.

"Mr. Thorn," he said, "is as well and 'arty as a man can be who is allers a-runnin' his head ag'in a science of some sort. He sends his love, and, what's ekal to a b'ilerful of affection, a couple of pounds."

Charley pocketed the two golden boys, and asked after Mops.

"Mops is gettin' on," said Filer ; "he ain't a young un, and the work was new to him ; but he's improvin' rapidly. If anything, he is too heager, for he's cleaned some of the knives until they ain't no thicker than a wafer, and the bill for boot-blackin' is rose double ; but he means well, and we treats him kindly."

By "we" Filer meant Mr. Thorn and himself, for Filer always looked upon himself as one of the family, a pleasant fiction which nobody cared to disturb.

"Well, I'm glad to see you, Filer," said Charley, "although your visit is so unexpected."

"I axed for a couple o' days," returned Filer, "just to take a peep at you. Have you heerd about old Phosey ?"

"Dr. Phosey—my old master ?"

"That's the willin."

"What's happened to him ?"

"'Arf his school made a clean bolt of it, and runned home, sayin' they wouldn't stand no more on it. He made 'em all so genteel, and put 'em into sech uncommon stiff collars, that none of 'em could play cricket, and lots fainted away at church. There's a long account on it in the county paper, in the form of a letter signed by a 'Hindignant Parient,' whose son went home with a mark round his neck as if he had been wearing mannikins."

"Manacles, Filer."

"Jes' so. I thowt it was summat o' that sort; anyhow he went home, and his parient fell into a b'ilin' rage, and being a kind o' fur'us old gent, hammered away at Phosey's door, who said he wasn't at home, until the perlice came and moved him on, which they did rough like, and chucked all his weskut buttons orf, and broke his heyeglass. Lor'! there have been a turn-up, I can tell you."

"Not sorry to hear it, Filer—it was a beastly crib, I hated it."

"I think Mr. Thorn is sorry he sent you there now, but he don't say so; perhaps them two suvrins is a kind of peace orphan."

"Offering, Filer."

"Ah! offering—there ain't much difference atween the words. Dash it! Master Charles, how you have growed!"

"Yes! I'm running up a bit," replied Charley, carelessly.

"Had any more fights?" inquired Filer, in a thrilling whisper.

"None worth speaking of," said Charley, laughing.

"Don't give way to none of 'em," advised Filer; "a young chap like you ought to pound 'em—slice—give it to 'em this way, straight from the shoulder."

And Filer favoured his young master with a few vague specimens of the fistic art.

"Had any whoppings?" he asked, after a pause.

"Yes."

"Many of 'em?"

"Pretty fair, Filer, but not more than I deserved."

"Was they stiff uns?" asked Filer, whose curiosity appeared to gather like a rolling snowball.

"Tol—lol, Filer; Mr. Crammer is neither a babe nor suckling."

"Do you take 'em quietly, or shin him?"

"Shin who?"

"Mr. Crammer."

"Dare not do that," replied Charley, laughing again, and shaking his head, "that's going a step too far."

"Is it?" said Filer; "well, I don't know much about it. I never went to school, but I thout that one now and then, jes' to tell him to draw it mild like, wouldn't do any harm; but you knows best. Lor'! how you have growed!"

"You said that before, Filer."

"So I did, but you seem to grow up afore me like Jack on the Beanstalk. I say, who's that party who keeps the lodge?"

"The porter?"

"Yes, the porter chap."

"That's Griddle."

"Nice name! he is sour like, ain't he?"

"Rather."

"So I thought," returned Filer, slowly; "him and I don't hit it, we can't hit it, and we shouldn't hit it."

"What's the matter with you?"

"Nothin' pertikler at present, but somethin' might come orf if he riled me much more."

"What has he done?"

"When I knocks at the door, on my fust arrival, he swings it back and stares at me as if I were dirt of the airth under his feet. 'Hallo!' he ses. 'Hallo!' ses I. 'Who are you?' he axes. 'Filer,' I ses, 'and I wants to see Master Thorn.' 'So you wants to see that himp,' he ses; 'are you his slavey?' I waves my hand lofty like, and tells him to show the way to the front parlour. 'I'll show you to the usual 'ception-room,' he ses; 'walk in, my hold himage,' which, put it as you like, Master Charles, is personal."

"So it is, Filer."

"I doesn't say nothin' to him," pursued Filer; "but I remembers them words, and I feels we shan't get on."

"I should think not, Filer; you and he are made of different stuff. But here comes the old duffer across the ground."

Griddle not only came across the ground, and entered the house, but sauntered into the reception-room, and bringing out a duster from his pocket, began to flirt with a little dust upon the table and books.

It is impossible to convey adequately in words the amazement and indignation which sprang up in Filer's face, or to give any idea of the frown which wrinkled his forehead and pursed his lips.

Charley, however, kept cool, and simply said—

"Griddle, don't you see that I'm engaged?"

"I can't help it, Master Thorn," doggedly returned the porter. "I've got my work to do; and I want to git it over a little airlier to-day, for it's my birthday. You've had a good 'arf-hour together."

"It's like your impudence to notice it."

"I must git done afore tea," said Griddle, "or I shan't have a moment to myself to celebrate my natal ewent. You let me alone and I lets you alone."

So saying, Griddle resumed his dusting, accompanying his movements with a soft but defiant whistling.

He had gone too far.

The patience of Filer was exhausted.

Turning back the cuffs of his coat with the utmost deliberation, he advanced upon the porter; and, striking a thrilling attitude, bade Griddle "Come on."

"I knowed we shouldn't agree," said Filer. " Put down that duster, and come on."

Filer was old, and about as fit for fighting as an infant in arms; but Griddle was a coward, and the bold attitude of the old man alarmed him.

"Call him off, Master Thorn," he cried, dodging behind the table. "You don't ought to bring bullies here, to timmydate a man o' my years."

"Get out of the room," cried Filer, making futile efforts to get at him; while Charley sat in a chair, and roared until his sides ached.

"I shall lay this afore Mr. Crammer," said Griddle, making towards the door. "It's ag'in' all rules. It's a——"

The rest of the sentence was never uttered; for he fled before a final charge from Filer, and left that faithful servitor master of the field.

"Victory—victory!" cried Charley, waving his cap over his head.

"Them as laughs at me laughs wrong," said Filer, wiping his heated face. "Ah! I knowed we shouldn't agree. Now, Master Charles," he added, looking at a watch—one of the old-fashioned sort, weighing a trifle over half a pound—"it's time to be orf. I've just half an hour to catch the coach; and, although I can, as you see, fight a bit, my walking ain't so brisk as it used to be."

Filer then shook hands with Charley, and they parted, mutually satisfied with the interview.

He encountered only one more difficulty on his way out, and that arose from Griddle, who, having locked the door of his lodge, had quietly hidden himself away, with the hope of annoying his enemy by creating a loss of time.

But in this he was disappointed.

A screwdriver was lying on a chair, with which Filer quickly removed the lock, and placed it on the table with the screws, and the following inscription in chalk—

"With filers complermits

I KNOWED WE SHUDENT HAGREE!"

which Griddle, half an hour later, discovered, to his overwhelming astonishment and rage.

CHAPTER XL.

GRIDDLE'S BIRTHDAY.

THE few words Griddle had let slip respecting the celebration of the anniversary of his birth did not escape Charley Thorn, who returned to his chums, to lay plans for the fitting celebration thereof.

The simple idea of Griddle having a birthday was bad enough; but that he should presume to keep it roused their youthful ire, and put their minds upon the rack, so that they might have, as Bob Martin remarked, "a finger in the old villain's pie."

"It is sure to be kept in the kitchen, I suppose?" Charley said.

"He would not hold high revelry with Mr. Crammer," rejoined Mat Langley.

"But he could keep it in his lodge—couldn't he, stupid?"

"Perhaps he could. But don't get abusive."

"All serene. Where's Tim?"

"Not back yet."

"Perhaps he has fallen upon Mr. Crammer."

"It would be just his luck."

This time, however, they were wrong, for in a few minutes Tim returned without any signs upon him of having fallen into the hands of the Philistines. Bob asked him what had detained him so long.

"I went after a particular article," he replied, "and I had some difficulty in getting it."

Charley then told him of Filer's visit, the money left, and the birthday of Griddle.

"If we can only be certain where it is to be kept," said Harry Leicester, "we can have some fun with him."

"I think we can," returned Tim, with a meaning smile; "but more of that by-and-by."

We will follow the example of Tim, and leave the subject for the time, skipping the intervening hours, until we come to Griddle with his day's work done, seated in the kitchen, preparing to do honour to his natal day.

He had not been a very great favourite with his fellow servants, but he was very desirous of being on a good footing with them, and he chose this opportunity to make a good impression.

"Cook," he said, "I shall spend an hour or two with you to-night. Everybody's in, and I don't think we shall get any visitors, and if they does come, we are sure to hear the big bell. So what does you say to making a merry night on it?"

"My lawks a mercy!" exclaimed the cook, "what have you got inter that foolish head of yourn?" What should we make merry with?"

"I don't think that a little drop o' summat short would hurt us," said Griddle, with a sly look.

"And who's to find it?" demanded the cook, sharply.

"Why, I will," returned Griddle; "for you see as how it's my birthday."

The cook opened her eyes and laughed, Mary giggled, and the boy who did the odd jobs of the house sniggered.

"You shut up," said Griddle, ferociously, addressing the boy; "as for you, Mary, arter wot hav taken place atween us, I'm ashamed of yer."

"I'm sure it's not worth mentioning," said Mary, with a toss of her head.

"Maybe not," returned Griddle; "but you needn't larf at me; it is my birthday. I suppose I've as much a right to one as any-body else."

"I don't know, Mr. Griddle."

"I *was* born once," said Griddle, "I'll take my oath of that, so drop that sniggerin'."

"And how old may you be?" demanded the cook.

This touched Griddle upon a tender point; he knew he neither looked, nor was, so young as he wished to be, so he proceeded to explain.

"I'm aweer," he said, "that I ain't worn well; knockin' about a 'ard-'arted world hev chipped some of my corners off; but I'm still far from my prime—in my yooth, I might say—I'm thirty-three."

A chorus of laughter followed this announcement, the boy going into a series of private convulsions under the dresser.

Griddle looked savagely around, undecided upon whom to fall. His eye caught the agitated form of the boy.

"Come out," he cried, hauling him up by the waist, "for it's a warmint you air, Dick. Laugh at me!—take that—you'll laugh at your father next."

"Or my grandfather," retorted Dick, dodging away behind the cook, who held her hand up and bade Griddle let him be.

"It's wexacious," grunted Griddle, sitting down, "werry wexacious, when here I am ready and willin' with a 'ole bottle o' rum and another o' gin ready to keep my birth-day, and all on you grinnin' like—like—grinnin' fools," he concluded, rather tamely, being in want of a better word.

"Well, don't be angry," said the cook, softening; "it is surely a proper time to laugh; but thirty-three. Ha, ha!"

"Ho, ho!" roared the boy, and Mary chuckled audibly.

"If I'd only a hodd boot," muttered Griddle, looking about for something to hurl at Dick; "but there—let be. Is it to be a hevening or isn't it?"

"I think so," said the cook, "and I think I can manage a little snack of some sort for supper. What do you say to a stew?"

"The werry thing," said Griddle, smack-ing his lips; "as a relish, nothin' beats a stew."

"Then I'll get it on the fire at once, and we'll have a drop of something nice and warm after it."

The ingredients were handy, and the cook put the saucepan on the heart of the fire. Mary leaned against the table, Dick sat upon it, and Griddle, pulling a paper a week old from his pocket, prepared to read.

"When I'm at hease," he said, "I like to pick a bit o' news, as a sort o' mentel relish."

"If you come across anything good," said the cook, "read it out."

"A breach of promise case," said Mary.

"Or a good murder in the police reports," suggested Dick.

"It ain't likely I should read out what *you* want," said Griddle, addressing himself to Dick; "so don't give me any of your cheek."

Dick forebore to make any reply, and Griddle, turning down the paper at a con-venient place, read about a very entertaining breach of promise case, where counsel, judge, jury, and the general public made excellent fooling out of certain love letters, which, in the eyes of many people, ought to have been held sacred.

Griddle stumbled though it, mispronouncing every hard word and galloping over the stops until he came to the end, when the announcement of fifty pounds damages for the devoted maid gave ample satisfaction to Mary and the cook.

"I'd damage a feller if he deceived me," said cook, stirring the stew furiously. "A parcel of scoundrels going about with smooth words and honey tongues, taking in poor girls."

"Sarve the gals right," growled Dick; "nothin's too bad for a gal, my way o' thinking."

"You'll know better," said the cook, "when you are growed up. Wimmingkind is a blessing—go on, Mr. Griddle."

"Here's something," rejoined Griddle, "which I think will amoose us all—

"'FAIRFUL EXPLOSHING AND LORSE OF LIFE.'—Steady a bit, while I fold it down.

"'Last night the neighbourhood of the Borough Road was startled by a loud report, which shook many windows out, and brought the inhabitants forth from their houses. For a time, the cause could not be ass——ass——dash the word!—ascertained; but it soon trans——transpired that the house of Mr. Fizzum, firework maker, was in flames. It seems, from what our reporter was able to gather, that Mr. Fizzum was sitting by the fire, when——'"

"Help! What's that?" screamed the cook.

Bang!—fizz!—bang, bang!

For a moment, Griddle appeared to be enveloped in flames, the next moment he was on his back, with the cook above him, scream-ing like a hurricane.

The room was dark, and full of smoke, hot ashes from the fire were strewn about, and in the corner stood Mary and Dick, lending their voices to the general confusion.

"What is the matter?" groaned Griddle.

"Dun know," cried the cook; "but I think

the house is blown up. Help!—help! Murder!—fire!—thieves! Help!—help!"

"Poof!" cried Griddle, "I'm choked, I'm murdered."

"What is the meaning of this disturbance?" screamed Mrs. Margery, as the door opened, and she entered, followed by Mr. Crammer, Mr. Pendulum, and some half-score of the pupils.

At first nothing could be seen but the dim forms of Griddle and the cook lying in front of the fire, but the opening of the door drove away the smoke, and the full extent of the disaster was revealed.

It was nothing very serious, after all : the fire was blown out of the grate, and the saucepan containing the stew was lying in the middle of the kitchen, the table was upset, probably by Dick during his hasty retreat, a few pieces of crockery were broken, and nothing more.

"Will you have the kindness to get up," said Mr. Crammer, giving his porter rather a vicious dig with his foot, "and explain this?"

"I can't say no more than this, sir," rejoined Griddle, rising ; "that I was a sitting by the fire readin' the noosepaper to while the hour away, when all on a sudden there was the most bustingest exploshing I ever knowed, and I was blowed bang up to the ceilin'."

"Ahem!" said Mr. Crammer, "gunpowder —but there is another peculiar smell in the atmosphere—like—like spirits."

"Rum and gin," said Mrs. Margery, with a short indignant sniff.

"And furthermore, it is about you," returned Mr. Crammer ; "at your old tricks again?"

"On my word," pleaded Griddle, "I haven't touched a drop to-night. Oh, lor!" he cried, clapping his hand to the tails of his coat, "here's both on 'em broke."

"Both of what?"

"Nothin', sir, pertikler," returned Griddle, evasively, "a night draught for the cramps, sir, nothin' more."

"Turn your pockets out, sir."

"But, sir, I—I——"

"Turn out your pockets."

Then, with much humility, Griddle removed his coat, and from the pockets produced sundry articles saturated with rum and gin, and the fragments of two full-sized bottles—reputed quarts.

"There's the mystery," said Mrs. Margery, "all of 'em queer. Cook, you leave this day month."

"As you please, mum," rejoined the cook, tossing her head, "and much good riddance to you, mum."

"As for you, Mary," continued the housekeeper, turning to the housemaid, "I would

pack you off at once, if I thought that you had a share in this."

"Don't be hasty," said Mr. Crammer, in a low tone ; "the girl and boy are entirely blameless."

Then, with much gravity of deportment, quite edifying to Charley, Bob Martin, and the others who formed the youthful portion of the audience, he read Griddle a severe lecture upon the evils of drink, pointing out how it would eventually undermine his constitution, and drive him to the workhouse, where he would undoubtedly perish miserably.

"Be warned in time," he said, in conclusion ; "and let your future sobriety atone for this night's debauch."

The boys, perceiving that his lecture was drawing to a close, quietly skedaddled, and shortly after Mr. Crammer returned to the solitude of his private room.

He was up early on the following morning, and out upon the roof.

He examined the lead, and found sundry footmarks leading to the chimney pots and back again to the trap-door.

"I thought so," he muttered. "I shall catch them one day, and woe to the ringleaders."

So Mr. Crammer was not deceived after all, and Charley, Tim, and Bob, the authors of the mischief, were much mistaken when they chuckled over the blindness of the master of Scarum School.

CHAPTER XLI.

THAT CONFOUNDED GHOST !—STRANGE NEWS FOR TIM.

A few mornings after the gunpowder feat, Mary, on going down to begin her morning duties, discovered the house to be in a state of extraordinary confusion.

The big clock in the hall had stopped, and the barometer was turned with its face to the wall. Every mat was gone, all the chairs were piled up, and in Mr. Crammer's room a large fire was burning in the grate.

Mary's first thought was to scream, her second to run to Mrs. Margery's room, which she acted upon, and startled that somewhat vinegary lady from her second sleep.

"Oh, mum!—oh, missus!" she cried, "I never did see such goin's on. I'm sure master will be drove clean mad."

"What is the matter, Mary?" asked the old lady, springing up and throwing a shawl over her head.

"Oh, mum! oh, missus! come down and see."

Mrs. Margery came down and saw, much to her rage, confusion, and dismay, but she only said—

"Let them be until Mr. Crammer comes down; and put the breakfast-room straight."

The whole affair was certainly incomprehensible.

If it was the work of any of the pupils, it certainly was a piece of unparalleled audacity; but Mrs. Margery could not bring herself to believe this.

Nor could Mr. Crammer, when he saw what was done, conceive it possible that any of the boys had created the confusion.

Now, who was it?

Who could possibly have entered the house and departed without being discovered?

Mr. Crammer half-suspected Mr. Tidd; but that gentleman's natural surprise, when introduced to the scene of disorder, placed him beyond suspicion.

And Mr. Pendulum was horror-stricken.

As for the domestic servants, including Dick, they slept in a part of the house solely accessible by a door of which the housekeeper kept the key; and Griddle reposed in the lodge.

It was a mystery.

Mr. Crammer secretly boiled over with rage, and felt inclined to call in the assistance of the police; but prudence forbade him to reveal too much of the internal disorders of Scarum School, and he resolved to watch and wait.

"I must have them one time or the other," he thought; "then, woe to them—woe to them!"

A little later, when he tried to put on a pair of boots, cleaned for him the day previous, he discovered therein two breakfast rolls, a corkscrew, part of a bottle-jack, a few screws, the handle of an old saw, half a brick, and a model steam-engine, the property of Master Toddy Crammer.

This added fuel to the fire.

Nor was his wrath assuaged when Mrs. Margery announced that the mats had been found carefully rolled up and packed away in the waterbutt, in company with a warming-pan and an old hat.

But he said nothing.

He bided the time when he hoped to make the culprits shake in their shoes.

These little events were, of course, fully known. Dick, who had been lately engaged as an additional help to the establishment, made them fully known.

Dick inclined to the supernatural, and declared it to be his solemn conviction that the place was "harnted," an assertion nobody cared to deny; it was so delightful to live in a horrible house, where everybody trembled as they walked in the passages after dark.

Many of our friends, especially Charley Thorn and Harry Leicester, laughed at the idea of a ghost; but they were, nevertheless,

to use their own expression, "fogged" by the strange events which had taken place.

Neither they nor any of their particular chums had a hand in it they knew, and looking round the school, they could not fix upon any one likely to carry out such a daring scheme.

"We must have a genius amongst us," said Harry; "some deep fellow among the slow school—but I'm dashed if I can make it out."

"How can you hope to," rejoined Bob, "when you know there is something wrong in the place?"

"Something wrong?"

"Yes, something very wrong; it's built upon bad ground—that's what it is—murderers sleep under it. Did you hear anything last night?"

"No."

"Well, I did, and so did Charley."

Charley nodded assent.

"What was it like?" asked Harry.

"Like what it was—something supernatural. In the middle of the night, something was walking up and down our dormitory slowly, between the beds, but so softly that you could scarcely hear it."

"Could you see it?" asked the sceptical Harry.

"No, for it was darker than pitch. I looked out of the bedclothes once, and not only could I hear it walking, but I could hear it *breathing*."

"Spirits don't breathe."

"But no man or boy could walk about as that did. Why, it was not walking, it was gliding."

"Dash it!" cried Tim, "do shut up; I shan't sleep for a week."

"Who frightened Panks?" said Charley, with a grin.

"Yes; but my story was gammon, and if he had waited another minute, would have ended pleasantly. But this is the truth, you say?"

"The solemn truth!"

"Awful truth!" rejoined Charley. "I lay and listened to it, until I felt as if I should swoon."

"No gammon, Charley," put in Harry Leicester.

"Upon my word and honour," returned our hero seriously, "it is true. Bob and I agreed not to say anything about it, as we thought it was a trick of some of you—in fact, we intended to give you one the next time it was attempted; but these things going on about the house give the matter a serious turn. I don't know what to make of it."

And that was the case with everybody—masters, pupils, and servants of Scarum School—they could make nothing of it.

Several days passed, and nothing worthy of note transpired.

The strictest watch was kept, but no discovery of the slightest importance was made.

After dark everybody went about with fear and trembling.

A knock at the door, or footsteps in the passage, were sufficient to give an alarm.

From the kitchen, from the schoolroom, from Mr. Crammer's study, perpetual excursions were made, ending in the discovery of naught but false alarms, and, not unfrequently, two parties encountered each other, to their mutual terror and confusion.

This feeling, however, gradually subsided, and the school settled down into a tolerably tranquil state—for a time, the ghost was laid.

And now an important change took place in the life of one of our heroes, Tim Turndown.

We have seen him in his poverty, for Tim without pocket-money was really poor—we have seen him struggling against the gradual decay of the skeleton suit ; we have seen him suffering from the treacherous nature of buttons, and compelled, in his hour of distress, to rely upon string.

All this we have seen, and marked how he had borne it, and now the change had come.

One morning, as he was wending his way to the breakfast room, Mr. Tidd checked his career, and told him that he was wanted in the private room.

"What have I done now, sir ?" asked Tim, who could only associate a private audience with "Tickler."

"Nothing," returned Mr. Tidd, in a gentle tone of voice. "Mr. Crammer has some news for you. I will accompany you."

They found Mr. Crammer seated in his chair, with a crumpled letter in his hand, and a mournful expression of face.

"Turndown," he said, "take a chair."

Tim was so overcome with this unexpected piece of hospitality that he fell into one all of a heap.

"Turndown," continued Mr. Crammer, "life is very uncertain. We are here to-day, and—and—gone to-morrow."

Tim opened his eyes very wide at this peculiar mode of address.

He strongly suspected his master of having imbibed strong waters at a too early hour.

"Turndown," said Mr. Crammer, "you had an uncle."

The heart of Tim beat fast.

He had an inkling of what was coming.

"Your uncle has been taken very ill, my boy."

Tears arose in Tim's eyes. He knew the truth now.

"He is dead ; he died suddenly, two days ago."

The old man had not been kind to the boy, but Tim was a tender-hearted little fellow, and he wept as bitterly as if old Ralph Turndown had been the kindest of fathers to him.

CHAPTER XLII.

GRIDDLE MAKES A DISCOVERY.

TIM did not go into school that morning, but was permitted to wander about the playground, and meditate upon the loss he had sustained.

The first outburst of grief was soon over, and, although Tim felt sorry for the sudden death of his uncle, he could not grieve for him as he would have done had the old man been of a kinder disposition.

He was to go to the funeral, that much Mr. Crammer had told him, and a tailor was coming from the town to measure him for suitable clothes, "by order of the trustees," the schoolmaster said, but who or what the trustees were, Tim had not the least conception.

Shortly before noon the tailor came, with tape and book, and skilfully taking the dimensions of our friend's proportions, sighed, and "supposed that he would like them to be as fashionable as possible."

"Then I'm not to have—have—anything like these ?" faltered Tim, indicating the skeleton suit.

"Oh! dear no," rejoined the tailor, smiling a sweet and gentle smile becoming the occasion ; "my orders are to provide whatever you may order, and let everything be of the very best."

This unexpected change of affairs was a little too much for Tim, and he was obliged to sit down a moment and think it over.

The tailor patiently awaited his recovery.

"Make them fashionable," said Tim, after a pause ; "and let the jacket be long—almost a coat."

"It shall be done, sir," returned the tailor ; "everything will be ready to-morrow at noon."

When the morning school duties were over, Tim met his friends, to whom he related all that had passed, not omitting the interview with the tailor.

"I was never so floored in all my life," said Tim ; "'Have what you like, of the very best,' said the tailor."

"Have you any relations left, Tim ?" Charley asked.

"None, that I know of," answered Tim, sorrowfully ; "I'm as good as alone in the world."

"When do you start ?"

"To-morrow."

"You will come back, of course ?"

Tim was startled; he had not thought of that before, and the probability of his having to bid adieu to Scarum School rushed upon him.

"I don't know, Charley," he said, "for I know nothing except this, that I am to go to the funeral. If—if I have no friends left, I can't come back."

"That's all bosh!" said Charley, impetuously; "you must—you shall—if you've no other friends in the world, there's my father, and all of us here."

"Well, we shall see," said Tim, smiling sadly. "Of course, I don't want to tramp about the world; but at the same time I don't like the idea of being a sponger—a pauper, you know."

To this Charley only said, "Bother!" and Mat Langley entered into a long argument to show how no "fellow who was helped by a friend" was a pauper; it assuredly was those who accepted public relief who deserved the name.

On the morrow the clothes of Tim came home, and gave every satisfaction, being a very creditable effort of provincial tailordom.

In the evening he went away by coach, escorted by Griddle, who grumbled all the way, and openly declared more than once that it was "p'ison" to him having to wait upon one who had done so much to make his life miserable at Scarum School.

"Which a himp you is," he said, "and allers will be; you was so in that old skeleton soot, and wot you'll be in fancy togs, I shouldn't like to say."

"Perhaps I'm not coming back," said Tim.

"Then there'll be one of the ghost party short," returned Griddle, meaningly; "ah! you may stare, but I know who the parties are, and I'll have 'em."

"You know too much," was all Tim said, as he climbed the coach, and was almost immediately whirled away.

Griddle charged Tim with being concerned with the production of the ghost, but in this he was wrong, for Tim and his friends were as much in the dark respecting it as Mr. Crammer himself; but Griddle, like all little wiseacres, whenever he got an idea into his head kept it there; and the idea he now entertained was that the mysterious visitor was the result of a deep organization on the part of the boys.

He had made up his mind to fathom it, and soon began to haunt the house, and shortly became as annoying as the ghost itself.

As several other outrages had been committed, the whole house was on the *qui vive* to discover the author; night watches, in which the masters and ushers shared, were occasionally kept, but to no purpose; whenever the watch was kept, the cunning ghost kept away, and as the watches were abandoned, it reappeared.

"But I'll have 'em," said Griddle, to the cook; "they can't go on like this for hever."

"It's my opinion," rejoined the cook, "that you had better leave it alone. What d you know about ghosts?"

"Real ghosts, nothin'," answered Griddle; "but Brummagem ones, a lot. Once, whe. I was a—a sort of junior magistrate in the country, the 'ole place was put in a funk about a ghost; everybody was skeered; it used to come to the four cross roads reg'lar arter dark, and caper about like winkin'; nobody wouldn't go nigh it. I orders my special consterbles, which I swore in for the puppis, to take it up, but they wouldn't. They said there wasn't a hact o' parliament to make 'em do it. It were the parson's work, they said, and so I was obliged to go myself."

"Alone, Mr. Griddle?"

"No, not 'zactly; I had a man or two with me—genelmen, in fact, who where staying at the inn for a week's fishing. We nails the ghost, and what do you think it was?"

"A willerwisp."

"No, cook, you can't nail them; it was the young squire, fresh from Eton for his holidays, with a turnip lanting on a pole—nothin' more."

"But that was a different ghost to this," said the cook, shaking her head.

"It's summat like it," returned Griddle, "and I mean to have it."

From that time he took to prying about the house, listening at the doors—especially that belonging to the schoolroom, where one day Charley and a few friends discovered him.

Some little dispute about the make of cricket bats prompted Charley to fetch his from the locker.

He was accompanied by Bob Martin and one or two more.

On their return they found Griddle kneeling on the ground, with his ear fixed to the bottom of the schoolroom door.

Such a favourable opportunity was not to be lost.

Rushing forward with the bat in the air, he cried aloud—

"Play!"

"Well hit, sir, well hit," shouted Bob Martin, after the manner of cricket players in the field.

"Who—who—struck me?" gasped Griddle.

"I did," replied Charley; "what are you lying there for?"

"Mr. Crammer wo—n't allow me to be knocked about."

"How should I know it was you?" demanded Charley. "I thought it was the ghost."

The porter retired muttering, considerably daunted by this check to his career of discovery; but he was not absolutely beaten, only made more cautious, and one morning when Tim had been away about a week, he knocked at the door of Mr. Crammer's study, and requested the favour of an audience.

"I wouldn't ha' troubled you now, sir," said Griddle, as he entered after receiving permission, "but it's a himportant matter. I've found out all about the ghost."

CHAPTER XLIII.

NOT CAUGHT YET.

The face of Mr. Crammer lighted up as he bade Griddle explain himself.

Here was the problem he had been working upon, solved at last. He felt grateful towards Griddle, and looked so.

"I hardly need say, sir," the porter began, "that I've the hinterest of this 'ere house at heart."

"I believe you have, Griddle; go on."

"When this 'ere ghost first showed his nose, I thought he wouldn't stop long, and I ses to myself, ses I, 'Here's a old game rewived, and it'll drop soon, like a hot pertater.'"

"Don't be too prosy, Griddle, but come to the point."

"Well, sir, arter I'd said that and lots of other things to myself, I looks about me to find the warmint, and in course of looking about, I received a buster with a cricket bat, which I spoke on, but which you couldn't see no way of interferin' in, as it was possible for them to have made a mistake in the darkish passage."

"Never mind that, Griddle; pray get on."

"I will, sir. Well, bein' of a parsewering natur', I ignores that buster, and watches agen and agen, listening at the door—which is a moral degrading; but bein' in your cause, I sacrifices my principle, and although it ain't considered in the wages, a little hextra present now and then would square it."

Mr. Crammer made no response to this gentle hint, and Griddle resumed—

"As I ses, I listens, sir, and this werry mornin', at this werry hour, I finds it all out."

He was so triumphant over his great discovery, whatever it was, that he was obliged to pause for breath, and Mr. Crammer, impatiently tapping his knuckles upon the table, bade him proceed.

"Mr. Tidd is in it, sir," said Griddle, in a thrilling whisper, "and Master Thorn, and Martin, and Langley, and Leicester, sir.

They are all in it, for on this werry mornin' and this werry hour, I heard 'em talking about how they should carry it on to-night."

"Be careful what you say, Griddle," said the master; "I shall treat this matter very seriously."

"It's true," rejoined the porter; "I stakes my reppitation on it, Mr. Crammer, sir. I saw Mr. Tidd with them young genelmen in the schoolroom—all together close like—and I draws up to the door, which was open a little way, and listens. I then hears Mr. Tidd say, plain as plain could be, 'Martin, you be the ghost to-night.'"

Griddle paused again and panted for breath, he was so overcome with triumph. Even in his days of beadledom such a glorious success had never fallen to his lot.

"Griddle," said Mr. Crammer, after a thoughtful pause, "are you sure you heard correctly?"

"I'm werry sure," rejoined Griddle, "and I hears more. Master Martin then ses, 'Thank you, sir; I think I can do the ghost!' Then Mr. Tidd ses, 'I believe you can. *Langley does it very well, but I'm sure you will do it better.*'"

"That's pretty conclusive," said Mr. Crammer; "you will take no notice of this. We shall catch these gentlemen in a trap. Be prepared to watch with me to-night."

"I'm prepared for anything in your service," answered Griddle, grovelling before his master; "and proud I am to be the means of putting this house in peace."

"The ghost is not laid yet," said Mr. Crammer, significantly; "when it is, Griddle, I will remember you."

Later in the day, Mr. Tidd startled his employer in another fashion. He requested permission to be absent from the house that night.

"An old friend of mine," he said, "is staying in the town; and as I shall be glad to see him, and talk over old days with him, I shall be glad if you will allow me to be absent for the night. I will return to-morrow in time to resume my duties."

"He wants to be absent to escape consequences, in case the plot is discovered," thought Mr. Crammer; "never mind—he may go. The ghost itself shall confess."

He gave the leave required, and Mr. Tidd left early after school hours, to spend the evening with his friend, who was an old associate of his in the days "when he walked the boards."

Not a hint escaped either master or man during the day; and when night came, they quietly took up a position in the bedroom of Mr. Crammer, who had elected to watch in the dark.

Confident of being on the right track, the

schoolmaster had no weapon but his cane, and Griddle was without a weapon as well, and there they sat for two hours or more, patiently awaiting the coming of the midnight disturber.

It was a quiet, still night, with a light breeze blowing off the land, which brought down to Scarum School the deep tones of the town-hall clock.

The watchers heard it strike twelve, one, and two; then Mr. Crammer resolved to go to bed.

"They have altered their plans," he said; "wait a moment, Griddle, until I get a light —I will then let you out by the front door."

Griddle, who was heartily tired of sitting in the dark, freely acquiesced in the change of the programme, and a light being obtained, they left the room.

"I object to the locking of the dormitory doors, in case of fire," said Mr. Crammer; "but this night, to make all sure, I shall do it. Hold the light, Griddle, I will do it as quietly as possible."

They went quietly from door to door, for which a single key sufficed, and, having secured the inmates, Mr. Crammer went down to the hall for the purpose of letting Griddle, who slept at the lodge, depart.

"As these tricks will, in all probability, be resumed to-morrow," said Mr. Crammer, "you must hold yourself in readiness. We have only our own counsel to keep, as I have sent my son away to spend a few days with a friend. [Master Toddy departed that afternoon.] You need not rise early in the morning. Mary can wait at the breakfast table."

Griddle thanked his master, and, bidding him good night, retired.

Mr. Crammer, having secured the chain and bolts, walked quietly up-stairs.

As he reached the top, a low moaning sound fell upon his ear.

He paused, and, despite his natural courage —for Mr. Crammer was no coward—trembled a little.

"Who is there?" he demanded, endeavouring to pierce the darkness with his eyes.

Something flew by, a large bird or bat it appeared to be, and the motion of the air extinguished the candle.

"Strange!" muttered the schoolmaster; "steady now, and let me think it out. The dormitories are all locked—Mr. Tidd, the archplotter, is away—something flew by and extinguished the candle; it might have been a bat, sometimes they get into houses—but this must have been a monster. The next question is—Am I awake?"

He pricked himself rather viciously, and was compelled to admit that he was in the land of reality.

Barely had he arrived at this conclusion,

when the groan was repeated, and something passed him with a swift gliding motion.

He had sufficient sense and judgment left to grasp at it, but he touched naught but the empty air.

Swift as thought, he took a match from the box, and igniting it, held it aloft.

The passage was empty!

Not even a mouse was moving.

He re-lighted the candle, and passed from door to door, trying them as he went.

All fast!

The mystery was deeper than ever.

He returned to his room, locked the door, and sat down with a cold, clammy dew upon his brow, the offspring of fear.

He could not ignore the fact, the strange, undiscovered visitor had completely cowed him.

He listened for some time, but nothing more was heard.

Then he crept into bed, and tossed about for hours, dropping off into a fitful sleep as daylight appeared in the sky.

In the morning he took Mr. Pendulum and Griddle into his confidence, both of whom were much disturbed by the intelligence— the former especially so, for he was a nervous man, with a faith strongly inclined to the supernatural.

"If the—the house is really haunted," he said, "I would rather leave."

"That is as you please," said Mr. Crammer, coolly; "but I think it rather absurd of men to fly from a shadow."

"I have no wish to fly," rejoined Mr. Pendulum, nervously; "but I have many things to consider—my own health, especially. I have not been well for weeks, and I pass most dreadful nights, dreaming of horrible things."

"Abjure suppers, and take a little physic," returned Mr. Crammer, "and you will be right in a week; in the meantime, I want your assistance in this matter."

He then told the head usher what Griddle had overhead, at which Mr. Pendulum laughed outright.

"You are merry, sir," said Mr. Crammer, angrily.

"I have cause to be," returned Mr. Pendulum: "and so would Mr. Tidd be, were he here. The ghost Martin performed, or rather read, last night. Mr. Tidd has established an evening elocutionary class, and last night the lesson was *the ghost scene in 'Hamlet'*. So much for Griddle's wonderful discovery. I was in the room last night when they went through it—Thorn played *Hamlet*."

Mr. Crammer coughed, and Griddle looked foolish—the wonderful discovery was but a mare's nest after all.

"Still I am convinced," said the master of

Scarum School, "that it is naught but a prank—well carried out, but open to detection, and I am resolved to get at the bottom of it."

"I sincerely hope you will," returned the usher; "for my part, I am willing to give you all the assistance in my power."

"And I, sir," said Griddle, "although I got hold of the wrong ghost, will do my best to unairth the right party. Through wheels and woes, I'm at my post, both ready and willin', Mr. Crammer."

CHAPTER XLIV.

NEWS OF TIM.—A DINNER-PARTY.

IN a week a letter came from Tim, addressed to Charley, in the rather irregular writing of our friend. It had been anxiously looked for, and as it was read aloud to the greater portion of the school, we violate no confidence by laying it verbatim before our readers.

Here it is :—

"DEAR CHARLEY,

"I am not the sort of fellow for bosh, and so I shan't write to you in a mournful style, although my uncle is dead and I have just returned from his funeral. Of course I am sorry, but nobody would expect me to be too much overcome after the life we lived to each other—you understand me, old boy. Now, sit down at this part of my letter, and prepare your mind for staggering news—*Charley, I am a rich man!* My uncle died something or other—I forget the word, but it means that he left no will—and I being the next of kid—I think that is what they called me—all his money is mine, and there is so much of it, that three gentlemen have taken it in hand, and *they* can't count it.

"I don't know much about it, except that I am to go up to London to see a judge, and let him see me, and that these gentlemen who have looked after me are to be approved of by the lawyers, and then all my tin is to be put in trust until I come of age. Ain't it a lark? and I am to have plenty of pocket-money—to begin with, a pound a week. A pound a week, oh! jiminy, won't we have some tarts? for I am coming back to Scarum School until the end of the year.

"They wanted me to go to a swell place, but I could not cut old friends all at once, and so I am coming back. Make up your mind for a go in, and remember me to all the boys.

"Your sincere friend,
"TIM TURNDOWN."

Great was the joy at Scarum School when this news arrived, and the return of Tim was hourly looked for; but there came a second letter from London, saying that the "judge was such a slow cove" that the business would not be over for some days, but he hoped to turn up by the end of the week.

As nothing could be done except to wait patiently, they patiently waited—and on Wednesday, the usual half-holiday, a merry party of youngsters assembled on the beach to discuss what sort of reception they should give Tim on his return.

"It greatly depends upon the day he comes," said Charley.

"He says the end of the week," rejoined Harry Leicester; "Saturday, most probably."

"If he comes on Saturday," said Charley, "we can do the thing prime. Now, I've got an idea—a stunner, I think—what do you say to a reception dinner in the smuggler's cave?"

"The very thing—hurrah!" cried Harry, tossing up his hat—an example followed by most of those who were present.

"We can get up a decent feed for a little money," continued Charley; "Tim is not proud, and he will put up with school fare, if he is rich. I've got nine shillings; let us choose a caterer, and those who have any money, hand over."

Bob Martin and Mat Langley were appointed as caterers, the cap of the former being the bank for the time being, into which the various youths poured their treasure.

Some had a little, some had none; but when Bob counted it over he found himself entrusted with the very respectable sum of thirty shillings—sufficient, he declared, to give them all "a royal tuck out."

"We must have candles, of course, suggested Grimmer.

"Torches," said Harry Leicester, "like the smugglers of old."

"Bravo, Harry!" said Charley. "Now, the next thing is to view the dining-hall, and see what can be made of it."

In a body they trooped to the cave, where they had assembled in former days of liberty, and, picking up a few pieces of paper and fragments of half-burnt wood—relics of their last gathering there—proceeding to make a fire to enable them to survey the interior.

"It's a chalky cave," said Bob, "and we shan't have much difficulty in fixing the torches, a staple will hold them, one fixed in each of these rough corners."

"Hallo—here!" roared Mat Langley, "I've found a bundle."

"Smuggled cigars," shouted Grimmer; and they crowded round Mat, who held up a blue cotton handkerchief protuberant with something within.

"Shall we open it?" he asked.

"Certainly! It's public ground."

He knelt down by the fire, and unfastening the knots, revealed a fair-sized basin,

A COPIOUS SHOWER RAINED DOWN UPON THE HEAD AND SHOULDERS OF GRIDDLE.

plate, knife and fork, a paper containing a pinch of salt and pepper, and a slice of bread.

"What's in the basin?" Bob asked.

"It smells like beef-steak pudding," replied Mat, "and smells very nice, too. I say—I'm rather hungry."

"So am I," said Grimmer, solemnly.

"And I! and I!" shouted the others.

"We did not steal it," said Mat. "It was found—fair spoil of the enemy."

"Oh, don't moralize," cried Bob, "pitch into it."

"Not here;" said Mat, "let us go to the Chyne."

The Chyne was a rent in the cliff, about half a mile away from the cave, a place promising much concealment to the youthful marauders; and thither they adjourned, partaking of the feast with all the zest which is proverbially attached to stolen fruit.

They had not departed more than ten minutes when a little coasting yacht, such as excursionists patronise, grounded on the beach, and two men, one about fifty and the other a little over twenty, landed, and drew the yacht up high and dry.

"I'm danged if I bean't hungry, Bill," said the elder; "and I du stick to it, for a nappytite there's nothin' like a run of a mile or two out to sea."

"Thee be right, feyther," returned the other. "What ha' mother made for our dinner to-day?"

"Beef puddin'," returned the old man, smacking his lips, "which be a dinner I'm moighty fond on."

By this time they had reached the smugglers' cave, and Bill, the younger, entered.

He was absent from his father's side until the old man, growing impatient, bawled out—

"Be sharp, Bill, for I'm peckish loike."

Then Bill came forth, very pale, and with eyes starting out of his head.

"Feyther, I cannot find the puddin'!"

"What?" bellowed the old man.

"I cannot find the puddin'!" roared Bill.

"Dang 'ee, thee must be lyin'!"

In rushed the old man, followed by Bill, and the two groped about in the well-known corner, like two frantic Jews in search of a lost diamond.

They groped in vain, knocking their heads together, and tumbling against each other in their agitation.

"Ha' thee got a match, Bill?"

Bill produced half a dozen from his trousers pocket, and a light was procured.

"Here be the basin," he cried, pointing to the middle of the cave, "and the hankercher, and the knife and fork; and what be this?"

He took up a piece of paper and turned some coppers into his hand.

Then, rushing to the entrance, he read aloud:—

"'Tuppence for the plate, old cock; we don't prig earthenware!'"

"It be boys," said the old man.

"Scarum boys," added Bill.

"They've turned the puddin' out."

"And have stole away to eat it, feyther."

"Ye be right, Bill. Dang it! I should like to come across 'em now. D'ye see 'em about?"

"There be some comin' out the Chyne."

"Call arter 'em, Bill."

"Ahoy! there, my lads—ahoy!" bellowed Bill.

"Do they hear thee, Bill?"

"Ay, and see me, too, feyther. One ha' put his hand ag'in his nose, and they've all runned away, feyther."

"Dang 'em! that be Scarum cheek. Hoist all sail, and be arter 'em, Bill."

CHAPTER XLV.

GRIDDLE MAKES ANOTHER WONDERFUL DISCOVERY.

FATHER and son ran after the delinquents, but it was a case of tortoises in chase of a number of hares too wary to sleep by the way.

The boys were also too cunning to make for Scarum School, but bolted straight into the country, and were soon lost in the fields.

Bill and his father were outpaced from the first—never got near enough to swear to any of the culprits, and, after ten minutes' hard running, gave up the chase.

"Let us go oop to school," suggested Bill.

"Na, na," returned the old man; "where be the good o' that? there be a soight o' boys there, and we can't ha' the lot whopped. Na na, Bill, we'll gi' 'em a turn one day."

These two seafaring men were the proprietors of a small pleasure yacht, the one they landed from, and made a very respectable income during the summer months by taking out excursionists and pleasure parties. In the winter they did a little fishing among the more regular fishermen, to whom they were known as Old Bill and Young Bill.

How these two gentlemen were finally avenged will shortly appear.

For the present, we leave them to recover their breath, and utter seafaring anathemas upon all schools, and Scarum School in particular.

Now, we are not going to defend the consumers of the beef-steak pudding.

From a strictly moral point of view, Charley and his companions had *stolen* it—nasty words, but, nevertheless, true; and had they reasoned over the matter, they would probably have felt very much ashamed of themselves.

But boys never did and never will reason; there is too much of the clown in their nature; they must have a feast of larking occasionally—although that larking, like the clown's, often takes a serious turn—or they would die.

"I don't think they recognized us," said Charley, as they pulled up.

"Not a bit of it," rejoined Harry Leicester. "Who's got the plate?"

Grimmer brought it forth from under his waistcoat, and held it aloft in triumph.

"It's ours," said Charley; "we paid for it, and I propose it be kept in memory of this day."

"Oh, bosh!" cried Bob Martin; "put it on a post, and have a shy at it."

This proposition met with general favour, and Old Bill's willow-pattern plate was put upon a post, from whence it was presently dislodged in a hundred pieces, and left in ruin to mingle with the dust.

The return to the school was made with as much caution as a party of Indians would exercise in a country swarming with enemies, Bob going forward as scout, examining every place likely to afford the enemy concealment; but neither Old Bill nor Young Bill wo visible, and they reached home without any mishap.

Griddle, as usual, let them in, his visage expressing more than the customary amount of distrust.

"Don't you feel any better?" Charley asked—not that he had heard of Griddle suffering from any indisposition, but because it was the best form of inquiry he could use.

"Go in," growled Griddle; "why don't you let me alone? I lets you alone."

"Who found the ghost?" cried Bob.

And a general laugh followed.

"You're a wicious lot," returned Griddle; "get out of the lodge."

"I say," said Harry Leicester, sniffing the air suspiciously, "here's a private still here; don't you smell rum, boys? Mind the exciseman, Griddle."

"If I smell it again," said Mat Langley, "I'll fine Griddle five bob on suspicion!"

"Will you go out?" asked Griddle, gulping down his passion; "how am I to do my work with a lot o' himps like you here? There ain't many men as would stand it for six bob a week and their board."

"I could get two beadles for that," said somebody from behind.

"Eh?—what? Who said anything about beadles?" cried Griddle, turning savagely in the direction of the speaker. "If anybody says *I've* been a beadle, why don't he come forward and do it; don't sneak behind there."

"I'm not sneaking," said the accusator, a boy known as Lively Benson; "you were a beadle in the parish of Upton-cum-Bawdor, and you got the sack for taking a bribe from a man who stole the parson's goose."

"Of—all—the—" Griddle began.

"It's no use your denying it," rejoined Benson; "I thought I knew you from the first, but I only recognized you a minute ago. Do you remember being whopped by the organ-grinder?"

"I don't remember no whoppings," returned Griddle, with dignity.

"No, I suppose not," continued Benson, to the overwhelming delight of his audience; "and you've forgotten the time when you got drunk on the Queen's birthday, and the tramps stole your staff and cocked hat?"

"Them's libels!" said the goaded Griddle, "and if I knows anything o' law, I'll bring a haction against your father, and get damages out of him."

"*You* know anything of law!" rejoined Benson, contemptuously; "who charged the man with bigamy when he stole a turnip?"

This last query was too much for Griddle. Seizing the poker, he charged upon the foe, and our friends, finding he was in earnest, prudently retreated into the playground,

leaving the insulted porter in a state of mind which can be much better imagined than described.

By this stroke of work, Lively Benson, hitherto one of the outsiders of the school, arose to distinction and became a hero. He was at once admitted into Bob Martin's "set," whom he delighted with a sketch of Griddle's career.

"My home," he said, "is within two miles of Upton-cum-Bawdor, and until the last two years I went to a private school close to the village. Griddle was the beadle, and a precious beadle into the bargain—a swipy, good-for-nothing old file, who, if he had done his duty, would have locked himself up for being drunk and disorderly at least three times a week."

This, and much more, at present foreign to our story, told he them, and gladdened indeed were their youthful hearts to have heard something wherewith to drive the unfortunate Griddle to distraction.

As the porter, an hour later, crossed the ground, they were ready for him. From under his jacket, Bob Martin produced a paper imitation of a beadle's hat and a stout staff, and there and then arrested Charley in true beadle fashion.

The sight was too much for Griddle; it called up painful memories of the past, and he fled.

"I'm a wictim o' circumstantials," he muttered, as soon as he was alone; "there won't be a moment's peace for me from this blessed hour. Or'nary life is a wale o' tears—mine's a wale o' wiciousness."

The feud between him and the boys waxed warmer from that hour. We forbear to name the number of cocked hats which suddenly cropped up like mushrooms in the school, for fear we should be suspected of exaggeration, but Griddle frequently saw as many as twelve or fourteen at a time round his lodge, which was now known as the round-house; and the number of prisoners brought to him for incarceration increased like the nails in the horse's shoes of the famous sum.

But more of this anon. Let us go back to the eve of the day when the boys of Scarum School partook of their ill-gotten gains, the rump-steak pudding of Old Bill and his son, in the Chyne.

A little event occurred which caused the disgrace of Mr. Jonas Tidd, and, although he was not dismissed there and then, his going was only a question of time.

Mr. Crammer, strolling about the house just before dusk, became aware of unwonted sounds—stamping, bawling, and falling—in the vicinity of the schoolroom.

He could understand noises there, the boys

never would be quiet, but this was something out of the usual way.

He walked slowly to the door and listened. Mr. Jonas Tidd was speaking in a loud and angry voice.

"Hence! wilt thou lift up Olympus?"

Then Bob Martin said something which he could not hear, and Mr. Tidd spoke again—

"Doth not Brutus bootless kneel?"

And then came the sound of a heavy fall.

Mr. Crammer, who had been joined by the head usher and Griddle, opened the door and rushed into the room.

The first thing he beheld was a confused mass of white heaving about the floor, which finally resolved itself into the forms of Mr. Jonas Tidd, Bob, Charley, and a few others, wrapped in linen, and apparently going through a deadly struggle.

"Mr. Tidd, sir!" thundered the master; "what tomfoolery is this?"

According to the play, Mr. Tidd, who was enacting Julius Cæsar, ought to have breathed his last, and lain still, weltering in his gore; but at the unexpected summons he cast off the conspirators, and sprang to his feet very much alive and kicking.

He made a pretty picture, so did the other actors, who, with sheets wrapped about them, and their faces very red, looked like ghosts suddenly smitten with apoplexy.

"Mr. Tidd, sir, will you have the kindness to explain?"

"My—y—eleco—cutionary class, sir," stammered the wretched actor. "I was playing Julius Cæsar—and these young gentlemen are the conspirators."

"What sheets are those?"

Mr. Tidd's eyes showed a tendency to start from his head, but he managed to reply—

"They were—were ta—taken from the beds, for a few moments, sir."

"You are a mountebank," thundered Mr. Crammer; "let there be an end to these scenes from this hour!"

And he stalked from the room, leaving Julius Cæsar, Brutus, Cassius, and all the other Romans very limp indeed.

"Just my luck!" muttered Mr. Tidd. "Martin, take these sheets back, and replace them."

"Can't I help ye, sir?" asked Griddle, who had remained behind, grinning.

Mr. Tidd looked at him for a moment, as if meditating what form of reply to give; suddenly, he laid hold of Griddle's nose, and twisted it in a wild and frenzied manner.

"There, knave!" he cried, letting him go; "and dare to be impertinent again, and I will wring it off."

Griddle made no reply, but retreated from the room with a sensation of suffering from a frost-bite about the nose, and it was only

when the blood came rushing back, accompanied with a severe pain, that he felt certain that the organ for smelling was safe.

CHAPTER XLVI.

TIM'S RETURN.—THE FEAST.

TELEGRAM from Timothy Turndown, London, to Charles Thorn, Scarum School, Winkle-by-the-Sea.

"All settled, coming down to-morrow (Saturday) by early train; be in at two o'clock."

"Hurrah!" cried Charley, waving the telegram aloft. "The very day and the very hour. Bob, purchase the prog for the feed in the smugglers' cave."

"I must send Dick for it."

"Can you trust him?"

"I think so; he seems to be turning out a decent sort of fellow, and he hates Griddle like smoke."

"That's enough. Have you made out the list?"

"Yes—here you have 'em : two large pork pies, from the ham-and-beef shop, five shillings' worth of tarts, two bottles of Cape sherry wine, four pints of Barcelona nuts, three shillings' worth of apples, and a pound of bull's-eyes."

"That's a good list."

"I should think so," rejoined the other, complacently, "there's enough to feed all who like to come."

"I should think so."

Dick was summoned to a secret council, and entrusted with the money for the things required, not forgetting the materials for the torches to light up the festive chamber.

"A little rope and a pound of tar is all we want," said Charley, "and those Dick had better hide somewhere outside."

"I'll hide 'em down by the notice board about bathing," said Dick.

"Do—the very place—and mark the spot with a circle of stones."

"A circle," rejoined Dick, scratching his head. "Be that square or round?"

"Round, you booby!" returned Charley, laughing.

It was Friday evening when these arrangements were made, and before they went to bed the eatables were under lock and key in the bedroom, and Dick announced that the materials for torches were stowed away as desired.

Then the talk of excitement set in.

There is not much in the prospect of such an affair, some will say, but novelty is everything to boys pent up in a boarding-school; and in the prospect of a feast in a real cave, where smugglers stowed away their contraband articles, there was novelty indeed.

Saturday was always a light day at Scarum school; studies were always over and dinner ready by twelve o'clock, to give the lads as much time as possible to themselves.

There is one thing which men, especially schoolmasters, will always declare to be unfailing, and that is a boy's appetite; but on the Saturday in question not half the lads made even a semblance of a dinner.

Some ate heartily; but these were the few who were either unable or unwilling to attend the cave feast.

The others ate scarcely anything at all.

"They don't look ill," thought Mr. Crammer; "and the food is as good as usual. Some freak, I suppose. A hamper arrived, or something of that sort."

But he was wrong, as our readers know full well.

As soon as the grace after meat was said, away scampered Charley, Bob, Harry, and half a dozen more, to the bedroom, where they secured the eatables and drinkables about them, and hastened towards the smugglers' cave.

Then the food was stowed away, and some of the willing assistants despatched by Bob for the rope and tar.

"Now, you fellows, get to work," said Bob, selecting half a dozen from the group. "All you have to do is, to cut off the rope about a foot long, dip it into the tar, and hang it up in the sun. I say, Lobby, you can dip them."

"I shall mess my clothes," rejoined Panks.

"You can either dip the ropes," returned Bob, "or have your head stuck in the pot."

This decided the question at once.

Lobby took off his jacket, and prepared for work.

"Keep at it," said Charley. "Harry Leicester will show you exactly what to do, and where to place the things. Bob and I are going to meet Tim. He comes from Harling station by the coach."

Leaving the workers, busy as bees, under the care of Harry Leicester, Charley and Bob sauntered off, arm in arm.

Tim was pretty sure to be punctual; for the ride by coach was a very short one, the rail passing through Harling, a few miles away; and a branch to run down to Winkle-by-the-Sea was in the course of construction.

They went into the town to the inn where the coach stopped, and were, after the manner of boys, half an hour before time, which they whiled away by watching the market people passing to and fro.

Shortly after two o'clock the coach, with a vast amount of horn-blowing, dashed up, with half a dozen passengers on the roof, with Tim such a swell, although he was dressed in black, that at first they didn't know him.

But they knew his voice, as he gave them a hearty hail; and, without waiting for the ladder, he dropped upon the ground, and embraced them cordially.

"How are they all?" was his first eager inquiry.

"Jolly!" said Charley; "and all anxious to see you, even your old enemy, Lobby Panks."

"Poor old Lobby! I shall take the shine out of 'em now," said Tim. "How's Crammer?"

"Much the same."

"He will draw it mild with 'Tickler' now, I bet," rejoined Tim; "and Mr. Tidd?"

"Fairish; but he got into a mess through being caught dying."

"Dying?"

"Yes, as Julius Cæsar. I had just stabbed him with the ruler, when Mr. Crammer showed up, and pitched into him strong."

"Tidd's an unlucky fellow," said Tim. "But what are you going to do with yourself to-day?"

"We thought of being on the beach," replied Charley, evasively.

The feast in store was a secret.

"Won't you have a tart or two?" asked Tim, jingling some money in his pockets, and grinning furiously.

"Not now," replied Charley, hurriedly; "I had such a heavy dinner. But do come down to the beach; the fellows want to see you. And we can come into the town by-and-by."

"Wait until I've seen after my traps," returned Tim, who spoke and looked amazingly like a man of property; "hoi! there —master!"

"Yes, sir."

"Will you send that black box and carpet-bag on to Scarum School?"

"All right, your honour," replied the man.

"And here, ostler, is a shilling for yourself."

"Thanky, sir."

"I like to treat those fellows liberally," said Tim, with an offhand air, as if he had been accustomed to piling silver upon ostlers from time immemorial; "they expect it of men in my position!"

"I say, Tim," said Charley, looking at his friend up and down; "you've got some tidy toggery here."

"Made in town," replied Tim; "those I had here were decent, but too provincial."

"Ha! ha!" roared Charley; "bravo, Tim; you are quite a man of fashion!"

"But they are bung up, ain't they?" rejoined Tim, resuming his old style; "lor'! wait until you see what I've got in my box —if that fellow loses it, I will murder him!"

"You've grown a bloodthirsty swell," put in Bob Martin.

"Have I ?" rejoined Tim ; "and why should I not, if I choose ? Isn't that Mat Langley on the cliff ?"

"Yes."

"What has he run away for ?"

"Perhaps he didn't see us."

"But he did—I am certain of it."

"Then he has gone to tell the fellows on the beach that you are coming."

"How many are there ?"

"Most of them."

Tim's heart beat fast, and his eyes filled ; he began to see that a more than usually cordial reception was in store for him, and being, as we have said, a tender-hearted little fellow, he was touched.

But a terrible momentary disappointment was in store for him. When he reached the edge of the cliff and looked over, there was nobody to be seen.

"Why, they have all gone !" he exclaimed, with a blank face.

"Hiding up, for a lark," suggested Charley.

"I'll tell you where they are gone," rejoined Bob, as if he had made a sudden and wonderful discovery ; "we shall find them in the smugglers' cave !"

"Hiding up to rush out upon us," added Charley ; "come on, Tim."

Tim would rather have met them at once, he could not understand their running away ; but he followed his friends down the slanting steps to the entrance of the cave.

"There's a light inside," said Charley ; "I think they must have made another fire."

He entered, followed by Bob and Tim, and then there burst upon them a scene which a newspaper reporter would have called of " wild-weird beauty."

Around the cave were about a score of torches, blazing away merrily, and lighting up every rent and projection of the old cave ; the drops of water draining from the land above shone like diamonds, and lent a fresh charm to the scene, but what Tim liked best, and remembered long, was the sudden rush of about thirty of his schoolmates, who, headed by Harry Leicester, bore down upon him with a ringing cheer.

Then ensued a vast deal of hand-shaking, and heartfelt congratulations such as only the young can give ; then came the crowning point.

The boys divided, and there, spread upon the ground, was the feast, which seemed fit for a king ; at least, so thought many of the Scarum boys.

A few newspapers formed a cloth ; sheets of writing paper, ornamented at the edges, served the purpose of dishes ; then came the pork pies, the tarts, the wine, the nuts, and the dry sandy ground to sit upon.

It was delicious—enchanting.

"Well, upon my word," said Tim, as soon as he could speak, "this is kind of you fellows. I shan't forget it."

"Sit down, boys," shouted Bob Martin ; "you have your places. Tim, you on my right-hand here. Charley on the left Mat, you take the foot, and I say, Harry, make yourself useful and cut up the pork pies."

CHAPTER XLVII.
THE SKELETONS AT THE FEAST.

HARRY LEICESTER took out his pocket-knife in compliance with the request, and was about to plunge it into the tempting dish, when a stentorian voice broke in—

"Hold off !—easy, youngster !"

The boys were silent in a moment, and looking up beheld three tall, powerful men hanging over them. The first impression was, that the ghosts of three departed smugglers had arisen to resent the insult of an intrusion upon their particular ground. Acting upon this idea, Lobby Panks fell upon the flat of his face among the guests, and begged to be forgiven ; but all thoughts of the supernatural were quickly dispelled.

One of the men, the foremost and eldest, took from his jacket pocket a stout piece of rope, with several knots at one end. He held it before Charley, who happened to be the nearest to him, and asked him "if he saw it ?"

"I do," replied Charley, now beginning to have a shrewd suspicion of the identity of the visitors.

"You know what it is, young un ?"

"A rope's end."

"Thee be right—bean't he, Jack ?"

One of the other men answered with a grin which would have done credit to a tortured chimpanzee.

"Now, I daresay you want to know who I am," continued the speaker, addressing the petrified boys. "Well, I'll tell ye. I am Old Bill, and this chap is a son o' mine, Young Bill—t'other's a friend of ours, and we've brought him to dinner. I hope thee has got summat nice, for my mate be a dainty chap. What's this—poork pie. Dost 'ee loike poor pie, Jack ?"

"I du !" answered Jack, readily.

"And thee, Bill ?"

"I du, feyther !"

Then Old Bill, with the rope's end in one hand and a knife in the other, removed the pie on the point of the latter.

"Take it, and sit thee down by the mouth," said Old Bill ; "and if any on 'em tries to cut lay into 'em."

Young Bill and his friend Jack then took up a position of 'vantage at the mouth of the cave, which we have already described as being very narrow; and Old Bill seated himself opposite the second pie, which he fell upon forthwith, and all this amidst the silence of the boys. Lobby Panks, who had arisen from the rest, staring at the unexpected guests, completely overcome.

Bob Martin was the first to recover and break the silence.

"I say, old man," he cried, "you let that pie alone."

"It be too good to leave alone," answered Old Bill, with his mouth full.

"But who are you? Haw dare you rob us of our food?"

"Young gentleman," rejoined Old Bill, bolting about four square inches of solid crust to make room for oratory, "I'm one of them as gives and takes. *If anybody prigs my dinner*, I don't object—*if I prigs theirn*, don't let 'em say nowt."

"But what do you mean?" asked Bob, looking as guilty as possible, while many of the others hung their heads.

"Do you ax me?" demanded Old Bill, looking around; "do you ax me, you Scarum boys, wot I means by comin' 'ere?"

"We do," said Bob, faintly making a last stand.

"Then I'll tell you," returned Old Bill, finishing off the remnant of the pork pie with wondrous ease. "T'other day I comed heer arter my dinner—that I couldn't find—I comed again to-day and I've dropped on it."

"Oh!" was all Bob could say, and the rest looked very blank indeed.

Tim alone was in ignorance respecting the tarts, but he saw that Old Bill had some ground for the deed he committed, and held his peace.

"Leave them tarts alone, young un," roared the old man, addressing Harry Leicester, who had made up his mind to begin with a raspberry puff; "you don't touch nothin' 'ere until I tell you, unless you wants the rope. Have a tart, Bill?"

"Yes, feyther."

"Come and take 'um, then; these light things ain't much, have hef a dozen—will ye try a few, Jack?"

Jack didn't mind if he did, and he and Young Bill swallowed nine each, one after the other, as if they were taking pills or oysters.

"I never takes *all* a man's grub," said Old Bill, rising, "so I'll leave you summat. I don't know as I wants anything else, unless it's a few nuts, for I do like nuts. Have any, Bill?"

"Yes, feyther."

"Then take 'um, lad."

Old and Young Bill then stowed away about a pint of nuts each in their pockets, and Jack, who had no fancy for nuts, contented himself with a dozen or so of apples. Thus supplied they calmly sauntered out and disappeared.

A blank silence ensued.

"A queer man!" said Harry Leicester, at length.

"Upon my word," cried Bob, "it was too bad!"

"And so were we too bad the other day," interposed Charley; "when we prigged *his* dinner we polished off the lot. I recognized him at once, and saw he meant mischief; he might have made matters worse, he has left us something."

"But did you ever see such a mouth for tarts as that Young Bill has?" said Harry, ruefully; "they went down like wafers."

"But what matters?" cried Bob, suddenly cheering up, "there's enough left for something all round, and he did not notice the wine."

Before you uncork it let me have a look out," said Charley.

He went cautiously to the mouth of the cave, and peered out.

"All right," he cried, "they've just got their little craft afloat and are bending th sails. Ain't they laughing though!—I can see them here."

"Of course they are," grunted Bob; "come on, old fellow, or every scrap will be gone."

Charley returned to his seat; and the feast, despite the untoward arrivals, was a merry one, and after a glass of Cape sherry round, everybody laughed and declared that they were glad Old Bill had shown up, for it was the jolliest game out.

"It would have been the best joke in the world," said Harry Leicester, "if he had left only a scrap of the pork pie."

"So it would," said Tim; "and it's not bad as it is. You won't forget his beef-steak pudding in a hurry."

So altogether the little entertainment passed off very well, and long before the torches had burned out every scrap of the good things had disappeared, and the empty wine bottles "shied" at with stones and broken into innumerable fragments. Then the boys we forth and scattered towards the beach—but Charley, Bob, and Tim, who had secret arrangements to go into the town.

"It is Saturday," said Tim, "and we have some fun with the yokels."

"There are no yokels nowadays," a Charley; "every countryman knows as mu as a town-bred bird. They don't stand sky-larking as they used to."

"We can try it on," rejoined Bob, briefly.

Bob illustrated his meaning by "trying it on" with a very bucolic gentleman in top-boots, who was comparing his watch with a clock over a watchmaker's door.

Going up to him with a grave face, Bob asked—

"Please, sir, how's your chine?"

"My what?" cried the farmer, aghast.

"Please, sir, what's the time?"

"A quarter arter five, lad," replied the farmer. "Dang it! I understood thee summat else."

Bob moved off with an imperturbable face, with Charley and Tim in an explosive state.

"That's not a bad trick," said Tim; "I shall try it on myself."

"Don't be in a hurry," returned Bob; "wait until I've shown you the right party to work upon."

In about a quarter of an hour they came to the market-place, where Bob saw the same farmer contemplating some books in a stationer's window. He thought it was an excellent opportunity for a practical joke.

"There's your man," said he to Tim, pointing the farmer out. "Try the chine dodge with him."

Tim, who failed to recognize the former victim, went readily up.

"Please, sir, how's your chine?" he asked.

"What, another!" cried the farmer, seizing him by the collar. "I thought I warn't mistaken before."

What followed we need not record, beyond this, that Tim came out of the struggle very much flushed, leaving the bucolic gentleman standing on one leg and holding the shin of the other tightly between his hands—why, we don't pretend to say. Perhaps he was endeavouring to find out the state of his chine—or, stay, perhaps Tim, in the frenzy of the fight, had given a "shinner"—very likely he had.

"That was rather too bad of you, Bob," said Tim, shaking his head.

"But who would have thought of you being taken in?" laughed Bob.

"Well, I ought to have known better," was Tim's rejoinder. "My eye! he's got a heavy hand."

"He's holding his leg still," said Charley, looking back.

"So would you if you were him," replied Tim, quietly.

"Oh! you don't do the trick right," said Bob, laughing. "Look here."

He walked straight up to a policeman, and staring at him, said coolly—

"You're a block."

"Be off," said the man, waving his hand.

"What's o'clock?" Bob asked.

The policeman looked at him steadily for a few seconds, but Bob never moved a muscle. The man was puzzled, but he thought he might have been mistaken.

"There's the town-hall clock," said the man, pointing to it.

"Thank you," replied Bob, politely; "I am a stranger here, and didn't see it. Good day."

"Good day, sir," returned the policeman; and Bob came away triumphant.

"Easy enough, you see," he said, with the easy air of one well versed in a mystic art.

"Yes, when you are not put on to the party who has been sold before," grumbled Tim, who could not quite forget his struggle with the gentleman of the agricultural interest.

It was pleasant work sauntering about in the cool of an early summer's day, and although the place was small, there was a good deal to see. The shops were decked in their best, and a good many strangers, bent on enjoying themselves, were about. Charley and Bob chattered like a couple of magpies, but Tim gradually became thoughtful and silent.

"What's the matter with you, Tim?" asked Charley, after a long silence on the part of his old chum.

"I've been thinking, Charley, that now I am rich I ought to do as other rich fellows do."

"So you can, can't you?"

"Yes, yes," replied Tim, slowly; "but there are some things which require a little consideration. Charley, don't you think I ought to *smoke*?"

A burst of laughter followed the question from both Charley and Bob.

"Smoke!" cried the former—"what next, old Tim? Wouldn't you like to drink gin, and stop your growth altogether?"

"But does smoking stop it?"

"Rather! My father says that the nicotine is poisonous to young flesh and blood."

"Still, Charley, I should like to try one cigar."

"Don't think of it, old fellow."

"I think I must, Charley; it is the aristocratic thing to do."

"Let him have one," whispered Bob, "on the heath—I don't think he will want another."

"*One* cigar," said Tim, thoughtfully, "can't hurt anybody."

"All right—try it."

Tim waited for no further encouragement, but entered a cigar shop, and put down a shilling upon the counter.

"A cigar, if you please."

"What sort—Cuba, Havannah, Henry Clay, or Pickwick?"

"One of your best."

"Mild, medium, or full?"

Tim was puzzled, but he answered, "Full," and received an ill-looking bundle of something supposed to be tobacco, and eightpence out of his shilling.

"I must have some lights," he said, remembering that essential to smoking.

A box was given him, for which he paid a penny, and now fully armed for the contest, he sallied out, and went towards the heath with his friends.

"I'll give you a last piece of advice," said Charley, who had great difficulty in repressing his merriment—"don't do it, Tim."

"I tell you it is all right," returned Tim; "a fellow with money ought to be able to do everything."

After this, no more was said, and Tim, sitting down on the grass, prepared for the important operation, Charley and Bob lying near, keenly interested in his every movement.

"I wonder which end you begin with," said Tim, looking at the ill-conditioned weed; "do you know, Charley?"

"You smoke with the pointed end," said Charley.

"Oh, that's it; but it won't draw."

"Bite the end off, stupid!" grinned Bob.

Tim bit the end off, and spat it out with a wry face.

"What a beastly taste!" he said; "if it smokes like that I'll soon turn it up."

After a moment's delay, Tim struck a match and went resolutely to work.

"How is it?" asked Charley.

"Prime!" replied Tim, sending out a volume of smoke; "there's nothing to be afraid of."

"Does it taste bitter?"

"No—sweet as a nut!"

"I think I should like to have a try," said Charley.

"Wait a minute," rejoined Bob, quietly; "see a little more of Tim."

"I had no idea smoking was so pleasant," said Tim, after a pause. "I wish I had brought you fellows a weed apiece."

"You are smoking rather fast," hinted Bob.

"It's jolly!" was Tim's rejoinder, as he smoked on faster than ever.

But the end was approaching.

The roseate hue of Tim's countenance suddenly died away; he fell back, and the cigar dropped from his fingers.

"Ill, old chap?" inquired Bob, bending over him.

"I don't know," gasped Tim, feebly; "I've turned so precious cold; and you—you are standing on your head, Bob."

"Nonsense; I'm on my feet."

"Is it Charley, then?"

"No—here I am," answered our hero.

"I can't understand it," muttered Tim, closing his eyes; "everything is going round and round."

"Finish your cigar," suggested Bob, rather maliciously.

"Ugh!" muttered Tim, staggering to his feet; "don't help me; let me alone."

They would have helped him, but he waved them off, and retired behind a clump of furze, from whence he presently emerged with a countenance ghastly white.

"I'm better now," he said, screwing up smile.

"And who would think," said Bob, thoughtfully handling the stump of the cigar, "that a little thing like this could cause such a change in a fellow?"

"Throw it away, Bob," gasped Tim, turning his head aside. "It must have been a very bad one!"

"It has taught you a lesson, Tim," said Charley. "When will you try another?"

"Never again," replied Tim, fervently; "but what a beast it was! You wouldn't credit the feeling, Charley—that you would not."

CHAPTER XLVIII.
TIM SCATTERS HONOURS AND REWARDS.

HALF an hour's walk restored Tim to something like his old self; and then, as the evening was drawing on, they returned to the school.

Griddle, who had heard of Tim's good fortune a few days before, was a changed man, for to him Tim was no longer "p'ison," but milk and honey.

"Lor', Master Turndown," he began as he opened the door, "it's quite a pleasure to see your cheerful face again. Only this werry mornin' I ses to myself, I ses—'The school ain't like the same place since he went; but thank goodness, he's comin' back to-day!' And here you are, the werry picter of 'elth and happiness!"

To which Tim only responded, "Shut up!" But once Griddle was set going, it was no easy matter to stop him.

"And won't Mr. Crammer be glad to see you," he went on; "and Mr. Peddleum, and Mr. Tidd; and Master Todman is comin' back to-night, so you will all be together agen in the old friendly way; and it's to be hoped that you won't forget them as stood by you, and cut 'em now you is rich."

"Did you stand by me?" demanded Tim.

"I did the best of my 'umble endeavours," replied Griddle, coughing gently behind his hand.

"Have you found the ghost yet?"

"The ghost," returned Griddle, "is still afloat and free, and fur be it from me to spy upon young gents, and spile a lark. What I ses is this, to you young genelmen—'Go it—have two ghosts—three if you like; I don't care—it don't matter to me.'"

"Thank you," said Bob Martin; "one is as much as we care about."

"It ain't badly done, I must say," rejoined Griddle.

"It's too well done," said Charley, gravely.

"You don't mean to tell me it's serus?"

"As ever ghost was on earth; we know nothing about it."

"Honour bright?"

"Upon our words, Griddle."

There was no doubt about the truth of the speakers; even Griddle could not do otherwise than place implicit faith in the denial.

"We pass a dreadful time of it," pursued Charley; "our dormitory is haunted every night."

"If I could only believe it was a real ghost," said Griddle, turning pale, "I'd give warning this very night."

"It's a true spirit," said Charley; "there is no gammon about it."

They left Griddle in a terrible frame of mind, for the conviction of the ghost's reality, which had gradually been dawning upon him, received confirmation that eve.

Later in the evening, when Tim's box arrived, he distributed a number of presents, principally books, and little knick-knacks, among his old friends; and he quite won the heart of Lobby Panks by the presentation of a knife with five blades, a file, a corkscrew, and a toothpick.

"Nothing like burying the hatchet," said Tim. "Lobby—your fist."

They shook hands warmly, and the tears came into Lobby's eyes.

He was touched to the heart.

The conduct of Lively Benson was named also, and for him Tim found a box of colours, which he had intended for Grimmer, but as Grimmer preferred a volume of "Arabian Nights," the colours fell to Benson's lot.

This generous conduct of Tim raised him immensely in the opinion of the boys, and he was then and for a long time after undoubtedly the most popular pupil of Scarum School—so high had riches and a liberal heart raised him up.

But Tim had other objects in his mind beyond his own immediate popularity; he had other scores to settle than those he had paid, and one was due to the son of Mike, the fighting sweep.

"Charley," he said, "I am going into regular training. You see I am not so stout as I was."

"Nothing like, old boy."

"That is the result of dumb-bells before breakfast. I shall go in for long walks and the horizontal bar. A doctor in London told me I had immense bones, and ought to make a strong fellow."

"I don't see why you should not, Tim."

"I'll have a go at it—plain living, good exercise, and in a month I'll knock that sweep out of time."

"You hav'n't forgotten him, then?" said Charley, laughing.

"Forgotten him—no! I'll put something black about him which won't come off."

"At all events, try, Tim, and I'll back you to do it. Here comes Mr. Tidd."

The usher, who had been out for the afternoon, now came in, and gave Tim a cordial welcome, which was fully responded to.

"Upon my word, Turndown," he said, "the improvement in you is wonderful. Money certainly works wonders."

"I shall be always glad to help a friend with it," hinted Tim.

"My dear boy," returned the usher, quickly, "don't be lavish with it. A too ready response to a beggar's cry helps to create a nation of paupers."

Tim felt that Mr. Tidd had divined his intention to help him; but Mr. Tidd was too proud in his way, had too much manly independence to accept help from a boy, although he was grateful to him for the implied offer.

Shortly after, Mr. Pendulum came in with his congratulations, and Mr. Cranmer followed with a warmth that was utterly confounding to Tim, who had not forgotten the days when "Tickler" was always ready upon so short a notice.

CHAPTER XLIX.

SQUARING ACCOUNTS.

IT was a bright afternoon, and the sun shed its genial rays upon the suburbs of Winkle-by-the-Sea—among others, upon the cottage of Mike, where his son, the pugilistic sweep, stood basking by the door.

The sooty youth was much given to sunshine and ease, when not up a chimney or in bed.

He was generally found--weather permitting, of course—in a reclining position in the sunlight, from which he had the very strongest objection to be aroused.

But it so chanced, upon this summer's day, that several noisy intruders, who would not be denied, trespassed on his peace.

The foremost was Tim, looking rather pale, but with a determined expression upon his face.

"Come out, smutty," he said.

The son of Mike turned slowly over, and eyed him lazily up and down.

"What do yer want?" he asked.

"To fight," replied Tim, firmly. "Come on."

In a moment the sweep was on his feet.

Next to the sunlight, fighting was his soul's delight.

"How many are there on yer?" he demanded.

"Five."

"I can't fight five."

"You are not wanted to. Fight me; that's all I want."

"You!" said the son of Mike, slowly; "ain't I fot you before? I think I have."

Tim made no reply.

The sooty one scratched his head, puzzled.

"I *know* we've had a touzzle," he muttered, "but when or where I can't tell."

"Get your backers," rejoined Tim, "and meet us on the green."

He then departed, with Charley, Bob Martin, Harry Leicester, and Mat Langley, who had come to "see him through it," and took up a position on the grass plot where the previous battle had been fought.

The son of Mike was not long behind him.

In ten minutes he appeared, with half a dozen louts at his heels, all bloodthirsty and hungry for the fray.

Without exchanging any of the courtesies usual to gentlemen who meet to settle difficulties, Tim and his antagonist stripped, the sweep still very much puzzled, and evidently trying to call to mind where he had seen our friend before.

"He's one of the Scarum chaps," he thought, "and I've fot a good many of 'em one time and t'other; but *which* is he?"

It was not the intention of either Tim or his friends to enlighten him, and they did not.

Tim, as soon as he was ready, stood forward in a position which showed how much he had improved by training.

The sooty one, with a heavy doubt operating in his mind, was not so active; but he advanced at last, and the fight began.

Both Charley and Bob had advised Tim to open the ball in a cautious manner; but he was so eager to avenge his former defeat, that he rashly rushed in, and received a stinger on his nose, which sent him to grass, and credited the son of Mike with "first blood."

"Tim, Tim," urged Charley, "this is not the way to begin. You'll be knocked out of time in a twinkling."

"Fence round him," said Bob. "The fellow can't stand sparring. He's a slogger; and unless he can go at it hammer and tongs, he's nowhere."

Leicester and Langley looked very glum; and they eyed the exultant yokels as if they would have liked to have had one go at them.

Tim was soon again upon his legs, and answered to the call of time a little sobered, but as determined as ever.

The sweep, fully assured of any easy victory, began the second round playfully.

First he dodged about a little, to sho. skill; then he feinted, and ducked.

But that moment was fatal to him.

Tim rushed in, and had him in Chance

A fierce, quick struggle, with a shower o blows from Tim, who showed wondrous acti vity, and the son of Mike, with a gory face and blinking eyes, rolled upon the ground.

The yokels came gloomily forward, and raised him up; and Tim walked proudly to his second's knee.

"Good!" whispered Charley, exultingly. "Not an ounce thrown away. You pounded him, Tim."

"I've cut my knuckles against his teeth," said Tim.

"Oh, bother your knuckles! A penn'orth of ointment will put them right."

"Time," cried Bob.

"It bean't up yet," roared one of the yokels, who was wiping the sweep's face with a bunch of grass.

"Time," repeated Bob, firmly. "Put your man up, or say he's licked."

"I ain't licked," bellowed the son of Mike, leaping to his feet. "Come on."

He looked ferocious, and his intentions were murderous.

Woe to Tim if he gets him in his power!

"Caution," said Bob, as a parting injunction. "Keep well away until he forgets himself."

This was a very difficult matter; for Tim's opponent, regardless of a storm of blows, was resolved to close.

But here, again, Tim strove wondrously, and displayed an agility hitherto foreign to his nature.

The son of Mike lunged and tore about until he was fairly tired out; then Tim permitted him to close.

Another struggle, and then, with a gasping sob—something between a cry of rage and a groan—the sooty one was down again.

Great was the exultation in Tim's corner, and deep the depression among the yokels—the latter but too plainly saw their champion on the eve of defeat; but they wiped his face, patted his back, gave him words of encouragement, and bade him "go in!"

"I'm fogged about him," gasped Mike's son; "I don't know him, and yet I've fot him before—that's the thing as is lickin me."

"Don't think on it," rejoined one of hi backers, "but give it to un hot!"

Excellent advice, easy to give, but hard to carry out; the sweep was fast caving in under the heavy punishment; Tim was rising under the exhilaration of imminent victory.

Another round—wildly fought on the part of the sweep, quietly but effectively on the

of Tim, who gave blows well planted in
:s where his hands had been before, and
:ooty son of Mike staggered under the
:iiction.

"I'm done!" he gasped, as his yokel
friends helped him off the field; "I can't
see, and there's a singing in my head."

"Another round," advised one.

"No; I've lost all my strength; I'm
licked!"

"Time!" roared Bob, and the yokel threw
up the bunch of grass in token of defeat.

Tim hastily donned his waistcoat and
jacket, and crossed over to his opponent,
who glared at him with half an eye—all he
had available in the optical line for the
purpose.

"We've squared accounts, now," said Tim.

"Who be ye?" muttered the sweep.

"Tim Turndown, of Scarum School."

"I don't know 'ee by that name."

"I used to wear a skeleton suit."

"Don't tell me," cried Mike's offspring,
rising a little with a struggle, "that you be
the fat chap!"

"I am," returned Tim, "brought down
by training."

"Licked by *him!*" growled the son of
Mike, in a tone of the bitterest anguish, and
fainted clean away.

It was on a Wednesday afternoon when
this encounter took place—an afternoon long
remembered in the school, and talked of as
the time when the bullying young sweep
turned over a new leaf, and fought no more
with the boys of Scarum School.

Tim and his enthusiastic supporters had a
little feast to celebrate the event, and a
bottle of ginger-wine was smuggled in and
drank that night in the dormitory, to the
health and prosperity of the genial victor.

Around the right eye of Tim a suspicious
ring arose, but his days of "Tickler" were
over. Mr. Crammer was blind to it, and the
ushers passed it by.

CHAPTER L.

COLD WATER CURE.

A DEADLY feud sprang up between Griddle
and Lively Benson.

Griddle could not and would not forgive
the revelation of his past life, whereby the
nakedness of his beadledom was laid bare before the school.

It gave rise to many practical jokes, very
harmless for the most part, but very exasperating to the object of these humorous displays
—anonymous letters, directed to "Griddle,
Esq.," came to Scarum School, and on being
opened in private by the recipient, were
found to contain nothing but scurrilous

verses and sketches, all bearing upon the
merits and demerits of a beadle's life—one in
particular, where he was depicted in the act
of arresting a child two years old for trespassing, especially raising his wrath.

The rhymes were very poor at the best,
but when a thing is purely personal, a little
ability goes a long way. There was one
commencing—

If I had a beadle what wouldn't go,
To take a dirty little tramp in tow,
I'd give him his pay and cry, " Now go
   To the School of Scarum."

This Griddle was half determined to show
Mr. Crammer, but remembering that his
past life was a veiled mystery to the schoolmaster, he prudently put it into the fire and
tried to forget it—but alas! the dart rankled
in his flesh, and others pierced him every
day.

"Who boiled the orphan?" Benson asked
him, one morning.

"What's that you say?" demanded Griddle

"Who prigged the cushion from the doctor's pew?" returned Benson, going on
another tack.

"I must put a stop to this," muttered
Griddle; "the character of no man ain't safe
among 'em. I'll speak to Mr. Crammer."

He accordingly intruded himself upon Mr.
Crammer, and said he had a complaint to
make.

"It seems that you have always a complaint to make," rejoined the schoolmaster
testily.

"I'm clean druv to it," pleaded Griddle
"afore I ventures to trouble you; but it's
the lies as worries me."

"What do you mean?"

"I'm accused of havin' fust murdered a
orphan, then b'iled him; then likewise with
havin' prigged——"

"Stolen, you intended to say?"

"Stolen, sir, the cushion of the doctor's
pew; and t'other day Master Martin said I
pawned a gallon of skilly—which your honour
knows is work'us porridge."

"I don't know anything of the sort, and it
seems to me that these are little stupid jokes
of the boys, unworthy of mention; don't
trouble me again with them."

Tortured and unable to obtain redress,
Griddle returned to his old habits, and the
lodge became once more aromatic with rum.
He no longer answered the taunts levelled at
him, but washed them down with insidious
liquor.

He waited at the dinner-table with a fixed
expression, his face indicative of inward
torture, unsatiated vengeance gleamed on the
very tip of his nose; and Bob Martin
reported that he had made a dummy boy
which he kept in the cupboard of his lodge,

"THEM WICIOUS VARMINTS HAVE MURDERED BILL."

and stabbed at stated intervals with a knife and fork.

"I think we had better leave him alone for a time," suggested Grimmer; "no knowing what a fellow like him might do when the worse for drink."

"I'm glad I always let him alone," said Lobby Panks.

"You are just the sort of boy," rejoined Charley, gravely, "whom he is likely to operate upon; he knows you wouldn't kick and struggle much, and it don't matter much who he kills so long as he kills somebody."

"I think I shall write home to my mother," groaned Panks; "there never was

such a dreadful place as this; only the other day, a man, whom I had never seen before, stopped me and said I had broken his window. I told him I had not, but he said, 'You come from Scarum School, and it was one of your lot, which is all the same to me,' and then knocked me about until I was giddy and sick."

"Why didn't you shin him?" said Tim, scornfully.

"He was such a big fellow," replied Panks, "and if I had he would have murdered me!"

"I wish he had," was all the consolation Tim vouchsafed to give.

10

The interrupted discussion about Griddle was resumed; some were for leaving him in peace, others were for carrying on the fun at any cost, and the argument was growing very warm when one of the boys came in, and reported that Griddle was at that moment in Mr. Crammer's private garden, seated among the flowers, singing a song.

This was enough, and a rush was made to the only point where the singer could be seen with advantage—a small room used occasionally for private studies.

Raising the sash cautiously, Charley peeped out, and at first thought that the bird had flown, but a voice immediately under the window undeceived him, and leaning over, he beheld the porter seated in the midst of a few choice plants, with his back to the wall.

He was murmuring to himself, but his voice gradually rising, his outpourings could be distinguished by his delighted audience.

"Why did I leave my native wale?" he cried, apostrophizing the air; "I were happy, nothin' to do but to walk about in uniform, and look in the wrong place for gipsies and tramps—ah! I knowed the wicious warmints. Catch me goin' among 'em!—not I—old Griddle warn't green enough for that; my pay warn't good enough for black eyes and bleedin' noses!"

"And yet," he added, after a pause, "there is wus things about than a beadle, and a beadle might do well if he didn't run up scores; mine, at the Fox and Goose," he added, "were three pun' ten and fourpence, and I never paid it—ha! ha! I never paid it!"

This idea seemed to tickle him immensely, and he chuckled over it for some time, and then he went upon another road.

"If them as I stood over once," he said, "could ha' seen me in another workus arter three months' tramp and livin' principally on turnips, how they would have rej'iced! but they never knowed, nobody; never knowed it—and nobody shan't know it. But it was werry 'ard, and their skilly was a long way behind the mark."

Then he grew mournful, and sobbed audibly, and after a time he sank gently to sleep, and snored fearfully.

"This is too good to lose," said Charley; 'we must wake him up a bit. Bob, fetch the watering-pot, it is kept in the outhouse, and fill it!"

Bob, delighted with his mission, hastened off, and speedily returned, with the green watering-can filled to the brim.

Charley held it over Griddle, and poured a little over his face. The porter opened his eyes, stared at the sky, muttered a curse upon the flies, and went to sleep again.

"It won't do, Griddle," said Charley, elevating the can; "we can't allow it!"

A copious shower rained down upon the head and face of Griddle, who woke again, sat for a moment like one dazed, then staggered to his feet a sobered man.

The watering-can was thrown into the garden, the window closed, and the operators fled.

"Ha! I don't want to look fur to know who did it," muttered Griddle, wiping his face; "confound 'em! they've taken all the starch out o' my handkercher, and my wesku. looks as if I'd tried to wash it. Ah! there goes the gate-bell—just my luck!—I wonder who it is?"

Hoping that it was nobody connected with the house, he went round the garden, and across the playground, making an effort to arrange his saturated apparel in something like presentable form; and, although he did his best, he looked no better than an intoxicated man in livery whom a kind friend had put under the pump.

To his horror, he found that Mr. Crammer and a gentlemanly-looking man about fifty were waiting for admittance. Mr. Crammer, as the door opened, was saying—

"You will find my establishment, sir, all you can possibly desire—airy, light, well-ventilated, plenty of sleeping room, an excellent diet, sober, well-conducted servants——"

Here his eye, and that of the gentleman also, fell upon Griddle, upon whom the rays of a setting sun shone, adding considerably to his disordered appearance, and showing him up in anything but a favourable light.

"Is that your servant?" asked the gentleman, distinctly.

"I regret to say he is," replied Mr Crammer, with much humility.

"I regret to hear it," rejoined the gentleman, gravely; "good evening, sir."

He turned loftily upon his heel and was gone, ere Mr. Crammer could recover from a state of angry astonishment.

The schoolmaster turned upon Griddle, who, not comprehending the scene, bowed and smiled feebly.

"You scoundrel!" cried he, shaking his fist at him, "you have lost me a pupil."

"How, sir? me, sir?"

"Yes! how came you in this disgraceful state?"

"Somebody chucked a pail o' water over me, sir—somebody as is given to wiciousness."

"Where were you?"

"In the garding, sir, sweepin' up the walk."

"Who was it?"

"I don't know, sir."

"You mean to tell me that it was possible for any one to—pooh! you are lying, you scoundrel."

"I wouldn't lie in your service, sir—I'm too dewoted."

"You have been drinking again."

"I've had nothin' but table-beer for a fortnight; which a barrel of it wouldn't hurt a babby."

This insult levelled at Mr. Crammer's extract from malt, combined with the disappointment he had received, was too much for the schoolmaster, and he knocked his devoted servitor down.

It was a fair blow, well delivered, and showed that once upon a time he had not been above a bout of fisticuffs. Having performed this feat, he left the lodge, and with an angry face hastened to the house, leaving Griddle on his back among the fire-irons.

"What's this?" he muttered, as soon as he was alone, "a blow! A beadle—dash it! no, a county magistrate, or wot is ekal to it—punched by a miserable schoolmaster! Where's the laws and pourwisions made for the purtection of its officers?" he added, sitting up. "A beadle struck—why, it's up to a revolution."

The door of the lodge opened, and Dick, the odd boy, entered.

"Now, Swipes," he said, "Mr. Crammer wants ye."

"You speakin' to me?" demanded Griddle, angrily.

"In course I was—come out of the fender, there, will you? I never did see sech a old man to roll about—allus in liquor—no wonder they wouldn't keep you for beadle!"

"Dick," said Griddle, huskily, "drop it."

"In all the faces of natur'," continued Dick, regardless of this exhortation, "I don't know a more painful pictur' than a buffy beadle."

"Dick," cried Griddle, rising in body and in wrath, "you'll wentur' too fur."

"I shan't never wentur' so fur as the workus, I hope," grinned Dick.

Griddle fell back with a frightened look upon his face, like one detected in a crime.

"What workus?" he asked.

"Any workus," replied Dick: "they're all alike; they keep a beadle to look arter you, and feed you on skilly, but some skilly's weaker than t'other."

What could the wretched Griddle say? The shafts struck home, but there was nothing he could seize hold of without exposing himself.

"Boys is boys," he murmured, "and their natur' is wenum. Dick," he added, with emotion, "may you never know the wicisitude hour of skilly. Tell Mr. Crammer I'll come directly."

Thoroughly satisfied with the assurance,

and certain of having obtained victory, Dick grinned again, and departed with the answer. Griddle followed shortly after, and had an interview with Mr. Crammer, in which he was, to use his own expressive language, "biled, skinned, and roasted, in a werbal manner," ending with an earnest assurance that, if he sinned again by an unwonted consumption of rum, he and Scarum School would part for ever.

"The slightest sign of intoxication in your eye or gait," said Mr. Crammer, "will be the signal for your instant departure."

The consequence was that Griddle, having the fear of this and another workhouse before him, went about with a sense upon him of his every movement being watched, and the position of his eyes and limbs a thing to be studied both hourly and daily.

CHAPTER LI.

THE TERRORS OF THE DEEP.

"I SAY," said Tim to Charley, "what a jolly day it is! How would you like a sail?"

"I don't care about sixpenny excursions," returned Charley. "I have a very vivid recollection of the last I indulged in; two-thirds of the people were ill."

"I don't mean that," said Tim. "Wouldn't it be stunning to have a boat all to ourselves, and sail out ten or twelve miles?"

"Glorious!" returned Charley; "but I can't manage a sailing boat; can you?"

"No," said Tim; "but then you know we can hire a man to look after the practical part of the business, while we enjoy ourselves."

"That would spoil the treat," said Charley. "I wonder if there is a fellow in our school who knows how to sail a boat properly?"

"I do."

It was the celebrated Lobby Panks who spoke, having strolled up and overheard the last of the conversation.

"You!" said Tim, grinning. "You! Well, I should like to place my life in your hands, certainly."

"All right," returned Lobby. "You needn't put yourself out of temper."

"Who taught you, Lobby?" asked Charley.

"My uncle in the country," was the reply. "He has a splendid yacht, and I lived on board nearly all last summer holidays."

"But you don't mean to tell me," said the dubious Tim, "that you could manage a yacht?"

"Of course not alone," replied Lobby; "but I could a small sailing boat, easily."

"Then we'll have a sail this afternoon, Lobby, if you'll come with us," said Tim;

"don't tell any one else, or it may get to the ears of old Griddle or Mr. Crammer."

"All right," returned Lobby. "What a jolly lark it will be! Hallo! there's the dinner bell, and I'm as hungry as a hunter. Come on, you fellows."

Justice having been done to the meal, and a few lessons yawned over, our three heroes were free, and lost no time in seeking the beach.

"I want a boat," said Lobby to a boatman, "for us three; not too small, you know, nor too large."

"Rowing boat, sir?"

"No—lug sail, and put a pair of sculls in case of accident."

"All right, sir."

In two minutes the boat was ready and launched, and Charley and Tim, under the protection of the celebrated Lobby, went on their wild career.

"We must use the sculls for a few minutes," said Lobby, who was tying himself up with the ropes at the bottom of the boat, in the attempt to arrange others. "You take one, Tim, and you the other, Charley."

This order from Captain Lobby Panks was promptly obeyed, and for a quarter of an hour all went on swimmingly, Lobby still struggling with the ropes and canvas.

"Now then, Lobby," exclaimed Tim, "how long are you going to be?"

"Don't flurry me," responded Lobby, "I'm getting everything ready. I shan't be a minute."

"The wind is rising," said Charley, "and we shall go along like one o'clock. Make haste."

The "lug" was at last hoisted, and the sculls laid aside.

A strong breeze, increasing every moment, was blowing, and the boat danced like a cork from wave to wave.

"How do you like this?" asked Lobby.

"Glorious!" said Tim, leaning back, and surveying Master Panks with admiration. "I'd give something to know as much about boating as you do."

"Well, you see," returned Lobby, proudly, "I've had great experience."

"So it seems," said Charley; "but does it not strike you that the wind and sea are rising very much? What's the matter, Lobby?"

"Good gracious!" exclaimed Tim, "why are you so pale?"

"Am I pale?" said Lobby, feebly.

"As white as a sheet," rejoined Charley; "if you are likely to be ill, we had better turn back."

"Ill!" cried Lobby, scornfully, the lustre of his eyes dimming every moment. "Who said I was going to be ill?"

"You look awfully queer," said Tim, "and I agree with Charley, that we had better turn back."

"Pooh!" said Lobby. "You're both af—af—oh!"

Lobby, ere he could finish the sentence, was fain to hold communion with the deep, and then sink, pale, ghastly, and helpless, from his seat to the bottom of the boat, where he lay with as much animation in him as is generally found in a log of wood.

"Here's a jolly mess!" said Tim. "Get up, Lobby."

Lobby's reply was a groan, and an intimation that he wished to quit this vale of tears, rather than suffer the agony he was enduring.

"But I say," cried Tim, giving the helpless sufferer rather a vicious dig in the ribs, "we don't know how to manage this confounded boat, not even how to get the sail down."

"Don't speak to me," moaned Lobby. "I'm dying."

"Nonsense!" said Charley, shaking him by the shoulder. "You're only sea-sick. Hold up, old boy, you'll be all right in a minute."

"How can I stand," gasped the unfortunate young mariner, "when the boat is upside down?"

"Charley," cried Tim, "leave Lobby alone a minute. Don't you hear a noise? It sounds like thunder."

"And thunder it is," said Charley, gravely; "we must get this sail down by some means. There's a knot between the pulley and the mast. Have you a knife, Tim?"

"No, I haven't," returned Tim. "Oh, lor'! here's an awful mess. There's the thunder again."

Charley again endeavoured to rouse the nautical Lobby, but all attempts were unavailing; and groans, gasps, and moans were the only replies that could be extracted from the unfortunate youth.

The billows increased in size every instant, and one foam-crested monster struck the stern of the little bark, very nearly upsetting it, and completely drenching its three occupants.

"We shall be drowned to a certainty," said Charley, "if I can't get the sail down. Don't leave the tiller, as you value your life," he exclaimed, observing that Tim was about to rise to his assistance, "and don't get broadside to the wind, or over we go."

Charley tugged at the rope with strength beyond his years, and at last the knot gave way, and the sail was safely lowered.

"Thank Heaven for that!" he said; "now we'll take a turn at the sculls. The tide is running in, and we may get ashore before the storm overtakes us."

"Oh, Lobby!" said Tim, shaking his disengaged fist at the sea-sick youth, "won't you catch it for this! I wouldn't be you for another pound a week."

The last words had scarcely passed his lips, when another wave playfully struck the stern, and deposited a foot of water in the boat, much to the discomfiture of Lobby, who, unable to rise, was compelled to take the involuntary bath.

"Help me up," he at last groaned. "I'm sitting in two feet of water. I'm certain I shall be dead before we reach shore."

"You won't have to thank yourself if you get there at all," said Charley. "You must sit where you are for a time; we can't help you."

"Wait till we get to shore," said Tim, meaningly, "we'll help you then."

They were now within a quarter of a mile of the shore, and now the sky suddenly became overcast by a legion of dark, angry clouds.

The wind roared, and wave after wave struck the boat, threatening destruction; but neither of the lads gave way to despair.

Charley plied the sculls manfully, and Tim handled the tiller like an expert coxswain.

The squall passed, and the sea becoming calmer, the boat floated much easier, and rapidly approached the shore; but although now safe, the youngsters had another trial to go through.

When within a few yards of the beach, and Tim had risen from his seat with a sigh of relief and thankfulness, a monster wave caught the boat, and Charley, Tim, and the helpless Lobby were jerked into the air, to fall flat upon the shingle.

Charley was the first to recover, and, looking round, beheld Tim rubbing his waistcoat and gasping for breath.

The luckless Lobby was lying on his back, his mouth and eyes wide open, looking, as Charley afterwards said, for all the world like a cod-fish that had been thrown ashore.

"Hullo, Tim!" cried his chum; "you are not hurt, are you?"

"I don't think there are any bones broken," gasped Tim; "but I'm bruised all over. Where's that fool Lobby?"

"There he is, look, to the right. Hullo! he's coming round at last."

Lobby raised himself on his elbow, and glanced vacantly at his companions in misfortune.

"Where am I?" he asked, feebly. "Tim, what are you turning round for?"

"Here, get up," said Tim, rising, and seizing Lobby by the collar. "Get up and walk about a bit. Now, how do you feel?"

"Much better, thank you, Tim," replied Lobby.

"Oh! you are better, are you?" said Tim. "What do you mean by telling us you were used to yachting, when first of all you didn't know how to fix the sail properly, and then doubled up like a stale fish?"

"I'm very sorry," said Lobby; "but, oh! I'm going to be ill again."

Lobby again fell prostrate on the sands, and when he recovered his eyes sought his companions in vain; but standing near was the boatman from whom the boat had been hired.

"Hallo! youngster," he said, "a nice mess you've made o' this 'ere job."

"What do you mean?" feebly inquired Lobby.

"Wot do I mean!" returned the boatman; "whoy, that you've done damage to my boat to the tune o' two pun ten. Mast half gone, both sculls a mile out to sea, and the bottom o' the boat stuv in."

"I had nothing to do with it," said Lobby, rising and backing.

"It ain't no use o' telling me," said the man; "you hired the boat, and you'll pay for the damage. I know you well, you are a Scarum boy, and to-morrow I comes up for the money, or sees the master."

CHAPTER LII.

OLD BILL AND YOUNG BILL.

IT is not to be expected that the little difference between the Scarum boys and the two Bills was settled when they had made an involuntary exchange of dinners.

As far as the old seamen were concerned, it was all over, and would have been forgotten; but boys are of a different temperament, and although they bore no particular spite, the memory of the interrupted plans rankled in their youthful breasts.

One day the old man went down to his boat and found many of its fittings gone—the handle of the tiller, the sweeps, odd sails, and a few other things, without which he could not put out to sea.

After an hour's search, he discovered the missing property carefully concealed in the chyne, with the compliments of Charley, Tim, Bob Martin, and others, pinned thereon.

Old Bill was terribly angry, for he lost an excursion party through it, and he took a line of revenge which, however satisfactory it might be to him, was scarcely just.

He seized every Scarum boy who crossed his path, and grievously assaulted them.

Size or age, no matter. A Scarum boy was always legitimate prey, and at least three-fourths of the school were introduced to the heavy hand of Old Bill.

Nor was this all. Young Bill, excited by the parental example, took unto himself a general smiting commission, and fiercely the war waged between him and our heroes, who, as the summer was now fully advanced, went down every day to the beach to bathe, under the care of either Mr. Pendulum or his brother tutor, Mr. Tidd.

After the bath the boys were allowed an hour's run, which they generally devoted to Old Bill and his son, when those worthies were ashore.

Sometimes they waited upon them at their little cottage by the cliff, the dinner hour now being the favourite time for these excursions; and it was no uncommon thing to behold either Old Bill or his offspring, knife and fork in hand, in full pursuit of the audacious foe, who was often bold enough to invade the interior of the old man's home, having first sent a scout forward to ascertain if he had fairly settled to his dinner.

It occasionally happened that the pea-shooters of the youthful enemy hailed their missiles down upon father and son and other members of the family in the midst of an energetic consumption of beefsteak pudding, or that, having partaken of the meal in peace, they came forth for a breath of fresh air, and were saluted by a shower of seaweed from a band of assailants hidden behind the water-butt and other points of 'vantage. These and other aggravations helped to embitter the relations between the parties, and an open, sanguinary war was declared.

The advice of the old man to his son was, " Hit 'em hard, Bill; and never venture out without a good bit o' rope," which Bill never did, and manifold were the assaults and dire the execution he committed.

One day Bob Martin encountered Young Bill escorting a party of excursionists down to the boat, several of whom seemed to be in no hurry to trust their precious carcases on the treacherous deep, and Young Bill was doing his best to drive their fears away.

"There bean't wind enough to move more than a feather," he said, "and the sea is smoother than 'arf the rivers. You couldn't be ill if you tried to."

Bob thought this would be an excellent opportunity to give his friends a rub. Sidling up as near to the party as he dared go, he shouted out, " Don't trust yourselves in that boat."

"Eh—what! Who spoke?" cried a nervous-looking fellow in a white hat.

"It was upset twice last week, and drowned a father and five children," added Bob.

"Get 'ee away," said Bill, angrily. "Bean't you had enough o' my rope?"

"I'm not afraid to speak," replied Bob, "when I see people going straight to a watery grave. You can swim; perhaps they can't."

Several of the party drew nervously back;

and the man in the white hat declared it to be his fixed intention to remain on shore.

"But sure 'ee don't mind that Scarum himp," urged Young Bill. "He belongs to the school on the cliff; and nigh mad it's driven by 'em we are. Feyther's away b'iling lobsters, or he would tell 'ee the same."

"But the boat is small," said one, looking at it with a critical eye.

"She's got a big keel on her," returned Young Bill, "and she's broad in the beam. She can carry double the sail we ever put on her; and there ain't no wind on to-day."

"It don't matter to you seamen being drowned now and then," said the man in the white hat; "you are used to it. But I'm not going out unless you've got another boat."

"That's right," said Bob. "You are the only wise man of the party."

Having said this, he retired in high spirits, whistling a popular melody.

The result was that funk carried the day.

The people would not go; and Young Bill, in a mad fury, kicked off his sea-boots and went in search of Bob.

A few minutes later Charley, Tim, Grimmer, Mat Langley, and Lively Benson appeared upon the scene.

As the coast was clear, the excursionists having strolled farther on, they searched the craft, and discovered Young Bill's boots.

Here was an opportunity not to be lost.

They brought them out and filled them with a variety of articles, such as young crabs, shrimps, star and jelly-fish, sand, sea-weed, stones, and so on; then, burying the uppers partly in the shingle, they went their way, leaving the boots' soles uppermost in the air

Being very stiff, and perfect monstrosities of the art of boot-making, they presented a very startling appearance; and presently Old Bill came upon them, in company with a gentleman who had been assisting him in " b'iling " the loosters.

The effect of Young Bill's boots was electrical.

Old Bill started back, and stared at them in a wondrous state of dismay.

His companion—a slow man at anything, but slowest at thinking—did not comprehend the backward movement until Old Bill trod upon his toes.

Even then he took a short time to reflect before he asked—

"Where be 'ee coomin' to, Bill?"

"See them?" cried Old Bill, pointing to the boots.

"I see 'em," replied the other, after due reflection.

"Them be Bill's boots."

"Be they?"

"Yes; and Bill had 'em on this mornin', to go out with. I thout summat serus would ome o' quarrelling with them Scarum boys· I knew it would be so, Jack."

Jack's face expressed the most profound indifference, or, rather, it was in its normal state, and had no expression at all.

"I knowed," pursued Old Bill. "Them wicious warmints have murdered Bill, *and buried him head fust in the sands*."

Jack's face expressed a dawning of something, but whether of wonderment, horror, or amusement, no man could have told, as he replied—

"You don't say so."

"Run for 'ee police," cried Old Bill, capering about like a dancing bear. "Oh, this be a job, and Bill such a favourite with his mother too !"

Jack slowly removed his hands from his pockets, and, having properly fixed the bearings of sea and land, was about to start off, at the rate of two miles an hour, when Young Bill appeared in person, blundering down the pathway cut in the cliff.

The next instant a dozen boys appeared on the summit, each armed with heavy tufts of grass, lumps of clay, and other missiles.

The appearance of Bill, too, showed that he had already been pretty severely handled, and that he was fleeing from a victorious foe.

"That be Bill," said Jack, about three minutes after Old Bill became perfectly aware of the fact.

Young Bill, in a great heat, came blundering towards his friends ; and the boys, perceiving that the enemy was now very strong, before retiring fired a final salute of grass and clay, a lump of the latter smiting Jack heavily on the breast, and causing him to stagger.

"Why, Bill, what be the move now?" asked the old man.

"One o' them lumps hit me," put in Jack, solemnly, having arrived at a knowledge of the fact.

"One o' them Scarums, feyther," returned Bill, "comed down and said our boat was that ere ricketty she upset three times, and drownded a mother of five families—I mean the family of five mothers—no, I don't know what I mean, for one o' 'em fetched me a crack behind t' ear as makes me silly loike."

"Look at thy boots, Bill !"

"Ay ! look at thy boots," added Jack.

Young Bill raised one of them, and the miscellanea—animate and inanimate—fell out ; he then emptied the other, and knocked the boots together for at least five minutes.

"Feyther," he said, when this charming process was over, "I do think I shall kill one on 'em outright if I get 'em handy."

"I don't think Bill's in them boots," remarked Jack, whose mind had travelled back to the original discovery.

"No—Bill's here, Jack," returned Old Bill ; "you get slower every day, old man. I do think, Bill," he added, addressing his son, "it would be a good thing if we took a party on 'em out and dropped 'em overboard."

"Fust get your party," said Bill solemnly, unconsciously imitating Mrs. Glasse.

Great exultation reigned in the bosoms of the pupils of Scarum School over the defeat of Young Bill.

It seemed that he had come upon Bob Martin by stealth, and captured him. While he was feeling for his piece of rope, Charley came up and smote him heavily with a piece of soft clay. Young Bill, bewildered, lost his prey ; and others coming up, heavily armed, he was obliged to beat a retreat, as we have seen.

CHAPTER LIII.

THE PASSION FOR JAM.

"A LETTER for you, sir," said Griddle, depositing a greasy envelope on Mr. Crammer's study table ; "and there's a man outside waitin' for the answer."

"What does he want ?" inquired Mr. Crammer, testily. "Is it a beggar ?"

"No, sir—it's a beachman ; and I has my suspicions that some of the boys has been up to some wicious game."

"Very well ; you may go. I will ring when I have the answer ready."

Griddle obeyed, and Mr. Crammer, opening the letter, read the following :—

"Honered Sur,—I rite to you to make a cumplante. Three of your boys hired a bote of me, called the *Lovely Jane*, which, honered sur, was the pride of my 'art. Two hours arter they had started, i found the *Lovely Jane* with her side bust in, a pair of waluable sculls gone, the mast broke, and the sale tore from top to bottom. Honered sur, I found a boy, one of them as hired the bote, with a pail face and fishy eyes ; the others were gone, but i shode know them again. I charge two pun' ten, and cheap toe, as the bote was the pride of my 'art.

"Your obedient servant,
"WILLIAM WHITE."

Mr. Crammer rang the bell, and requested Griddle to show the beachman up.

"Sit down," said Mr. Crammer, and the man seated himself on the extreme edge of a chair.

"Where is the owner of the injured boat," inquired Mr. Crammer, after a pause.

"He's 'ere afore your eyes," returned Bill White. "I thought it best to write, 'cause I didn't 'xactly know as how you'd care about seein' me."

"You say," continued Mr. Crammer, referring to the epistle, "that you could point out the boys who committed this outrage. If you can do so, your claim shall not only be considered, but the offenders severely punished."

"Thank'ee, sir," returned the beachman. "I on'y want my money; I'll leave the whacking to you. It might ha' been a haccident, but that's nothin' to me. Boats' sides mustn't be busted in at a shillin' a hour."

"Griddle," said Mr. Crammer, "tell the boys to hold themselves in readiness to come to my study. Send Master Panks up first."

Griddle, delighted with his mission and the prospect of seeing his youthful tormentors in trouble, hastened to the playground, where they were assembled.

"Now then, you boys," he cried, in a voice of Bumbledom authority, his eyes sparkling with delight, "stop your game, and attend to me."

"You be hanged!" said lively Benson. "Shut up, and hook it. You are not talking to charity children."

"No himperance," cried Griddle; "I am sent by Mr Crammer——"

"To look for your cocked hat, I suppose," interrupted Benson. "What a pity it is, Griddle, they didn't make you a present of it when you got the sack! I hope it fitted the new man."

Griddle replied not aloud, but muttered something intermingled with questionable adjectives, and went in search of Lobby Panks.

"You're wanted in Mr. Crammer's study," he growled, when he had discovered that youth.

"What's the matter?" inquired Lobby, who was intent upon a game of marbles.

"I don't know," returned Griddle, "and what's more, I don't care. My instructions is, to send you up, and I does my duty, and leaves you to find out the rest."

"I say," shouted Bob Martin, as the porter turned to depart, "there's an advertisement in this morning's paper about you."

"About me?" gasped Griddle, turning. "What do you mean, you himp——?"

"Imploring you to return the ticket for the gold lace you pawned, as it is wanted for the new beadle's hat."

"Werry good. Go it," gasped Griddle; "you'll suffer for this. Mr. Crammer sent me down to say that every boy was to be ready to go to his study when called upon."

During this conversation Lobby Panks was wending his way slowly towards Mr. Crammer's study, and, entering, started back on beholding the boatman.

"That be him," exclaimed Bill White; "that's the warmint as hired the *Lovely Jane*."

"Hush!" said Mr. Crammer, "I cannot allow such expressions to be used here. Now, Panks, what is the meaning of all this? Here is a bill charging you with two pounds ten for damage to a boat."

"If you please, sir," snivelled Lobby, "I went out with Thorn and Turndown. I was taken ill, and they drove the boat ashore, and did the damage, and then ran away and left me on the beach."

Mr. Crammer summoned Griddle and bade him send up Charley and Tim.

When they arrived the story was repeated by Lobby.

"Now, Thorn and Turndown," said Mr. Crammer, "what have you to say to this?"

"Nothing, sir," returned Tim. "Simply this, the whole affair was an accident, and I am willing to pay my share."

"And you, Thorn?"

"The same. Lo——, I mean Panks, sir, was taken ill, and we were driven ashore. I am also willing to pay my part."

But not so with Lobby, for when Mr. Crammer put the question to him he snivelled out a reply to the effect that it would be a shame to charge him anything, when he had nothing to do with it, and also intimating that he had no money.

"Nevertheless, the boatman," said Mr. Crammer, "shall be paid; but I think thirty shillings will more than cover the damage. If this meets your view of the case, Mr. White, here is the money, and you may depart."

Mr. White was not the man to haggle, and taking the proffered coins he slouched out of the room, leaving the three boys standing before the table like so many prisoners in the dock.

"Thorn and Turndown," said Mr. Crammer, "you are aware that I have warned and cautioned you against venturing on the sea; but in the face of my desire and instructions, you have done so on the first opportunity. I should severely punish you were it not that I believe you have spoken openly and truthfully; you will therefore each of you write me out a hundred lines during the recreation hours to-morrow. Panks will remain for a short time."

Charley and Tim left the study, delighted at getting off so easily, but scarcely had they turned their backs upon the study when sounds of anguish issued from it.

"Lobby is catching it warm," said Tim.

"And serve the sneak right," replied Charley. "Crammer is a brick."

Lobby was at this moment thrust into the passage with all the show of a thrashing fresh upon him, and he stood for a few seconds rubbing the afflicted parts, and moaning out threats of vengeance.

"You got off with a few lines," he snivelled,

"I've been beaten within an inch of my life. Never mind, I'll serve you out for all this."

"It must have been hot," grinned Tim; "I can see where 'Tickler' brought the dust out all down your back."

"And bruised me from top to toe," groaned Lobby.

"But no matter," laughed Charley; "a little vinegar, brown paper, and a good night's rest, will do wonders."

"Let him be," said Tim, "there goes the bell for tea. Come on."

They left the afflicted Lobby in the passage, and hastening to the tea room, found the majority of the boys actively engaged with the somewhat thick slices of bread and butter, and steaming cups of tea.

Large quantities of these were disposed of and the boys rose and went to the schoolroom to study the lessons for the morrow.

"I say, Tim," said Bob Martin, "you're looking thinner."

"I hope so," returned Tim, proudly. "That beastly skeleton suit would hang about me like a sack."

Lively Benson entered the room, and whispered something to Tim.

"You don't mean that?" said Tim.

"Fact."

"How is it to be done?"

"Through the small window at the side," returned Benson.

"But who is to do it?" asked Tim.

"We must cast lots," said Benson. "Stop! Who have we here—anybody likely to peach?"

"All as true as gold," replied Tim.

"Well, then, you fellows," said Benson, aloud, "if you like, we can have a lark to-night, and a feast into the bargain. There's a new stock of preserves brought in to-day. What say you? Shall we take the pantry by storm?"

None objected, and the lots were cast; and Tim drew the fatal number.

"We must cast again," said Benson. "You'll excuse me mentioning it, Tim, but you're too fat to get through the pantry window."

"Oh, am I?" said Tim indignantly. "That's all you know about it. At any rate, I'll have a try at it."

"Think of the consequences, if you should fail," urged Benson.

"Do you think," exclaimed Tim, "that I'm going to shirk the work? It ain't likely. The number fell to me; and if the window was only half the size, I'd try it—ah, and get through it, too. I'm losing flesh fast."

"Very well," said Benson; "just as you like. Now to work. I will watch on the staircase; and Charley Thorn shall take the pantry end of the passage, and give you a lift

up and down. If any one comes, we will whistle."

Tim, removing his boots, crept cautiously down the stairs, accompanied by his two scouts.

The passage leading to the pantry was not a long one, but it was dangerous for an enemy to traverse; and servants hurried to and fro all day long.

But in the evening it was different.

The labours of the day being over, the girls sat down to their needlework, and listened to Mr. Griddle reading the paper, or devoured some fearful ghost story, and shivered when they thought of the sounds heard and sights reported to be seen in that same house.

Tim's progress was, therefore, not interrupted.

He could hear the servants laughing in the kitchen; and, by the tone of the celebrated Griddle's voice, concluded that he was the cause of the mirth.

The pantry was gained, and the little window—a small glass wicket is a better name for it—was opened; and Tim, assisted by Charley, mounted, and inserted his head, and, after a struggle, got his arms and shoulders through.

"How are you getting on?" inquired Charley. "Tight work, isn't it?"

"I believe you, my boys," rejoined Tim, "but I think I shall manage it."

"Don't make that noise," whispered Charley; "you're grunting like a litter of pigs. If you can't get through, come down again."

"I can't move," groaned Tim. "I am wedged in, and can't stir one way or the other. Oh! Don't pull my legs like that. You'll break my ribs."

Charley was about to reply, but was prevented from so doing by a hand which was placed over his mouth, while another lifted him by the collar from the ground, and bore him away upstairs to the schoolroom, where he was released, and beheld, to his discomfiture, Mr. Crammer.

"I will attend to you by-and-by," he said, significantly, taking a cane from his desk; "but first I will settle with the trapped burglar."

While this was going on, Tim, in his uncomfortable position, was struggling to free himself, and calling on Charley to bring relief, but, receiving no replies, deemed that his friends had deserted him in the hour of need.

"But, no; Bob and Charley wouldn't do that," Tim thought. "No; there's a footstep. Hurrah! I shall soon be free. Charley!"

There was no reply.

The footsteps ceased; and it was growing darker every moment.

The thought suddenly came into Tim's mind that the ghost might find him in this plight, or perhaps had already seized upon Charley, and would return to him.

"Charley! Bob! Charley!" the trapped youth cried, kicking and struggling, but without avail. "Drop your larks, and get me out of this."

"How came you there?" asked a deep voice.

"Oh, lor'!" gasped Tim. "I came after some jam, but stuck, as you see, half-way. Whoever it is, help me out. I can't stand much more."

The next instant he received a terrific cut from "Tickler," followed by a dozen terrible brother stingers; and the passage and hall rang with Tim's yells of agony.

"Now," said Mr. Crammer, pulling Tim out as if he had been a huge glass stopper, "perhaps you will give up any further attempt at burglary in my house."

Tim made no reply, but fled to the school-room, where he found Lobby Panks rubbing his hands, and grinning with delight.

CHAPTER LIV.
LOBBY PANKS IN TROUBLE.

Now the holidays were drawing nigh, and as the time of the book slavery decreased, the spirits of the Scarum youths rose in proportion.

Old Bill and Young Bill had a terrible time of it—they suffered a martyrdom. The most timid ventured to play some prank upon them; even Lobby Panks, who was incited thereto by the evil counsels of Tim.

"Do something to distinguish yourself," said our friend. "You oughtn't to let the half go without getting your name up, Lobby."

"What shall I do?" asked Panks, his soul feebly burning with a desire for glory.

"Could you put a few pins into Mr. Crammer's chair?" suggested Tim.

Lobby shuddered, and declined the proposition—"Tickler" he had an especial fear of.

"Then trip up Griddle with the tea things," pursued Tim.

"It couldn't be done," said Lobby, "and besides, they would be sure to find me out."

"You must do something," returned Tim, artfully. "Only the other day Charley was saying that he was sure you had plenty of pluck, and you only wanted a little bringing out."

"I'm rather nervous," replied Lobby, with a faint smile.

"That's nothing," said Tim, "I'm nervous, but that's soon got over—nervousness is not downright funk, and I am sure you can get over it."

"Do you think so?" rejoined Lobby, doubtfully.

"Certain of it, Lobby; and as I said before, you must do something—in or out of the school, which is it to be?"

"I'd rather do it out of the school."

"Very good. What do you say to paying a visit to Farmer Baker?—his hens are laying well, now."

"Didn't you get into a mess there, Tim?"

"Nothing much," replied Tim, indifferently; "all over now."

"I don't think I dare go there, Tim."

"Then you must look up Young Bill or Old Bill—they're safe sport. If you just keep out of their reach, they can never get near you; both of 'em got such precious feet—like elephants'."

"You are quite certain that they can't catch me, Tim?"

"Bet any money on it, Lobby."

"Then I'll do something to them," rejoined Lobby, valiantly.

"And do it at once," added Tim.

But Lobby wished to put it off for a time; this Tim, however, would not hear of, and furthermore volunteered to accompany him to the place of action.

"Saturday," he said, "is one of their quiet days, and they always go home to tea about this time; and you can always tell when they are at home, when the door is shut—at other times it is open."

Tim left the playground, where the above conversation had taken place, and went upstairs, where Charley and Bob were busy colouring a sheet of characters, and informed his friends of the proposed expedition.

"What's your game, Tim?" asked Bob.

"Don't know yet," returned Tim, "but I daresay something will turn up. Will you come to see the fun?"

"We will follow in a few minutes—if Panks sees us all together, he will be suspicious."

"All right," shouted Tim, and retired, with the object of keeping Panks up to the mark.

He was made of metal which quickly cooled.

Pouring insidious flattery into his ears, Tim led him forth by the arm, towards the cottage where the persecuted pair of Bills resided.

The little hut was built in the shadow of the cliff, out of the reach of the tide, and surrounding it was a low stone fence, formed by bits of stone roughly piled upon each other.

Just outside the enclosure was a small wooden building with a crazy chimney-pot in the corner. This was the sanctum devoted to the boiling of lobsters, shrimps, and other marine produce.

"The door is shut," said Tim, taking a survey of the cottage; "so they are at home."

"But what shall I do?" asked Lobby, timidly.

"Well, I don't care," replied Tim; "open the door suddenly, and shy that old tin kettle among the tea things."

"Perhaps they will break," said Lobby.

"That would be the cream of the joke," rejoined Tim; "go in, or come home and be a coward for ever. I will wait for you behind this boiling crib."

Lobby, supported by a strong desire to distinguish himself, crept with a palpitating heart round the fence and through the wooden gate.

The weapon suggested by Tim lay directly in his path, and he took it in his hand.

Tim waited carelessly to see the result of Lobby's movements, which were very slow indeed. He was too far away now to be talked to, for fear of arousing the enemy, so Tim cast his eyes about in other directions, in search of something to while away the tedious time of waiting.

His looks fell upon the chimney of the boiling-house; it was old, and very much awry—a tempting object to a skilled marksman. Tim could not refrain.

A tuft of very tough grass was handy, he raised it, sent it towards the object, and smote it heavily.

It rocked, reeled, then rolling down the roof, came with a crash to the ground.

He heard a shout, the bursting open of the door, and both Bills came out heated and furious. At the same moment, Lobby had got one hand upon the cottage latch—his other holding the aged kettle.

Upon him the eyes of the furious fishermen fell.

Tim was hidden by the sheltering hut.

The ensuing movements of the fishermen were skilful and rapid—that is, skilful and rapid for them.

Young Bill darted through the gate. Old Bill remained outside to prevent Lobby from scaling the wall.

Poor fellow!

There was little fear of his flying; fear had petrified him—he could neither move nor speak—and he clung as tenaciously to the battered kettle as if he designed it for a birthday present for Old Bill.

When he was captured, Old Bill went into the enclosure, and together they bore the hapless Lobby into the interior of their home.

At this moment, Charley and Bob, unconscious of what had taken place, came up and found Tim alone.

"Where's Lobby?" asked Charley.

"Hush!" replied Tim, putting a finger on his lip.

"Good gracious!" cried Bob Martin, "what's all that howling inside there?"

"Lobby Panks," replied Tim, "they've got him."

"Too bad, Tim."

"On my word I didn't mean it—I only thought—well! I don't know what I thought."

"Can't we effect a rescue?"

Tim laughed—a rescue, against two such powerful fellows!

"Look out, Tim; the door is opening."

The trio promptly hid behind the wall, where interstices in the stonework enabled them to see what was going on. Lobby came out in a very rumpled condition, and Old Bill followed him as far as the porch.

"Get 'ee back to school," he said, "and show 'em wales about yer body. Tell 'em all that we'll sarve 'em so when we get 'em."

Then the door closed, and Old Bill disappeared like the cuckoo of an old-fashioned kitchen clock.

Lobby came limping out, and saw his friends waiting to receive him—upon his face an angry scowl appeared, and he was sulkily passing on when Tim went up and put a hand upon his shoulder.

"I'm sorry you were caught, Lobby," he said.

"What's the good of your being sorry?" returned Panks, "will that make me any better?"

"Did you get it warm?"

"I'm sore all over—both of 'em laid into me with a rope—while an old woman kept thumping my head with her knuckles."

"Never mind, Lobby," said Tim, winking at his friends; "next to being successful comes the glory of being a martyr. Where's the kettle?"

"Oh! the little children took it away," returned Lobby, sulkily, "and played on it like a drum."

"While you were being wolloped?"

"Yes, while I was being wolloped."

"You have suffered in a common cause," said Charley, "and deserve the sympathy of your comrades."

"Which, as far as I'm concerned," added Tim, "shall take the form of a tart or two, and some ginger-beer."

"Going to stand treat?" asked Lobby, brushing away his tears.

"Yes, old fellow."

They took him away to the confectioner's in the town—not the one Lobby visited on the memorable first of April, but to another shop much patronized by the young. There Lobby ate unto repletion, and topped up with a couple of bottles of ginger-beer.

Amicability restored by this means reigned during the rest of the time they were out, and as a concluding piece of salve or ointment for Lobby's wounds, Tim walked home with him arm-in-arm.

As they approached the school grounds a frightful uproar saluted their ears—an uproar undoubtedly the offspring of riotous fun.

"What can it be?" cried Charley, running forward. "Confound the door! it's fast—give me a leg up, Bob."

The desired leg was given, and he was hoisted to the summit of the wall. The others stood in a panting state of excitement below.

"Here's a lark!" cried Charley; "oh, lor! I never saw such a go."

"What is it?" cried Bob.

"Old Griddle—ha—ha! ho—ho!"

"Give me a leg up," said Bob, impatiently to Tim; "now then. Thank you."

Once on the summit of the wall, he joined Charley in a fit of convulsive laughter. Tim in his turn becoming impatient, requested the favour of "a leg" from Lobby Panks.

It was given, and then Tim saw the cause of his friends' merriment. Griddle—the hapless Griddle, was staggering about the grounds with a metal chimney pot—cowl and all complete—fixed upon his shoulders.

CHAPTER LV.

MAT LANGLEY'S JOKE.

A NUMBER of boys surrounded the unfortunate porter of Scarum School, each bent upon adding to the misery of his involuntary confinement—peas, pebbles, cricket-balls, tops, stones, anything that was handy, they rained upon him, keeping up an incessant hail upon the metal pot and cowl.

"I can't keep out of this," said Charley; "over you go, Bob."

Over went Bob, and Tim only waited to give Panks a lift up, and then he dropped over too, leaving Panks in a doubtful state whether he dare risk a jump from the summit of the wall.

"Go it!" cried Bob.

"Hurrah!" broke in Mat Langley, "here they are. Did you ever see anything like this? He can't get it off. If you go close you will hear him swearing."

"A wicked old man!" said Charley, aiming a piece of brick at the metal cowl, which made it twirl like a teetotum.

The strenuous exertions made by Griddle to obtain his release were certainly very comical, and his voice, increasing every moment, now swelled into an angry roar. This only increased the joy of his persecutors, who, abandoning themselves to the feelings of the moment, danced around him like freshly imported savages in a travelling circus.

This unseemly proceeding was put an end to by the clanging of the gate bell. It was an angry ring, and the boys knew it. Probably Mr. Crammer or Mr. Pendulum was at the gate.

Having a strong objection to meet either of those gentlemen just then, they fled in a body, and took refuge in the general schoolroom—all but Lobby Panks, who, mustering a little courage, at last dropped from the wall, and obsequiously went to open the door of the lodge.

"I haven't seen a bit of fun like this," said Bob, wiping his heated face, "since I've been at Scarum School."

"I did it," cried Mat Langley, exulting over his villany; "it was brought in this afternoon to put over the study chimney—where the pot came off during the gale a short time ago."

"However did you fix it so?" asked Charley.

"He was sitting in his chair," replied Mat, "with his head thrown up. I fixed it on suddenly, and I fancy it caught his chin and the back of his head."

"It must have hurt him."

"Anyhow, he isn't smothered."

"Oh! here's an awful thing," cried Lobby Panks, bursting into the room. "It will be very serious for somebody."

"Is the cowl spoilt?" asked Mat.

"It's not the cowl," replied Lobby, "but Griddle—he is dying."

Mat Langley turned as pale as a sheet, and quietly sank down upon a form.

"Mr. Crammer was at the gate," continued Panks, "he was so angry that he knocked the chimney about with his umbrella, and all the time Griddle, thinking it was some of you——"

"Of us," said Charley.

"Well, thinking it was some of us, Griddle swore at him dreadfully; at last it came off, and Griddle fell down insensible."

"Then Mr. Crammer killed him?" cried Mat.

"I can't say anything about that," replied Lobby; "but he's lying on his back in the grounds, and Mary's gone for a doctor."

In a moment every available window was filled with heads, and then the boys beheld the prostrate Griddle lying on the ground—Mr. Crammer kneeling by his side, sprinkling his face with water.

Mat alone kept behind, in a pale, trembling state; he had not the courage to look out upon his murderous work.

"Here comes the doctor," cried a score of voices, as Mary hurried into the ground with

THE HAPLESS GRIDDLE WAS STAGGERING ABOUT WITH A METAL CHIMNEY-POT FIXED
UPON HIS SHOULDERS.

a portly old gentleman. "Come and look at him, Mat."

"Let me be," groaned Langley; but they would not let him rest, and kept him well up in the particulars of what was going on.

"The doctor's feeling his pulse. Mary's gone for another doctor. No; she's only fetched in a man to help—they are carrying Griddle into the house. Isn't the doctor puffing? One of Griddle's shoes is off—they've put him down to rest," and so on.

Then an impressive silence followed: it was broken by Mat.

"I can't bear it," he groaned; "will nobody go down to see how he is?"

"Who dare intrude?" asked Bob.

"Listen at the door, or on the staircase."

"I'll go," said Tim, "and keep quiet, boys, so that I lose nothing."

They were as quiet as mice, scarcely whispering all the time he was away, although Tim did not return for more than ten minutes. He came back at last with a handkerchief before his face.

Breathless silence.

Not a sound; their eyes never even blinked. Mat Langley sat like a culprit awaiting his sentence.

"Poor Griddle!" murmured Tim. "I wouldn't be him for a trifle."

" Is it—is it—all over ? " stammered Mat.

" Not quite so bad as that," replied Tim, " but I heard the doctor's opinion, and he said that Griddle's illness is—ALL GAMMON."

What a shriek of joy and exultation arose ! Mat turned a wheel and knocked down Lobby Panks, who happened to be in the way, with his feet. Charley and Bob embraced Tim affectionately, and many others performed uncouth dances typical of their joy.

In the midst of the hubbub Mary appeared with " Mr. Crammer's compliments, and he'd be amongst them directly," a message which tended to smooth down their exuberance, " Tickler" being a great leveller upon all occasions.

A little later a scout informed the main body of pupils that Griddle had retired to his lodge with the battered chimney top, and that Mr. Crammer was gone out again.

This was an opportunity not to be lost, and a party sallied forth.

The lodge, however, was barricaded, and the window-blinds drawn down, which prevented any triumph over the fallen Griddle, except through the keyhole.

Through this medium a great many personal reflections, taunts, and innuendos were conveyed, but for a time to no purpose.

At length an allusion to an unpaid score, contracted in his time of beadledom, brought forth Griddle, armed with a poker.

He expected the boys to flee, but to his astonishment they remained stock still, knowing well that he dare not strike them with such a weapon.

" Why don't you let me alone ? " asked Griddle, pursuing his favourite argument. " I lets you alone. I lives the life of a wild Injun on the war trail in his wigwum. You ain't Christians, you are young savages— rantin', roarin', tearin' savages, allus a swoopin' on a man who's had a fall in life."

" Who sold the sign-post ? " demanded Bob.

Poof ! from Tim, and a pea smote Griddle on the chin.

" If it wasn't for a haged father," returned Griddle, " as I keeps in snuff and bacca— which ain't allowed in the work——ahem ! in the establishment where he's a sort of under overlooker—I'd turn up my sitivation and foot it through the country ; but what's haged fathers to *you*, himps as you is, from the holdest to the youngest ? "

" Who kept pigs in the pound ? " asked somebody in the rear.

" I've seen a sight o' boys in my time," returned Griddle, ignoring the question, " but never anything like you ; the most wenomous tramp that ever hit a man over the head with a turnip is mild and wenerable compared to you."

" What have you done with the chimney-pot ? " asked Charley ; " don't sneak it away and sell it for old metal."

" I'll have your tin tile," added another joker.

Griddle turned from one to the other like a wild beast at bay ; he had borne much in his time, but never so much as he had that day endured. He wanted to fix upon one, and he decided upon Lobby Panks.

" You fix a thing like that on my head agen," he said, " and I'll wrop you up in a sheet of tin and bury you alive.

" Why I helped to take it off," returned the injured Panks.

" Yes," sneered Griddle, " after you had put it on. I hate sneakin' ways. If *I'd* fixed it on *your* head, *I* wouldn't ha' took it off. My principles is straightforrard."

" And yet you prigged a pig," said Bob.

" Prove it," returned Griddle, warmly, " prove it ; but I'll make some o' you pay for libels."

" What is all this disturbance about ? " interposed Mr. Tidd, as he walked through the lodge.

Griddle proceeded to explain.

" This werry day," he said, " I've had my head stuffed in a chimney-pot—which thunder was nothin' to the row when they hit it with a brick—and arter being drawn out of it by Mr. Crammer like a tooth, they falls foul o' me in this place, and drives me to that—"

" Boys," said Mr. Tidd, interrupting the eloquent speaker, " it is time to retire. Griddle, will you get the supper ready ? "

" If I had the selectin' of their wittles," muttered Griddle, as he crossed the ground, " there would be a nettle or two among it, or maybe a dose of strichnine, and think it no crime neither."

Mr. Tidd looked as if he were displeased, but he did not mention the subject, and at the usual time the boys retired.

By that time Mr. Crammer and Mr. Pendulum had both returned.

The master and the two ushers held a consultation ere they went to bed.

" My boys," said Mr. Crammer, " grow worse every day, and I am sure I do not see my way clear to better it, unless we keep a stricter supervision over them."

" If you cramp the young too much," returned Mr. Tidd, " you are apt to spoil them —growing plants want room and air."

" But see," said the master, angrily, " to what an extent they carry their pranks ! "

" Mr. Crammer," replied the usher, " will you allow me to point out one thing ? "

" Certainly, Mr. Tidd."

" Once upon a time we were boys."

" Certainly, ah ! certainly," said Mr. Crammer.

"And I think, sir, if you look back upon our youth, we committed many egregious follies."

"Well, ahem! I believe so."

"It was our nature," pursued the usher, "and it is theirs; of course I do not defend all their acts, nor stipulate for their having a licence to pursue what course they please. If discovered in any of their tricks, let them be punished, sir; but to bind down the whole school for the acts of two or three— and those acts spreading, as we know, over a considerable space of time, for as a rule the boys are not so bad, would be unjust—unjust I say, sir, to them, and unworthy of you."

"What is your opinion, Mr. Pendulum?" asked the schoolmaster.

"I cannot agree exactly with Mr. Tidd," replied Mr. Pendulum; "I do not hold with pranks in any shape or form. My boyhood was free from them; I could never see the object of making a fool of myself, and annoying other people."

"How do you propose to act in the present instance?" asked Mr. Crammer.

"Make an example of the first you detect," was the reply, "and dismiss him from the school."

Fatal words—destined to be carried into effect in a most unexpected quarter.

That night the ghost of Scarum School was rampant again; Mr. Tidd's face was blackened in his sleep, Mr. Pendulum lost his boots, and in the bedroom of Mr. Crammer quite a little crockery shop was discovered in the morning, a vast amount of earthenware belonging to the dormitories having been collected there, and arranged in rows—very pretty in point of effect, but decidedly annoying to the master of Scarum School.

Nor did the mischief end here; a new hat, belonging to Mr. Crammer, left in the hall, had been carefully brushed the wrong way, and the hands removed from the clock; added to this, one of the eyes of Mr. Crammer's portrait was knocked out, and the stump of a cigar fixed in it, with the addition of a stout pipe in his mouth, which, to say the least, had a very peculiar effect.

Great was the rage and indignation of the master and ushers, vast the surprise of the boys; but nothing came of either indignation or surprise, the time for discovery, although close at hand, had not yet arrived.

CHAPTER LVI.

ANOTHER MYSTERY.

"AHA!" said Griddle, throwing himself into his special chair in the kitchen—"aha! this is a relief after the trials and troubles of to-day."

"Why, what has been the matter, Mr. Griddle?" inquired the cook.

"Them wicious warmints o' boys, as usual," returned Griddle; "I shall be the death of some of them, I know I shall. They ain't satisfied with cheekin' their superiors, but they must fix chimbley-pots on their heads. What next?"

"Ah!" said Mary, taking a chair and sitting down opposite Griddle, "what next, I wonder. But boys will be boys, and I sometimes think, Mr. Griddle, that if you were not so cross they would behave much better."

"Tush!" said the porter, waving his hand, "do you think I would give way an inch to the wicious brutes? Not I. You forget yourself, Mary, you forget yourself."

"Well, I don't know," Mary continued, smoothing her apron; "but I've often thought so, and, as I always speak my mind, if you don't like what I have said why——"

"There, there," the cook chimed in, "this is not the time for quarrelling. Mr. Griddle is tormented by the boys, but perhaps he is a little hasty."

"We all have our weaknesses," said Griddle.

"Yes, and show 'em pretty often, too," retorted Mary, who was not to be put down by the cook.

Griddle said never a word in answer to this, but gulping down his wrath, looked round the kitchen, and then smiling, said—

"As cook says, this is not a time for quarrelling. Now, ladies, I am at your command. What is it to be, the police reports or the last report of the servant gals' meetin'?"

"I don't care to hear about the servants," said Mary, snappishly;" and it's my opinion that if they kept at home and attended to their work, they'd be better off in the end."

"And so I think," said the cook. "Suppose, Mr. Griddle, that you leave the paper till to-morrow, and tell us a good story. You must have seen and heard a great deal in your life."

"Ah! that would be better," returned Mary, at last condescending to smile—"the very thing. Now, Mr. Griddle, if you please."

"I ain't much of a story-teller," said Griddle, "but I'll do my best. It was at the time I was acting as assistant magistrate at —well, never mind where, that there was a great talk about a ghost which was said to walk on the high road from sundown to sunrise."

"Lor'!" cried the cook, "what was it like?"

"People as seed it," Griddle went on, speaking slowly and solemnly, "said it was the figger of a man *without a head!*"

The cook gave a little scream, and Mary

turned pale and glanced suspiciously over her shoulder.

"To resoom," said Griddle; "as I observed, there was a great talk about the spectre, and at fust we magistrates thought some one were doin' it for a lark, so we offers a reward of fifty pounds for the willain, dead or alive."

"Was it a ghost, after all?" asked Mary, whose eyes and mouth were open with excitement and horror.

"I'm a comin' to it directly," returned Griddle. "One night I had been dinin' with the sheriffs, and was goin' 'ome. It was very dark, and so I walked in the middle of the road, and jest as I got in sight of the workus——"

"You were on your way home, weren't you?" asked Mary.

"I see something white a-comin' dancing up the road to meet me," Griddle continued, waiving this personal reflection.

"Oh, good gracious!" exclaimed the cook, "don't go on, I'm sure I shall faint if you do."

"It came dancin' and jumpin' from one side of the road to the other," Griddle went on, taking no heed of the cook's interruption, "and I stood still, my blood a freezin' in my veins, and the 'air of my 'ead standin' out like wires on a bottle-cleaner. But, says I to myself, 'Is it you, Mr. Griddle—Mr. Griddle, a magistrate, a justice of the peace, and member of the Poor Law Board—is it you, Mr. Griddle,' I says to myself, 'that allows your knees to knock, your teeth to chatter, and 'air to rise? I can't believe it.'"

"What did you do?" asked Mary, wiping the perspiration from her face.

"What did I do—oh, lor'! if there ain't the bell for the drawing-room."

"Bless me! so it is," said Mary and the cook in a breath; "I wonder what's wanted?"

"They can't rest a minit," returned Griddle; "it wouldn't matter but Dick's out. Mary——"

"Eh!—what?" exclaimed that young damsel; "you don't think I'm going to answer the bell, do you? If you do you are greatly mistaken."

"Think of the trying day I've had," pleaded Griddle; "think of the hagony I've suffered through them warmints."

"I shan't think anything of the sort," said Mary. "It's your place to answer the bell when Dick is out, and if you don't like to obey orders, why you must take the consequences."

"Oh! the ingratitude——" began Griddle.

But Mary tripped him up by asserting that no one owed him gratitude, that she did not believe one word of the magisterial business, and that the ghost story was simply an invention on his part.

"You're afeard," said Griddle, as white as any ghost could be, "to answer the bell—you know you're afeard."

"No more than you," rejoined Mary; "for you know you have been frightening yourself by your own lies. Now, then, what have you to say to that? Why don't you go upstairs? Ah! there's the bell again. Master will be down directly."

"I'm not well," gasped Griddle, "or I wouldn't hesitate; I've been bruised and beaten to-day. Cook, you I know will——"

"Certainly not, Mr. Griddle," returned the lady addressed; "it's nothing to do with me."

Ding, dong, ding, dong, dingle!

"You will certainly lose your place," said Mary, maliciously. "Hark! Listen to the wind. Hark how it moans, just like some one groaning on the stairs."

CHAPTER LVII.
GRIDDLE AND THE GHOST.

THE unhappy Griddle rose to answer the bell, and with tottering footsteps made for the door; but ere he could reach it, a hollow-sounding voice, unearthly in tone, rang through the kitchen.

"Griddle! *Griddle!* GRIDDLE!" cried the voice, "why don't you answer the bell?"

Mary and the cook screamed and rushed towards the porter for protection; but the unhappy Griddle seemed incapable of taking care of himself. He stood leaning against the dresser, his eyes and mouth wide open, his face of a light green hue, and his knees in constant collision.

"What was that?" he gasped at last. "I thought I heard some one call my name?"

"Oh! Good gracious, yes," cried Mary, "and it was no human voice."

"There goes the bell again," said the cook. "Oh! what shall we do?"

Again the voice rang out in hollow, sepulchral tones—

"Griddle! *Griddle!* GRIDDLE! Why don't you answer the bell?"

At this juncture both Mary and the cook showed signs of hysterics, especially the cook, who became suddenly limp, and fell into Griddle's arms, much to that gentleman's discomfiture.

"Hold up, cook! hold up, Mary!" he cried; "this 'ere is another game, I'll back."

"You lie!" cried the voice. "*Why don't you answer the bell?*"

After this, there was a prolonged roar, such as an infuriated bull might have given vent to. The cook collapsed. Mary sank into a chair and hid her face, and Griddle's legs became weaker and weaker, and he felt that his taxed nerves could stand but little more.

Again the bell pealed furiously, and again the mysterious voice inquired the reason it was not answered.

For a minute after this, all was still; but suddenly a footstep sounded on the stairs, and Mr. Crammer burst into the kitchen.

He started back when he beheld the scene. Vague and strange ideas flashed through his brain.

Had they been poisoned, assassinated, or was it possible that Griddle had introduced the ardent spirit into the kitchen, with such dire effect. Mr. Crammer seized Griddle by the collar, and shook him until his teeth did duty for a pair of castanets.

This operation had the effect of bringing the porter to his senses, and he smiled feebly as he recognized his master.

Mr. Crammer was about to enquire the reason of the sudden collapse of the domestic household, when the terrible voice, cried—

"What became of that poor family you turned into the streets? Was there ever an inquest?"

The man of learning's hold relaxed on Griddle's collar, and staggering, he cannoned against a couple of chairs, and measured his length on the floor.

"This is some infamous trick," he gasped, hastily rising, "and if I find the delinquents, I'll—I'll——"

"Where's that beadle?" inquired the voice.

"Who is that?" roared Mr. Crammer, in a tone of mingled terror and fury.

There was no reply, but a sound resembling smothered laughter followed, then a noise of falling tiles and bricks, and all was quiet.

"Now, Griddle," cried Mr. Crammer. "Come. Don't be foolish. I have found it out."

"The family weren't anything to me," responded Griddle, feebly. "What with six of my own, and a haged father, I had enough to do."

"What are you talking about?" cried Mr. Crammer. "Wake up."

"The lace fetched four and a tanner," Griddle went on, a ghastly light in his eye; "and I hown the score at the pub was never paid."

"Merciful Heavens!" cried the distracted Mr. Crammer. "The man has lost his senses. Mary, cook—some of you—anybody—run up-stairs for help."

Mary moaned, and the cook kicked feebly.

As a last resource, Mr. Crammer rushed to the pipe, and filling a pail with water, distributed the contents amongst his domestics.

Mary was on her feet in a twinkling, the cook opened her eyes, screamed, and Griddle,

under the impression that he was being attacked by his old tormentors, called Mr. Crammer "a wicious warmint!" but recovering himself, instantly became the Griddle of old.

"Oh! lor, sir," cried Mary, "has it gone?"

"Has what gone?" cried Mr. Crammer. "There has been nothing here. Some of my pupils have succeeded in terrifying you by calling down the chimney."

"The young warmints!" said Griddle, under his breath. "Wengeance—wengeance!"

"And you," said Mr. Crammer, turning to vent his rage on the unhappy porter—"you call yourself a man to be frightened by a few foolish boys. Pooh! I am ashamed of you."

"It's werry 'ard," murmured Griddle, "that a man as has seen better days should be first frightened out of his life, and then bullied."

"Silence!" cried Mr. Crammer; "I am going round the rooms to investigate this disgraceful affair. You will accompany me."

Griddle brightened up wonderfully. This was just what he wanted—a chance of being avenged of the long list of ills and insults he had received at the hands of the pupils.

Accordingly, upstairs master and porter went; but in every room they found all quiet, nothing disturbed, and what was still more astonishing, Mr. Crammer could find no spot from the windows where the roof could be gained.

Suddenly a thought struck him, and leading the way to an unoccupied room at the end of the corridor, he beheld a small trap door leading to the point of vantage.

A short ladder was procured, and Mr. Crammer struggled on to the roof.

Here he found convincing proofs that the roof had been assailed.

Footmarks, tiles dislodged, and near the kitchen chimney a remnant of black cloth, apparently torn from some garment.

Mr. Crammer descended, and dismissing Griddle, went below to the schoolroom, where the boys were busy in getting up the morrow's lessons.

He walked up and down between the desks, and at last pounced upon Mat Langley, and dragging that youth up by the collar, hauled him out of the room without saying a word. Charley looked at Tim and winked.

"It's all up," he said, "somebody has told. Poor Mat!"

"It will be our turn next," groaned Tim; "I wonder how he found it out?"

"Wait till Mat comes back," Charley returned; "we shall hear all about it then. Perhaps Lobby has been playing the sneak again."

"If he has," said Tim, clenching his fists, "I'll lick him within an inch of his life."

But as we know this was a mistake, we will now return to Mr. Crammer and the unfortunate Mat.

Upstairs, and along the corridor, did the schoolmaster drag that hapless youth, saying never a word until his study was reached, into which he pushed Mat, and locking the door, bade Mat sit down.

Mat did as requested, and sat staring at the master, his eyes and mouth wide open, and a sinking sensation creeping over him, well knowing what was coming.

"Langley," said Mr. Crammer, "your jacket is torn. How did it happen?"

Mat breathed again, yet he wondered why so much violence should have been used about a torn jacket, a thing so common at Scarum School.

"An accident, sir," he replied.

"When did it occur?"

"Th—th—this evening, sir."

"How?"

This was a clencher for Mat, and for some seconds, he sat ruminating on the reply he should give.

Mr. Crammer relieved him.

"Langley," he said, "I can tell you how that jacket was torn, where and how. Come here!"

Mat rose, and stood before his tutor.

"Take off that jacket and pass it to me," said Mr. Crammer.

Mat obeyed, and passed the fatal jacket over the table.

To his horror, he saw Mr. Crammer fitting a small piece of cloth into the torn place, and which corresponded to a nicety.

"I thought so," said Mr. Crammer, rising to his feet, and taking "Tickler" from a drawer. "You know," he continued, aloud, "why I am going to punish you, Langley, and therefore the least said the better."

For several minutes Mr. Crammer held the unfortunate youth, and smote him, hip and thigh, but not a cry or groan did Mat make until he was free and on his way back to the schoolroom, and then for a moment only did he sit down on the stairs, and, writhing with pain, gave way to his agony in a burst of tears.

"The vicious old brute!" he groaned. "And yet it serves me right. I wonder how he got that piece of cloth."

In the schoolroom he found Charley and Tim waiting his arrival with anxious faces.

"How did you get on?" inquired Tim.

Mat replied by rubbing the afflicted parts.

"I'm awfully sorry," said Charley, compassionately, "that you should come in for the lot."

"Never mind," returned Mat, brightening up, "it's all the same. I should have been in for something to-morrow. But I say, what did you do with the speaking trumpet?"

"Hid it under my mattress," Charley replied. "It's safe enough there."

"I fancy I can see Griddle," said Mat Langley, breaking into a laugh. "Did you hear him groan?"

"Yes, and Mary and the cook screamed as if the house was on fire," said Tim. "Poor Mary! I'm sorry for her, she has often done us a good turn."

Just then Griddle put his head into the room. There was an expression of delight on his countenance, which told that he had heard of Mat's downfall.

"Good evenin', gentlemen," he said. "Hopes as how you are pretty comfortable."

"What do you want?" demanded Charley.

"Was coming past, and thought as how I would look in to see how you was a-gettin' on," returned the porter with a grin.

"Cut it," cried Tim, "if you have any respect for that thick head of yours."

"I weren't addressin' you, Master Turndown," said Griddle; "so you had best hold your tongue."

Tim seized a red-ink bottle and emptied the contents into Mr. Griddle's face, who, beating a hasty retreat, met Mary on the stairs.

At first Mary was under the impression that Mr. Griddle had been driven mad by the boys, and, in his despair, had attempted suicide, and, giving a slight scream, turned to run for assistance, when the porter called her back, and said, pathetically—

"Behold the work of warmints!"

Mary did not reply, but bit her apron; and something like a smile played over her face.

"Warmints," continued Griddle, wiping his face. "Wicious warmints, as has no respect for hage. Wot they'll be in a year or two, I ain't hable to say; but I knows this, that if they go on like they do now they'll be the death of a dozen Christians, and Mr. Crammer 'll have to engage a couple o' blacks."

This was quite a speech for Griddle; and having delivered it with great emphasis, he turned on his heel and went his way to cleanse his smeared countenance.

CHAPTER LVIII.

SOMETHING FOR GRIDDLE.

"IF it could be done," said Tim, with a kick of delight, "how jolly it would be!"

"I tell you it can, and shall be," returned Lively Benson.

"Here comes Charley," exclaimed Tim. "We must tell him. Oh, lor! what a lark it will be! I can fancy I see him. Somebody hold me, while I have my laugh out."

Lively Benson declined that office, but

"TAKE THEM OFF! TAKE THEM OFF!" SCREAMED LOBBY.

smote Tim's broad back with a heavy hand, bringing that gentleman up sharply.

Charley here strolled up, and inquired the reason of Tim's mirth.

Lively Benson took him by the arm and whispered something in his ear.

Charley immediately became convulsed with mirth, and declared that it would be prime.

"Then I'll write off to-night and have it done," said Benson.

"Do," said Tim, who had laughed till he cried, "it will be the greatest lark that ever happened."

A few mornings after this conversation, there stopped at Mr. Crammer's gate a parcel delivery cart.

The man in attendance rang the bell, and Griddle appeared.

"Now then, sleepy," said the man, "open that gate, will you? Here's a hamper for 'Griddle, Esq.'"

The porter's hand trembled as he shot back the bolts.

"Who is it from?" asked Griddle, faintly.

"What's that to you?" returned the man. "You ain't a 'squire, are you?"

"My name's Griddle," said the porter, loftily, "and I don't want any of your imperence."

"My eye!" returned the man, "a 'squire in shorts and bright buttons. Well, my buck, I s'pose you are the man I want. Sign the bill, and hand over four and eightpence."

"How much?" cried Griddle, aghast.

"Four and eightpence."

"Who sent the hamper?" said Griddle, looking at it dubiously.

"Thomas Jenkins, of Upton-cum-Cawdor," replied the railway official, after consulting his bill. "Now, look sharp; I've fifty places to call at, and ain't done then."

"What!" exclaimed Griddle, joyously; "old Tom ain't forgot me then."

"And sent you something strong to drink his health in, or I'm much mistaken," returned the man.

"And yet," said Griddle, "I wonder how he found me out."

"That's nothing to me," cried the cart attendant, savagely. "Am I to have the four and eight, or is the parcel to go back?"

"I'll fetch the money in a minit," said Griddle, and darted into the house, returning soon with the requisite sum.

"In the holden time," the man said, contemplating the coins in the palm of his hand, "'squires were liberal, but times is altered."

Griddle fished out another sixpence, and the man departed.

"Here's luck!" exclaimed Griddle, meeting Mary in the hall. "A hold friend of mine have sent me a hamper of wine and some game. Won't we have a jolly time of it below!"

"My!" exclaimed Mary, opening her eyes to their fullest extent, "what kind friends you must have!"

"I'm a broken-down gentleman," returned Griddle, mournfully, "but there is them as have never forgotten the time when I was flush."

Mary departed to communicate the news to the cook, and Griddle staggered upstairs with his burden, to unpack it.

Reaching his own room, he closed and locked the door, and fell on his knees beside the precious hamper.

"If it's wine or sperrits," he muttered, "I'll crack a bottle afore I go down."

Producing a knife, he cut the cords and threw open the lid, springing at the same time to his feet with a cry of joy.

There were at least twelve bottles, neatly corked, and snugly packed in the straw.

"Three o' brandy," said Griddle, as he pulled them out, "three o' gin, three o' rum, and three o' whisky. Hullo! what's this at the bottom?"

A shade passed over Griddle's face as he brought the object to light.

It was a battered cocked hat, dirty and old, and deprived of its gold lace.

"Tom were always a funny chap," Griddle murmured. "It's a lark o' his, that's what it is. Now then for a taste o' one o' these bottles—whisky, that'll do."

Griddle's knife boasted of a corkscrew, and the bottle was soon opened.

The porter sat on the edge of the bed, and raised the bottle to his lips.

A painter might perhaps do justice to the change in the expression of that countenance, but it is impossible for the pen to do so.

It was half-doubting, half-convinced, with a dash of rage and sorrow thrown in.

"Dash it!" said Griddle, putting his eye to the neck of the bottle. "Wot's the meaning of this?"

As no reply came, he rose, and pouring a quantity of liquor from the bottle into a glass, took a sip.

"Sold!" cried Griddle, dancing with rage, and dashing the bottle into a thousand pieces against the wall; "sold! It's coloured water, and it's a trick o' them wicious warmints."

Then the thought came how he had parted with five shillings and twopence, and he stamped and swore, and plucked at what little hair Nature had left him.

"What'll Mary and the cook say?" he moaned. "They'll larf of course, and the news 'll fly like a house o' fire; them wicious warmints will get hold of it, and shan't I lead a miserable life!

"I'll see Mr. Crammer about this affair," he gasped. "There's laws ag'in' a thing o' this sort. And yet I can't prove anything, the wicious warmints are too knowin' and cunnin'; they're like foxes."

Slowly and sorrowfully Griddle left his room and sought the kitchen.

The cook and Mary hailed him with delight, but the housemaid, when she heard the doleful story, had the cruelty to laugh.

"What boys they are!" she said; "really they does one's heart good to hear of their pranks."

The cook also had been endeavouring to stifle her mirth, but now found it impossible, and taking up the cue, laughed till the very plates and dishes on the dresser rang with the sound.

This was, as may be expected, very exasperating to the feelings of Mr. Griddle, who commenced a volley of abuse, but was cut short by Mary pushing him out of the kitchen.

"The old fool!" she said, sitting down and beginning to laugh again; "I don't wonder at the boys serving him out. Oh, dear! what an awful thing, to pay four and eightpence for twelve bottles of coloured water and a battered cocked hat."

The laughter at last became so loud that it reached Mr. Crammer's ears, who was in the schoolroom.

"I won't allow this sort of thing," said Mr. Crammer, rising; "I will not allow this shouting in my house. Griddle, what is the meaning of that noise?"

"They're larfin' me to scorn, sir," said the porter, who was standing outside on the landing.

"Doing what, sir?" exclaimed Mr. Crammer, in astonishment.

"They larf, sir," Griddle replied, "because I'm an unfortinet man—the wictem of wiciousness."

"Explain yourself, sir," said Mr. Crammer.

Griddle told his story. Mr. Crammer listened with a serious face, but his eyes twinkled, and he could have laughed as loudly as either Mary or the cook.

"It is no use coming to me," he said at last—"no use whatever. I cannot accuse any one, unless you can bring me positive proof of who the guilty parties really are."

"I know it's one of 'em," said Griddle, desperately.

"How can you assert that?" demanded Mr. Crammer. "Some foolish acquaintance of yours in the country has probably done this."

Griddle shook his head, and said—

"'Tain't likely, and yet it may be as you say, sir. Thankee, sir, speakin' to me; if I can make out anything, I will let you know."

"And you may rely upon my taking the matter up warmly," said the schoolmaster, a curious twitching playing round his lips. "But I do not think this is a trick of any of my pupils."

"P'raps not—p'raps not," Griddle murmured, as he moved away, "but them warmints are up to anything."

That night of course all was known, as it had been long before by a certain number of boys, and that night the youths of Scarum School sang songs of joy at the downfall of their enemy.

Griddle came up for the lights as usual, and by the time he reached the room in which Charley and Tim reposed, his face was pale with the trials he had undergone.

"Here's the wine-merchant," cried Tim, as the door opened; "I say, Griddle, what's the price of the best Cognac brandy?"

"You'll wear the cocked hat on Sundays, to oblige us, won't you?" asked another.

"I tell you what I will do," cried the tormented one, who was by this time mad with rage, "I'll settle one or two of yer, if yer ain't quiet."

"Try it on," cried Tim, sitting up in bed; "yah! why didn't they send the lace?"

"You've been in my room," roared Griddle.

"Of course we have," returned Charley; "and enjoyed ourselves with the contents of your hamper."

"Look here," groaned Griddle, "I shall do some of you a mischief—I know I shall. I've been worked up to a hawful pitch, and mark me, summat 'll come of it."

"Too bad!" cried Lively Benson, "I say, Griddle, what a lot you might have done by putting that four and eight on the Derby."

At this moment Mr. Crammer's footstep was heard on the stairs, and Griddle beat s retreat to his own room, vowing revenge.

The next day, and for many days after, did Griddle endeavour to get a clue to whom the culprit was, but without avail, and after a time the matter died out, and was heard of no more.

CHAPTER LIX.

THE LOBSTER TRADE.

SOMETIMES, in the height of the season, sales of fish took place upon the shores of Winkle-by-the-Sea. Then it was that certain luggers anchored close in shore, and boats laden with shrimps, lobsters, crabs, plaice, skate, and other fish, were landed on the beach, and hoarse-voiced men mounted upon rough rostrums built of old boxes, barrels, &c.

Sometimes the fish was scarce and sold readily, at other times it was plentiful, and buyers wary of purchasing. Upon these occasions the fishermen generally had some left upon their hands, which they either carted away for manure or took home, and in their own expressive vernacular "b'iled."

These sales were much patronized by the boys of Scarum School when they had the chance, as affording an opportunity for cheap excitement and a little fun. Sometimes the boys were merely spectators, at other times bidders—and high ones too—but never buyers.

One morning a party of the boys were on the shore, and mixed themselves up with the throng surrounding the auctioneer.

Fish changed hands very rapidly, and the selling of an entire cargo sometimes takes less than half an hour.

On this particular morning, there was a scarcity of fish of every class, except lobsters, which were abundant.

Old Bill was in the crowd, and Charley, who was of course with the boys, noticed that the old seaman's eyes were fastened on one particular hamper of fine lobsters.

The auctioneer mounted his rostrum, and commenced business.

"Now then, gentlemen," he began, "the market this morning is empty, but I have a few very fine little lots for sale. Who says fourteen shillings for that lot of soles?"

"Eight," said a voice.

"If I know the trade at all," the auctioneer said, smiling, "they will not let such a fine lot of soles go for eight shillings."

" Fourteen," exclaimed another voice.

" Who bids fourteen?" inquired the auctioneer, opening his eyes very wide.

No reply.

" I'll wait on you in a minute, young gentlemen," said the auctioneer, fixing his eyes on Tim. " I don't want any of your tomfoolery here. Be off."

" What have I done?" demanded Tim; " I haven't opened my mouth."

The auctioneer went on with his business.

" Now, gentlemen, how much for these soles? Eight—eight and six—nine, thank you; any higher bidder than nine shillings? Down at nine."

The sale would have been completed, but a voice at the moment cried—

" Don't have them. They are not fresh."

The auctioneer charged into the crowd, but as may be supposed, came out empty-handed, his tormentors having escaped easily.

About an hour after this, Old Bill appeared, struggling along with a hamper of lobsters, and placing it on the ground, some distance from the auction ground, returned for something else he had purchased, and as luck would have it, Charley, Tim, and Lobby Panks at that moment neared the spot.

" I'm awfully tired," said Lobby. " It's much too hot to play cricket, and I've been at it ever since six this morning."

" Sit down, then," said Charley.

" The sand is so awfully wet, or I would," Lobby returned.

" There's a hamper," said Tim. " Sit down and wait till we call for you. We shan't be long."

The unsuspecting Lobby approached the hamper; Charley darted behind and raised the lid, and Lobby fell amongst the lobsters.

The terrified youth recovered himself as soon as possible, but there was no escape for him. Lobsters, when confined in a hamper or fishmonger's shop, are wont to fasten on each other for the want of an enemy, and it is not, therefore, astonishing that several remained clinging to Lobby Panks.

" Oh, lor!" screamed that youth. " Pull them off; they are tearing my flesh."

" They won't come off," cried Tim, pulling at one monster, which had fastened upon a fleshy part of Lobby's frame. " I never saw such a beast to hold on."

" Look out!" cried Charley; and Tim, turning his head, beheld Old Bill charging down upon them.

" Hullo!" he roared; " what be thee up to there?"

" A poor young fellow has fallen among your lobsters," Tim replied. " Look at him."

" Oh, take them off! take them off!" cried Lobby, dancing with pain.

" Scarum boys, o' course," said Old Bill, wetting the palm of his hand. " Now, look here. Them lobsters couldn't get out of that hamper, that's clear. The fact is, the young warmint fell in among 'em as a hartful way o' stealin' 'em."

" I didn't," cried Lobby. " I don't want them. Take them off."

" I sha'n't do anything of the sort," replied Old Bill.

Charley and Tim screamed with laughter, but Lobby's scream was from a very different cause.

" Oh! lor, Mr. Bill," he cried, " take them off—do please, sir; they're biting me dreadfully."

" That's good news," returned Old Bill, grinning. " I shall take ye oop to the guv'nor jest ye are."

" Oh, my!" yelled Lobby Panks, clutching at the lobsters in despair, " what shall I do? My arms are black and blue, I know."

" Coom on," cried Old Bill; " the sooner we reach Scarum School, the better for you."

Sneak and coward as Lobby was, his two schoolfellows could not stand there and witness his despair, without attempting a rescue; but Old Bill produced a rope's-end, and kept the boys at bay.

" Coom a leetle nearer," he said, enticingly; " and I'll leave the marks on ye that ye won't rub off in a hurry. Coom a little nearer, lads."

Charley and Tim declined the invitation, and made good their retreat behind a volley of seaweed, and left the unfortunate Lobby to settle his own affair.

" Werry good," cried Old Bill. " I shall have yer one by one. I've got one warmint, and I means to keep him."

" Oh! do let me go," cried Lobby.

" Don't waste words, lad," said Old Bill, seizing Lobby by the collar and leading him away.

Lobby's appearance created no little sensation in the streets of Winkle-on-the-Sea.

Such a sight as a beachman leading a youth in Lobby's state was not often seen, and by the time Scarum School was reached a crowd had collected, and hooted and cheered in turns.

Mr. Crammer heard the commotion, and went to a window to ascertain the cause, and to his horror and indignation beheld that one of his pupils had caused the uproar.

Griddle was in ecstacies, but his transports became somewhat moderated when he saw Mr. Crammer at the window.

The window opened, and the schoolmaster bade Griddle admit Old Bill and the captive Lobby, but to be cautious that none of the crowd passed the gate.

Griddle felt himself once more a beadle,

as he proceeded to execute this order. His eye became brighter, his nostrils dilated, and his step was firmer and more official in its stride.

"Now then," he cried, waving his hand, "stand back there. Stand back, will you?"

But the crowd wouldn't, and continued to press forward, hoot, yell, and cheer louder than ever.

"This must be some terrible dream," groaned Mr. Crammer. "Scarum School disgraced in this style. "Why don't you open that gate?" he screamed to Griddle.

"Ah! why doesn't he?" exclaimed a greasy butcher lad. "Now then, Guy Fox, don't you hear what the guv'nor ses?"

The crowd had by this time squeezed both Lobby and Old Bill flat against the bars of the gate. Several of the lobsters relaxed their hold, and were seized and carried off by members of the assembly; but others of a more revengeful nature held on, and, as if inspired by the shouting, nipped Lobby's limbs more unmercifully than before. Not a muscle in Old Bill's face moved, nor did he speak a word save at their arrival, when he demanded admittance. He utterly ignored the crowd, and stood with his heavy hand on Lobby's collar, waiting for Griddle to open the gate.

The ex-beadle was in a sad plight; he knew that to open the gate would insure a rush of the British populace, while on the other hand Lobby and his captor could not be kept out all day.

"What am I to do?" he inquired of Mr. Crammer. "If I open the gate, they'll bust in and overrun the place, like a 'erd o' wild bulls."

"Send for the police!" roared Mr. Crammer in a state of frenzy.

"P'raps you'll go round by the back and drop over the cliff yourself," growled Griddle. "The police wouldn't stand no chance with sech a mob."

Probably the force (three in number) were perfectly aware of this fact, and viewing the assembly from a safe distance, had sought a more peaceful clime.

The crowd were becoming impatient, and sundry suggestions were made.

One hinted that he knew of a chimney-sweep not far off, who would lend a short ladder willingly; another thought it proper that the gate should be "bust;" while a third, a gentleman smoking a short clay pipe, black to the stem, remarked, with sundry adjectives, that if Griddle had any respect for his life, the gate would be thrown open at once.

And how felt the unhappy cause of this turmoil—miserable? No. Lobby heard the shouts, saw the forms of Mr. Crammer, and Griddle, and Old Bill—became aware that the upper windows were filled with the heads of his schoolmates, felt that he was fast undergoing the process of mangling by the crowd, but all without any sense of fear or apprehension.

Lobby was too far gone for that; vague ideas filled his head that it was a lark, but everything was misty and undefined.

"I tell you what," roared Griddle, seeing that the crowd showed no signs of dispersing; "I tell you what, my lads, if you are not off I'll have the b'ilin' lot on yer locked up."

A roar of laughter followed, but they fell back, and Griddle approached and unbarred the gate.

What followed he could not remember, but he felt his head come in contact with the wall of his lodge, stars and bright lights danced before his eyes, and then all was blank.

When he recovered he was in the kitchen, the cook standing near him with a basin of water in her hand, and Dick close by with a bottle.

Griddle snatched at the bottle, and applied it to his mouth, but, alas! it was vinegar, and he cast it from him with an expression of rage, and staggering to his feet, inquired if Mr. Crammer and the "warmints" had survived the crowd.

He heard then that at the moment of peril a "blue" had arrived, and the crowd dispersed, and that Lobby was at that moment in the hands of Mr. Crammer.

CHAPTER LX.

GRIDDLE PROPOSES AGAIN.

"Mary—Mary. Will yer have me? I ain't a man to be put off, and I axes you once ag'in."

These words were uttered by Mr. Griddle, in Mr. Crammer's kitchen.

"Don't make a fool of yourself," said Mary. "Get up." It should have been stated that the lover had assumed a kneeling position. "What do you think people would think if they saw you?"

"I don't care," exclaimed Griddle, desperately. "Oh! Mary, if you could only look on me with a favourable heye!"

"But I can't," returned Mary, "so it's use. If you bother me again I shall tell M Crammer."

"I've a sprained hankle," said Griddle, softly, "through a warmint as tied a bit o' string across the stairs, and now I've a broken 'art; there's nothin' left for me but the grave."

"Don't talk nonsense," said Mary, "but go on with your work."

"I will," said Griddle, "the work of destruction. Where's the nearest chemist?"

"They're all shut up," Mary replied, laughing. "Won't a rope do as well?"

"Go it, Mary, haim your harrows at my bustin' 'art. You never had a bustin' 'art, did yer?"

"Now, once for all," cried Mary, "will you cease your stupid prate? You have been at that beer barrel again. If you want to hang yourself, why go and do it, I won't stop you."

"Werry good," said Griddle. "If them's your sentiments, wot have I to hope or live for? Good bye, Mary—good bye. You won't forget my last words—I loves yer."

Griddle left the kitchen and staggered upstairs, and Mary sat down to laugh.

"But what if the old idiot was to hang himself!" she thought. "He is anything but sober. I think I'll go and see if he is in his lodge."

Mary let herself out and ran across to the lodge, but the place was in darkness and no Griddle was there.

Mary hastened back, and ran upstairs to the schoolroom, hoping to find the love-sick individual there; but no, Griddle was nowhere to be found, and Mary became pale and faint with fright.

"Good heavens!" she exclaimed, "what can have become of the man? Oh! if he should have hurt himself I should never forgive myself. What shall I do?"

Mary then thought it better to communicate with Mr. Crammer, and ran swiftly down-stairs to carry the thought into effect.

On the first landing she stopped and uttered a scream which ran through the house, for there, hanging to the door opposite to her was the figure of a man suspended from the door by a piece of rope.

Hiding her face in her hands, and screaming as she ran, Mary fled down-stairs to Mr. Crammer's study, the door of which she threw open, much to the astonishment of that learned gentleman, who was at that moment concocting a new plan to torture the youthful mind.

"What's the matter?" exclaimed Mr. Crammer, rising from his seat. "Are you mad, girl?"

"Oh! no, sir. Griddle,—that is Mr. Griddle—pro-pro-posed to me, sir, and I refused him, and he's gone and hung hisself, sir."

Mary, having delivered these words, burst into tears.

"Hanged himself!" cried Mr. Crammer. "Unhappy man! Wretched girl, do you know I am ruined? Where is the—the—"

"He's hung on the door of the second landing," cried Mary. "Oh, lor! oh, dear!"

Mr. Crammer, white as a sheet, took the lamp from the table with a trembling hand, and bade Mary conduct him to the remains of the unhappy Griddle.

Mary complied, with many tears, sobs, and sighs. Mr. Crammer started back on beholding the fearful object, but the next instant burst into a loud laugh and smote the hat of the—dummy, and revealed a figure cleverly stuffed with straw!

Mary gave a scream of delight, and a husky voice inquired—

"Is that you, Mary?"

It was Griddle, who came stumbling down the stairs and fell involuntarily at the feet of Mary and Mr. Crammer.

"What is the meaning of this, sir?" demanded Mr. Crammer.

"It's all ri'," returned Griddle, attempting to rise. "We hold uns are fond of a drop a' times. Good health, sir."

"You drunken scoundrel?" roared Mr. Crammer, "you shall leave the house a month from this day. And now, Mary, you will go back to the kitchen while I investigate this matter."

Mr. Crammer did his best, but nothing came of his investigations; but that night it was noted that sounds of suppressed laughter came from Lively Benson's bed.

CHAPTER LXI.

APPROACHING THE BREAK-UP.—THE DISCOVERY OF THE GHOST.

AND now the month of June was well advanced, and the Midsummer holidays were approaching. Writing books were undergoing the process of cleaning, blots erased, and finger-marks removed with india-rubber, diabolical productions of the pupils, called drawings, passed through the ushers' hands for finishing touches, and a general relaxation of discipline gladdened the hearts of the boys of Scarum School.

Even Griddle showed up literally bright, and was seen to smile occasionally, and once Mr. Crammer detected him in a corner in the act of chuckling over something.

Being questioned, he confessed that th "holidays were comin' on, and he naturall felt light and gay."

As Mr. Crammer felt happy also, he did not reprove his servitor, beyond hinting that if Griddle indulged in many such performances, it might lead strangers to doubt his sanity.

Last, but not least, the ghost—that mysterious unknown midnight visitant, having lain quiet for a week, came out as vigorous as ever.

"MR. TIDD—TID!" THUNDERED MR. CRAMMER, "WHAT TOMFOOLERY IS THIS?"

It crossed the ground during the darkness, and stopped up the keyhole of Griddle's lodge, so that our worthy friend was unable to get out in the morning; it hung pieces of carpet, sheets, and other articles out of the window; it haunted the dormitories, and spread a vague terror through the whole house.

Mrs. Margery, the housekeeper, never went to bed with less than two female attendants, who, having safely seen her between the sheets, scampered through the corridor to their own room. The boys told horrible yarns to each other until the very hair of their heads was lifted up—in fact, the whole house was in a fair way of being demoralized.

Only two men maintained their composure, viz., Mr. Crammer and Mr. Tidd.

The former despatched his son quickly to a friend's house a few miles away, and went earnestly to work to put an end to these pranks at once and for ever.

He bought a stout life-preserver, an extra cane or two, and with these lay down every night, resolved to spring up as soon as he heard a sound; but as always happens in such cases, he dropped into a sound sleep, and the ghost continued his rampageous course unchecked.

"This is monstrous—incredible!" he said, one morning to Mr. Pendulum; "the door of my room was opened last night, and somebody cried out—'Get up, Crammer—don't come the sluggard dodge!' Now that was no ghost."

"Certainly not," said the usher, gravely.

"Then what is it?"

"That's the question, Mr. Pendulum, and we must find it out. It has gone past a joke. The whole house is made restless and uneasy with this foolery. You look far from well."

"I'm very poorly," replied the usher; "my digestion is bad—has been for years—but lately it has grown worse. I am troubled at night—these disturbances haunt me, and I sleep very badly. I scarcely rest at all."

"No wonder," rejoined the schoolmaster; "the events here are beyond the whole experience of my lifetime."

"If the culprit is discovered, sir, punish him heavily."

"I intend to do so."

Nothing more was said that day, and Scarum School enjoyed a quiet night; not a sound was heard—but in the kitchen the shadowy visitor had been up to something: apparently endeavouring to make a dumpling, for a basin full of flour and water, partly mixed, was found, and a cloth ready on the table for the boiling.

A saucepan was also placed over the empty grate.

When this discovery was made, the cook and the other servants, except Dick and Griddle, went straight to the housekeeper and gave warning.

"They couldn't a-bear it any longer," they said; "and what could be expected of a house that was built over a smugglers' cave, where lots of murderous villains were buried, which Master Thorn had read of in books."

The housekeeper conveyed this intelligence to Mr. Crammer, who bit his lips in quiet fury, and having sent for Charley, gave him a dose of "Tickler," to take the romance-reading propensities out of him, and then sat thinking for some time, until Mr. Tidd unexpectedly made his appearance.

The usher was very pale, and he hesitated in his walk as he advanced towards the master, who saw at a glance that something was the matter with him.

"Have you been disturbed in the night?"

"I was aroused early this morning," returned Mr. Tidd, pointedly.

"By whom?"

"*The ghost!*"

Mr. Crammer stared.

A clue appeared to be coming at last.

"Could you see it?"

"Yes, sir."

"And you know it?"

"*Well—it was Mr. Pendulum!*"

Had he told the master of Scarum School that it was a white elephant in top boots, he could not have looked more astonished; he was overwhelmed.

"I know I ought to be careful what I say," pursued the usher, "but I have good grounds for the charge. I believe the ghost to be r. Pendulum, and no other."

"But belief is not evidence."

"Hear me, sir, and judge for yourself. It was growing light this morning, when I suddenly awoke as if I had been loudly called. I am a sound sleeper generally, and this made it more astonishing. Sitting up in bed, I looked towards the part of the room Mr. Pendulum occupies, and perceived that his couch was empty."

"Ha! that was strange."

"I thought so, sir; and while I was pondering on it the handle of our door was turned slowly and silently. The light was strong enough to see that, and, resolving to feign sleep, I lay back again and quietly composed myself as Mr. Pendulum entered."

The usher paused to give impression to this announcement.

Mr. Crammer gazed upon the speaker with an absorbing interest.

"He came in," pursued the usher, "with a steady step, closed the door, and crept into bed, where he lay *chuckling like a schoolboy who has played a successful prank.*"

"Did you speak to him?"

"No, sir, although I was tempted to ; but second thoughts told me that such a course would be injudicious."

"Perhaps it would have been."

"What could I say ? What could I prove ? A simple denial on his part would suffice to refute any accusation I might make."

"True."

"As it is, he does not suspect that he is discovered, although I am convinced that he is the author of all."

"But naturally of such a sober temperament !"

"A mask, sir !" rejoined the usher, warmly ; "a mask such as I have known a hundred men to wear. My ways of life have led me among many classes of people, and I have known even the most seriously disposed (apparently, of course) guilty of the grossest follies."

"I have heard of such things, Mr. Tidd. What would you propose doing ?"

"Watch him—watch him keenly, day and night."

"But he may suspect us."

"Leave the night to me ; in the day I shall be glad to be relieved."

"He certainly has changed very much of late," said Mr. Crammer, musing. "He carries with him a weary, tired look, and I have more than once detected him dozing during school hours."

"The want of sleep," said Mr. Tidd, triumphantly. "Every piece of evidence in favour of my accusation."

"He shall be watched," returned Mr. Crammer ; "but we must have the evidence of more than one. Should he leave his room again, do you think you can come quietly to me ?"

"I will try, sir."

"So be it. For the present, not a word to any one."

"Not a word, sir."

Throughout the day Mr. Crammer keenly watched his head usher. Mr. Pendulum certainly looked as if he had been up all night ; yawning frequently, and occasionally dozing off, soothed by the murmuring of the boys over their lessons.

The schoolmaster ventured to allude to this when the day's duties were over.

"You look very much fatigued," he said.

"I am, sir," replied the usher. "I suppose it is the heat of the weather—the glass was eighty-eight in the shade to-day."

"So warm !" exclaimed the master, with an air of surprise.

"It was, sir," replied Mr. Pendulum, looking at his principal out of the corners of his eyes ; "and heat always overcomes me."

"You sleep but little, you told me."

"My rest is broken," replied the usher, "but I do not lie awake."

"No," thought the master, "but you walk awake ; and it shall go hard with me but I make one in your next perambulation."

He then bade the unsuspecting usher good evening, and went for a walk to think the matter out.

CHAPTER LXII.

THE GHOST'S LAST WALK.

AT the usual hour, the various inhabitants of Scarum School retired to rest.

In the dormitories there was little or none of the usual skirmishing, no bolstering, no invading rival sanctums, no punishments of sneaks and other culprits.

The ghost had a quieting effect upon all, and made bed a most desirable resting-place ; for there sheets drawn over the head shut out half the terrors of the midnight visitor.

Mr. Crammer, as usual, resolved to keep awake, and, in accordance with his established custom, was speedily sound asleep.

He was aroused by a hand upon his shoulder, and a voice in his ear—

"Get up at once, sir."

"What is it ?"

"Hush !" returned the voice of Mr. Tidd. "He is up, and at his usual work."

Mr. Crammer then comprehended the position, and softly arose.

The room was very dark ; but he managed to find his slippers, made of soft list, and especially purchased for this night duty.

And, taking Mr. Tidd by the arm, they crept quietly from the room.

"He went down-stairs," whispered the usher ; "and I heard him strike the match upon the wall."

"Did you observe the light ?"

"No. I came straight to you."

By this time they were at the head of the stair-case, and, guided by the banisters, proceeded slowly down.

Half-way, they suddenly observed the flash of a light below, and halted.

"He is coming," whispered the usher.

Mr. Crammer leaned over the banisters, and by this means commanded a view of the hall below.

The light grew stronger, and he beheld Mr. Pendulum, in night attire, emerge from a passage leading to the kitchen, with a candle in his hand, and a sack upon his shoulder.

It was empty ; and having spread it upon the floor, like a door-mat, he retired the way he came.

"What is he up to ?" whispered Mr. Crammer.

"No telling, sir," replied Mr. Tidd ; "but we had better remain here. He will return."

The usher was right.

In about a minute—a very long one it seemed—Mr. Pendulum came back, with some fire-irons in his hand.

These he placed carefully in the sack, and, putting down the light, performed an idiotic dance round his prize, and again disappeared.

"How idiotic !" said the schoolmaster. "I can scarcely credit the evidence of my senses."

"You never know the nature of a man," softly returned Mr. Tidd, "unless you have an opportunity of watching him when he fancies he's alone."

"Perhaps not."

The return of Mr. Pendulum checked conversation for the present ; and this time he was laden with sundry boots, which he placed in a row, and contemplated with much apparent satisfaction.

He then placed them one by one in company with the fire-irons, and disappeared once more.

"Shall we go down now ?" asked Mr. Crammer.

"No, sir. Let us wait and see the end of his contemptible folly."

The two ushers had never been friends ; and Mr. Pendulum had tried very hard to obtain the discharge of Mr. Tidd.

Judge, then, of the satisfaction the latter experienced at this state of things.

Foolish as all the movements of the head usher were, the two watchers could not help feeling a breathless interest in all he did ; and when he returned with a leg of mutton, intended for the schoolmaster's dinner on the morrow, and put it into the same receptacle, they watched the process as carefully as if he were hiding the body of a ruthlessly-murdered victim.

The mutton deposited, they lost sight of him again ; and they sat down upon the stairs to rest.

Five minutes, and no Mr. Pendulum.

The old clock below ticked off the moments slowly and laboriously.

The wind from the sea whistled musically through the keyhole.

The murmuring of the restless waves fell upon their ears.

But all else was still.

Ten minutes and no Mr. Pendulum.

The old clock seemed to sound the passing time slower and slower.

The wind died away, as if it waited, breathlessly. like the two men, for the usher's return

The sound of the waves seemed softer ; and the stillness of the house became oppressive.

A quarter of an hour, and no Mr. Pendulum.

A little French clock in Mr. Crammer's bedroom struck one, and the tiny tintinnabulation floated towards them.

They could endure no more.

"I must go down," said Mr. Crammer. "He is perpetrating some folly in another part of the house."

They went down with extreme caution.

And it was well they did so ; for they had barely reached the hall when they heard the usher return.

Shrinking behind a large piece of furniture —an old wardrobe, and general receptacle for odds and ends—they awaited his coming ; and presently he appeared, carrying a spade upon his shoulder.

His object was now plain.

Having collected the articles together, he intended to bury them.

Shouldering the sack with much care, the midnight joker wended his way to the back garden, where he had already dug a very respectable apology for a grave.

This accounted for his long absence ; and Mr. Crammer marked with rage that it had been dug in the middle of his favourite bed of geraniums.

But he let Mr. Pendulum go on.

The candle, the usher left in the hall ; but what was done, the faint light of a waning moon enabled Mr. Crammer and his brother watcher to see.

With the utmost care, Mr. Pendulum deposited his burden upon the side of the grave, and lowered it. Then he performed another dance, looking strangely grotesque in his night apparel, and proceeded to fill it in.

He was very careful about this part of the performance, and frequently jumped into the hole to stamp the earth down with his slipper-encased feet. But he was very reckless with regard to the geraniums—shovelling them in with the rest as if of no value whatever.

"Now we will get back to the house," whispered Mr. Crammer, "and when he comes for the light accuse him of his folly."

"Very good, sir ; but why not now ?"

"I want to see his face: we should lose the effect here."

This Mr. Tidd did not attempt to deny, and they returned as softly as they came, taking up their position behind the old wardrobe.

The candle had now burned rather low, and the top of the wick presented the appearance of a bloated spider, who had terminated a murderous career in the flame.

The clock was ticking faster, or it seemed so, as if to celebrate the downfall of the wicked joker, and the wind was whistling again quite merrily.

"He is a long time," said Mr. Crammer, fidgeting, after a few moments.

"Putting away the spade, perhaps."

"Can he possibly have seen us?"

"No; I cannot think that."

"Or heard us?"

"We watched as quiet as mice; my feet are only stockinged."

"Hush! what's that up-stairs?"

"I heard nothing."

"I am as nervous," muttered the school-master, wiping his face, "as if about to arrest a murderer!"

"I certainly feel like a burglar or a police-officer," said Mr. Tidd. "I don't know which."

"Quiet! I hear him."

The soft sound of Mr. Pendulum's footsteps was distinctly heard, but he seemed in no hurry, apparently, halting here and there as a traveller might, when there are many objects to attract his curiosity; once he coughed, but in so stealthy a manner that it showed how careful he was about alarming the house.

"I should like to knock him down!" muttered Mr. Crammer.

"I should be most happy to execute the commission," whispered Mr. Tidd.

"Perhaps he might prove violent."

"We are two to one."

"You are right, Mr. Tidd. He shall be knocked down, but the pleasure of the task must be mine!"

"I would rather do it, sir."

"No doubt; but I have prayed almost for this moment, and would rather not be baulked of the pleasure. Can you hear him?"

"Yes; he is coming nearer. Did you hear that?"

"No; what was it?"

"He was chuckling!"

"I'll chuckle him!" muttered Mr. Crammer; "support me when I rush forward."

"I will, sir."

"The dastard might strike me a foul blow."

"Most likely, I should say."

"Be silent, now—I can see him."

With a slow and stately step, like the ghost of Hamlet's father in deshabille, Mr. Pendulum emerged from the darkness, looking straight before him.

There was a self-satisfied leer upon his face, and he patted his hands together, in a way betokening quiet enjoyment.

All this was very exasperating to Mr. Crammer, who rolled up the cuffs of his dressing-gown to the elbow, and nudging Mr. Tidd to support him, prepared to rush forward.

The second usher had never removed his eyes from his rival after he appeared, and the angry triumph he felt was at the first intense. But it slowly died away—there was

something in the face of Mr. Pendulum which caused a revulsion of feeling, and as Mr. Crammer was about to rush forward, he threw his arms around him.

"Hold off, for Heaven's sake, sir!" he whispered.

"Let me go!" gasped Mr. Crammer; "my leg of mutton—my geraniums—my boots! I will not be threatened! Are you, too, in this conspiracy?"

"No, sir," returned Mr. Tidd; "but if you touch that man now, you may kill him! Don't you see, sir, that he is WALKING IN HIS SLEEP?"

CHAPTER LXIII.
DISMISSAL OF THE GHOST.

THE terrified cry of Mr. Tidd startled the master of Scarum School. Walking in his sleep! What a revelation of all the mysteries of months past! At once a conviction of proof and innocence.

The flood of thought which passed through Mr. Crammer's brain quickly overwhelmed him, and he stood with eyes and mouth open, a counterpart of the sleep-walker—his double, as it were—and the appearance of the two horrified the usher, who seized his superior by the arm.

"For goodness' sake, sir," he whispered "make an effort to recover yourself."

"Walking in his sleep!" muttered Mr. Crammer. "What a horrible idea!"

"Hush! sir," returned the usher; "draw aside for a moment, he is going ups-tairs."

"Would it not be better to waken him?" asked the master.

"That waking might be his last," replied Mr. Tidd, solemnly, "especially to a man of a naturally nervous and irritable temperament. Mr. Pendulum could not bear the shock."

"Shall we follow him?"

"Yes, sir!—but as cautiously as possible Heaven alone knows what crime he might commit in this unconscious state."

This thought had struck them both; and pale with a terrible misgiving, they slowly followed the head usher, who was leisurely ascending the stairs.

Despite the ludicrous events of the evening —or rather night—there was a solemnity about this man, moved to walk and act by some unknown power, which made both the hearts of Mr. Crammer and Mr. Tidd quake within them.

At another time, and under other circumstances, they would have been amused with the appearance that Mr. Pendulum presented —his long-night dress, his night-cap rakishly on one side, lit up by the candle he bore, made him a very comical object indeed.

There was yet another surprise for the watchers. Reaching the landing, Mr. Pendulum suddenly blew out the light. They heard a slight rustling of his footsteps, and all was still.

"Now where is he gone?" whispered Mr. Crammer.

"To bed perhaps—let us see."

The road was familiar—and they entered softly. Pausing a moment, Mr. Tidd struck a light, and held it aloft. Mr. Pendulum's bed was empty.

"We must look him up at any risk," said the schoolmaster, nervously. "I could not return to rest with his movements any way in doubt."

"Certainly not, sir," returned the usher, "and I think we may retain the light."

"Decidedly so."

They went quickly through the passage and down-stairs. The boys were peacefully sleeping, and they found no sign of the sleep-walker; they went again below, but he was not there—they returned to his sleeping-room, and failed to find him.

"Now this is the greatest mystery of all," said Mr. Crammer, puzzled.

"He has escaped from the house by some means."

"Perhaps walking on the roof."

They went up to the roof, but he was not there, and, their anxiety terribly increased, entered Mr. Crammer's own room.

As they passed the threshold, a ponderous snore saluted them.

They fell against each other, the candle dropped from the stick, and they were once more in darkness.

Mr. Crammer was the first to recover—indignation brought him round.

"He's in my bed!" he growled; "get a light, Mr. Tidd."

The usher sought the box of matches, which had fallen with the candle, and obtained a light. There, snug between the sheets, and very much at home, lay Mr. Pendulum in his employer's bed!

"Let him be there," said Mr. Crammer, after a pause; "in the morning he will awake and find himself there, which will convince him that something is wrong, and what I have to say will do the rest. For my own part, the night is warm, and a rest upon the sofa in the study will do for me."

They retired and left him—Mr. Tidd immediately seeking his own couch and making up for his disturbed repose.

When the morning bell sounded and he awoke, he was astonished to find Mr. Pendulum in his usual place. He awoke, yawned, and proceeded to dress as calmly as usual.

Mr. Tidd was astounded, and could hardly believe his eyes or his ears when Mr. Pendulum remarked—

"I think I have slept better than usual." It sounded so much like a piece of bravado—as if he knew of his nightly wanderings, and was resolved to brave them out.

To this observation Mr. Tidd made no reply. It was just possible he might commit himself, and what there was to say had better be said by Mr. Crammer.

That gentleman, after tossing about on his strange couch for a couple of hours, had fallen into a sound sleep, and was only awakened when Mary came in to dust the room.

The girl was, of course, much surprised to see him there—especially as an empty bottle happened by accident to be on the table—but as Mr. Crammer made no remark, but simply walked out to get a breath of air, she reserved her opinions on the point for the edification of the kitchen.

He encountered Mr. Tidd on his way out for a breath of air on the cliffs, and the two joined company. Then the master of Scarum learned of the sleep-walker's return to his couch.

The question arose whether the usher was "foxing" or not. There was a possibility of it; but, looking at his general character, it did not seem probable.

"Anyhow," said Mr. Crammer, "he leaves my establishment this very day."

Accordingly, when breakfast was over, and Mr. Pendulum was making his way to the schoolroom, Griddle interrupted him with an intimation from Mr. Crammer that he was wanted in the study. Thither the unsuspecting usher went.

"Mr. Pendulum," said the master of Scarum School, gravely, "take a chair."

The usher took one; and perceiving the expression upon his employer's face, looked very grave.

"Mr. Pendulum, I have found the ghost."

"I am glad of that, sir," returned the the usher; "but are you sure?"

"Certain this time; but I am not sure that you have any particular cause to rejoice. Pray who do you think it is?"

Mr. Pendulum ran over a list of names, including the principal school culprits, Mr. Tidd, Griddle, and the boy Dick, but received a negative to all.

"Then on my word, sir," said the usher, "I have no idea who it is."

"Prepare for a surprise," returned Mr. Crammer. "The ghost is no other than—yourself."

"Impossible!" cried the usher, starting up. "What new calumny is this? Mr. Tidd is at the bottom of it."

"Be not so hasty, Mr. Pendulum, but

TIM STOOD LIKE ONE PETRIFIED.

listen to me. Are you aware that you are a sleep-walker?"

The usher suddenly turned very pale, and a frightened look leaped into his eyes.

"As—as—a boy," he stammered, "I—I—believe I left my room occasionally."

"And not since?"

"Not that I have heard of, sir."

"Then the habit which so long slumbered in you has awakened here—there can be no doubt. I watched you myself last night. You buried various things in the heart of my geranium bed. You can see your own work, if you desire it."

Mr. Pendulum buried his face in his hands, and seemed much agitated. It was some minutes ere he looked up again and spoke.

"But the tricks are so wanton and foolish," he said. "It is possible they could have been committed by me—a man?"

"Do we not dream foolishly at times?"

"True, sir. Well, I suppose I must accept my fate. What is it, sir?"

"You must leave at once—a change is necessary for us, and may be beneficial to you. It is the only cure for somnambulism—at least I have heard so. At any rate, I could not retain you here; and you are not so unreasonable as to expect it?"

"I am not, sir," replied the usher, "and will go at once."

In two hours he was gone, and not until he was well on his way, did Mr. Crammer give a brief sketch to the boys, informing them that the ghost was discovered and now laid at rest for ever.

*   *   *   *   *

And now the time drew near for parting. Another night, and Scarum School would be deserted. Packing up is a tiresome affair, but with boys about to realize the delights of holiday and freedom, there is nothing more delightful.

Let us then take a peep into Charley and Tim's room. Here those two young gentlemen, and the other occupants of the spacious chamber, are busy at work.

Discarded school-books have a hard time of it; they are trodden under foot, thrown as missiles, and those tyrants which speak of the mysteries of Euclid and Algebra, a short time since so terrible, are now divested of their power, and treated with the greatest contempt.

Garments of all descriptions are thrust indiscriminately into trunks and boxes, the boys well knowing that the task will have to be performed again when the housekeeper comes round, but they like to torment that good lady.

"Hullo, boys!" cried Tim, suddenly. "Look here. Here's my old friend."

Tim held up the skeleton suit, and the boys roared with delight.

"Bless it!" Tim pursued, "I wouldn't part with it for a hundred pounds."

"Have it stuffed," cried Lively Benson.

"What a jolly Guy Faux it would make!" cried another.

"Glorious!" exclaimed a third, "if it only had its owner in it."

Tim replied not to these satirical remarks, but went on with his packing.

"How are you getting on, Langley?" inquired Charley. "What are you looking so glum about?"

"Nothing particular," returned the youth addressed, "but I can't find a whole pair of socks, they're all odd ones, and the toes are all out of those. Oh! shan't I have a lecture when I get home!"

"Never mind, old fellow," said Tim, looking up. "Get on, for the dinner bell will ring directly."

In a few minutes every vestige of clothing except that which was being worn was under lock and key, and the boys chatted, and laid out their schemes for the holidays, until the bell rang to summon them to dine.

They rushed from the room shouting and laughing, and commenced sliding down the banisters, jumping down stairs, and endangering their lives by committing other acts expressive of joy, when they encountered their old enemy, Griddle.

His face was pale, and it was evident he had suffered intensely that morning. Over one shoulder he carried a warming-pan, but whether for defence or whether he had been requested to carry it up-stairs cannot be said, but when he beheld the legions of tormentors, he waved the instrument on high, and without waiting for the attack he smote Lively Benson on the cranium, and brandished the weapon again on high.

The metallic sound of the pan falling heavily upon Benson's head rang through the house, and brought another troop of youths to see what was the matter.

A glance was sufficient, and they rushed up-stairs to support their companion.

Griddle knew now that he must fight or suffer; and uttering a yell of defiance, raised the pan and succeeded in smiting Tim on the ——well, on the extremity of his jacket behind, causing the afflicted youth to descend half a dozen stairs at a miraculous speed.

"Get close to him and he's helpless," said Charley, leading the way.

But Griddle was too quick, and again a loud note rang forth from the pan as it made acquaintance with another youth's back.

The combat, however, was not of long duration, and Griddle was soon overpowered and held captive.

"What shall we do with him?" cried Tim, rubbing the afflicted part.

"Give him a dozen with his own weapon," cried a voice.

"Bravo!" said Charley, "a good idea. Now, boys, stand back, and let me speak to the prisoner."

"I'll be the executioner," roared Benson; "he hit me first."

"Very good," said Charley, passing the pan, and then turning to Griddle, said, "Prisoner, thou hast heard thy doom; prepare to meet it."

"What d'yer mean?" exclaimed the unhappy wretch, becoming paler than before.

"The sentence is that you are to receive a dozen whacks with an instrument known as a warming-pan," said Charley, gravely. "No time is to be lost. Prisoner, bear the punishment, meekly or it will go hard with you."

"Stand out of the way, you warmints," cried Griddle, dashing at the boys and upsetting several of them.

But, like elves in the fairy story, they swarmed round him, and held him tight.

His hands were held, and he was thrown over the banister, and hung there in a most undignified manner, like an article of wearing apparel hanging out to dry.

"Oh! you wicious young brutes," cried Griddle. "I'll p'ison some on yer, I will. Oh! let me go. There, the blood is rushin' into my 'ead."

"Executioner, advance," said Charley, "and wait for the word of command."

Benson advanced with a martial stride, and poising the instrument of torture, waited for the signal.

"One!" said Charley, dropping his hand.

Bang!

Griddle uttered a yell of mingled rage, pain, and despair, and the boys literally shrieked th laughter.

"Two!" said Charley.

Bang!

"Three!"

Bang!

What is the meaning of this noise?" inquired a well-known voice from below. "Really, boys, although it is a joyous time, I cannot suffer such an uproar to take place."

"They're a-murderin' o' me," groaned Griddle; "they've smit me with the warmin'-pan until they've bust it in."

Bang went the pan again; then it was thrown down-stairs, a sound of pattering of feet followed, and Griddle was alone.

Griddle sat down on the stairs, but immediately got up again, tears springing into his eyes.

"If I hadn't the disposition of a hangel," he said, "there'd be murder in this 'ere 'ouse afore the day was out."

"Griddle," shouted the master, "why don't you come down? the boys are waiting for dinner."

"If I'ad the management on 'em," muttered Griddle, as he descended, "they'd have to wait a long time for their grub."

Mr. Crammer knew that to attempt to check the spirits of the pupils on this day of days would be perfectly useless, and it was for that reason he had not replied to Griddle's complaint; indeed, when the afflicted individual arrived in the dining-room, the pedagogue was observed to smile, and even Griddle, as the minutes flew by, softened, for he consoled himself with the thought that soon he would be left in peace.

Ample justice was done to the meal, and the boys rushed into the playground.

"What shall we do this afternoon?" cried Tim.

"What do you think of cricket?" said Charley.

"Too slow," said Tim." Let us go down to the beach and pay a parting visit to Old and Young Bill."

"If we can find them," Charley returned; "but it is all the same to me. Here comes Benson and Langley—they'll go, I know."

"And if we could only induce Lobby to accompany us, the party would be complete," said Tim, laughing.

"I'll manage that," said Benson, as he strolled up. "You fellows go down to the beach, and in ten minutes I'll be with you and bring Lobby, or perish in the attempt."

CHAPTER LXIV.

AN EXCURSION TO THE BEACH.

BENSON was as good as his word, and ten minutes after the others arrived on the beach, he arrived leading the passive Lobby.

"I told you he would," Benson said. "It wasn't likely that he would be out of this lark —the last, perhaps, we may ever have together."

"I've had enough of your larks," Lobby returned, "and I wouldn't have come if I had known your game. You said you were going for a quiet walk."

"And have I not kept my word, most potent Lobby?" said Lively Benson. "Did I assault or chaff any wayfarer on the way from the school?"

"No, you didn't," Lobby replied, "and I'm not going to give any of you a chance to get me into any more scrapes. I'm off."

"Not so fast," said Tim, catching Lobby by the arm. "Why won't you go with us?"

"Because I don't feel inclined," said Lobby.

"The fact is," said Tim, "you're afraid."

"I'm not!"

"Then come with us."

"I shan't."

Our hero Tim here produced a slip of sea-weed of a species resembling a leathern thong, and quite as hard.

Lobby eyed this weapon, and well knowing how soon it would be applied on a tender portion of his frame, consented to become one of the party.

"That's right," said Tim; "and now let us be off. We shall just catch him boiling the lobsters."

Lobby Panks sprang back in horror.

"What!" he cried, "going up to Old Bill's. Not if I know it."

"Come along, Lobby," said Charley, "there's no time to lose."

"I tell you I won't go," Lobby exclaimed, shrinking back, "no, not if you cut me to pieces," he went on, as Tim drew forth and flourished the sea-weed whip.

But Lobby's nature was not a hard one, and a couple of stingers were enough to make him alter his opinion, and follow his tormentors.

"Here's a mess!" groaned the hapless youth. "Old Bill will half kill me if he catches me again."

"We're all in the same boat, for that matter," said Langley. "Old Bill loves us all alike."

"Don't talk to him," said Tim. "There's the cottage, and look, smoke is rising from the chimney. It's all right, he's sure to be at home."

The five precious youths surrounded the cottage, approaching cautiously, as it was well known that Old Bill kept sticks and other weapons in ambush; but all was quiet.

A whispered consultation was held, and it was resolved to send a scout to reconnoitre. Charley volunteered, and creeping cautiously up to the cottage, peered into the nearest window.

During all this Lobby had remained in an agony of fright. In his mind's eye, he saw himself a victim to Old Bill's fury, and when he saw Charley suddenly drop on his hands and knees under the window he could scarcely suppress a cry.

But nothing had occurred, and Charley beckoned his comrades to approach, which they did with the utmost caution, crawling through the grass Indian fashion.

"Anybody at home?" Mat Langley asked, in a whisper.

"Yes."

"Who is it?"

"Young Bill. He's sitting before the fire, waiting for the water to boil."

"Then look out for Old Bill," said Tim, "he's sure to be somewhere about."

"Hush! don't speak so loud," Charley returned, "I don't think the old man is at home. I expect Young Bill is waiting his return."

"We'll try it," said Tim. "Keep your eye on the door, Charley, and you, Lobby, see no one is coming up or down the road."

Tim rose to his feet, and approaching the window, pushed it open, and hoped that Young Bill was well.

"I don't know as 'ow I'm any better for seein' thee," was the ungracious reply. "Cut it. Feyther will be 'ere d'rectly."

"Sorry to hear he's out," Tim returned; "I trust he still enjoys his usual good health."

"Dang 'ee for a haggravating warmint!" cried the youthful lobster-boiler. "Will 'ee cut it, afore I do 'ee a mischief?"

"How's the lobster trade?" inquired Lively Benson, putting his head in at the window.

"What! be there more on ye?" exclaimed Bill the younger. "If ye bean't all off, I'll shy some hot water over ye."

"Say not so, sweet and gentle youth," said Benson; "let not thy angry passions rise. Think of the days of our youth, our rambles on the seashore, where oft in heedless——"

This pathetic appeal to the feelings of Young Bill had no effect whatever; on the contrary, it seemed to exasperate him, insomuch that he flung a pipkin at the head of the poetic youth.

But the missile took a wrong direction, and passing through a couple of windows, smote the unsuspecting Lobby on the small of the back.

Naturally, this made matters worse, and Young Bill, seizing a formidable cudgel, made for the door, with the intent of charging the hated youths of Scarum School.

But again he was defeated.

Mat Langley, during the conversation, had gently opened the door and possessed himself of the key, which he now turned to advantage by locking the door from the outside.

Young Bill danced and capered in his passion, and sad to relate, used sundry adjectives of a questionable nature.

"Oh, wait till feyther comes," he cried; "he'll come up to Scarum Schule, and half murder some on ye."

"Do you see any one in the road?" asked Tim.

"No," replied Lobby; "there's a man in a cart about a mile off."

"That's feyther," cried Bill junior, joyfully; "he's comin' 'ome from market."

"Thanks, for giving us such timely warning;" and then, turning to Mat Langley, said, "Have you stopped the keyhole?"

"Yes," replied that youth, grinning; "and thrown the key over the cliff."

At a signal, the five conspirators scampered off, leaving the inmate of the cottage to vent his rage upon empty air; but Bill's feelings were such that he felt he must kick something, and falling upon a weak rush-bottomed chair, kicked it out of shape, and then sat down again to await the return of his parent.

Old Bill, riding quietly homeward with a cartful of live lobsters, suddenly espied the party of Scarum boys coming towards him.

"Them warmints," he muttered, "hev been up to the 'ouse, and there ain't a doubt but as how they've been pitchin' inter Bill. But they're too strong for me alone, the warmints don't stop at anythin'; they wouldn't mind haulin' off the net, and lettin' all the lobsters run loose—not a bit."

This soliloquy brought him up to the boys.

"Good afternoon," said Tim.

Old Bill answered with a growl.

"You're looking very well, sir," said Charley. "How is the fish trade?"

"That's a nice horse of yours," cried Benson, "you will make something of his bones after he is dead."

To all this Old Bill replied never a word, but jogged on, looking straight ahead.

"I say, look out," cried Langley, "there are three spokes out of one of the wheels."

"Which?" cried Old Bill, for a moment off his guard, and pulling up sharply. "Which wheel?"

"A slight mistake of mine," said Langley. "All right. Go on ahead."

Old Bill swore a little, shook his whip a great deal, and smote the unfortunate animal behind which he was travelling with all his might.

"Hold hard," screamed Tim, "the back of your cart has fallen down, and the lobsters are tumbling all over the road."

Not a muscle moved in Old Bill's face; he lit his pipe, applied the lash once more, ignoring his tormentors.

"It's a fact," roared Charley. "We're not joking. Look behind and you will see for yourself."

"They're creeping into the ditches," cried Benson. "You'll lose the lot if you don't look out."

Still no reply from Old Bill.

Without heeding a word, he drove up to his cottage door, and called to his son to assist im to unload.

"What be thee comin' through the window for?" he cried. "Bean't the door big enough?"

"Feyther," snivelled Young Bill, "there hev been Scarum boys, and they stole the key o' the door, locked me in, and throwed the key over the cliff."

"Dang em!" said Old Bill. "Sartenly I shall be the death of some on 'em; dash—

if they ain't enough to drive a man mad. Hallo! who's been bustin' the winders?"

"Scarum boys," replied the untruthful Bill.

"Well, lad, it can't be helped. Get out and lend me a hand."

Young Bill scrambled through the window, but his feet had scarcely touched *terra firma* when he gave vent to a most unmelodious howl of despair.

"What be the matter?" roared Old Bill.

"Oh! feyther," cried the son, "look behind."

"Who's comin'," cried the parent; "Scarum boys?"

"No. no. Look, feyther, the lobsters; they're all over the road."

Old Bill turned his head, and immediately a cold perspiration burst out upon his face.

"Dang it!" he muttered, "them warmints spoke the truth for once; what a fool I was not to look round!"

The board at the back of the cart, as Charley and his associates asserted, had given way, and the greater part of the lobsters had availed themselves of the opportunity to tumble out and and escape.

"Get thee a shovel, lad," roared Old Bill, "I'll lead the horse back while thee gathers them up."

"But, feyther," returned Bill, "there must be a lot gone, the Scarum boys hev cut and run wi' a heap on 'em."

"Dang it!" cried the irritated fisherman; "what be the use of crying over spilt milk? Get thee a shovel and basket, or the lot will be gone!"

Young Bill complied with alacrity, the ground was gone over again, and every vagrant lobster visible picked up and replaced in the cart.

"Bill," said the parent, "I shall leave thee to look arter the fish. I be goin' oop to town again."

"What for, feyther?" inquired his dutiful son.

"About these Scarum boys," said Old Bill; "I be goin' to see Mr. Fellowes, the magistrate. Danged if they won't drive me mad!"

"I know they will me," responded Bill the younger; "they bust the windows, locked the door, stopped up the key-hole with mud, and chucked the key away. Then they shied whopping big stones at me, and one on 'em 'it me in the harm and nearly broke it!"

"The warmints!" gasped Old Bill; "where be the stones, Bill? I'll show 'em to Mr. Fellowes."

Young Bill, who had been fibbing with respect to the stones, did not know how to reply for a minute or two, but at last he said—

"I shied them out of the winder ag'in, feyther."

"That be a pity," said Old Bill; "but never mind, I'll go down and ax Mr. Fellowes to lock the whole b'ilin' lot up!"

"D'ye think he'll do it?" inquired the son.

"O' course!" replied Old Bill, "and be glad o' the job; but get thee in, lad, and in with the lobsters, and be werry careful with 'em, for they be as fine a lot of fish as ever came out of the sea."

Young Bill promised obedience, and his father, after assisting to unload the living cargo, turned his back on the cottage and walked towards the town; the purpose of his visit our readers are already acquainted with.

He walked smartly along the shady side of the road, and when within half a mile of the town, he thought he heard the sound of voices from a field on the opposite side of the road.

Creeping softly across, and peering through the hedge, he beheld the party of Scarum boys seated on the grass in a circle, admiring something, which Old Bill could not see.

"My eye!" exclaimed Tim; "what a beauty! Wouldn't he give you a nip!"

"Ah!" rejoined Lobby; "I know from experience what they are!"

"They've got one o' my lobsters!" muttered Old Bill, between his teeth. "Werry good. We'll see about it in a minit!"

"I wonder what Old Bill will say when he gets home?" said Benson. "I say, Langley, it was hardly right to throw the key away."

Old Bill took particular notice of Mat's features, and jotted down several notes upon his memory.

"Oh! bother!" said Mat; "that's nothing. Just fancy Lobby coming out so strong, and collaring a lobster, after his adventure with Old Bill!"

"Bravo!" cried Tim, laughing, but the expression of his face changed the next instant, and uttering a cry of alarm, he scrambled to his feet and sped away.

Charley, Mat, and Benson, did the same, but Lobby was not quick enough, and fell a prey once more to Bill the elder.

"So, I've got ye ag'in?" said the fisherman, shaking Lobby after the fashion a terrier does a rat; "I don't take thee up to the school this time—oh! no. Thee shall spend a night in the lock-up, danged if thee shan't!"

"What have I done?" snivelled Lobby.

"Come on," said Old Bill, "we'll 'ear what the justices hev to say. I've been tormented by you and the other warmints quite long enough. Come on, I say."

"I won't," cried the struggling Lobby. "You—oh!"

The now desperate Master Panks, with some wild hope of escape, had made an on-slaught upon the fisherman's shins, and thus caused that cry of agony.

"You warmint!" cried Old Bill, smiting Lobby, heartily; "take that, and that, and that! I'll teach thee to bark people's shins. That shall go down to the charge, too, or my name ain't Bill. Now, then, are you comin' or am I to drag you afore the justice?"

"I haven't done anything," snivelle Lobby; "and won't go."

"Didn't you collar my lobsters t'other day?" exclaimed Old Bill; "and hain't you prigged one this afternoon?"

"No, I d—d—did not," returned the tearful Lobby; "the first time was an accident, and this afternoon, I picked the lobster up on the road."

"You knew it belonged to me," said Bill.

"W—w—we called after you," Lobby went on, "but you wouldn't look round."

"I don't care anything about that," persisted Old Bill; "I've found you with one o' my lobsters, and I locks ye up on a double charge, first for priggin', the second for being a nuisance, and worryin' an' assaultin' my son Bill."

"I didn't," roared Lobby, "the others made me come and keep watch to see when you came."

"I ain't goin' to waste no more words," said Old Bill; "are you comin' peaceably—Yes or no?"

Lobby tried to wrench himself from the grasp of Old Bill, but he might as well have attempted to get out of a vice.

And another attack on Old Bill's shins having proved a dismal failure, Lobby threw himself on the grass, and, shading his face with his arm, kept up a movement with his heels, highly suggestive of a youth's first lesson in boxing.

"For the last time," said Old Bill, "are you comin'?"

"No, I am not," roared Lobby; "you are not a policeman, and have no right to take me."

"That's true," muttered Old Bill, surveying the prostrate Lobby with anything but an expression of friendship. "I ain't a bobby, and wot's more, I hain't no wish to be. I've got an hidear."

"Get up," he said to Lobby; "I ain't a-goin' to take you afore the justices."

Lobby rose instantly, but still shading his face with his arm, as if expecting Old Bill's heavy hand.

"I ain't a-goin' to lock you up," Old Bill pursued; "I'll gie ye a chance. You know my son Bill?"

Old Bill might as well have asked Lobby if he knew "Tickler," that instrument of torture so ably wielded by Mr. Crammer.

"Well, ye see," said Old Bill, taking

CELEBRATING THE BIRTHDAY OF GRIDDLE.

Lobby's nod for a reply in the affirmative, "Bill 'as often said, ses he, 'Feyther, if I could only cotch one o' them Scarum boys alone, I'd show 'em who was the best man !'"

Lobby shivered visibly at these words.

"And 'ere's a chance," continued Old Bill; "you and Bill can 'ave it out in the wash'us, and I'll stand by and see fair, and if I interfere I wish I may be b'iled as red as any lobster."

Lobby did not reply, but shivered more and more.

"What d'ye say, lad ?" said Old Bill, after waiting in vain for a reply.

"I never aggravated your son, and I'm not going to fight him," gasped Lobby.

"Then Bill shall whop you as you warmints have done him."

So saying, he seized Lobby by the collar, and flinging him on his back with as little ceremony as he would have handled a basket of crabs, trotted off towards his cottage.

This kind of travelling Lobby found uncomfortable, and implored to be let down, saying that he would walk quietly.

To this Old Bill acceded, and the rest of the journey was performed without any further interruption.

Young Bill was actively engaged with the lobsters when his father and his prisoner arrived.

When his eyes fell upon the form of the hapless Lobby, his face became one huge grin, and turning up his shirt-sleeves very tightly, he sallied out to meet the captive.

"Where did ye catch 'un, feyther ?" inquired the young torturer of lobsters and shellfish in general. "My eye ! ain't his ears red ! Have ye been whopping him, feyther ?"

"Not much," said Old Bill; "he kicked my shins, and I guv 'im one or two busters, but nothin' to speak of. I've brought 'im 'ere for thee, Bill."

"For me, feyther ?"

"Aye, lad ; thee and him shall have it out in the wash'us. What say thee, lad ?"

The dutiful son spat on his hands, re-adjusted his shirt-sleeves, and squaring scientifically at the terrified Lobby, pronounced himself quite ready.

"Then come on," said Old Bill. "Dang it ! if this ain't what I've wished for this last six months past."

"Wait a minit," said Young Bill. "I've got a b'ilerful o' lobsters on."

"Wang the lobsters !" cried Old Bill. "A ton o' soft-b'iled uns ain't ekal to this. Come and settle this warmint, and dang it ! if thee lick him properly, thee shall hev a new weskut, and a shillun to spend."

"I'll lick 'un fast enough," said Young Bill. "Come on. I'm heager to pepper his heye and smeller."

But Lobby was not quite so ready to pepper or be peppered, and shedding tears, promised to behave better in future ; but Old Bill was deaf to all entreaties, and dragging him into the out-house, closed and locked the door.

CHAPTER XLV.
A BATTLE ROYAL INTERRUPTED.

To depict the expression on the unfortunate Lobby's face when he beheld these preparations for his destruction would have taken a clever artist.

He screwed up his features, holding the most prominent one in his hand, well knowing that it would shortly be smitten by Young Bill's anything but genteel fist.

"I tell you I shan't fight," he moaned. "If you knock me about I'll speak to father, and he'll have you punished."

"Dang it !" cried Old Bill, slapping his thighs with delight ; "this be worth a crown. Thy feyther must be proud of thee. Now then, Bill, are you ready ?"

"Quite, feyther," cried the dutiful son. "Stand out of the way."

Old Bill complied, and his son squared scientifically up to the hapless Lobby.

The victim felt the blow mentally, and was preparing to give a shriek of agony, when a circumstance occurred which postponed the unequal combat.

Before we explain what caused the interruption we must go back to Charley, Tim, Mat Langley, and Benson.

At the moment of excitement and flight neither turned to ascertain if Old Bill had secured a prisoner ; but when out of danger, and finding Lobby was not one of the fugitives, a shade of consternation passed over their faces.

"What do you think has become of him?" said Benson.

"Old Bill has got him," rejoined Tim. "Poor Lobby ! he's always getting into some scrape."

"Old Bill will half murder him," said Charley. "I vote that we go back and rescue him."

This resolution was seconded by Tim, and carried ; and the four boys returned to the spot where they had admired the fatal lobster.

But neither Old Bill nor a fragment of Lobby could be found.

The boys looked at each other with faces of blank horror.

Could Old Bill, in a frenzy of rage, have thrown Lobby over the cliff, and thus revenged himself for a long list of insults ? or might he not be at that moment cruelly torturing that youth in some corner ?

Tim was the first to speak.

"Look here, you fellows," he said; "if you'll come with me, I'll show you where Lobby is."

"Where's that?" cried Charley.

"Why, the whole thing is as plain as daylight," said Tim. "Old Bill's dragged him up to his cottage."

"You don't think Old Bill would be so cruel as to boil him, do you?" inquired Benson.

"Boil, be blowed!" cried Tim; "Old Bill has got him at home, and a nice whopping Lobby will get if we are not quick."

"Come on, then," cried Charley; "but first let us get a thick stick each."

A hurdle was broken up, and armed with the rough stakes, the boys set out on the war trail.

On their way they met several lobsters wandering helplessly about, looking, as Tim, said, as if it would be an act of mercy to boil them.

These had escaped Old and Young Bill's eyes; indeed, thirty or forty were picked up, and one ingenious rustic went home with the wonderful news that the clouds had been raining lobsters!

But to proceed.

The cottage was soon reached, but as the reader knows, no one was there, the father, son, and Lobby amusing themselves in the outhouse.

"There's no one at home," said Tim; "what can have become of Lobby?"

"Oh! here's a jolly mess," said Benson; "I should never sleep again if anything was to happen to him. What fools we were to run away."

"It's no use talking like that," said Charley, "the question is—where is he? He must be found at any risk!"

"What's that?" exclaimed Tim.

"What's what?" cried Benson; "you're as pale as a ghost, and as nervous as a kitten!"

"I thought I heard a groan."

"Rubbish, Tim!" said Charley; "at the worst Old Bill will give Lobby a good thrashing and let him go."

"I am not so certain about that," returned Tim; "Old Bill is a venomous old brute! He——There it is again, and that was Lobby's voice."

"Where can he be?" inquired the boys, in one breath, for they had all heard the sound this time; "he's hereabouts, some where."

At this moment they distinctly heard Lobby's voice proclaiming that he didn't like fighting, that he couldn't, and he wouldn't fight.

The faces of Charley and his companions brightened up immediately.

"Stay here!" cried Charley, "I'll bring him out in a minute."

Creeping cautiously up to the door he applied his mouth to the keyhole, and roared in a loud voice—

"Fire! fire! the cottage is on fire!"

The ruse had the desired effect.

The door flew open, Old Bill tumbled out, followed by his son, and Lobby lost no time in joining his companions, who made the best of their way back to the school.

CHAPTER XLVI.
A GUY OUT OF SEASON.

OLD BILL, having boiled over with wrath at the hoax and Lobby's escape, boiled his lobsters, and sitting down before the fire, pipe in mouth, to watch them, soon forgot his wrongs.

But not so with Young Bill—nothing could pacify him. He longed for a sanguinary encounter, and went about during the rest of that day squaring at the empty air, blacking imaginary eyes, and drawing blood from visionary noses.

These attacks on the imaginary parties seemed to afford him the greatest satisfaction; indeed, on taking his seat by the side of his father, he made a remark to the effect that "he hoped he'd had enough, if not, he could cut and come again."

But what was Old Bill's life to that led by Griddle?

The party returning from Old Bill's fell upon the porter, and, after asking him numerous questions respecting his beadleship, wound up by joining hands and executing a wild dance of triumph round him.

"Now then," cried Griddle, "stash it, will yer, afore I does yer a mischief."

The only reply was another wild shriek of triumph, and more inquiries as to the health of the immortal cocked hat.

Griddle, who during the last day or two had been wound up to a pitch of desperation, could stand no more, and, dashing in amongst them, seized the nearest and smote him heavily.

This was Tim, who returned the compliment by butting at Griddle ram fashion, succeeding in upsetting that functionary.

"When a man's down keep him there," is a very old saying; and probaby the choice youths of Scarum School remembered it, for they fell upon the prostrate Griddle as did the Lilliputians upon the sleeping Gulliver.

"What shall we do with him?" cried Benson. "Wouldn't he make a splendid guy?"

"Happy thought!" cried Charley. "Let us make one of him."

"What?" roared Tim, grinning with

delight. "Paint his nose and all that? All right, I'll soon fetch my colour-box."

"Fetch a rope first," cried Charley. "Wou-would you?" (this to Griddle) "keep still, old hoss, till we get the harness on!"

"Sit on his head," said Mat Langley. "That's the way they keep fallen horses down in the street.

"Shame! shame!" cried two or three voices.

"I was only joking, you idiots," said Langley. "Here comes Tim, with the rope and colour-box. Hurrah! gentlemen. Here's the eighth wonder of the world!—the living Guy Fawkes!

" 'Oh, please to remember
The fifth of November,
    Of gunpowder treason and plot.
I see no reason
Why gunpowder treason
    Should ever be forgot.' "

"Shut up!" cried Charley. "Do you want to have Mr. Crammer amongst us?"

It must not be supposed that Griddle submitted to these indignities quietly; on the contrary, he struggled, used a sprinkling of bad language, and expressed a decided opinion that murder would be committed if he was not instantly released.

But his words were wasted. He was securely bound, and placed in a chair produced by Mat Langley.

"Now then, my cherub," said Tim, "hold up your head and be painted, like a good boy."

Griddle yelled with rage; but his cries and expostulations availed him nothing.

He was bound as helpless as Mazeppa was on the back of the wild and untamed steed.

Doubtless it was wrong of the boys, but they gave the matter no consideration.

A lark in the eyes of boys is harmless, and exceedingly funny, but we doubt if any of Griddle's tormentors had been in the position of that worthy porter, whether they would have seen the joke.

Tim ornamented Griddle's face with patches of vermilion and blue, and having finished his task, called upon Benson to make a fool's cap.

This was manufactured, and the guy was complete.

"If he would only consent to hold a bundle of matches," Mat Langley observed; "how stunning it would look!"

"Now he's finished, what shall be done with him?" said Tim.

"Chair him, of course," returned Charley.

Accordingly, after many efforts, the chair and Griddle were hoisted aloft, and borne three times round the school ground, amid the applause and laughter of the boys.

It was well for the boys, and unfortunate for Griddle, that Mr. Crammer was out, otherwise the living guy would have had a terrible revenge.

During the chairing and shouting, Griddle did not struggle, but when one of the boys suggested that he should be set down at the gate and exposed to the public view, he set up a most doleful yell, with which he mingled oaths, threats, promises, and entreaties.

But alas! of what avail were his cries? The suggestion was adopted, and the unfortunate being found himself at the door of his own lodge, next the road.

The first wayfarer to arrive was an old gentleman of exceedingly nervous temperament, who, on beholding the hideous object, flung up his umbrella, dropped a parcel of books, lost his hat, and fled up the road at a pace that did him credit for his years.

A nursemaid, trundling a couple of youngsters in a perambulator, next appeared, and took flight in the same direction as the nervous gentleman, screaming with all her might.

The young damsel's screams naturally brought several of the inhabitants out to inquire what was the matter, but the nursemaid being in the first stage of hysterics, could do nothing but point towards the school gate and gasp.

"What's the matter?" asked a gentleman of the coal-heaving persuasion. "Who's a been and frightened you?"

"There! there!" cried the girl. "Oh! it's awful!"

"What's hawful?" inquired the coal-heaver.

"Oh, my! don't ask me," the damsel went on. "It's terrible, indeed it is."

"If it's at the schule," the bewildered coal-heaver went on, "them warmints is up to some game. I'll go down and see."

At this moment, the gentleman who had first seen Griddle, returned with a policeman, and, joining the coal-heaver, went to investigate the matter.

"Now then," said the officer, looking sternly at the helpless Griddle. "Wot's the meaning of this houtrage? Come out o' that," meaning the chair.

"Though much I wish, I can't," said Griddle. "It's them warmints of boys as have done this, they fell on me like a swarm o' flies round a honey-pot, give me some busters in the ribs, and then brought me 'ere."

"Scandalous!" exclaimed the nervous gentleman. "Policeman, you will make a note of this disgraceful affair, I hope."

The officer touched his hat, and promised obedience.

"Do you know the boys' names?" inquired the policeman.

"Do I know my own ?" Griddle rejoined. "In course, I do ; but wot's the use o' that ! You can't lock fifty on 'em up, can you ?"

"I'd like to try," said the policeman. "For of all the warmints——"

"Wicious warmints," interrupted Griddle.

"That ever I seed," the officer went on, "them Scarum boys is the wust. Hullo ! the gate is locked. Where's the key ?"

Griddle's face paled through the paint as he heard this.

"One o' them warmints have collared it," he groaned. "It were in the lock jest now. Get hover the gate."

"There's spikes on the top," observed the officer ; "and the walls is topped with broken glass."

Then ring the house-bell, for mercy's sake !" roared Griddle. "There's a knot o' this cursed rope in the middle o' my back, tormentin' me awful."

"What is to be done ?" exclaimed the old gentleman. "The man can't remain in that position."

"Get a ladder," groaned Griddle.

"Where from ?" asked the policeman.

"I don't know, and I don't care," said Griddle. "You're an officer, and hain't no right to leave me 'ere."

"My good man," said the old gentleman, "you must not be so impatient. The officer is doing his best."

"Wot's it to do with you ?" roared Griddle. "You needn't stand grinnin' there. 'Ook it ; I don't want your sympathy."

The nervous gentleman did not reply to this ungrateful remark.

"I tell you what it is," said the coal-heaver ; "I'll jolly soon be over the wall, if you can get me a sack."

"A sack !" exclaimed the nervous gentleman. "What for ?"

"Why, to chuck across the top of the wall," returned the man ; "the glass can't cut through that."

"A good idea," said the gentleman.

The officer, however, made no reply.

He was thinking it was far from improbable that the suggestor had used other sacks to advantage, but he said nothing, and, running to the nearest house, fetched a sack, which was thrown upon the wall, and the coal-heaver mounted.

He had scarcely reached the top when a voice from the road thundered—

"Come down, sir ! How dare you, sir ? Are you aware, sir, you are trespassing ?"

It was Mr. Crammer who uttered these words, having observed the preparation to enter the sacred precincts of the school, almost speechless with indignation.

"My dear sir," said the nervous gentleman, approaching the schoolmaster, and smiling blandly—"my dear Mr. Crammer, let me entreat you to be calm."

"Calm, sir ! I will not," cried Mr. Crammer. "Officer, I give that man in charge."

"If that's the game," said the coal-heaver, "I ain't goin' to interfere."

"Mr. Crammer," the nervous gentleman went on, "I assure you this is a case of necessity. Your porter has been ill-used and maltreated. Come to the gate and see for yourself."

Mr. Crammer complied, and staggered back when he saw the object before him.

"Who has done this ?" he almost screamed.

"About forty on 'em," returned Griddle. "They're all in it, and all bad alike."

"I will see about that," cried the enraged schoolmaster, and then, turning to the coal-heaver, said—

"My good fellow, I beg your pardon. Will you kindly mount the wall. I have no wish for any of the other servants to behold this ridiculous figure."

"No, I won't," said the gentleman in the coal trade, "and that's flat. I ain't a man to be bullied for nothin'. Get up yourself."

"I'll do it," said the policeman.

And up he clambered, fell somewhat heavily on the other side, and released Griddle.

It now came to Mr. Crammer's turn to climb.

The nervous gentleman gave him a leg up, jerking him completely over the wall.

If Mr. Crammer was hurt, it did not become his dignity to admit it ; he, however, attacked Griddle with might and main, called him a "drunken idiot," and sundry other epithets, all of which Griddle bore patiently.

The boys were in their rooms when Griddle and Mr. Crammer entered the house, but they soon knew of their arrival when the bell rang out for them to assemble in the schoolroom.

They went trooping down, looking the picture of innocence.

Mr. Crammer stalked in, cane in hand, followed by Griddle, with a face red with rasping in getting the paint off.

The schoolmaster smote his desk with his cane, and in a loud voice demanded silence.

"Boys," he said, "I must and will know who are the ringleaders in this outrage ! Griddle tells me you all joined in it. If I do not discover the instigators of the villanous plot, it will be my painful duty to punish all !"

A suppressed groan rang through the room, Lobby looking very dejected and miserable.

"I will give you five minutes," Mr. Crammer said ; "five minutes, no longer, understand, to decide."

A minute, two, three, four passed, and yet no one spoke.

"Well," said Mr. Crammer, "the time is up!"

Tim stood up and said—

"I was the ringleader, sir."

"You are not the only one to blame," cried Charley, "for I was as much in it as you."

"And I! And I!" cried Benson and Langley.

"That is sufficient," said Mr. Crammer; "the other boys may go; you Thorn, Turndown, Langley, and Benson, will remain behind."

There was a rush to the door, Lobby being one of the foremost.

"Now," said Mr. Crammer, when he had shut and locked the door, "I regret that so disgraceful an affair should have happened on the last day here, yet I am pleased to find you so honourable as to exonerate your schoolfellows. To flog you would be useless. I have determined upon another plan. You will remain here six hours from this time, and execute the tasks I will give you."

This was not cheering news for the boys, but they comforted themselves with the remembrance that to-morrow would bring their freedom.

Mr. Crammer having prepared the tasks, departed, leaving the prisoners to their studies and meditations.

"He's gone!" said Charley, throwing down the book; "what shall we do to keep ourselves awake? I shan't touch a line!"

"A ghost story would be stunning," observed Tim; "but who's to tell it?"

"I remember a short story," said Benson, "which my uncle used to tell. He lived in America a number of years, and when he returned he told us a number of yarns."

"Go it, then," said Charley.

"I know it word for word," said Benson, "so here goes:—

"On the wild and turbulent Swift River, there is a spot that bears the name of this sketch.

"A name more fitting could hardly be found for so gloomy a locality.

"The dark rocks rise up from the depths below, stern and forbidding.

"Giant hemlocks tower aloft and throw their branches across the stream, until their arms are firmly interwoven together, shutting out the light of day.

"The river, dark and deep, moves up to the brow of the falls, and then goes plunging down into the abyss below, where a pool of unknown depth, and boiling like a seething cauldron, receives it.

"The road through the valley runs a mile away, and between it and the river is a dense and unbroken forest.

"There are but a few inhabitants in that section of the country, and all of them shun the falls as though they were an uncanny thing.

"A man was once murdered there, and to this day they say the spot is haunted by his restless ghost.

"They see it, they say, in the night time, when the moon is shining brightly, for it was at its full when the wicked deed was done.

"At such times they see it floating in the white curtain of mist that is for ever coming up from the seething pool below.

"One time my uncle chanced to be in the valley, and an old resident told him the story of the murder :—

"It was more than thirty years ago, in a time that has since been known in these parts as the great land speculation, that a stranger came into the valley for the purpose of looking at the timber, and buying largely of land should it suit him.

"He wanted a guide who knew all parts of the country, to pilot him about; and he found one in the person of Jacob Hill.

"People wondered that he chose such a companion, when others were ready, and even anxious, to accompany him; but then there was no denying that Hill was well posted, and could perform well what was expected of him.

"He lived alone in a cabin about a mile from here, and the most of his time was spent hunting in the forest.

"It was all the way he had of obtaining a living, for he raised nothing on the little bit of cleared land he had about his cabin.

"The stranger made his home with him when the stormy weather drove them in, so it was very little that the rest of us saw of him.

"None of the people hereabouts liked Hill, and that was another reason why they saw so little of the stranger.

"It was seldom that any one paid a visit to his cabin.

"One day, about two weeks after the stranger had come, Hill came to my house, and in answer to my inquiries, told me that the stranger had got through his explorations and had gone home.

"I had no suspicion that all was not right, but I could not help wondering why it was that Hill should have taken such pains to come and tell me, as he made no other errand at the time.

"It was about a month thereafter, as near as I can remember, when two men came into the valley making inquiries after the stranger.

"One of them was his brother, and they had traced him here, but could not find that he had been seen afterward.

"Hill told them the same story he had

A SURPRISE FOR MR. CRAMMER.

related to me and others, but it did not satisfy them. They did not like his looks, and their suspicions were aroused. They made what inquiries they could, but nothing was discovered.

"They had taken two or three tramps through the forest, and on each occasion Hill had persisted in accompanying them, notwithstanding that I and one or two more were along with them. It looked to me just as though he was afraid to have them out of his sight.

"One day we went down to the river. The brother of the missing man seemed somehow to be impressed with the idea that he had not gone out of the valley alive, in spite of the repeated declaration of Hill to this effect.

"We struck the river half a mile above the falls, and as it was good fishing there we thought we would try our hand for trout as we went down. As we neared the falls I could not help thinking but that Hill was growing more and more nervous.

"I watched him narrowly, for since the men had come I could not help suspecting him.

"At the top of the falls his uneasiness was still more apparent, and he suggested that we should fish no farther.

"The brother of the missing man was standing on the edge of the rock, and he declared that he would go down and try the pool below, for it looked to him as though there must be plenty of trout there.

"It seemed to me that Hill turned a shade paler at this, and again he tried to dissuade the stranger from going. But it was no use. He was determined to go, and already he had commenced to clamber down.

"We all followed him, and after considerable trouble we stood upon the well-worn rocks which formed the barrier of the pool. We threw in our lines, and soon were taking out the speckled trout faster than we had done before.

"We had been at work in this way for perhaps ten minutes, when an impatient exclamation from the brother of the missing man fell upon our ears. He had caught his hook in something beneath the black waters of the pool, and could not free it.

"At last he gave the line a jerk, in hopes of breaking the hook or line, but he did not do so. Instead, the object into which it was fastened began slowly to rise towards the surface.

"He pulled slowly and steadily upon it, and presently a large body neared the surface. A moment more and a cry broke from his lips, such as I have never heard before or since.

"'Great heaven! it is my brother!' he cried, his face white with the agony he felt.

"We all looked that way.

"There was the outline of a face amid the dark waters, and a hand was thrust up, as though imploring me to take it from its watery grave.

"Another cry broke upon our ears, and glancing about, we saw Hill, with a face of ashen hue, kneeling upon the rocks.

"'I killed him! I killed him!' he cried in terror; 'and now he has come back to accuse me of it!'

"The next moment the brother of the dead man was upon him, and had caught him by the throat with a grasp like that of a giant.

"'Die, murderer!' he cried, in a terrible voice. 'I would that you had a dozen lives, that I might take them all!'

"He would have strangled Hill then and there, had we not taken him off and assured him that vengeance should be meted out, and that it was not possible that Hill could escape us.

"We bound the murderer so that escape was impossible, and then turned to the task of recovering the body from the water.

"I went back to the settlement for help, and by nightfall we had conveyed our prisoner and the body of his victim thither.

"As his own words had condemned him, Hill confessed all.

"Watching his opportunity, he had pushed his victim from the summit of the rocks, and he had disappeared in the pool and was not seen again.

"In vain it was that he searched for the body, that he might obtain the money for which he had done the deed. So after all, it availed him nothing.

"In due time Hill died on the gallows; but the ghost of his victim haunts the falls still."

CHAPTER XLVII.
CONCLUSION.

BENSON had scarcely finished speaking, when the door opened and Mr. Crammer entered.

"Well, boys," he said, "how are you getting on?"

There was no reply.

Tim became absorbed in the numerous spots of ink on the floor, Benson retired within the first book of Euclid, and Charley gazed at a map of the world in a most studious manner.

"What have you been doing?" demanded Mr. Crammer.

Charley was the first to speak.

"Nothing, sir. We can't work at breaking-up time."

A TALE OF A TUB.

Instead of the thrashing the boys expected, Mr. Crammer smiled, and said—

"Well, well; perhaps not. Come down to tea."

With a joyous shout at their good fortune, the boys bounded from their seats, and in less time than it takes to write it, had joined their friends in the tea-room.

Whether the idea of parting softened the boys' hearts, or the thoughts of home had kept them employed, it is certain that Griddle, for once, was not annoyed.

Indeed, that gentleman hovered round the table with a smiling face, offered to make any amount of toast, and whispered to the cook not to cut the bread and butter so thick.

The hatchet of war was buried, and Griddle smoked the pipe of peace with his enemies.

The weapon was never dug up, for an occurrence happened that night which made Scarum School known by that name no more.

Mr. Tidd was the first to hear the uproar, and rising from his couch, threw open the window, and inquired who was there.

"Now then, sleepy," cried a shrill juvenile voice; "are you going to keep me here all night?"

"What's the matter?" demanded the usher.

"Telegram for Mr. Crammer," repeated the boy. "Look sharp, it's beginning to rain."

Mr. Tidd hastened below, took the telegram, and rushed with all haste to Mr. Crammer's apartment.

Mr. Crammer was at that moment in the power of the nightmare, and when aroused by Mr. Tidd's entry, the thought flashed through his brain that some evil-minded person had entered the room with a view to his assassination.

He sat bolt upright in bed, his eyes glaring upon the intruder.

"What do you want?" he cried, preparatory to shouting for help and the police.

The next instant, he recognized the usher, and inquired in a calmer tone, the cause of the intrusion.

Mr. Tidd replied by delivering the telegram, and remained in the room, watching the effect on Mr. Crammer.

"I wonder," mused Mr. Crammer, as he tore open the envelope, "who this can be from; I hope no one is ill. Eh! what's this? 'From Messrs. Jingle and Moses, Chancery Lane, to Mr. Crammer. *Come to London at once. Ezekiel Crammer died last evening, and bequeathed his property to you, leaving you sole executor!*'"

Mr. Crammer dropped the telegram upon the counterpane, and gazed at Mr. Tidd in helpless surprise.

"God bless me!" he said at last, "what an astonishing thing!"

"Who's Ezekiel Crammer?" inquired Mr. Tidd.

"An uncle of mine," returned Mr. Crammer. "I never saw him but twice in my life, and I was quite a boy then. Mr. Tidd, call the boys, let the house be roused, and we'll celebrate this event."

The boys of Scarum School, as may be imagined, were not a little alarmed and surprised at hearing the bell calling them up at such an unearthly hour; but Mr. Tidd soon relieved them of their anxiety, by circulating the news of Mr. Crammer's good fortune, and in ten minutes all had assembled in the dining-room.

Mr. Crammer shortly after appeared, and was greeted by a volley of terrific cheering.

"Boys," he said, when the noise had subsided, "you have heard the news from Mr. Tidd. As I am well advanced in years, it is only natural I should need repose, and it is therefore my intention to discontinue the school. You will depart to-day to your homes, and I wish all of you a happy and prosperous future. A circular will be prepared and sent round to your parents."

Another burst of cheering, which made the room ring and the windows shake.

Half an hour after, Griddle, Mary, and Dick appeared bearing coffee, and announced that breakfast would be ready at seven precisely.

The boys then turned out into the playground to amuse themselves and discuss the news.

"I'm awfully sorry, Tim," said Charley, laying an arm upon his friend's shoulder; "I was looking forward to next half. But now Crammer is rich, and the school broken up, we may never see each other again."

"Nonsense, old boy," said Tim. "Don't you think I shall run down and see you, and

bring you back to stay with me? Of course I shall."

"But perhaps I shall go to college, or be sent abroad," said Charley, still somewhat dolefully.

"Well," returned Tim, "what then? Can't I go to college too? and if you go abroad, why shouldn't I too? I've plenty of money —or that is, I shall have."

Charley grasped his friend's hand.

"My dear old chum," he said, "I ought to have known better than to speak of parting. We will never part!"

"Never!" repeated Tim; "but I say, talk of parting, what's to become of Griddle?"

"I haven't the slightest idea," returned Charley. "I daresay he will find something to do."

"We have worried him awfully," Tim went on. "What do you say, shall we get up a subscription for him?"

"But we have no money," said Charley.

"We shall have when Mr. Crammer pays us our travelling money," Tim replied.

"All right; I'll give five shillings," said Charley. "Let us hear what the other fellows say about it."

The others were all agreeable, and just before breakfast, after the money had been paid, Griddle found himself possessed of a goodly sum.

"Genelmen," he said, "we hev 'ad many hups and downs this 'arf. There hev been chimbley-pots chucked down on people's 'eads, and groanin's down chimbleys a frightenin' people hout o' their senses. But it air all forgiven. If you was wrong, its certain I weren't right to pitch inter you, sometimes, I hown, without the slightest occasion—the warming-pan for hinstance Genelmen, we part friends, and I thank ye kindly for your proof of affection to yours obedient."

*   *   *   *   *

Years have rolled on, and many changes have been made in Winkle-by-the-Sea.

There is a cottage by the cliff, the porch of which is covered with honeysuckle and jasmine.

A hale and hearty old gentleman is engaged in the garden.

It is Mr. Crammer.

Now comes the sound of boys at play, and Mr. Crammer turns his head and smiles as they pass, and walks to the gate to shake hands with Mr. Pendulum, their master, who has settled in Winkle-by-the-Sea, and is doing well.

*   *   *   *   *

"How the years have slipped by. It seems but yesterday, Tim, that we chased Young Bill down the cliff."

The speaker was a fine young fellow, in the undress costume of an officer.

By his side, another young fellow, no less handsome, stood, his eyes upon the house which had once been Scarum School.

The speaker was Charley, and his companion Tim.

"It almost brings tears into my eyes," Tim said, "to think of the old days. I often wish I was there still. Come, let us pay Mr. Crammer a visit."

They went up, arm-in-arm, to the cottage with the honeysuckle and jasmine creeping round it, and accosted its owner.

At first, Mr. Crammer did not know them, but when he recognized his old pupils, the old man shed tears of joy, and gave them the heartiest of welcomes.

Charley and Tim spent the day there, recounting their adventures during the Indian mutiny, and listening to stories of those they had known in days gone by.

Griddle, it appeared, had obtained a situation in a school in London, but returned in a week, it being supposed that his propensity for rum had ruined his prospects.

He was now beadle of the church at Winkle-by-the-Sea, and took especial delight in smiting noisy charity boys, or stirring up with his cane a sleepy pauper.

"But he's a great favourite with the old ladies," said Mr. Crammer, in conclusion; "and gets no end of sixpences."

* * * * *

Reader, the story of Charley and Tim is told. You have followed the boys through their school-life, and we would fain that you should follow them further still. But our story was one of school-life.

We have done our duty to our heroes, to our readers, and to ourselves, and yet write with a trembling hand,

www.ingramcontent.com/pod-product-compliance
Lightning Source LLC
Chambersburg PA
CBHW080832250626
47160CB00008B/2909